Conduit to Infinity

I0611168

Caspian Vesper

First published in 2025 by Blossom Spring Publishing
Conduit to Infinity Copyright © 2025 Caspian Vesper
ISBN 978-1-0684329-6-5
E: admin@blossomspringpublishing.com
W: www.blossomspringpublishing.com

Dedications

Timothy Clarke, my stepson. He was diagnosed with Type 1 diabetes in December 2010. Since then, I have watched this disease slowly take everything from him until there was nothing left. Rest in Peace, Tim. I am so sorry our relationship was not what it should have been; it was hard on all of us. I hope you are somewhere free of this god-awful disease at last and finally able to pursue your hopes and dreams. I hope this book will portray your imperfect but ultimately good nature and will allow you to be the heroic individual we all knew you were.

My long suffering wife, Ginny, the best person I have ever known.

To my aunt Maura, who recently passed away.

My friend Fiona, a beautiful individual inside and out.
We are sunlight, we can sparkle and shine, and our dreams are what we're made of-Dio

Contents

Prologue Part One

In approximately 75,000 BCE, there existed the zenith of the first human civilization. There was no 'most powerful' nation in these times. The concept itself was redundant as they were all working together. Yes, they had their differences, but these differences were respected, and the nations on the earth respected each other, all living to a single golden rule. The vast majority of humanity at this time were intelligent enough to know objective truth, and that what does harm to one does harm to all. People still got gaslighted and lies were told, but not on a scale to threaten societal stability.

An average lifespan of 130 elemental cycles was the result of a diverse gene pool, and although madness and disease did exist as a significant problem, those afflicted could not breed by default. In some cases, dangerous individuals would be locked up to protect society, but inside, they were treated well, and every effort was made to turn things around in that individual's life. Over time, the average lifespan had steadily increased, and this was matched by subtle improvements in physiology and mental function.

As they spread throughout the world, they had for the most part learnt from their mistakes, exercising population control through enlightened and magnanimous means. All of the drinking water on earth, with cooperation from all nations, was treated with a compound that was able to reversibly sterilise both genders. If a couple wanted to have a child and to be treated with the reversal agents, they both had to prove there was no mental illness, drug abuse, violence, sexual deviance or other antisocial traits in their character or family history.

Although this meant the children born were likely to be physically and mentally healthy, the main reason was to ensure that the child was not abused. A society that allowed children to be abused and neglected eventually rotted itself to the core and self-destructed. This was one of the biggest lessons learnt from the distant past. The couple wanting to breed also needed to prove that their finances were stable and not compromised. Robust social safety nets did exist which helped and empowered people, but they were still just safety nets, and the people making use of these safety nets were not permitted to breed.

Modern humans were distinct from other humans who existed at that time, of whom there were two types: first, there were the children of the frost – strong and durable humans who had adapted to survive the cold temperatures, and second, there were the first fire bearers – the tall ones who had adapted to the open steppes and could run. These humans were all smart, as was required for their survival, but these adaptations were too specific and lacked versatility. They were physically stronger than modern humans, but they lacked the spark required that allowed humans to gaze at the stars with wonder as well as just use them for navigation.

Modern humanity's darkest times saw those other humans they shared the earth with systematically slaughtered almost to extinction. Eventually, light was able to overcome the darkness as treatment of children began to improve. Now the other humans' decimated populations were recovering, but an irreversible genetic bottleneck had been imposed. They were allowed to live on swathes of land given to them by the nations of the earth. Trauma, bitterness, hatred and lack of a good gene pool made these places dangerous. Even their specific adaptations, which once had given them a physical advantage, were compromised and largely redundant.

Some who were blessed with good physical and mental attributes were welcomed into main human society, but they were only an unlucky few. They had to work extra hard to be trusted not to take revenge by getting to trusted positions only to commit sabotage. The modern humans did everything they could to make amends, but all over the world, every modern human generation after this bloodshed was burdened with a guilt and a fear that they would ultimately reap what they had sown. Their fear was going to come true.

After an accumulation of many aeons, the world governments were more united than ever before. And they needed to be. At the edge of the old world in modern day Sumatra, seismic activity was consistently spiking and had been for over 20 elemental cycles. Around the world, everyone was united in fear of what was about to happen and the scientific projections of the consequences. And for 20 elemental cycles, whilst humanity awaited its fate at any second, the world governments were funding everything from space travel to underground complexes and survival bunkers in many bids to somehow escape or survive humanity's shared fate.

It was a desperate rush, resulting in corners being cut. One of the bungled projects was something everyone thought was their only hope until the last second. A phenomenal underground compound of 10,000 square miles was constructed in modern day Siberia. To construct this, labour was sourced from enclaves containing descendants of ethnically cleansed primitive humans. Many in this pool of labour already held a grudge against modern humans, for obvious reasons. This grudge was only made worse by poor working conditions and mistreatment by modern human supervisors.

This complex contained DNA samples of vast populations of different flora and fauna, as well as a huge population of scientists, engineers, tradespeople and the unskilled. In theory, the people would be able to build a viable, functioning economy for an indefinite period of time. When the time came to move back to the surface, humanity's retained knowledge could be used to rebuild the world and their society. As a result of deliberate sabotage during construction, it had suddenly subsided one day, killing all inside and destroying all the samples. The samples could be duplicated, sure, but above ground, it was all only academic.

Still, not all of the hope was placed on one single endeavour. As spacecraft were added to and built upon in the skies above, containing the same samples, a different project was being feverishly worked on. Scientists were trying to harness the very power of the universe to do their bidding.

The hypotheses were viable. If the fundamental particles of which everything was made could be programmed to carry out specific tasks with optimal energy efficiency, then the results would be so far-reaching that reversing or even stopping the impending global extinction event would be made possible. After that, humanity would be propelled forwards to an era where nothing was unattainable, and everyone would have everything they could possibly need in order to flourish, both as individuals and as a race.

Despite their dark and evil past, this civilization was moving in the right direction. There was, however, the collective sense that humanity had thus far avoided its punishment, and that this must be endured before there was any hope of redemption. Total self-destruction by their own hand was not a serious notion that anyone entertained. In the present day, however, deep down, we have a primal memory of this, and it is infused into the collective psyche, even if nobody knows exactly why.

The science already existed to harness the power inside the elemental units of creation, but this was only used for energy, and even this had been phased out many generations ago. Some crude elemental weapons were made. After the damage caused by a single detonation in an ancient war in modern day Northern India, any further production was prohibited, and this decree was signed by all nations. Only a single world leader knew of their location at any one time, as they did not know what to do with the weapons other than to keep them hidden in a remote, dark place.

Once knowledge was passed from one world leader to another, the previous one had this information wiped from their mind This was possible using a highly classified technology implemented as a neural implant which interfaced with organic brain matter. If the current knowledge holder was killed or incapacitated, the information would automatically pass to another designated leader, randomly chosen. Nothing was stopping the designated leader from telling someone else, and they were simply trusted not to do this. No leader had ever betrayed this trust.

Prologue Part Two

Near modern day Braşov in theCarpathian Mountains

Gathered in a room were some of the finest scientific minds of the world, some with experience stretching beyond 80 elemental cycles. They were sleep deprived and overworked to begin with, but upon hearing of the subsidence of the underground compound, they were collectively devastated. Unfortunately, ancient humans were more gullible in that they had not suspected sabotage, only that the labour pool from the enclaves would be grateful for the work and would do it well. The scientists were in their armour-plated and life-sustaining safety gear. All checks had been completed. This final test was a rushed affair, like all others, but they had no choice.

Using advanced solar energy capture, they had synthesised tiny organic molecules, which when activated, could rearrange themselves to be catalysts for any reaction deemed necessary by the controller to any predetermined stereospecific ratio. This would drastically lower the activation energy for any given reaction better than any catalyst, biological or otherwise.

Not only that, but these molecules, when activated, could synthesise any substrate necessary for these reactions from almost any matter, provided the building blocks were there. Unstable waste products could also, in theory, be conjugated safely and even reused as the activation energy required for even this purpose would be drastically reduced, provided the activation process went according to plan. But preparations were rushed, with important quality control checks bypassed.

The unprogrammed proto-particles ranged between 200 to

500 grams per mole equivalent in modern measurements; any higher than that and instability was potentially a major problem. Some of the smaller weight molecules were to have the sole purpose of repairing higher weight molecular machines, maintaining their function. They could even work together to create more of themselves to counteract the unabating process of entropy and the forces of environmental degradation.

The compounds were all suspended in place using power electromagnets in a vacuum, primed for programming. The scientific community at the time had spent years understanding and trying to isolate the most fundamental particle which gives specific mass and determines the nature of matter and thus the very laws of physics themselves. This mysterious particle they deemed 'the particle of creation', and its properties showed how the fabric of existence was fine-tuned. And they wanted to locally alter this fine-tuning. There were fears in the public discourse that this could go badly wrong and get out of control, and the public were not even aware of the unnecessary risks being taken.

Also discovered was what was deemed 'the ghost particle'. This was without attractive force or mass, but the vibrational energy that could be isolated from this ubiquitous particle was practically limitless, dwarfing even what could be harnessed from the sun using the most advanced solar energy capture technology. The scientists hypothesised that the energy harnessed from the ghost particle could allow for the manipulation of the creation particle to programme discrete but precise commands to alter the fine-tuning of nature within the proto-particles so they could be controlled. And then anything would be possible. Anything.

Using advanced solar capture, they planned to accelerate the particle of creation and the ghost particle in opposite directions, close to the universal speed limit. The energy harnessed would allow this pre-programmed artificial manipulation to manifest in the proto-particles.

The lead scientist was satisfied that all gear safety checks and parameter checks were done and initiated the process with the push of a button. Her finger hovered above the button. She had a bad feeling, but she could not think straight. None of them could. The results would be known once the particles were accelerated to speed, providing the energy needed for the predetermined parameters to be initiated. They were observing the chamber from a safe distance behind triple-glazed reinforced glass, as it was anticipated that a lot of heat energy would be emitted.

As soon as it was indicated on the wall panel that the final command was ready to be given, the lead scientist looked around at her wide-eyed colleagues, all of whom were aware that a huge risk was being taken, but a world-ending natural disaster could occur at any second. No time and energy could be wasted in maintaining the acceleration. The final command was given and implemented. Now they waited.

A circle in space, which contained the suspended proto-particles, started to glow and ripple. The luminosity within this circle slowly increased, and with each ripple, the circle seemed to bulge inward, further each time. Once the fourth or fifth ripple occurred, the bulge inward became more pronounced, and at this time, the luminosity seemed to start decreasing. In the middle of the circle, once the illumination had gone, a perforation suddenly formed. This caused a jump scare for the scientists. And from the perforation, many tears formed, moving to the outer edge of the circle.

Red visible light was seen coming from behind the perforation and the tears. The dimensional boundary disintegrated, and beyond this, another world presented itself.

"Shut it off!" the lead scientist ordered at the first sight of the monstrosity, which caused something to uncoil in her stomach.

Everyone was frozen to the spot.

"SHUT IT OFF!!!!" she screamed.

When there was no response, she charged towards the emergency shut-off lever. She was held back by the rest of the captivated and curious scientists, but she pushed them out of the way and managed to get to it. It did not matter, though. Without the original power source, the circle showed signs it was trying to collapse, but it maintained for now. Some disgusting, indescribable horror, even though it appeared to have its back to them, was eating alive another abomination. And the screams of this thing, although muffled, caused a fear none of them had ever felt close to feeling before. It was slowly dawning on them that they had made a terrible mistake.

They could make out a rocky, barren landscape with all manner of filthy life crawling upon it. Also, there was a red sky, with human-sized winged creatures. Each lifeform they saw was more of an obscenity than the last. The scientists were frozen in place, all feeling utter ruin inside. Another atrocity, further away, came into view and was looking right at them. This thing was mottled with a greenish hue and was around ten feet tall. Although humanoid in appearance, it was asymmetrical, deformed and distorted. It was stooped over, with deep red and featureless eyes full of hostility.

The feeling of malevolence emanating from these creatures was profound, ancient. The first observed creature froze in place as it let its still-live prey go free. It limped, screeching, into the distance. The first creature, also mottled but with a bluish hue, started to slowly stand up. Even its movements, like a real-life creepy stop-motion animation, filled the viewers' hearts with desolation and existential dread.

"How did this happen?" the lead scientist whimpered, even though she already knew.

"W-w-w-well," replied her deputy.

None of them took their eyes off the hellish sight. A crowd was gathering, as word had spread through the facility. Inside the chamber, the portal was trying to close, one reality trying to expel the abhorrent invading reality. As the first monster approached, others were coming into view, all approaching.

Her deputy continued. "The creation particle – it … it governs our reality. It has been distorted into how it governs another reality. It is fine-tuned, yes, but now the distorted reality, as it is, has manifested because of this. It is trying to correct itself as two realities cannot exist together, but local distortions may be able to cross over."

A tear rolled down the lead scientist's cheek.

A leg tentatively crossed the portal as the creature climbed through, its face scanning the chamber as its skin rippled.

It contorted into an even more corrupted shape, arched its back with all limbs stretched out, and a sound came out of this thing that could only come from hell. All the scientists were brought to their knees by this god-awful sound as it went on for thirty seconds or so. The thing dropped to its knees and wheezed a few times before looking back into the portal, now at three-quarters its original size. The team composed themselves and were watching again, observing a crack in the first pane of the triple-glazed reinforced glass.

The affront to creation looked at the portal, noticing it had shrunk, and attacked with all its teeth and claws the others trying to cross over but was quickly overwhelmed. Two more made it through. Then five. Then ten, twenty, thirty. They all ran a few yards before falling, rippling and screeching for thirty seconds at a time, making a total of around fifty so far. The next one that got through was enormous. It was all the bright colours against a background of the darkest, combined in the most grotesque way imaginable. They all radiated evil and malice that simply did not belong in this world, and they had been given a most welcoming invitation.

The enormous one writhed on the ground for a while and went still, dead: clearly too large to adjust to the new reality. Although all were equally disgusting, they varied in shape, size and features. A miasma of colour schemes on their skin was infused with mottled brown and patches of black hair. Most had horns. All had featureless eyes of a single colour, although this varied between individuals. They had various arrangements of serrated yellow teeth. Their limbs were asymmetrical, with angular joints and claws that could eviscerate an elephant with ease. They all hissed, growled and swiped at each other.

Just as the hole was a quarter of its original size, another giant made it through, but not quite as big. As it began screeching in what was obviously an adaptation process to the new reality, a *huge* arm came through after it and grabbed the giant. Three hag-like creatures, distinctly feminine and similar in size to the smallest of the creatures, stepped in calmly past the giant arm, confident as if they had done this before. These three were different from the rest, with long thin brown hair and pronounced chins and noses. Their eyes were sunken and human like but with no iris and a bloodshot sclera. Their bodies and faces were wrinkled and crisp looking, and they did not need to go through the adaptation process. It was like they were all expecting this to happen. They looked around them, heads jerking and cocking to the left and right like birds.

There was only around two feet of space available in the portal, and around thirty or so one-foot tall imp-like creatures squeezed through until no more space was available. One imp was unlucky enough to try and go through at the wrong time and was slowly cleaved in two.

The smooth reddish-brown arm hinted at a body ten times the size of any of the others. It had a black claw protruding from a bony elbow, with a dark green and brown liquid dripping from it. Each joint in its hand was pronounced, angular and hard looking. It had only two fingers and a thumb, with a short black claw on the thumb and longer claws on the fingers. It squeezed while the fifth guest screeched louder than all of the others combined, claws ripping its flesh to the bone as more dark green fluid poured onto the floor of the chamber.

Just then, the portal closed, severing the huge arm below the shoulder. A whump sensation like a change in pressure was felt and heard, although seemingly in reverse from when it had opened up. The giant threw the severed limb to the floor. Now that all the screeching had stopped, the lead scientist watched with tears streaming down her face as the first and second pane of glass became a spiderweb of cracks. The third held. She could hear the alarm and order to evacuate as echoes in the distance. What she had just seen, she could feel it as her mind broke, and she knew that mentally, she could not recover from this, especially as it was her fault.

Someone pulled at her arm, but she could not move. Each second was orders of magnitude more awful than the last. The creatures were now feasting like mad dogs on the huge severed arm, fighting over every morsel with pure rage as though they were settling a score and had an insatiable appetite. The giant corpse was left, and this was next on the menu.

Eventually, whoever was pulling her arm gave up, and she heard receding footsteps. The facility was now beginning its countdown: five minutes until this facility imploded and buried itself deep in the earth. The creatures, using what could only be tongues in varying degrees of deformity, licked the green liquid off their 'faces'. There was nothing left of the arm or the giant corpse. Then each one glared at every other with hatred as ancient as it was evil. The hags stood off to the side, spaced throughout the chamber, all with their arms raised. Malicious but somehow less primal. One thing was for sure. They all *detested* each other.

They were circling and looking ready to attack when one seemed to point out that they were in a chamber. The first and second panes of the reinforced glass were just glass, but the third was a two-way mirror. Another monster pointed at her, but she knew they could not see her, and it was obvious they had noticed the cracks. She was able to look down now and ripped off the helmet of her protective suit. She dropped to her knees and simply whimpered, "What have I done?" as all these hell-spawned insults to creation started screeching in unison.

Prologue Part Three

Three months later

A handful of the creatures had not made it out of the facility unharmed or before the implosion. The giant one had been severely injured, with one arm cleaved from the main body. With the other arm, the limb was reattached, and the injuries had healed quickly. Most of the entities had been slightly wounded in the implosion, especially the smaller ones, but they also healed quickly. All of the survivors scattered to all points of the compass once they had escaped.

Despite their hatred for one another, some still stuck together in small groups. All three of the hag-like creatures had survived with serious injuries but also healed easily. They stayed together, held their arms up, flickered and vanished. The lack of a military presence outside the facility was because of how remote it was, and military command became chaotic with viewing of the footage.

Two of the entities and the giant were forced to work together and figure out what to do next. They were on the eastern slope of Mount Tâmpa in the modern-day Carpathian Mountains, having fled to this remote area. They expected hostility, this being the default in their home world, and the denizens of this plane did not take too kindly to their arrival. It was high summer, and a light breeze from the south caressed the contours of this peak.

It was an alien world to them, with a blue sky that was objectively beautiful. Although they no longer had the capability to appreciate beauty in this capacity, they were certainly jealous of the denizens of this world who could. And they wanted to take it from them. With a lightning strike, one of the smaller two snatched a multicoloured bird out of the sky and regarded it with curiosity. As the other two advanced on it, it consumed the bird without chewing, still alive.

They all eyed each other with their normal hatred, but they had a collective need to understand what had happened to them, where they were, and what to do. They spoke in their own language, and each one's voice carried variable traits of deep growling, which gave away their baleful natures.

The lead scientist, just before the facility's implosion, had already been in a weakened state when the first monster to get to her demanded answers in its own language. Hearing this, she just started screaming, "I'M SORRY!" over and over again. This one on the mountain, the bird swallower, now mimicked her voice for the amusement of the other two, which it had been doing repeatedly for the previous three months.

They all possessed this ability, which was part of the reason their world was so parasitic. Nothing could be truly trusted to be what it said it was. Doing this, along with their other abilities, to varying degrees, used up significantly more energy than in normal function and could not be maintained for long, although mimicking a voice was relatively easy.

Their abilities varied notably between each individual. These abilities, especially shapeshifting, were not conducive to a virtuous and fair society if they were ubiquitous amongst the population. Humans could lie and deceive but were relatively transparent compared to this. On this plain, the monsters were at a distinct advantage to get what they wanted and act out their hateful desires, fooling the denizens of this realm with ease.

As of this moment, however, the entire earth knew of

their existence, and they were being tracked, so first priority was to ensure they were not killed or sent back. When this threat was eliminated, the real carefree fun could begin. Loud booms were heard above them as gravity defying objects came and went with a speed completely unknown to the outsiders. Just as soon as they were gone, slower levitating objects rose to their eye level at a safe distance and appeared to study them.

This lasted for a short period of time before booming voices emanated from these machines in a demanding tone. They could not understand, so the bird swallower just telepathically said, "I'M SORRY I'M SORRY!!!" mimicking and mocking the main scientist again. The original scene had been seen and reported the world over as the mocking entity had crushed the scientist's head in its clawed fist. This was broadcast repeatedly, censorship never being an issue in this society.

The taunt appeared to elicit an angry response from the occupants of the levitating machines, in the form of streaks of blue fire directed at them. The combined attack impacted every single invader, causing extreme injuries but nothing they could not recover from. And they healed quickly, long before the gravity-defying machines could recharge their weapons. It dawned on the pilots that they had acted in anger when they had all made the stupid decision to fire and completely drain their weapons at the same time.

The giant focused its will on a randomly chosen attacker, snaking its psychic tendrils into the pilot's mind with ease, as humans had not evolved any mechanism of defence to this kind of violation. It saw itself on the mountainside from the pilot's point of view and felt the fear as autonomy was taken completely. The foreign presence absorbed all of the knowledge contained within the pilot's mind, including how to control the gravity defying machine. The pilot, on the edge of the formation, was now totally hijacked by the foreign psychic parasite. The pilot slowly turned the aircraft ninety degrees to face the others in the formation. The weapons systems had now fully recharged, and the blue fire easily destroyed the rest of the machines in the formation. The psychic parasite then directed its puppet to fly the only remaining machine into the side of the mountain.

After this, the giant psychically shared its new bounty of information with the others. It said to the others in its own language, "I know what to do! We now know the things they fear the most, and we will make them all happen. Their world will be ruined and we will make them suffer."

They all whooped in celebration, screaming at their beautiful new blue sky. The world watched with devastation and helplessness a live feed from the space station after it had positioned itself in a geosynchronous orbit above the chaotic scene.

All races of humans on earth as well as those primitive humans in the enclaves were united in existential dread, and all hope was collectively lost. More primitive weapons from other fast-moving flying machines were soon unloading their ordinance at the unwelcome visitors, but this was done in anger and did not make a difference. If the plasma weapons did not destroy them, the primitive weapons were unlikely to have an effect on these horrible creatures. When the air cleared, nothing remained on the side of the mountain. They had made their escape using the smoke as cover, with any injuries probably well on their way to healing already.

Prologue Part Four

The leaders of all the world governments were desperate and frightened. The space programme was now the only hope that their great and hard-fought civilisation had of surviving, and it was running into constant problems in regard to materials, technology and labour. It was more urgent than ever, and problems were occurring because of the same reasons their other endeavours had failed. Samples were being destroyed, and some technological failures had resulted in loss of life of extremely important individuals who had possessed rare knowledge and skill. Some had possessed skills no one else did. The humans from the enclaves had played a major role in the unskilled factory-line construction of important components for transport to the space station, and there were plenty of opportunities for sabotage.

An indescribable horror had been released upon the world. People the world over were being tormented and killed in the most brutal displays of bestial cruelty imaginable, and some of these were brazenly public. Some people in great positions of power had fallen victim to these creatures, prompting unprecedented security measures to be implemented. All important people in power were now coated with their own individual electromagnetic shields, which protected them from all manner of attack. They were more or less safe except when on the move, and even that was kept to a minimum.

The leaders were meeting from each of their respective fortresses via holographic means using the electronic planetary web of knowledge, with electromagnetic shields temporarily disabled to prevent interference. To each leader, it would seem that all the other leaders were in the same room at a round table with a map of the world. On this map, it showed the location of all attacks from these vile, otherworldly beings, each timestamped. The current designated speaker for the world council, Baltonovia, looked around at the bewildered faces and decided to begin. He banged his gavel and began to speak.

"So, you all know why we are gathered here at this time. We are facing the greatest threat our civilization has ever known. In dealing with this threat, we have not only failed to rise to the challenge but have created a new, seemingly infernal threat. We have unwittingly invited creatures from a dark and mysterious underworld, full of degenerate evil. They have not succumbed to any of our weapons, and less than a few dozen of them have caused untold suffering, fear and terror, seemingly without purpose, other than for the thrill and enjoyment of these things. Today we need to discuss our options. My learned friend Caltroth from our most populous and militarily industrious nation, it would seem prudent that you be the first to speak."

"Thank you, Speaker Baltonovia. We, with the help of all nations, have been tracking the activities of these creatures as much as we can. Three of the creatures seem to be the most prominent and powerful and have stayed together. Two are of average size in comparison with the first wave, around eight feet tall, and the third one is huge, at around twelve feet tall. We have decided to call them the Malefic three, and their names are Moloch, Baphomet and Kronos the Titan. All of the monsters that got through, we will call the Echthroi, the ancient enemy. The Malefic three appear to be responsible for the worst of the atrocities and do not even try to run when confronted with our most destructive weapons. We can track their activities, but beyond that, we seem to be powerless." He paused to gather his thoughts.

He continued. "There are also the twins, two of the Echthroi, who are on average around half the size of the others. They seem to be responsible for random tornados of destruction, disappearing before any armed forces can be summoned. And we never know when or where they will turn up next; it could be anytime, anywhere. We have decided that these particular entities, whilst extremely dangerous, are not pursuing any particular agenda other than arbitrary suffering.

"Encouragingly, an intense attack of conventional weapons on the miniature goblin-like creatures, which we are calling the Faerie, can inflict pain and death. They can be gotten rid of, but it takes a lot to kill even one of them. Due to the large amount of ordinance required to do so, significant collateral damage occurs every time. Due to the effectiveness in our responses, despite the collateral damage, the attacks from the goblins are lessening in intensity and frequency. They, like the twins, are almost impossible to track. There are many more still out there, but for the most part, they seem to be lying low, doing God only knows what.

"We believe the three hag-like creatures, who disappeared on the day they entered the world, are directly responsible for children going missing all over the world. There is only circumstantial evidence of this, but we believe there is causation and not just correlation taking place. And when they are seen, which is not often, they are able to escape using optical illusion and sleight of hand. That being said, the hags also don't seem to have a specific agenda, for now. I have a feeling that they do, but the threat from the Malefic three is more immediate.

"They all have preternatural, occult abilities to varying

degrees, none of which we can explain rationally. They can communicate telepathically as well as read minds. The Echthroi can absorb the knowledge, fears and weaknesses of those unfortunate souls whose minds they invade. As the world saw from the mountainside and the blue fire, they were able to directly control the body of the pilot to turn the blue fire upon his comrades and fly his aircraft into the side of the mountain. This is a terrifying ability. All data, however, suggests that this is a crude ability, which does not allow for fine movement and can only be used for a matter of seconds at a time. It is very energy intensive on their part, but when used, it cannot be resisted. It does not seem that this ability would be useful except in the rarest of circumstances.

"All of these abilities diminish sharply with distance, and your electromagnetic armour, we postulate, should protect you from this. Unfortunately, logistics and costs dictate that we cannot assign these shields to the rest of humanity. The creatures can also shapeshift but cannot do this indefinitely. There are other capabilities, but these three are our greatest threat. There are specific abilities falling under the banner of telepathy, such as the power of suggestion, but this depends on the mental composition of the individual.

"The holographic nature of this meeting ensures that if one of us falls victim to these abilities, the others will know and cannot be affected. We have determined that the maximum time they can shapeshift is one part in forty eight of each rotational cycle. The Malefic three appear to have a purpose and strategy. We believe they are trying to find the projectiles. They know our greatest fears and appear to keep returning to Batak Toba, that particular place being the source of the existential threat.

We believe they want to expedite the inevitable catastrophe but cannot do this without the projectiles. The twins have also been spotted at Batak Toba on a number of occasions.

"Currently, their growth cipher is being mapped using samples retrieved from the site of the incident. It is still in early stages but preliminary reports disturbingly show a quadruple cipher spiral with unfamiliar and numerous complimentary elemental units. Please speak freely now, my learned delegates."

They all looked at each other knowingly. They knew what the question was, and the answer.

"The projectiles, charged with the power of the universe," stated Artemis of Carpathia, the leader of the world's second most populous nation. "Who knows their location?" she asked.

They all contemplated in silence that one of the leaders present knew this, but they knew they must not reveal it.

"I will ask that the learned delegate in question reveals this information once this summit has concluded, which we will deem to be one part in twenty-four of the rotational cycle. A vote will take place to determine the will of the council at that time, even if the decision remains that of the delegate in question. Desperate measures are needed now, and eventually the Malefic three will find the projectiles. On that assumption, we must be brave, take the initiative and use these weapons."

"I know where they are," President Brugat of Europa calmly stated.

The rest of the leaders gasped in unison as Brugat bowed his head. An unholy, guttural moan could be heard from the direction of the holographic Brugat. They all recognised this growl, as did most of humanity. The window to the world in the majority of domiciles throughout civilization showed the countenance of all of the prominent invading putrid lifeforms as well as the frightful noises they emitted.

This, along with footage and first-hand stories of their arbitrary wickedness and cruelty, was too much for many hundreds of thousands, who would choose to end their own existence to avoid even a tiny chance that they would encounter any one of these things, especially with most of them relatively unaccounted for. All of the other leaders were frozen to the spot despite their relative safety, but Brugat rose to his feet, closed his eyes and turned to face the sound as it grew louder.

It was the largest of the Malefic three, which had earned its own masculine name; Kronos the Titan towered above any living human to about fifteen feet, which ironically was his greatest weakness. It was very hard for him to move undetected. But he could take the form of whatever he wanted for about one part in forty-eight of the rotational cycle. He was never completely convincing, though, just as with all of them, so in human form, he kept a low profile. This also drained his energy on account of having to essentially crush himself down to size, so he also needed a safe place to rest when he transitioned back to his true form. He possessed the other abilities, also, having been the one who had hijacked the bodily autonomy of the pilot on that fateful day on the mountainside.

He was mottled with differing shades of brown in a completely random pattern, with sparsely placed, coarse black hair. He was barely even humanoid in shape and seemed to be in a constant half crouch but bipedal, with legs that seemed unable to straighten completely but with powerful-looking thigh and calf muscles. His legs and crotch area were grey and slimy with more random areas of course black hair. This black hair completely covered his crotch, and his legs ended in black hooves.

He had angular arms with three claws on the end of each one, each arm similar but on a much smaller scale than the one that had tried to grab it through the portal. The face was the worst of all, a singular manifestation of all of humanity's nightmares, past, future and present. Beady black sunken holes for eyes exuded an impenetrable, endless dark hatred for all of creation and rage for his miserable, tortured existence.

The only thing that took the edge off his wretchedness was the destruction of anything and everything around him. In his home world, the satisfaction only went so far, as he could only cause suffering to life forms already miserable and incapable of being happy. He never imagined he could find himself somewhere so beautiful and full of thriving, happy beings working together to improve their lives more as time went on. The fear and pain and destruction of the denizens of this plain of existence gave him gratification he had never thought possible, allowing for at least a fleeting relief from his own suffering.

A series of hard, keratinous black protrusions emerged from various points on his face, some merging together and some bigger than others, but all finishing at nasty-looking sharp points either pointing straight out or curving inward. All oozed a black toxic-looking substance. These growths caused his features to be even more distorted and asymmetrical. What passed as his mouth was nothing but an opening, its edges conforming to the growth with countless small and large deep-yellow and brown teeth pointing in different directions. This thing was a true desecration and defacement upon all of creation, which is why Brugat could not look at him.

As Kronos raised an arm towards Brugat's face, the president of Europa simply stated, "Do not let my sacrifice be in vain. Never forget Operation Tartarus." With that, Brugat bit down on something, slowly dropped to his knees and slumped forwards, dead.

Kronos regarded the president of Europa for a second before snapping his head around towards the sound of several dozen heavy metallic thumps in quick succession. In infiltrating Brugat's fortress, he was at great risk of being found out. And one of Brugat's loyal followers had seen his filthy transition without Kronos knowing. Then a pre-recorded voice sounded on their speakers. It was Brugat.

"Here, vile defiler of humanity, we outwitted you. We saw you coming. Our sacrifice is small to imprison you here. You will never get out. We have overcome you, and I hope that this realisation tortures you for aeons. I implore you, fellow world leaders, please do not let this evil overcome us. Please undo this terrible mistake and vow to never try to manipulate the fabric of creation again. Let this be our lesson but not our extinction. The laws of creation are in place for a reason and must be respected. My love for Europa and all of humanity."

Kronos looked shocked, if that were possible. Then he seemed to smile and let out a deep and guttural cry while appearing to be contorting himself to make the bellowing more horrible and disturbing. It was like watching footage of a sunset, though; it could only disturb them but not harm them, as staring at the sun in a film would not hurt the eyes. They were all left in no doubt that this debasement in sound waves would induce insanity if witnessed firsthand. He extended an arm and clamped the claw on Brugat's head.

Brugat began to seize violently and was changing before them, his flesh bubbling and melting and rearranging itself into a grotesque and blasphemous humanoid appearance, one that looked horribly bloated, mutilated and deformed. The claw released the head, and this thing that used to be Brugat stood up slowly and smiled at the delegation. He looked animalistic, muscular and ape-like in gait, as if some sort of evolutionary regression was part of the transformation. Kronos simply said, "Do not worry, your hero is long gone. I am only using what he left behind."

He looked off into the distance and continued. "Looks like there are plenty of fallen heroes here I can use. You had better hope I never get out of here, and I hope that this fear will haunt you forever."

Just then, the president of Europa's holographic feed was cut off, leaving nothing but a black circle behind.

After what seemed like an hour of silence, Chancellor Hariquonal of the Island Coalition spoke up. Her voice quivered, but she drew on all the spiritual strength within her to simply state, "This possibility of Kronos escaping, it need only haunt us."

Location data of the projectiles had automatically been transmitted into her mind instantaneously upon the death of Brugat. "We need to call upon the old ones. Let the human spirit triumph over despair. Let us emerge redeemed from this hopelessness."

The others were silent, this silence confirming that they all agreed and that this was their only hope.

Prologue Part Five

Not all the old ones were to be awakened at once. There had been no need, up until now, for their activation. They were titans of war, part human and part machine, and served no purpose in peacetime. After the ancient wars had ended, the old ones had not gone silently into stasis. As with the projectiles, it was seen as a better option to hide rather than eradicate should they be needed further down the line.

The risks of the latter were much greater if their inactivation and stasis were a viable option. The titans were all sentient, much more than had originally been intended, and they were seen as being too much of a danger to humankind after the ancient wars had ended. Hundreds of thousands had died bringing the titans to heel, and they had not even been given a chance to prove they were not a threat.

Right now, technicians responsible for maintaining the stasis of the old ones in the huge underground complex were busy attempting to wipe the memory of humankind's betrayal of Talos. The wiping and reprogramming of the synthetic nervous system was relatively easy compared to that of the intertwined biological nervous system. There was no guarantee that this would work, and the mind of Talos might still be active despite the stasis. Talos could, in theory, purposefully employ trickery which could fool both the technicians and the devices remotely connected to both parts of the nervous system.

The reprogramming was to re-emphasise the original programming, and this was subtly changed to ensure that Talos would fight on behalf of and protect all humans and not just those of the Great Northern Empire. The events since the disastrous opening of the portal and the filth that had come through was fed into the mind of Talos, and also the new objectives: to retrieve the projectiles, prevent them from falling into the claws of the Echthroi, and to help humanity use those projectiles to destroy the Echthroi.

All the footage of the Echthroi was played into the mind of Talos, instilling a sense of disgust and repulsion and a desire to want to destroy them, instead of only doing what he was told. This would vastly reduce the possibility of Talos retrieving the memory of his betrayal and turning on humanity. There was still a chance of that, but there were no other options. All memories not deemed to be risky to humans did remain, though, including all the help he had given to advancing society before the betrayal.

The principle was simple. Ice in its crystalline structure destroyed biological cells as well as metallic structures. Rapid cooling to ~130 Kelvin and increasing the pressure to 3 atmospheres inside the steel sarcophagus maintained an amorphous structure of ice, preventing it from becoming crystalline in structure. This meant that both the biological and synthetic nervous systems, as well as all other systems, would, in theory, retain their viability.

Talos was chosen as he was the easiest to take down via electromagnetic pulse but was theoretically the best titan to fight the Echthroi. Much of the knowledge of the old ones, their capabilities and their nature had been lost over time or was potentially incorrect. But they had to go with the information available. Use of an electromagnetic pulse (EMP) was a last resort. And still it was not a guarantee. It was not a built-in weakness and had only been discovered as the best way to disable Talos for long enough to induce cryogenic freezing. And it would only disable him for a very limited period. As long as the Echthroi did not figure this out and were not able to use an EMP, they would meet their match in Talos.

The wiping and reprogramming were complete, and now the five-minute countdown to the rapid thaw had begun. Five minutes for humanity to change its mind. A flashing red light and a robotic voice emphasised the risks of this action. "BEWARE, TALOS MAY TURN, TALOS MAY REMEMBER, PLEASE RECONSIDER. THIS ACTION MAY ONLY BE JUSTIFIED IN DESPERATE TIMES. PLEASE HAVE EMP ON STANDBY."

This was repeated over and over until the last twenty seconds, when the voice simply repeated the word "WARNING! WARNING!" The last five seconds were simply a countdown. The holographic conference of world leaders watched remotely as the scene unfolded before them. None of them spoke a word during these five minutes, and the emperor of the Great Northern Empire simply bowed her head.

Emperor Kuafiral knew every detail of her country's history. The war of old against the Island Coalition. She remembered Talos fiercely defending his country, and the endless fight with the old one of the Island Coalition, Ása-Þór. Eventually, the mighty armies of both countries had stopped fighting and made peace as neither titan was showing any signs of winning or losing, and the same could be said for both mighty armies. After 20 long elemental cycles of war, they had realised the futility.

In world history, this was seen as the first step towards world peace as humanity came to the collective realisation that if they as a species stood any chance of success and happiness, they had to reconcile and work together.

The old ones did stop fighting on command, but these sentient creations, like humans, needed purpose. Just as an immune system without stimulation turns on its host, it was thought by many that if there was no fight for the old ones, then they would create their own fight. Humanity tried to placate the old ones with purposes such as construction of great citadels and carrying out dangerous missions to remote places to advance scientific discovery. Originally, though, the old ones had been made to fight, with no thought given to when they would not be needed anymore. Over time, humanity's fear and paranoia overcame their willingness to harness the strength and abilities of the old ones.

This building fear and paranoia was manifested in the hysterical belief that humanity's punishment for the genocide of the distant past, long before the great wars, would be at the hands of the old ones. Eventually, the great united armies of the world preemptively attacked the old ones in a sickening act of coordinated betrayal.

No one would ever know what would have happened if the old ones had not been betrayed or whether the preemptive attack had ever been necessary. Everyone did know, however, exactly what would happen if the memories of Talos's betrayal were not successfully wiped. The world watched. Nothing was classified in this enlightened age, as the human race at this time was mature enough to not panic en masse if given full disclosure of all good or bad news.

The rapid warming was completed, and Talos began to move. The sarcophagus cracked open with a hissing sound as soon as the rapid warming was completed, and Talos took one step outside. Talos stood at his full height of one hundred feet and looked around the huge subterranean chamber. He had a black exoskeleton of tungsten carbide, which could change colour for camouflage depending on the environment. He was humanoid otherwise, and his eyes were like those of a cat, with vertically slit pupils and a reflective retina. Synthetic night vision could improve night vision even further if necessary.

Behind thick tungsten carbide bars were a hundred men dressed in the uniform of the Island Coalition's army at the time of the ancient war. The old programming was to destroy any human wearing this uniform, so if he tried to attack the people behind the bars, then the awakening of Talos would have been a huge failure. Talos did not attack, only looked confused. He simply asked in his deep, bellowing voice, "Where are they? The Echthroi. Where are they? And where are the projectiles?"

The decision had been made not to give Talos the available data on the location of the Echthroi. Talos was to be transmitted this information as well as the location of the projectiles only when it had been determined that the wiping and reprogramming was a 100% success. Which it appeared to be. For now.

Prologue Part Six

The brain of Talos, being part biological, needed regular temporary dormancy. The artificial brain also needed to charge from the energy of the great light source of the heavens. So he went into dormancy during the day, to rest and recharge both components of his nervous system. He had made his way to where the projectiles were hidden, deep inside the cold northern wastelands, currently without nationhood.

The northern wastelands hosted a sparse, primitive population who lived as they had for millennia, with all the nations agreeing to leave them alone. This agreement was made after the projectiles had been hidden. Talos had made his way towards the tomb in a random pattern, scanning far around him before and during every movement for possible threatening biological signals. He was going to get there without being seen by the Echthroi, seemingly invincible beings which terrified him beyond belief. But he would save humanity and be the hero of all time.

There were things about humanity he did not like, but these inhuman things filled with concentrated evil and malevolence had to be destroyed. They had no place here, and it was his job to secure the projectiles charged with the power of the universe to prevent them from falling into the hands of the Echthroi. He hoped that humanity would finally learn their lesson not to recklessly interfere with the inner workings of the universe; no good had come of it.

If all went to plan, he would try to use the projectiles to destroy the Echthroi, using one ill-conceived venture to destroy another. It needed to be a decisive victory far from civilization. It was stipulated that he could take them on himself, but as next to nothing was known about the scope of the abilities of the Echthroi, then extreme prejudice was the only way.

He awoke at sunset after a quiet and motionless dormancy lasting one third of a rotational cycle, most of it filled with a horror from the darkness of betrayal by those he had bravely fought to protect, people he had trusted and who had revered him as a hero. Being sentient and needing to lay dormant regularly, it was inevitable that these horrors from the darkness would manifest themselves from time to time. He knew it was not real. But it *felt* real. Betrayal was his greatest fear.

Talos was able to blend into his surroundings well enough in a rural area as long as he remained motionless, which was not a problem for him. He had dispatched some of the smaller Echthroi by ambush on his journey through the wastelands. He had removed the heads of some of the larger ones. However, this might not have been enough. At that time, though, his priority was the projectiles, so all he could do was create a large distance between the heads and bodies, obliterating the heads as best he could.

From a distance, he watched the foothills of Batak Toba for any Echthroi activity with a series of cameras and sensors that alerted him of activity during dormancy, or if there was activity on the unseen side. He had the projectiles stored inside his lower leg, and he knew how to retrieve, arm and detonate the weapons within a few seconds if necessary. He would gladly sacrifice himself if it meant annihilating the Echthroi.

Here was not the place for any detonations, though, for obvious reasons. His plan was to destroy any of the

Echthroi he could if the opportunity presented itself. Another option was to lure them to a remote place and immobilise them one after another. Then he could destroy them using the projectiles and spare human lives. He could not destroy all of them himself, though, and the plans would not go without a hitch, but the humans were wanting to see some tangible results before reawakening the other old ones.

There they were: the twins. Miniature grotesque entities similar in appearance to that of Kronos the Titan, who was now buried in a prison deep in the earth. They were moving around, stopping at regular intervals for who knows what reason. The twins and others of the Echthroi regularly visited the foothills of Batak Toba. The most popular theory for their regular visits was that they were aware of humanity's greatest fear.

It excited them to be near it, the indirect reason the Echthroi were able to escape their hellish realm to this paradise – a paradise where the pleasure of inflicting suffering was infinitely more gratifying than where they came from. This was especially true as humans were much less able to defend themselves, felt pain more intensely, and expired with ease.

The twins acted as a single organism, able to communicate anything with a single look, experiencing joy in the knowledge that vulnerable humans all over the world could see their biggest regret cavorting around on their biggest threat while knowing that they were completely at the mercy of both, mercy which would never be forthcoming. They were laughing at all of humanity, at their lack of ability to do any real harm to the Echthroi at all. Mankind was completely unprepared for the ruin they had unleashed upon their own world, of which they had had dominion since they came down from the trees.

And there was nowhere to hide for humans but in inhospitable wastelands where only death awaited. As the twins were mindlessly revelling in the potential for the decimation of humanity beneath their feet, two huge metallic hands grasped each of their heads. They were lifted off their feet. Talos had made the decision to attack. He believed the twins to be the lesser threats, and the risk was justified. Cracking and squelching could be heard as Talos squeezed with all his might, surprised at both their weight and how hard it was to crush their heads. With each destructive crack, he could *feel* them healing under his grasp.

He was struggling, but at this moment, they were no threat to him. He jerked them around violently, and he could feel what was unmistakably a vertebrae cracking in his right hand, soon followed by the crunch and grind of it attempting to heal. He violently and repeatedly smashed them on the ground. They were now hanging limp from his grip. They were still healing, but now much more slowly. They did not stand a chance. Humanity watched this scene play live and were overjoyed that these hateful things had finally met their match.

Talos put the bodies of each one under his feet, stamped down hard and felt satisfied as he felt the physiological scaffold of these abominations give way. He then pulled each head with every ounce of strength that he had, and one of the twins heads came off in the most satisfying way.

But then Talos felt a twinge from deep in his subconscious mind, and in an instant, a horrific scene played out in his memory. It was over as soon as it had begun, and Talos froze as he held the decapitated head of one twin in one hand and the still attached head of the other twin in the other hand. The twin that was still in one piece began to heal very slowly.

Talos felt a pain as if a blade had been plunged into his head, and with that, all of his buried memories surged into his consciousness. All of them. Including that of the betrayal. He dropped the broken flesh of the twins as his hands opened. He was frozen in disbelief that he was fighting for the survival of this disgusting and perfidious race.

Baphomet and Moloch

The Malefic two of the Echthroi, now with the names Moloch and Baphomet, were watching as the cretinous twins were taunting humanity, which they had no problem with, of course, but the twins were of no use to them. This metallic giant was slowly destroying the twins to well past the point of healing.

Moloch and Baphomet were both mottled in appearance, with various patches of coarse black hair, but Moloch seemed to be mainly blue and Baphomet, mainly green. They were of a similar height of about eight feet, asymmetrical, with wiry arms and torsos with protruding ribs. On the end of each finger, thumb and elbow joint were dirty brown and black claws, each one covered in dried blood. The dried blood was also present around the mouth of each.

Moloch was reptilian in appearance, with sunken yellow eyes and a constant snarl. An open mouth with rows of yellow-brown merciless-looking teeth that looked like they could pierce steel. Baphomet was hideous too, and could not be compared to anything found on earth. One side of the face had a caved-in appearance, with a circular mouth on the other slowly opening and closing, intermittently revealing the same coloured teeth as Moloch but bigger and less numerous. The entire mouth seemed to be on its cheek. One red eye bulged out on the caved-in side and was without a pupil. The eye on the other side was smaller and red and did indeed have a pupil, full of pain and fear and ancient hatred.

They could not gain psychic control of the giant no matter how hard they tried, so they burrowed deep down into his biological brain component and found memories held under psychic lock and key using programming in the artificial component. This meant that a psychic attack was not necessary. A psychic attack involved the manipulation of electrical signals in the brain, very low voltage signals, and because of this, they were unable to manipulate electrical signals within artificial creations to any significant degree. This particular artificial nervous system was specially designed to transmit signals in the millivolt range in order to interface with the biological component. Despite this, the interface by its very nature was something alien to them, and figuring out how to gain sustained manipulation took time they did not have.

The Malefic two were able to interfere with the signals maintaining the programming for just a split second, but that was all they needed. This tiny interference compromised the programming for long enough so that access to these memories was returned in a flood, and even when the programming was automatically restored, it was too late. The memories had escaped their prison.

Moloch and Baphomet cackled at the shared thought that if there had been no interference with the memory of

Talos, they would probably have been at his mercy. They could not have exerted sustained psychic influence, and on an even playing field, he would have ended them. Their claws and teeth were no match for his reinforced metallic exoskeleton and his size.

*

Talos regarded the rippling, crumpled heaps of biological corruption before him in the realisation that he had no friends in this world. No one was like him. He was an artificial creation, and his creators had simply turned on him when his use had expired. And now they needed him again and knew he would only do their bidding if they violated the sanctity of his mind. Talos saw this for what it was: one betrayal on top of another. He knew his creators would betray him again once this particular job was done. He felt hurt, violated and filled with rage. He did not want humanity to succeed.

Previously, any loneliness he had felt was somewhat offset by the bond forged in trust with humanity, but this was all a lie. They had created him, a sentience not dissimilar to that of their own, not to forge a relationship of mutual benefit but one of subjugation and treachery.

He could see that the head of the twin he had decapitated was knitting back onto the neck. It was essentially in one piece. He had only one thought: humanity had made their own bed in calling forth the Echthroi, and now they were on their own, just like him. He grabbed both twins again and held them tight in both fists. He began to climb Batak Toba, still with the elemental weapons in his lower leg.

Talos was designed to withstand sustained attack with

conventional weapons; that was his whole purpose. Considering that there had been no focus on developing weapons of war since he had been put into stasis, there were no new weapons that could easily take him down. Not that they even tried, especially considering his cargo. No EMP weapons were nearby, as it was thought that these would only be needed when Talos was awoken, if at all. And considering the age of the elemental weapons, an EMP could detonate them.

No matter what they said, what promises they made and all of their pleading apologies, Talos did not slow for a second as he charged towards the rim of Batak Toba, intent on his vengeance. All over the planet, people received the emergency broadcast. In a sickening twist of irony, the imminent disaster had been expedited. Now it would be made so much worse because of mankind's catastrophic and ill-conceived attempts to avert the oncoming calamity.

Prologue Part Seven

The dispirited council of leaders were once again hastily convened and all watched helplessly as Talos rapidly ascended the slopes of Batak Toba. They were out of options and were hoping for but not expecting a miracle. The writing was on the wall.

President Artemis of Carpathia put her hand to her ear and nodded. "Learned delegates, I have news from the laboratory of our nation's most gifted growth cipher specialist. May he please address us all?"

Some nodded, most did not respond, and some just stared ahead at nothing in particular. Some gazed at the black circle once occupied by the brave president from Europa.

The population of Europa were not satisfied by the lie told of the fate of their leader, and too much chaos had followed for a replacement to be appointed. Artemis took their lack of response as a yes and pressed a discreet pressure plate in front of her. The footage of Talos and yet another plan going completely wrong was replaced by that of a man in high-risk scientific protective gear similar to those worn by the so-called experts who had accelerated the ruin of their civilization. He took his helmet off and placed it on the floor beside him. He did not look at ease, nor was he comfortable in this gear.

"Please cool the room for my valued expert!" Artemis stated impatiently.

The expert closed his eyes and took a deep breath as the cold purified and dried air hit his face, and he was instantly at ease.

"Please speak in your own time, honoured expert Bhagalet," Artemis said respectfully.

He gave a brief smile and started. "As you know, we have been studying the never-before-seen quadruple growth cipher spiral of the life forms which have invaded our reality, bringing untold suffering upon the world. Compared to humanity's four complimentary elemental cipher units, the Echthroi have many more within their cipher. There is an unknown amount as yet, but we have identified twelve novel complementary cipher units so far."

There was no reaction from the world leaders, so Bhagalet continued. "Through trial and error, within fourteen rotational cycles, we were able to identify patterns within the complementary elemental units. These were identified through the simulated integration of these patterns into the human growth cipher. The simulations showed many millions of disastrous outcomes. We have not tested it yet on humans, but the simulations have never been incorrect once they predicted a positive outcome in specific manipulations of the human growth cipher." He looked around and saw devastation and despair on each face.

Artemis simply stated, "Please continue; you are doing brilliantly. Can you please explain the predicted real-world manifestations of these manipulations?" She smiled warmly at him.

"Thank you, my leader. Yes, I can explain. We needed to manipulate such that the effect on the human growth cipher would result in improvements in the human function whilst keeping the subject human. The desired traits would be the telepathic traits of the Echthroi along with the ability to resist psychic attacks, as well as the strength, durability and life extension."

Now the world leaders were starting to pay attention.

"If we could give these traits to humans using an inactivated pathogenic occult life form, we would stand a chance of defeating the Echthroi. Any further manipulations would be too much of a deviation from the human form."

Chancellor Hariquonal interjected. "But what about after we defeat them, if we can defeat them? What would we be then? Humanoid parasites feeding on one another?"

"No," Bhagalet stated calmly.

Artemis sensed he was mentally tiring. "I volunteered. I had the prototype sample administered two rotational cycles ago. As of yet, I still feel like myself," she said. She pulled an ancient handheld combustive device used to propel metallic projectiles at high speed. This had not been in widespread use for a thousand elemental cycles. Before anyone could utter a word, she placed the device under her chin and pulled the activation lever, resulting in a loud bang.

They all flinched except for Artemis, who placed a hand under her chin and removed a piece of distorted metal which had originally had a streamlined design.

Hariquonal spoke. "He is at the summit. My apologies to President Artemis. Please return to the feed of Talos."

Instantly, they saw Talos standing on the rim of Batak Toba, still holding the twins. The pilots of the numerous aircraft circling continuously around Talos loudly begged for his forgiveness, made promises and apologised, stating that humanity had learnt from its mistakes. Talos knew all this was genuine for now, but he knew that eventually, perhaps after many generations, their ancestors would decide once again to let their fear overcome them, and once again, they would turn on him.

He reached out and dropped both twins into the vent of Batak Toba, and the world watched as the glowing molten earth showed that nothing was too strong or too evil for the earth itself to destroy violently. He turned his back to the vent and fell backwards into peaceful oblivion, his revenge on humanity giving him solace during the final seconds of his existence.

Talos sank into the hard molten glowing earth, his metallic exoskeleton slowly being destroyed as he sank further into the vent. The projectiles were now out of reach of anyone and were quickly reaching critical mass. The delegation of leaders watched with a feeling of utter helplessness. All aircraft and any mobile vehicles raced away from Batak Toba, some faster than others, as well as a sea of humanity that were fleeing on foot. But they were only buying time. There was no escape.

All of the world leaders observed their feed going completely white for a significant time. The whiteness faded eventually to reveal a landscape of complete and utter ruin. The rim of Batak Toba was spilling its tainted filth at high velocity into the stratosphere, red lightning pulsing through, around and outwards. Red hot rocks were already pelting the ground.

"My, my, we have truly failed, haven't we?" said Artemis. She was surprised at herself as the rest of the delegation looked at her in shock. "I'm sorry, but dark humour is all that we have left in the absence of hope."

They all understood, worrying that the alterations to her growth cipher spiral might be causing subtle personality changes.

"She is right," stated Hariquonal.

Baltonovia, Caltroth and Kuafiral all nodded in agreement. Kuafiral pressed a pressure plate in front of him and spoke briefly. Behind him, an assistant brought forth a small container. Kuafiral thanked the assistant and quickly dismissed her before upending the container to reveal paraphernalia as well as little bags of mostly white distillates, all labelled accordingly. Kuafiral got busy preparing a cocktail of injectable distillates, as well as several sticks which would be slowly combusted for inhalation. They all realised what Kuafiral was doing, and they all called in their assistants for the same purpose. Nothing to lose.

They were all redundant now except Artemis of Carpathia. She still had a role to play. For a very long time.

When Kuafiral had administered the distillate parenterally and begun the combustion for inhalation, he asked, "So when can your growth cipher spiral therapy be rolled out en masse?" He inhaled deeply and closed his eyes.

All the other leaders manipulated their paraphernalia excitedly.

"Not possible," stated Artemis. "We are too late. Batak Toba has erupted. Not only that, but as a result of the ancient ones manipulating the fundamental universal particles and thus creating the elemental weapons, the debris from the eruption will emit the decay of this manipulation, and this will reach *everywhere*. Already, communication networks are starting to break down, and this conference feed will be cut off. I promise you that I will use my abilities to protect the remains of humanity and help them not to forget the Echthroi, which most certainly have plans to terrorise all humans left behind. Even if it takes me millennia, I will find a way to get rid of them."

"How?" stated Baltonovia.

They all wanted to know.

"The growth cipher spiral treatment will allow me to live indefinitely without a ..."

The feed was cut off.

Chapter One

Kaitlin

The year was 2026. Kaitlin had just turned 23 and started the last semester of her microbiology master's degree, living at home again to save money. She was far from confident about the outcome of her tertiary educational endeavour. This inner battle had her deeply ingrained imposter syndrome constantly trying to convince her to give up. Her stepdad Tommy had told her many times that even if she believed in her heart that she would fail, it was better to fail than not to try. He would also say that pleasant surprises might be in store as she was likely remembering more and understanding more than she thought.

She had just arrived home and was looking forward to seeing her border collie, Maia, and her three cats. Jesse and Violet were black and white, and Akasha was a tuxedo cat. Jesse was by far the oldest, and having been treated well his whole life, was a truly happy and gentle creature who had welcomed the other two cats without the slightest hint of aggression. The same could not be said about Maia, who was four years old and wanted to be Jesse's friend, but Jesse had never encountered dogs before and they were a long way from becoming friends (if it would ever happen at all).

Violet was a truly beautiful creature with a feisty attitude, and although she did swipe, the first swipe was always just a warning with the claws retracted. She only had eyes for Jesse and tolerated Maia. This was because she was only a kitten when introduced to Jesse, but an adult when introduced to Maia. Akasha, or 'Kash' for short, trusted all humans unconditionally and was not aggressive to the other cats. She was essentially just a kitten, though, and saw the other cats and Maia as playthings, always trying their patience. Maia had been around since Akasha was a kitten, and she was the only cat completely at ease around her. Kash would regularly use Maia for body heat when sleeping, and Maia would happily oblige, sniffing Kash gently before going back to sleep.

Her brother Tim had gone to Weybourne railway yard at Great Yarmouth an hour before Kaitlin arrived home, and it was decided that although Maia should not be left alone if at all possible, it was only for an hour. She had the run of the house with plenty of food, water, treats and toys. Kaitlin would be alone until the late evening, when her mum Ginny and stepdad Tommy arrived home from work. Her mindset was conflicted between wasting time on the internet or getting organised and studying.

In the end, she decided she would study and organise for two hours, and then she would maybe reward herself with some Xbox time. Maia was relaxed, and Kaitlin just let her snuggle under the blanket beside her for now, as she'd had a couple of walks that day already. She could hear Violet's collar bell outside. Violet was the only cat with a bell, as after moving to the countryside, she had embarked upon a murderous spree. The gifts of half-dead or dead birds and rodents to her human family were plentiful, to the point where it got very stressful. The collar had solved the problem, though.

Kaitlin was peripherally aware of world events but overall quite disinterested. Tommy seemed almost obsessed, which was downright annoying. He would also get annoyed with Kaitlin for not caring, especially with things as bad as they were. She did know that Donald Trump, re-elected after defeating Kamala Harris about a year ago, had wasted no time in withdrawing from NATO and forming a new alliance with Russia, China, The Philippines and North Korea. He had stopped all military aid to Ukraine, but the Ukrainians had no intention of surrendering and were making every artillery shell and bullet count.

The existing alliances had not been broken, at least for now. Due to voter apathy and a tiny turnout, Rishi Sunak had been re-elected prime minister eighteen months ago. He and Trump maintained the UK-USA alliance, but it was far from solid, as the relationship between Britain and Russia was increasingly volatile. Eventually, America would have to choose.

Britain was especially vulnerable in the world due to Brexit, which had been quite some time ago, but the supply chains were slowly and insidiously deteriorating due to a lack of trade agreements and crippling inflation. The sinister progression of endless new variants of COVID-19 were also to blame. Instead of a mindless virus, it seemed like a sentient parasite slowly destroying humanity and causing prolonged suffering. The scientific community was beginning to realise that COVID-19 might be linked to a change in human behaviour for the worse. However, research into this possible link was only in its early stages.

Food prices were on a constant rise, with supermarket shelves increasingly scant. Kaitlin was worried about the political strife all over the world, but she was trying to be the eternal optimist she had always been. She hoped that cooler heads would prevail eventually before things went too far.

After the two hours of study time, with perfect timing, Maia woke up. Kaitlin gave Maia and the cats their dinner and let Maia out into the garden to do her business. Not long after, Kaitlin settled down to play the Xbox, with Maia's chin on her lap as she gazed up at her with loving brown innocent eyes. Jesse was sitting behind her head on top of the couch, and Violet was on the other side of the room, both cats still wary of Maia but getting slightly less so every day. Kaitlin tried to text her mum asking what would be for dinner, but there did not appear to be a signal at all.

The internet was still there, but the signal was getting weaker. There were only a few lights on in the house, but those lights started to flicker. The red LED light at the bottom of the TV turned off and on a few times. It looked like no Xbox for tonight without a consistent power supply. Kaitlin was worried about a full power cut in the fading sunlight of this January afternoon. It would be very creepy out here in the countryside, and she was not used to the silent darkness far from the city.

There was nothing else for it but to go and have a nap. She found the headlamp that Tommy had bought and held it in her hand, waiting to drift off. Her phone was charged, and she had a fully charged 50,000 mAh power bank in case of emergencies. Maia had curled up in the tiny cat bed, Jesse and Violet were settled on the couch, and Akasha was batting something unseen around the floor. The sound of Akasha playing made her smile in the darkness. The pets were nursing their full stomachs, but not Kaitlin. It would not be long before Ginny got back and cooked her something. Just as it seemed everyone would soon be sound asleep except for Akasha, Maia suddenly stood up, fully alert, and started whimpering.

Kaitlin put on the headlamp, turned it on, and could see across the room that both Jesse and Violet were awake with their ears back, pupils fully blown even in the bright light. Jesse was silent, and Violet was emitting low-frequency, hellish noises from deep in her throat. They were angry, ready to face down something. Akasha was nowhere to be seen. Maia jumped onto Kaitlin and put her full weight on her, getting in as close as possible with her tail between her legs. Kaitlin then heard what sounded like a far-off crack of thunder, but the sound had a sinister, unnatural edge to it. She could tell it was far away, but loud, wherever it was. Violet hissed for a few seconds, then stopped, now seemingly only on high alert.

Maia was still terrified, so Kaitlin comforted her by talking softly about things Maia liked, mentioning words such as 'ball', 'shitbags', 'park', 'lead', 'harness' and 'shop'. Each word caused a tilt of the head in adorable expectation. As always, it worked. Kaitlin loved this dog, as did anyone who came across her. Truly one of a kind. Kaitlin noticed that the LED at the bottom left of the TV and the other lights in the house were now off. The power was out. Strangely not scared, Kaitlin wondered what was going on. The cats had calmed down, but their pupils remained fully dilated, even when she shone the light at them. Innocent little Kash had resumed her playing.

Whatever Kaitlin had felt and heard, her pets had sensed tenfold. Kash eventually stopped her playing after tiring herself out. She jumped up on the couch beside Kaitlin. Violet sat on her other side, and Jesse stayed where he was. Maia remained nestled in Kaitlin's lap, with her head on her shoulder. She was becoming calmer by the second. Maia and the cats discreetly changed their demeanour to watchful and vigilant. Kaitlin was simultaneously delighted and creeped out when she noticed this was the first time all the pets were in such close proximity to each other without being aggressive, having formed a protective phalanx around her. *What are they protecting me from?* she thought.

Kaitlin was growing uneasy, counting down the seconds until Ginny and Tommy got home.

Chapter Two

Ginny and Jane

Ginny

Ginny had really landed on her feet this time. She had just completed the finishing steps of electronic DNA analysis for emailing to clients. Her staff had tested samples sent in by the owners of several Cavalier King Charles spaniels to see if they were carriers of the faulty GlyT2 recessive gene. If expressed on both alleles, this could cause episodic falling. If any of them were carriers of the faulty gene, then any offspring could not be sold. If the faulty gene was not present, a certificate would be generated to confirm this, which was invaluable for the breeders.

Ginny usually took Maia with her to work, and her colleagues also brought in their dogs. They played together and always had their lunchtime walks in the woodland surrounding the trust. Maia had seemed quite tired that morning after a long walk the previous day, so Ginny had decided to leave her at home with Tim.

Ginny was Head of Genetic Services at the British Pet Guardianship Society in Downmarket. Although she had previously worked with human samples, the science itself was still fascinating. It had the potential to help pave the way for advancements in human genetic sampling and analysis in the future, the ethics of which was another conversation altogether. All Ginny cared about right now was that she was helping to advance the science of genetics for the future.

The future, Ginny thought as she shook her head and sighed. She did not really care about global politics, but her husband, Tommy, talked about it a lot, which could be quite tiresome. Having said that, thinking about the 'New World Alliance', or NWA, as it was called, between the USA, Russia, China, The Philippines and North Korea, sent a shiver down her spine. There was no more NATO, so when it came to the crunch, would the US support the UK?

America was increasingly becoming a terrifying place in the minds of most Britons. In half the country, abortion was now illegal, and Trump was doing his best to make it illegal for the whole country. He did not even care and was only pandering to the religious extremists who gave him his power. America was becoming a Christian fascist state, and if the USA did protect the UK, would it be worth the price they would have to pay?

Typical, Ginny thought. Things were going great for her and her family, but if the world had no future, neither did they. All she could do was hope that things got better, as it was completely beyond her control. It was after 2.30 p.m., and Ginny had given the staff the rest of the day off. Their work was up to date, and they had worked hard to help the lab pass the recent intense round of inspections. Catherine had agreed to this as a one-off, as it would help staff morale. Emma, the last member of staff in the building apart from Ginny, stuck her head round the door to say goodbye. Ginny liked that people did this; it meant they did not hate her, at least.

Ginny was a really nice person, which conflicted with her duties as a manager at times, and she had to take the hard line on occasion, but she believed she had reached a good balance. She decided to text Tommy and Kaitlin to let them know she was staying a bit late to finish the analysis. She had taken the hard line with them too, recently, by not cooking their meals anymore, and they were fine with this, but they did not eat well and she had gone back on her word to avoid them getting scurvy.

No signal. At all. Unusual, Ginny thought, but nothing to really worry about. The internet was still up, so she would finish the analysis. Then two things happened. She heard some sort of a blast or detonation. It was big, but it was not close. And there was probably a delay between the detonation and when she heard it, which explained no phone signal and slow internet. Ginny could not believe she was thinking logically at this point as what was happening was alarming, reinforced by the trembling beneath her feet like a small earthquake, but not nearly enough to cause property damage or be any risk to her safety, and it was over as quickly as it started.

Ginny was acutely aware that she was not terrified, with the knowledge that she should be. She then heard the deafening sound of many, many jets screaming past, very close to the ground. She rushed to the glass bridge which connected the two laboratory buildings and looked up. There were literally hundreds in the air, and they continued screaming past for what seemed to be a full minute. Then they were gone, and all was silent. Time to go home, right now. She went to turn off all sources of electricity before she went and realised all of the lights were out. All the power was gone.

The only source of light in the complete darkness was her fully charged phone, which provided comfort, even though the signal was gone. She did not want to be alone in this place, in the dark, and the daylight was already fading fast. Her decision to leave was expedited by the sounds of screaming and gunfire, far enough away for her to be safe for now, but too close for comfort.

Ginny used the torch of the phone to guide her to the

staff kitchen, where she grabbed the biggest and the smallest knives. She then stopped by the lab and put on some gloves. She grabbed the five-litre concentrated hydrochloric acid solution, brought it to the fume cupboard, and slowly decanted it into a 200 ml empty plastic water bottle she found in the bin. She replaced the lid, which she realised was non-spill, and if primed could be squirted by squeezing the bottle. *How the hell am I thinking so clearly?* she thought. She then made sure the lid was properly fastened and closed and went to the freezer to grab one more thing – three one-litre glass bottles of 100% ethanol.

She barely managed to fit all this into her backpack along with a can opener and all of the canned food she was able to find in the kitchen. The smallest knife went in her coat pocket, the biggest one was strapped in place on the outside of the rucksack, the 200 ml of hydrochloric acid in the side pocket. She hurried across the car park to get to the second love of her life, her white Nissan Juke, and was extremely relieved when she remembered she had filled it with diesel that morning. Ginny remembered Tommy's words to engage the central locking as soon as she got in, and she did just that. Then someone tried the front passenger door.

"GET THE HELL OUT!!!!" shouted a young man around seventeen years old, in typical chav gear, including the baseball cap. His face seemed full of rage and hate, almost inhuman. He then started punching the window over and over, oblivious to what must have been pure agony. He was screaming, and she became aware of the cacophony of screams from what must have been about five people in this gang that she observed in her rearview mirror. The smashing of the rear left window snapped her out of her frozen state.

She stepped on the accelerator and pulled away with a hard right. The guy that had smashed the window, with his fist reduced to mincemeat, had got his arms and upper body into the car but was thrown back out the window, scraping up his torso on the way. He held on for a few seconds but had to let go. The gang gave chase, throwing anything they could get their hands on. She heard something hitting the car, but thank God, she had got away. In her rearview mirror, she saw one of the gang waving her hands and mouthing the words 'help me'. She was running faster than the rest, who were now chasing *her*. Ginny stepped on the breaks.

Jane

Not ten minutes ago, Jane had been in the corner of a field with her friends, all sitting around a fire in the dying light, smoking high grade ~18% purple punch skunk, with Andy holding on to the harder stuff they planned to do later. They all heard the far away explosion and felt the mild earthquake but were unfazed and too high to take it seriously. Jane had a bad feeling, though. Her friends looked up in awe when the fighter jets roared by above their heads.

When they had all passed, Andy stood up, screamed at the top of his lungs with his arms up, and ran towards the woodland. The sound was inhuman. The rest followed. Jane was confused and could think of nothing better to do than follow. She caught up quickly due to her athletic build, which still remained despite the booze and drugs. They were going crazy, whooping, screaming in each other's faces.

Andy turned around and screamed at her. He wasn't Andy anymore. He was pure rage, all else gone. His pupils were dilated with barely an iris present at all, with the sclera so bloodshot as to be completely red. They all stopped and looked at her. All of their eyes were the same. Instinctively, Jane screamed as loud as she could and threw her hands in the air. She exhausted her vocal cords trying to make it seem inhuman, but it worked. They seemed happy with this and resumed their madness. They eventually made it to a car park adjacent to the nearest building and saw a lady power walking to her car with a purpose.

Andy stopped and watched her for a second, as did the rest, and then they took off in the lady's direction, this time in complete silence, like a shared thought. The lady was oblivious. She made it to her car in good time and closed the driver's door, and Jane could hear the central lock engaging. Andy tried the passenger door a split second later, and when it did not open, he started repeatedly punching it. The lady looked frozen in shock and fear

When Derek broke the rear passenger window, the lady snapped out of it and pulled up to the right and sped off, but not before Derek almost made it inside the car, being thrown out as she pulled off. They all gave chase. *Now or never.* Jane gave chase on foot and easily passed her 'friends'. After she was well enough in front of them, always making the effort to increase her distance, she started waving her arms and silently mouthing, '*help me*'.

They now appeared to have given up on the car and were chasing her. Her legs were burning as she surged with all the adrenalin she had, hoping the lady in the car had seen her. Then the car slowed down to a brisk walking pace. She used her last reserves of adrenalin to reach the car and jumped through the windowless rear door on the passenger side.

Chapter Three

Jonah and Cele

Jonah was depressed. There was no better way of putting it. Until recently, he'd been living in Spalding, Lincolnshire, with his pregnant girlfriend's parents, but they had had a falling out. None of them worked apart from the father, and they were driving each other crazy at the house. Celeste, or 'Cele', was driving Jonah back to his mum Ginny's and stepdad Tommy's rented house in Wymondham, three hours away, and they were an hour into the journey. The purpose was to cool off for a while and then go back.

Jonah just wanted to earn money, and with every rejection and ghosting he got, he became more and more demoralised and fed up, especially if he perceived that an interview had gone well. Nobody could even be bothered to send a rejection email or communicate at all. So spineless. Cele was still in the first trimester and not showing yet. She was completely honest about her pregnancy with prospective employers, and she knew at least one company did not take her on purely because she was pregnant. It was an eye opener. Discrimination was still alive and well; the only difference between now and 40 years ago was that it was done openly back then, and now it was always hidden behind a 'legitimate' reason.

They heard the far-off concussive blast, which was barely perceptible, but there was still no doubt that it was *big*. Cele stopped just in time to feel the earth rumbling ever so slightly. She got out of the car. In the distance, she could hear something loud in the sky, and it was getting closer.

She saw a huge number of fighter jets flying towards

them, and they were being bombarded by what was obviously anti-aircraft fire when about fifteen or so exploded in the sky. The rest kept going and passed them. More were exploding. They were trying to escape. A full thirty seconds later, coming from the same direction, more fighter jets were following, but these sounded different.

From the east, more of the first type appeared and in unison all let off their rockets, flying towards the pursuing jets. All fifteen or so were torn to shreds by the anti-aircraft guns and missiles following them, seemingly fired from elsewhere. The pursuing jets were closing their distance and started ejecting little balls of light which seemed to attract the rockets fired from the interceptors. The rockets exploded harmlessly amidst the little balls of light. One of the pursuing jets caught damage from anti-aircraft fire after they passed overhead. Cele guessed it was done unintentionally and it looked like the pilot had ejected but they were kicking and screaming in their seat. *What the fu…??*

Cele snapped out of her trance when a full wing landed in the middle of the road. It was blue camouflage with a red star and white outline. Jonah had woken up and came over to her. "What does the red star mean?" she asked.

"Russia," Jonah replied.

Neither of them had any idea what was going on, but Russian jets exploding above English airspace gave them enough of a clue.

Then they realised a man was running towards them, eyes full of black rage and a machete in his hand. They jumped back in the car and started the engine before he could get to them. As they pulled off, the guy gave chase, but there was a middle-aged woman in the middle of the road in front of them. She was smiling, with blood flowing from her mouth and covering the front of her professional business suit. Cele slowed down, beeping the horn and trying to change her direction to swerve around, but the woman kept moving to stay in front of them.

The machete man was gaining on them.

"Just bloody well run over her!" Jonah screamed as Cele sobbed with fear and started shaking.

"I can't!" she replied.

"Just breathe and sodding drive or we are DEAD!" At this point, Jonah wished it was him in the driver's seat, but there was no time to change over. "GO! NOW!!"

Cele stepped on the accelerator and sped towards the woman, reaching 30 mph as they hit her.

Her knees buckled and her lower legs bent unnaturally. Her head cracked the windscreen as it impacted, and her head completely caved in. She went over the car and landed behind them like a rag doll. Jonah looked in the rearview mirror and saw her trying to move, her brains spilling out of her head. Cele sprayed screenwash on the cracked windscreen to wash off the brain matter, and luckily it appeared that despite the crack, the windscreen was maintaining its integrity, and the cracks were on the passenger side.

"Jonah, what the hell is going on?" she asked, looking for reassurance even though Jonah knew just about as much as she did.

"I don't know exactly what's happening, but it looks like my wildest dreams are coming true!" he said, grinning.

Cele was shocked to hear this and she glanced at Jonah.

The grin was not that of Jonah. It was unrecognisable.

Jonah could not believe what was happening. All he knew was that he had gone to sleep and woken up to see the world burning. As he looked around, the smile stubbornly stayed on his face. Suddenly, he felt hit with the most extreme adrenaline rush he had ever felt, out of nowhere. All of the negative emotions a person could feel welled up inside him. But not just that. He also felt his ability to experience positive emotions burning itself away.

He looked over at Cele, who was looking at him for as long as possible and glancing back at the road, then back to him. She had a look of terror and disbelief and confusion, but inside, just felt ruin. Slowly and with as much calmness as she could muster, she said, "What the hell is wrong with your eyes, Jonah? STOP BLOODY SMILING AT ME! WHAT IS WRONG WITH YOUR EYES?!"

Jonah was starting to lose his ability to experience empathy. He knew he was turning into one of *them*. What felt like a slow lightning bolt of pain contorted his entire body. He felt blood trickling down his chin due to his incisor puncturing his tongue, but he had bigger problems.

Anything inside him that was good started to circle the drain even faster, but with a jolt, his cognitive abilities flooded back. He looked at the makeup mirror and his eyes were going from completely black to normal again. He looked over at Cele.

"Thank goodness those black eyes are gone!" she cried.

"If it was just the eyes, I could barely handle it, but with the smile, I was already looking for something to stab you with!"

Jonah used the final fragments of his humanity to scream at Cele.

"LOOK AT THE GODDAMN ROAD! DO NOT LOOK AT ME AGAIN OR I WILL KILL YOU!"

Jonah thought he was losing himself, but the deep guttural rasp at the edges of his voice made him realise he was being replaced. And this was also the reason he did not have to tell Cele twice.

"SPEED UP AND FACE FRONT AND DO NOT STOP NO MATTER WHAT!" He released his seat belt, opened the door, and with the last of his humanity, he hurled himself out the door. He changed his mind and decided he was going to kill her and his unborn child. But it was too late. Cele was already going at 60+ mph as he tried in vain to grab onto any part of the car to haul himself back inside and quench his hatred.

When he finally stopped rolling, he tried to stand up. Not only was his left knee dislocated, but his lower left leg was degloved. He inspected the damage. He felt no pain, but it was impossible to stand on a dislocated knee, pain or no pain. He pulled the skin back over the knee, only for it to snap back into place below the knee. It was filled with gravel and dirt. He felt his nose, and this also was dislocated or broken. Everywhere else had only scrapes and cuts. "I WILL FIND YOU AND KILL ALL OF YOU!!" he screamed. This sounded at least ten times louder than any volume he could have mustered before.

He turned to look behind him and bore witness to a scene right out of the *Night of the Living Dead*: an army of former humans, growling intermittently as if to murmur interest. He was not afraid of them. He did not even pity them. But he did not hate them. There was nothing to hate. He knew on a primal level that these mindless things were his subordinates, to do his bidding in order to focus the raw destructive power of their potential. He also sensed that these beings were temporary, and depending on the damage done in the meantime, they would return to normal in a few days.

A switch had been flipped inside of him, and this was permanent. They wanted something from him, but he did not know what it was or why they did not try to just take it from him. Maybe they did not know, or maybe they thought he was in some way stronger? Just then, a white-coated figure came running through the crowd, a stethoscope around her neck and the usual blood and gore around her mouth. She was carrying a bag and knelt down beside him. She stopped and looked him in the eye briefly before putting her head down. Jonah grunted an 'Okay'.

She clamped her hand down around his lower thigh. In a normal human, this would have brought pain and discomfort, and they both knew that. With her other hand, she clamped down on the lateral malleolus for leverage. Then with a single sudden movement, she pulled with her left hand and pushed with her right, and a sickening crunch could be felt. Jonah felt nothing, of course, so he tried to stand up and found that he could. A guttural roar rose within him and percolated through the demonic horde, which Jonah noticed had grown bigger.

The doctor creature motioned for Jonah to get down, and she gently bent the leg at the knee. She rinsed out the visible dirt and gravel from his degloved knee with spring water which she happened to have on her. This was not the type of procedure normally done at the side of the road. After re-rinsing everything with a limited amount of sterile saline wound irrigation solution, she pulled the skin over his knee and meticulously sewed the skin from his lower leg to the upper leg. Jonah then stood up and lifted his knee. He was back in one piece but knew he needed to be extra careful to avoid tearing the stitches, especially if he could not feel any pain anymore.

The doctor thing just stood there.

"Well, piss off, then! Thanks for the repair, but kindly piss off, please! I need to figure out what's going on and you're staring ..."

In an instant, the good doctor clamped her teeth onto his arm, seemingly taking a mouthful of blood. After she'd finished, she pulled her head back and screamed the most demonic scream he thought possible. Jonah now knew what they wanted as they started moving in on him. He also knew that they had seen the doctor thing take it without permission or consequence.

He was not afraid. He clamped his hand on the back of her neck and squeezed. Once he had a firm grip on her backbone, he used his other hand to rip away the rest of her throat. He pulled her head off with ease, as well as part of her spine. Then *he* screamed the loudest he could, holding up the head and backbone as a message. He fed on the blood falling from the severed head, and it tasted oh, so sweet. They fell to their knees, clasping their heads. Blood flew out of the sides of some of their heads and they fell limp. Jonah stopped. They had got the message. But Jonah knew he probably would have to send more messages in the future.

He needed their blood to live; they needed his blood to stay undead. Thankfully not too much in one sitting, no more than a mouthful. They were not loyal, but they feared him and would need regular, perhaps pre-emptive messages. They would do his bidding, execute every command, every single command except *go away, leave me alone*. Not that he wanted that. He felt something he had never felt. *True power.*

*

Cele slowed to 40 mph. Night had fallen, and fog was drastically reducing visibility. She felt protected by the car, but it was not much use upended in a ditch. Jonah was gone and had used the last part of what remained of him to save her and the baby. When she turned the corner, she had seen those things descend on him en masse. She knew now she had to get to the university. Any of the family not completely destroyed would know to go there. Two hours. She had to ensure her own survival and that of Amelia, or Jonah had sacrificed himself for nothing.

Chapter Four

Howell's Pharmacy

The bang in the distance. The tremor. The aerial conflict raging above them. All the staff and customers had gone outside and tried to make out what was going on, but in the dying light, all anyone could see was a distant chaos of tracer bullets and explosions. The intensity eventually died down until some thirty jets started screaming into the further distance, closely followed by about ten or fifteen more with endless tracer bullets flowing towards the escaping jets. More explosions were heard, but this fight quickly disappeared below the horizon. The remaining jets also turned and screamed over the opposite horizon. Then silence.

The staff of Howell's Pharmacy of Stratton River and its customers, totalling around fifteen people, looked at each other in silence for what seemed like forever but was only about ten seconds. Everyone who had a phone had it out to find out what was going on, but there was nothing, no signal at all. Everyone went back into the pharmacy, and upon realising there was no power, four customers ran out of the shop, jumped into their cars and sped away, with the realisation that their prescription for antibiotics or antihistamines to combat the sniffles or a booboo on their finger was not worth it.

Everyone knew this was serious. It was now impossible to find out where any prescription was if it was not already bagged on the shelf, so if it was not, all the staff could do was ask patients what medicines they were on and just grab it off the shelves. The staff had decided to lock the door at this point and give the present customers what they needed. It did not occur to any of the elderly patients to take more than a single box of what they needed.

But it did occur to Tommy, the on-duty pharmacist. By the time the last customer was gone, the staff had locked themselves in the shop and Tommy's rucksack was full of inhalers, antibiotics, prednisolone, pregabalin, tramadol, promethazine, diazepam, as well as controlled release and normal release oxycodone and morphine. Tommy did not take everything, only what he thought he would need for the foreseeable future if things were as bad as they hinted they were going to be. The staff realised what he was doing pretty quickly at that point.

Although they were initially bothered by how quickly he made the decision to do what he did, they understood and quickly followed suit, taking everything they thought they would need, even taking tablets out of the boxes to make room in their bags. Even after the staff had taken what they needed, they agreed to leave a lot of antibiotics, Ventolin inhalers, morphine solution and prednisolone at the front counter. They knew once they left that, people would come looking, and these would be the kinds of medications they would be looking for. There were still medicines remaining that staff could not carry in their bags, and they did not want to be going back and forth to load up their cars. Everybody still had an ample supply of everything they would need.

"What do we do now?" asked Holly.

"Well, it's pretty simple," Tommy said. "We either stay, or we go. And each person, if they want to go, had better do so now before whatever is happening gets worse." Tommy's family home was an hour away, and everyone except Kaitlin was away from home, at work or otherwise.

"I'm staying until I can decide what to do. I think if you live close, you should try to get to your family."

"Well, I think I'm going; my kids are at school," said Holly.

Diane and Wendy also decided to leave as all three lived close by, all with kids at the same school.

"I'm staying," said Suzanne. "I live close by, but my husband's working an hour away. I think I would be safer here until I decide what to do, like Tommy."

The staff unlocked the door. Holly and Wendy and Diane walked out, got into their cars, and left. Outside was deserted, with strangely no activity from the surgery next door. There were still cars in the car park. Instead of going straight back in, Tommy decided to investigate.

"What the hell are you doing?" Suzanne asked.

"I'll be back in thirty seconds. I just want to see what's going on next door, as they're strangely silent in there."

Bastard idiot." Suzanne shook her head and locked the door, peering out as Tommy crept over to the main entrance of the surgery.

"Bugger off, you twat," Tommy said under his breath as he went over.

He peered in the front entrance and saw no one there. A woman dressed like a receptionist came running out of a hall adjacent to the front entrance with a big pair of scissors in her hand. She then hid behind the reception desk as a deranged-looking middle-aged man in a suit and tie came from the same direction. *Was that a stethoscope around his neck?*

He had a wicked smile on his face, and Tommy could see that he was talking as he approached the reception desk. He went around the back of the desk, his smile broadened, and he dived towards where the receptionist was hiding. He emerged ten seconds later, staggering backwards with the scissors embedded in the middle of his chest. He then fell backwards and was still. Tommy then saw the receptionist's hand flop down and a pool of blood spread from behind the desk.

Suzanne saw the terrified expression on Tommys' face as he staggered backwards and then ran back to the door. She unlocked it, let him in, and relocked it. "What did you just see?"

Tommy just stood frozen in place, trying to get the words out.

"WHAT DID YOU SEE?" Suzanne shook Tommy physically until he stopped looking through her and then looked directly at her, snapping back to reality.

"I think I just saw a receptionist and a GP kill each other ... Locking the door is not enough. Get the shutters down, now."

Suzanne went to the back door and pulled down the shutters manually while Tommy did the same at the front door. They were designed so that you could see out but not in.

"What is happening?" Suzanne said.

"Let's face it, we're under attack. That skyward display we saw in the distance? Let's hope that we were the victors in that one."

"Have you any idea why a receptionist and a GP would kill each other?"

"Clearly it's related, but I don't know how," Tommy said.

There was something about the way Tommy was speaking to her that was pissing her off, like he thought he was better than her. So what if he was a pharmacist? She worked just as hard as him, and on a much lower wage.

"Who the hell do you think you are, Tommy? Just because you're a pharmacist doesn't make you better than me!"

"What the hell? I hardly think that's constructive! Can we put that aside for n…"

Her anger was building exponentially, and after more perceived patronisation, she lunged at him, punching him on the jaw and knocking him to the ground. She straddled him. Tommy definitely did not want that. He was still too shocked to respond. She continued to rain down blows upon him as he automatically held up his arms in defence. She landed a blow on target and felt his nose break with a satisfying, sickening crunch. She just wanted to kill him so badly. She felt herself sliding helplessly backwards down a tunnel, watched from the top by her own vicious countenance staring down at her, smiling through bloodstained teeth.

Tommy was not a fighter. He had seen this scene play out in so many movies. He was on his back, nose broken, essentially being water-boarded by his own blood flow. There was no weapon to the side he could use to get her off him. The blows stopped once his nose broke, but immediately, she opened her mouth, going for his throat. All he could do was grab the hair on both sides of her head and push back, but she seemed to be a lot stronger than she should be. Tommy was not going to stop her this way and he needed to get off his back, to get her off him.

He decided to gather all his strength, kept hold of her hair, and threw her off him. Once she was off him, he got to his feet fast. She was still getting up, so he quickly got behind her and put his right arm around her neck. He grabbed his right wrist with his left hand, his first attempt at a real-world choke hold. On a possessed lady. He squeezed and pulled back. Tommy was unfit and was already exhausted. She did not get back to her feet due to Tommy's weight but thrashed around with inhuman strength. If she overcame him before she passed out, he was done. Just when his arms were burning to the point he would have no choice but to let go, she finally stopped thrashing and passed out.

Tommy let go and kicked her away from him. He lay on his back, gasping for about a minute until he could use his arms again, and then she started groaning. Tommy knew where there were zip ties for sealing totes filled with medicines to send to other branches, and he ran out the back, looking for them. He could not see them and was looking under everything, in every drawer, every nook and cranny. He stopped, took a deep breath and opened his eyes. They were on the shelf beside him. He had not seen them originally due to his panicked state.

He grabbed a handful, racing back to Suzanne, who was quickly regaining consciousness. If he did not restrain her, she would easily overcome him. He lifted her to a seated position and pulled her hands behind her back. He had never used zip ties previously, but they were self-explanatory, and in no time, her wrists and her ankles were restrained. He made a mental note to check for blood flow as he was not taking any chances with her getting free, and they may have been too tight. He grabbed the biggest pair of scissors he could find, pulled out a customer seat and sat opposite her. She was awake and looking at him.

"Care to explain yourself?" Tommy asked.

"I hate you and I'm going to kill you, you piece of shit."

She was squirming to get free, and it looked too

painful for a normal person to endure. He then realised she did not seem to feel pain. Tommy confirmed in his mind what he had originally expected. There had obviously been some sort of nerve or biological attack, and only some were susceptible. But that was more than enough for whoever saw fit to disperse it. It clearly involved hyperstimulation of the sympathetic nervous system.

Tommy immediately went and got 200 mg of carbamazepine to suppress action potentials in the nerves, 160 mg of propranolol to counter the effects on the adrenergic receptors, and 20 mg of diazepam to activate the GABA receptor and thus counter the hyperstimulatory effects. *Throw some shit at the wall, hopefully some will stick*, Tommy thought. He approached her.

"You think you're going to make me take them, you pathetic arsehole?"

"Trust me, Suzanne, if this works, you will thank me."

"I will not stop until I kill you, you pig fondler!"

Tommy grabbed her hair and pulled her head back. He let go and held her nose closed, pushing back against the wall so she could not move her head. She had no choice but to open her mouth. He threw all the tablets in and used his knee under her jaw to hold her mouth closed, with the top of her head pressed into the wall so she was fixed in place. The rest of her body was squirming, and Tommy felt his energy draining as he tried to hold her in place.

"Swallow the goddamn tablets!"

"MMMMMMMMMM" was all she could muster.

"Swallow the bastard tablets if you want to breathe again!!"

She swallowed and he let go. He thought she was faking and would spit the tablets back at him, but luckily, that did not happen. Over the next fifteen minutes, she slung the worst verbal abuse imaginable towards Tommy, but she gradually stopped squirming and started to weep, still threatening to kill him. After twenty minutes, she passed out. Twenty-five minutes after she had taken the pills, she regained consciousness. She looked at Tommy, whose face was covered in dried blood, nose obviously broken. He was soaked in sweat, still breathing heavily and white-knuckling a pair of huge scissors. She could not move her arms and she was in pain from head to toe, like she had pulled every muscle in her body. She felt drowsy and could barely speak. "What the hell happened?" she whimpered.

Tommy used the scissors to free her hands, and she was rubbed the ligature marks on her wrist, where the skin looked like it was about to come off with the slightest trauma. Tommy gave her some Savlon, and she applied it to the area.

"We both nearly sodding well died," Tommy said. He grabbed a vial of cyclimorph and broke it, drew it up into a 1 ml syringe and re-sheathed the needle. He did the same with a vial of diazepam 10 mg/ml and gave both pre-prepared injections to her. He tossed them to her. He wished he had thought of this in the first place. He figured that anything to counteract the overstimulation of the sympathetic nervous system would work.

"You'll need these."

"What the hell happened?!"

"Well, obviously, you're susceptible to whatever nerve or biological agent we've been exposed to, and I'm not. The *second* you start to feel angry or weird again, inject both of these into the muscle on your thigh. I don't know if you've been temporarily or permanently cured, and it's pretty clear we have to determine which before we leave."

She pictured herself in a room full of people, all of them her, giving that familiar bloodstained smile and shuffling closer with each passing second. In the middle of that room was the hole she had just got out of. Tommy guessed if it was a small molecule nerve agent, she would be okay once it was metabolised. She would not be so lucky if this was biological. She nodded her head in agreement. All Suzanne could remember was Tommy coming back from the surgery, locking the door, and then she was sliding feet first backwards down the hole. Then nothing.

Chapter Five

Tim Clarke (RIP)

Tim loved trains. Partly due to the fact that his dad did, also. His dad had passed away from metastatic stomach cancer almost sixteen years ago. Six weeks from when the lump was noticed until death. Ironically, it was not caught earlier because of the human body's ability to adjust and function normally, until it couldn't. And then it was too late. Tim, being the oldest, had taken it the hardest and had had to endure bullying in secondary school because of it, because people are just *awful*. His younger two brothers also got bullied.

Tim was type one diabetic, and there was a school of thought that suggested the stress caused by his father's passing triggered the onset of the disease. Tim did not get on well with Tommy, his stepdad, a lot of the time and had good reason not to. They had never got on, and he was the polar opposite of what his stepdad was. But Tim, being an adult for most of the time Tommy and Ginny had been together, had to accept that he shared the blame as to why they did not get on. He had also driven his mother to the brink of insanity at times and sparked off a lot of the arguments Tommy and Ginny had.

But Tommy was forever the one to overreact to things and did so often, so Tim could not be blamed for that. His relationship with Tommy was okay these days, due to the fact that Tim was working full-time and making an honest living. Both Tim and Tommy suffered from severe depression, the one thing they had in common. When Tim was not working or looking after himself, this had a tendency to trigger Tommy.

Tim was volunteering at the rail yard of the transport

museum on his day off. This was where he was happiest. Tim and the customers in the rail yard experienced the far-off explosion, the jets screaming overhead, the minor tremor, and the phone service and electricity getting cut off. Tim sensed that this was where he was supposed to be at this moment. Anywhere else, including at home, he would have freaked out.

An old lady and her husband, whom Tim had been talking trains with ten minutes ago, looked at him, and he looked back. The old lady, who had been carrying a pamphlet for the yard, just let it drop as she turned to look at her husband. Tim saw something change in her eyes, which had gone almost black due to extreme pupil dilation, and the whites of her eyes went red. Where before Tim had seen in her eyes a lifetime of positivity and kindness, he now observed an abyss of endless hatred and madness.

The husband was still oblivious and looking at Tim, as if Tim could give an explanation purely because he worked there and had displayed great knowledge of steam trains during their exchange not ten minutes before. The lady grabbed what remained of her husband's hair and pulled his head back, exposing his throat. She put as much of his Adam's apple and throat into her mouth as would fit and bit down with all her might. Tim was frozen in place, peripherally aware that around him, things were kicking off and people were fighting.

Tim was focused on the couple, convinced he was having a hallucination. The man silently mouthed the word 'help'. Tim snapped out of it and ran towards them. When he got to them, the lady locked eyes with him. An evil grin spread across her face, boring into his soul. This grin was made worse by the blood all over the lower part of her face, intermingling with the yellow of her teeth.

Tim had no clue what to do and so just grabbed her hair and pulled with all his might. She shrieked, but not with pain. It was a shriek of pure pleasure and excitement. All the husband could do was let out a gurgling sound. As Tim pulled, she also pulled back with all her might, and the gurgling got more panicked. It took Tim only a second or two to realise he was helping her and not the husband, but then it was too late. Before he could stop pulling, he felt a release and was sprayed with blood. She had managed to bite out the entirety of what she had in her mouth. It was inhuman.

All three of them fell to the ground. The husband was seconds from death and could not be saved. She got to her feet quickly, but Tim was still stunned. She spat her husband's throat out and looked down at Tim. She grinned the same way again and dived at Tim, face first and mouth agape. Tim rolled away, but the old lady had not put her arms out to break her fall, even though she had plenty of time to do so. Any regard for her own safety seemed to have been taken from her somehow.

Her open mouth planted on a wrought iron steel track, and she went still. But only for a few seconds. She got up and was clearly bleeding out from her smashed lower jaw. She attempted to grin again, but this was not possible as the entire structure of her jaw and face were destroyed beyond repair. *Why the hell was she not in agony?* Tim could see at least ten bloodstained teeth on and around the track.

He sprinted to the loco shed, where he knew there was an array of potential blunt force weapons. He unbolted the door and grabbed the first thing he saw, which was a bigger than average spanner. The weight felt good in his hand, and he turned around. She was right behind him, swaying as she bled out. She had chased him but was clearly no longer any real threat. He used the spanner to put her out of her misery.

He slowly became aware of a battle raging outside the loco shed. It was a quiet day in January, and he estimated a total of around forty people were outside, fighting to kill or to survive, some unable to adjust to the situation in time and just submitting without resistance. A lady was on her knees, crying as a toddler used their teeth to take apart what was obviously her partner, who lay still and bloody on his back. A big guy was on top of another average-sized guy, bringing a hammer down and destroying the man's face with blow after blow. The man was just laughing, however, and struggling under the bigger man's weight, and he had *the eyes*. The man on top looked terrified, but his eyes were normal, seemingly wanting the man under him to just be still. Despite all this, in the numerous fights and assaults taking place, it was not necessarily that easy to see who was affected and who was not.

"Tim!!!"

Tim recognised the voice as that of the operating superintendent, Ethan Caldwell, who was standing at the entrance to the engine shed. He also had a wrench, as these were in abundance here. Tim saw a man approaching Ethan. Ethan grabbed the man by the shoulders and looked closely at his eyes. Ethan let the man into the shed. A split second later, he had to cave in the head of a young teenage girl who ran at him. Ethan used the momentum of the girl running towards him for a better impact, lifting her off the ground. She lay lifeless seven feet from the engine shed, her face a non-viable red mess.

Tim took off running over the couple of hundred feet to the engine shed. As he approached, he slowed as Ethan raised the wrench. Tim let Ethan examine his eyes.

"Get in!!" Ethan said.

Tim raised his wrench. "No, let me help," he said.

Ethan nodded, and Tim stood at the other side of the door.

The large man who had been beating up the other man approached. His eyes conveyed a broken mind, but the pupils were not dilated, and Tim could see a person behind them. "I JUST BEAT MY HUSBAND TO DEATH!" he screamed.

Tim and Ethan told him to get in the shed, but he just asked, "Have you got another one of those wrenches?"

Ethan reached into the shed and handed him a big one.

"COME ON, YOU DEAD-EYED BASTARDS!!!" the man screamed.

He screamed as he ran into the fray. About five more unaffected people who were huddling nearby rushed into the shed after a quick eye inspection. The man seemed competent in knowing who to attack and managed to cave in five skulls in thirty seconds. The rest of the unaffected ran into the shed, and when Tim and Ethan saw that only the affected were outside the shed, they ran over to help the unknown man. The affected had decided to attack him en masse. Ethan and Tim took out about two more before the man was completely overcome. He clearly was not prepared to live through the mental trauma which would inevitably follow.

He lay still as they continued to rain down more punches and kicks and bites all over his body. Tim and Ethan looked at each other and slowly backed towards the engine shed door, hoping the affected would remain distracted for long enough to let them get inside the shed and shut the door. They reached the shed without being noticed, but as they started to close the engine shed door, it creaked. The mob stopped and looked in their direction, causing Tim and Ethan to freeze in place for a microsecond. The mob then started sprinting at the door but did not get to it before Tim and Ethan got it closed and bolted shut.

Tim and Ethan looked at each other by the dim light of many phone screens and the small window, not knowing what to say.

Ethan broke the silence. "This is actually happening, isn't it? This is real!"

"Well, it feels real, but at the same time, I cannot believe it is happening. I don't know WHAT's happening, though," Tim said.

"My mummy and daddy are out there," a little girl said from somewhere inside the shed.

"My kids."

"My friends."

"What happened?" someone asked, clearly not having heard Tim and Ethan express that they did not know. Everyone in the shed was looking at them, seemingly putting them in charge by virtue of the fact that they worked at the rail yard and had got them safely into the shed.

"Look, we know as much as you do! Did you not hear us? We have no idea what is going on either!" Ethan put his hands up. "I'm sorry, I know you were probably being rhetorical."

It slowly dawned on Tim and Ethan that they were the only ones to have not just lost family members and friends in the most awful way imaginable. Not only that, but the last thing they would remember about their loved ones would be nothing but black demonic eyes full of hatred for them, tainting all of their memories. This was utter devastation. And everyone in the shed knew deep down that things would not get better. This was just too sinister.

"Does anyone have a signal on their phone?" a man said.

A resounding "No" from everyone was the reply.

"You have a radio in here?" asked a middle-aged man holding the right side of his face, blood seeping from between his fingers.

"Yes, we do!" Ethan said with hope. Then, straightaway, his heart sank. "It's not battery powered. If we can get to a car and turn on the radio, we might be able to get some information."

A man took out his car keys and shook them. "I'll go to my car."

He was mid-20s and looked fit and capable. He was dressed smart casual, but with blood staining the right leg of his cream chinos. "It's not mine, don't worry," he said as he saw Tim looking. "Can someone come with me?"

"I will, but first can we get my insulin out of my locker?" Tim said.

"No problem, it's the least I can do," he said. "I'm Greg."

Ethan was still standing by the door when he realised that despite the fact that the affected had been sprinting at the door when he'd closed and locked it, there was no impact. Just silence from outside. "They're waiting. How well can you use a wrench, Greg?"

Greg took it from Ethan. It felt good in his hand. "I think I'll have to learn quickly," he said. He nodded at Tim.

Tim nodded back and slowly started unbolting the

door as quietly as possible.

"Wait," Ethan said. "I think they're waiting quietly on the other side of the door. We should go to the roof. It's only eight feet high. We can surprise them."

Tim cursed himself silently for not realising this. Quietly, they went up the ladder, and Ethan carefully removed the roof hatch. He passed the hatch down to Tim, who gently put it on the ground.

Ethan whispered, "One person at a time - I don't think the roof is particularly strong."

"Is there a ladder to the ground?" asked Greg.

"No, but you can lower yourself slowly, and the grassy area will ensure the sound is absorbed," Tim whispered. He was proud of himself.

He was right; they were all able to soundlessly make it to the back of the shed, one at a time, but they would still need to take on these things. With wrenches. Ethan calmly buried his wrench in the head of an individual sneaking up on Tim. It was pretty quiet, but the affected must have heard the soft *crump*, as there was a sudden sound of running footsteps.

"Tim, go and get your insulin! Now!" Ethan shouted, but Tim was frozen in place. "GO!" Ethan shouted again. This was not an act of heroism, just saving time.

Tim ran towards the locker room, pursued by three of the affected.

Greg and Ethan decided the last thing these things were expecting was for them to run straight at them. So they did. At the end, they had seven caved-in heads on the ground. Ethan was clutching his neck as blood ran through his hands and down his arm.

Greg had lost an entire chunk of his cheek, with his teeth showing through the hole. He looked down and realised his ring finger had gone, along with his wedding band. It was a bad omen. Would his wife still want him after this? He put his tongue through the hole in his cheek. He had no pain, but he knew that would come later. He felt something move as he moved his head. He slowly put his hand up to his right ear and he realised it was hanging on by a tiny amount of skin. "Oh, for Christ's sake," said Greg.

Ethan was on his knees, looking at Greg with a resigned expression. His whole hand, arm and his clothes on the right side were saturated. He slowly took his hand away and revealed that not a slice, not a puncture, but a large portion of the left side of his neck was now gone. Blood spurted from the cavity with noticeably less force each passing second. Ethan simply said the words *"Hotel, reception, helps,"* and pointed in a random direction. Then his arms fell limply by his sides and he fell face-first onto the concrete, dead.

Greg just stared at Ethan and took his car keys out of his pocket. He looked up and saw another ten of those things circle around the building. "Where the hell did you come from?" he shouted. He knew the answer. He felt a bit stupid for not realising that the whole world was like this, for all he knew. These ones obviously came from nearby. He could not get to his car now. He decided quickly to test their intelligence. He screamed at the top of his lungs and sprinted around the back of the engine shed, and yes, they all followed him, and not one tried to intercept him as he circled around the other side to the front of the shed. The way to the carpark was now clear.

He kept running and boosted his speed even more. He tripped over a stone and stumbled forwards but did not allow himself to fall. They were around twenty feet behind him and closing. His key was in his hand, ready for the ignition. He unlocked his vehicle from twenty feet away. When he made it to his pickup truck, he started the engine and engaged the central locks. They kept running at him as he gunned the engine. He smiled like a horror movie villain, the hole in his cheek stretching to show all his teeth on one side as blood continued to drip from the gouge.

He caught two with his bull bars at 15 mph, breaking many bones as he sent them flying backwards. Then he just drove over them slowly, feeling the chest cavities and skulls give way when the truck dropped. Two used the slow speed to their advantage and climbed into the pickup bed. "Stupid bastards!" he screamed. He put the truck in gear and sped up to 40, the most he could get to in the carpark as far as his own safety was concerned.

He slammed on the brakes and watched them sail over the truck. The fence protecting the adjacent wasteland with an overhang and a combination of razor and barbed wire was ready for them. One of them hit the sharp overhang with its belly, resulting in a full impalement and entanglement in the barbed wire. One simply got entangled but hit the overhang with their sternum. That one went limp and slowly slid to the ground, the wire causing awful post-mortem injuries. The other one was screaming and flailing, slicing itself open, with blood pumping from the impalement. Eventually, the impaled one also went limp. The bleeding seemed normal in both of them. Obviously, those monsters needed a beating heart.

He put the truck in reverse and quickly felt it run over two or three of them. When they came into view in front, he saw it was three of them. Two started crawling, and one kept trying to get up with one intact leg and the other broken. He laughed, clapped his hand and lifted his fists into the air in victory. "Stupid pricks, I wasn't even trying to hit you!" he shouted. He could see two more standing in the car park where he had been initially. He reversed and turned quickly to face them.

He raced towards them, again smiling the supervillain smile. He decided to go to 50 and connected with them full force, then floored the brake pedal, skidding satisfyingly to a stop. He watched them bounce off streetlights, trees and kerbs until they came to a rest around two hundred feet away. They started moving, but they were a crumpled heap of bones, and now he had grown bored. He felt a pang of guilt until he looked at his missing finger and at his face in the rearview mirror.

There, he saw Tim with his wrench, dripping with gore. He looked very happy with himself. Greg disengaged the central locks. When Tim got in, he had a small cooler with a red cross on it slung over his shoulder. He also had a second bag, most likely paraphernalia like needles and so on. Tim had a fresh, badly broken nose, his eyes starting to blacken. He was holding his left hand delicately. The little finger was maybe dislocated.

Without saying a word, Greg grabbed Tim's left hand and aggressively forced the finger back into place. Tim's face went red, his eyes closed and he let out a keening sound as he leant forwards, obviously suppressing a scream. Eventually, he leaned back and angrily looked at Greg.

Greg just raised his fingerless left hand, and Tim realised he should be glad he still had all his fingers.

"Let's see what's on the radio, shall we?"

Tim gave a nod.

*03:15 hou... ... No comment from Pres... ... Trump...
... Russ... ... hydro... ... deton... ... respo...... Kreml......
destr...... Putin......*

"Urgghhhh, what the hell is happening??" Greg shouted in frustration, holding his cheek, head lolling forwards. He snapped backwards again, but his eyes were rolling back in his head.

"You're in shock," Tim said. "Here, take this."

He ripped open the sachet of Glucogel, an emergency concentrated glucose gel for those suffering from acute hypoglycaemia. He reached across and squeezed it into his mouth. It tasted good, so Greg did not resist. From the first aid kit in the car, Greg wrapped a bandage around his head to hold his ear in place. Tim had been stealing his mum and stepdad's medications for around a year, just skimming off the top, unnoticed. He had managed to pilfer around 50 pregabalin 100 mg capsules, 28 tramadol 200 mg modified release capsules, and 105 tramadol 50 mg normal release capsules. Greg was coming around, but he needed something to calm him down.

"Here, take this," said Tim.

He handed Greg a single red 100 mg pregabalin capsule. Greg looked confused.

"Don't worry about it," Tim said. "Stick it up your arse as far as you can get it." Tim opened the glove compartment, relieved to find baby wipes, opened but almost full and resealed. Tim hoped this was not for a baby, because if it was, there was a good chance it was orphaned.

He set the baby wipes on Greg's knee and opened the window. He rested his head on the door and lit a cigarette. He handed it back to Greg, who said, "'I don't smoke!"

"Yeah, you do," Tim responded. He felt the cigarette being taken from him, and Tim lit one of his own.

He heard first a ten-second coughing and wheezing fit and the sound of belt and zippers being undone. Suddenly, Tim got the urge to giggle. Nothing was funny here, yet he laughed. He tried to hide it, but it was obvious from his Muttley from *Catch the Pigeon* sounds and his shoulders rapidly going up and down.

"What is shhoo fulney?" Greg slurred.

Tim responded, "Well, let me see ... You're about to butt chug a drug you've never taken, judging by how you look at it, at the same time smoking your first cigarette." Tim did not look back. "Judging by the sound of you, you'd better get on with it."

Greg was feeling woozy from the cigarette and took another drag, still coughing and wheezing.

When this was over, he took about five or six deep rapid breaths, making him even more woozy. He looked one last time at the red capsule on his right index finger and in one swift movement, stuck it up his arse as far as it would go. He pulled his finger out, and the smell hit them both.

Greg opened his window and started vigorously wiping his finger and whole right hand with the baby wipes. He pulled up his chinos and redid his belt and zipper when he felt the wiping was complete but still stared in disbelief at the offending finger. Luckily, the fragranced wipes replaced the offending odour of arse, and he found himself having another long drag on the cigarette. "Thish dishgusting pieth of cancer causig sit is really thakin the hedge ofth my self-violashion."

"Yeah, it does," Tim said as he turned around to see Greg with the cigarette in his mouth, still staring at his finger. He tried not to laugh as he saw the smoke billowing out of his cheek hole.

"You know, I want this finger arrested. I did not consent," Greg said with complete clarity.

"Greg, throw the dirty wipes out the window!"

"But that's littering!"

"Who bloody cares at this point?"

Greg realised the absurdity, grabbed them and threw them out. He decided to give his hand and finger one last vigorous wipe.

Just then, the radio spat out a few words: *around 10% of the popul…… dark-eyed…… murderous rampa… … country slipping into chao…… Do not engage but hide… … Government assures that communication infra…… all NATO members except the USA have invoked Article 5…… Protests have erupted in Los Angeles, Chic…… …ew York.*

Greg switched off the radio, the partial snippets hurting his head. The cheek gouge and finger stump started to really hurt, and this pain level was rising quickly due to the adrenaline wearing off. The pain and the panic were building to a crescendo, but before this was reached, he felt a warmth start to spread lovingly from his lower abdomen, which in no time engulfed his entire body in a pleasant embrace. It spread over his gouged-out cheek and finger stump, converting the pain into a slow and pleasant throb.

"You need antibiotics. Don't worry, you can take these by mouth," said Tim.

Greg had a serene look on his face, with his eyes mostly closed. Tim handed him two flucloxacillin 500 mg capsules from his stash of unfinished courses from countless infected diabetic lesions. Greg swallowed them with a little more of the Glucogel. Tim decided to take 200 mg of tramadol with the bottled water he spied on the back seat. He drank quite a bit and then handed it to Greg, who looked at the bottle with suspicion.

"Go on, it's not the end of the world," stated Tim.

Greg took the bottle and drank greedily, finishing it off. They sat in silence for around a minute.

"Let's drive as close to the engine shed as possible," said Tim.

Chapter Six

Pandora

Professor Ronal Cawl sat on the couch in the fallout shelter underneath the Planck Building at the School of Chemical Engineering at the University of East Anglia (UEA). This basement was not on any blueprint, for good reason, but not really kept a secret. Anybody who did know of its existence did not care enough to talk about it, so the knowledge did not spread too far. Here, he had access to the security footage of the huge car park, the main entrance to the university and the sports park. Generally, all these would capture a lot of happy coming and going, but this had all changed suddenly six hours ago to what essentially looked like static photos on a screen. The university was littered with corpses, some moving in place while they died or elbowed themselves slowly in a random direction.

The activity he did see in the initial hours after he had decided to flee underground were staff and students fleeing on foot and by bike, scooter and car. Then, soon after, what appeared to be foreign soldiers running around all over the place, killing anyone who got in their way against the backdrop of artillery explosions and automatic weapons fire. It seemed like they were looking for something. He had assumed Russian because who else could do this to England? They eventually left after a few hours, but before this, it seemed they were constantly harassed by unarmed ordinary-looking British citizens who seemed happy to give their lives in vain. This seemed heroic, and quite a few soldiers were taken down, but it was ultimately suicidal.

In the shelter, he eventually found an old battery-powered radio which would have plugged in, but no lead was in sight, and after a thorough search, he found every size battery except the one he needed for the radio. It had not been used in years, but he managed to listen to the BBC World Service for a few minutes before it died.

Those few minutes were enough to learn of the rabid humans (which explained who was attacking the Russian soldiers), the invasion and airburst fusion bombs in London and Moscow. Why were the soldiers so interested in the university? After six hours, nothing. Total silence. Nothing but crawling and slowly dying rabid humans, a label he himself decided to use in his own mind. With everything happening, he saw no point in leaving as the university's generators were still going strong, and he knew there was enough diesel for at least a week if the building's occupants were economical with use of electricity. And he was the only one there.

He saw no point in going home as his only friend, a cat named Max, had had to be put down due to a blocked urinary tract not one week before. He had lost touch with his family and was the epitome of an eccentric loner. He had never been happy before, but had rarely felt despair until recently with the loss of Max. He was in the pits of it, as twelve hours after the distant blast, he saw on the monitors the appearance of dirty brown mottled clouds and was aware of a nasty smell of burnt hair which penetrated the bunker. He had an abundance of tinned food, but he did not want any of it, with the nausea building insidiously since the clouds had come. He had held off engaging the air filtration system. It was on now, but he knew intuitively that the damage was done.

Around this time, the silence was broken by blood-curdling screams. He had witnessed a group of rabid humans chasing an individual, and when they caught the person, they beat them senseless and tore them apart with their teeth. Then they left them to slowly die. When the mob left the person there, Cawl could still see the person moving weakly for around two hours until they finally stopped. Professor Cawl did not enjoy this but also was numb to it. He was a coward and did not care if he lived or died, but primal fear had stopped him coming to the person's aid. For now, all was quiet. But this did not mean all was well.

He had been doing a lot of soul-searching for the best part of a year as to whether or not his research and breakthrough should see the light of day. He had more or less accepted the fact that if there was even a small chance his research should fall into the wrong hands, it was an absolute certainty. Even if it fell into the right hands, the road to hell is paved with good intentions. It had unlimited potential for benign applications, but he knew all too well of the dark heart of humanity. It mattered not now because it looked like the end of the world out there, with him as a spectator.

Using quantum computing, nanotechnology and 3-D printing, he had been able to produce an edible clove of garlic using ash – yes, ash. Ash was used as it is a low energy, unreactive substance, full of freshly made high energy bonds and low energy byproducts. Thus, it made sense that if the right amount of energy was applied and focused properly, bonds could be broken and reformed at the direction of nanomolecules, in which vast amounts of information would be stored using quantum computing. Potentially, they could elegantly lower to near nothing the activation energy of any reaction. This did not sound like much, but this property alone would change the world.

The use of quantum computing allowed for storage of virtually unlimited data between the classical binary digits of 1 and 0, and information could be stored at the atomic level instead of at an elemental level. The stability of this quantum computer depended on programmed molecules being in a dark vacuum, and with the application of a magnetic field, this held the programmed molecules in place and thus kept the data viable. Unfortunately, this was inherently less stable than a household PC.

If applied and programmed to certain parameters, the quantum computer would then be able to synthesise pre-programmed and free-moving molecules from the precursor building blocks supplied. These would then be replenished when they ran out. The synthesised molecules could then carry out a specific task and keep doing so until the task was completed, the precursor building blocks ran out, or if a stop signal was sent. But what if the stop signal did not work? And what if the quantum computer was able to replenish the precursors from the surrounding environment to continue synthesising indefinitely? Even worse, the quantum computer could evolve to integrate itself into the environment itself and do whatever it wanted. Something this advanced would necessarily be mediated by self-aware AI, and maybe even the singularity would manifest itself. Part of the reason would be that due to its inherent instability, it would need to develop its own mechanisms to keep itself stable.

By definition, if we humans created something more intelligent than us, it could also improve upon itself without our input. This would inevitably lead to self-awareness, and the nature of this self-awareness could not be predicted, whether or not the singularity occurred. It would also essentially be indestructible once able to keep itself stable. He had not thought of a way to ensure that the stop signal did not fail. And for it to be effective, it needed to autonomously use the resources in the surrounding environment to synthesise the precursor building blocks. Eventually, it would need to become the surrounding environment itself. For all these reasons, he had decided to name his prototype device 'Pandora'.

At this point, all his research had been put on paper, but here and there, he had made slight changes that only he knew about which rendered the data meaningless. He also left out a few crucial equations. Not even his mysteriously disappearing American PhD student knew, and no one on this earth was qualified to reverse engineer Pandora. He was very fond of Adam and had looked forward to working with him every day. The student's sudden absence a few weeks ago did not help Ronal's current mental state. If anyone wanted to replicate his work, they would hit a dead end. If the ethics question in his own mind were to be removed, he would be much further on in his research. But no breakthroughs were without ethical consideration.

As it was right now, the nanomolecules could only work in a completely dark vacuum, and even then, they degraded quickly. Through trial and error, the molecules functioned optimally at -14.7°C. The cold temperature did not allow for speed, and at the very least, he needed nanomolecules which would function at room temperature and not degrade. As it happened, the same ash was used by the quantum computer to make the functioning nanomolecules. The actual quantum computer functioned at room temperature but used a vast amount of electricity. It had to quickly churn out the rapidly degrading nanomolecules in order for the task to be completed, and the national grid could not sustain this.

When actively producing the nanomolecules, it was not enough to just be 'plugged in', and it required electrical engineers to figure out a way to get the quantum computer the energy it needed safely. It also took a whole month to create a single clove of garlic, which did not taste great and degraded quickly. This was partly due to the fact it was created in a subzero temperature. He knew how to overcome all of this, but this was only in his own mind and not written down.

He also knew where to go to implement his findings, both what was in his mind and what was written down. This place had a particle accelerator. The people working on this particle accelerator were old rivals of Cawl, who had eventually understood he was intellectually out of their league and the smart thing to do was work with him and not in competition with him. But he had alienated them. He did know, however, that if he contacted them and fully revealed his findings, they would quickly get over any discontentment towards him.

As it was right now, the world was safe from the fruits of his research. But a lot had changed in a very short time. He could not help thinking that the world could actually benefit if rebuilding were needed. He knew he did not have the resources here to continue his research. Should he correct the intentional errors in his notes? Should he add in the missing equations? He had a lot to think about, but he knew that being by himself, he was not thinking clearly. He needed at least one confidant he could trust. Not a scientist, but an individual with a solid moral compass and a good memory. And they needed to be physically capable of traversing the land to get to the facility which housed the particle accelerator.

On the screen, a white Nissan Juke with a broken rear

passenger window and flecks of blood and gore down the driver's side pulled slowly into the front entrance. It went slowly because the front and rear wheels on the driver's side were on their rims, sparking on contact with the tarmac, even with the slow movement. A young lady with athletic build stepped outside carrying an AR15 assault rifle and walked along the side of the road with the car, keeping the slow pace. He could tell no one was looking for trouble, though, and the young girl looked terrified. He had absolutely nothing to lose by reaching out to these people. He opened the door to the bunker, ran outside and started waving his makeshift white flag, which he had fashioned using fabric and furniture he'd found close by.

Chapter Seven

Adam Looks into the Void

McMahon's Irish pub, Washington D.C., mid-December 2025

Stephen Miller gave Adam Long the creeps. Donald Trump had single-handedly taken apart the intelligence network to the point where Adam was now, in his capacity as an undercover spy, reporting to the chief advisor of Donald Trump rather than the House Intelligence Committee, not to mention the fact that he was being made to spy on a supposed ally. Adam had grown fond of Professor Cawl and slowly gained his trust. Adam was thirty-two but looked nineteen. He had a degree in chemical engineering and nanotechnology from M.I.T. and thus was perfectly placed to gain the professor's trust and access to his research data.

When he was able to make copies of all the research data, despite his protests that he did not have everything he needed, he was pulled back by an excited Stephen Miller, who was too eager for his master's approval to be patient. Miller wanted to meet here as he was too paranoid to have the information sent electronically, even through channels secured by the NSA. Stephen Miller approached Adam, who was sitting in a private booth, out of the way of the other customers and out of earshot.

Adam looked into dead eyes that had the look of a highly medicated psychotic individual, with the medication only focusing the evil and making it more productive. Adam guessed methylphenidate or something similar, probably not prescribed. Miller had a constant sneer of contempt, which he regarded everyone with.

Miller sat down and set his drink down. He smiled broadly, an action in which his eyes took no part.

"So, you got something for me?" Miller asked.

Adam hesitated. He did not want to give him the USB stick with photos of Professor Cawl's research. He hoped he was right about some crucial data being altered and something important being missing. "What do you want it for? It makes no difference telling me now; I'm bound by a lifetime NDA, plus I'm just curious." He tried to sound relaxed and hide his disgust and fear of this truly demonic individual.

"This is a new world, and the life of the world reflects the life of the individual. We grow apart from friends, relationships begin and end, and loyalties change." A smile crept across Miller's face, and he paused for a second or two to relish Adam's reaction. "The balance of power changes, and just like always, some draw the long straw and some draw the short. That is all I will say." He took the USB and promptly got up and left. His smile disappeared as he walked away, and he nodded to a huge guy who had been watching them the whole time.

Adam pretended not to notice his impending death and thanked himself for his backup plan. He nonchalantly went to the bar, pretending to stagger drunkenly. He left his drink and belongings. He asked the barman to watch his belongings and drink while he went to the bathroom and very obviously pointed to the booth. The barman seemed annoyed by this unusual request but nodded okay to Adam. Adam purposefully staggered to the bathroom slowly and even stopped to check his phone, pretending to laugh at something and almost banging into a huge, unfriendly looking guy. Quite an abundance of them around here, it would appear.

Once in the bathroom, he approached the window with bars on the outside. The previous night, he had got his ex-Green Beret brother to use a quiet power saw to cut through the bars top and bottom, leaving them in place but easily removed. He had gone round the edges of the glass with a pencil grip cutter. Adam had seen where his brother had gone around the edges, and he simply pushed the pane so that a perfect square of glass removed itself. He slowly guided it back through and gently laid it on the tile floor. He did the same with each bar and easily climbed out. His brother's Charger roared to life from a parked position halfway down the back alley. He jumped down and the Charger came and stopped beside him. He wasted no time jumping in, and he and his brother sped away to safety.

Chapter Eight

The Man with the Tape Has Bone Cancer

The Kremlin, Moscow, January 4th, 2026, 9.30 a.m.

Putin sat in his private office, eagerly awaiting a visit from the Kremlin's chief scientific officer, Dr Mila Turgenev. There was a knock at the door, and Dr Turgenev came in, flanked by two FSB officers. She avoided eye contact, and her shoulders were hunched in a way that showed she did not have the news he wanted to hear. He did not mind, though. He knew plan B would be so much fun. He motioned for her to sit whilst the FSB agents left to wait outside the door. Mila was quite beautiful, with pale skin, jet-black hair with a purple streak, and big green eyes. However, she did nothing for him, as she was not a little boy.

"I am sorry, sir. Everything we have tried has hit a dead end. There is something big and important missing, and we believe some parts have been made incorrectly on purpose, probably because he did not want the likes of us recreating his work."

"Are you not a scientist? Do you not have the best scientific minds of Mother Russia working under you?"

"Yes, sir. But Professor Cawl is on another level. He even took deliberate action to avoid anyone recreating, reverse engineering or finishing his work. On several occasions, we actually thought we were getting somewhere, but he is such a genius, he structured his notes to seem like it could be understood, only to lead us to yet another dead end. His genius is truly one of a kind. Our best scientists could only reach the conclusion that the man's moral compass is such that he deliberately slowed his own research and kept the most important parts in his head, which he could take to the grave if he so wished."

"So what you're saying is ..."

"We need Cawl, or his fully complete notes," Mila said.

"Keep trying," Putin said as he dismissed her with a wave of his hand. She had always done right by him, and he believed her. She got up and left, still with her shoulders hunched and head hung in shame.

He had already consolidated his power. On the surface, he was in good health, but he could feel himself getting weaker by the day. Although he had time, his recent diagnosis guaranteed that this would not be quality time. He winced at the random, deep metacarpal pain travelling to his wrist, up his arm and across his collar bone, becoming a hand under his skin which gripped his windpipe. This lasted for ten seconds, and he could not breathe. The pain could start at any part of his body but always ended with the hand under his skin, gripping his throat. The frequency and intensity were increasing by the day. Eventually, the subdermal hand would grip his throat and not let go, unless he found what he was looking for.

Recently, his intelligence service had received reports from the chief adviser of his ally, the orange deviant. A scientific breakthrough had occurred with far-reaching implications that could benefit him in numerous ways. He had quickly begun to covet this. The orange ape also wanted his hair back instead of what looked like a piss-soaked rag on his head. Trump was in his 80s, with terrible health, so he could certainly benefit too if he towed the line. Trump finally had the consolidated power he had coveted, with Project 2025 already under way. He wanted to experience this power indefinitely instead of knowing he could drop dead at any second. A lot of people hoped he would.

He lifted the remote and put on his favourite tape. He picked up the phone and dialled the orange ape, who answered on the first ring.

"Hel…" Before he got out the first word, Trump heard the all-too-familiar tape in the background, and he knew he would have to do whatever he was told.

In perfect English, the man with the tape said, "The NWA is one of the greatest alliances in history, is it not?" He did not wait for an answer. "We cannot recreate the work; we need the professor. Operation Red Claw is a go. Do NOT interfere, or you know what will happen." He hung up on the ape. A deep pain began moving up his breastbone from his ribs. He closed his eyes and waited for the hand.

Chapter Nine

The Mouth-Breather-in-Chief

The White House, Washington D.C. 13:00 hours, day one of hostilities

This was a meeting which should have taken place hours earlier, and the impatience and agitation of the cabinet members in the Oval Office was palpable. Trump loved this. There was nothing they could do about it. A year into his second presidency, his power was consolidated due to Project 2025, and he was more untouchable than ever. He kept his cabinet around for entertainment when he defied them. People got angry, people said things, people leaked to newspapers, but there was nothing they could actually do. And the people that could do something did not, as they were only out for themselves.

He wanted some executive time that morning, to communicate directly with his base and eat a lot of crap, truthing nonsense the whole morning with not a word about the atrocity committed against America's oldest ally. Because why not? He was 80; what did it matter at this point? He was feeling a little sluggish after his less-than-productive morning, but a few lines of Adderall saw to that. His guts were full of gas, which he had no qualms letting go of in a room full of his cabinet and other important people. He could have opened a window, but he wanted them breathing in the gas produced by the toxic, impacted sludge in his large intestine.

He saw the NWA as a huge achievement on his part, despite the fact that he was manipulated, blackmailed and influenced by the only real threat that he had ever encountered. Talk of deviance at this point was only hearsay, with no real evidence possessed by any media outlet or journalist. People more or less believed he was a pervert, but there was still a tiny enough amount of plausible deniability that he could hold onto his power and retain some semblance of dignity. A single disgusting act caught on hidden camera at a prestigious Moscow hotel in the late '90s had made him Putin's lap dog for life.

Trump had proudly pulled out of NATO soon after re-election, under orders from Vladimir Putin, who was the man with the tape. The tape would be the thing to finish Trump. It was humiliating, yes, but rumours of it were not enough to finish him. The real thing would, though. Also, under orders from Putin, he had been distancing himself from America's oldest ally. The United Kingdom was in a sorry state. Supermarkets could not stock shelves, inflation was growing fast, homelessness and poverty was worsening by the day, and for the first time in a hundred years, actual starvation of significant numbers of people was becoming a problem in this first world country, the country which had once had the mightiest empire in history.

Russia had attacked the UK. Militarily, the UK was holding its own, and it appeared to be winning. It had a better navy, more state-of-the-art fighter planes, and a modern volunteer army. This morning, Russia had airburst a fusion bomb over Westminster, and this had destroyed half of London. The UK government had received enough of a warning, and the prime minister and cabinet were in a safe location. The UK had responded with a single fusion bomb airburst over the Kremlin, which had pretty much destroyed most of Moscow. Russia must have seen this as an acceptable loss. No further detonations were reported. Because let's face it, even the most evil, power-hungry bastards wanted something left to have dominion over.

The UK had what they had militarily but were not in a position to continue manufacturing to replace losses, whereas Russia did, even if the military hardware was not state of the art. In the last five years, Putin had invested in proliferating his nuclear stockpile like never before. Israel, France, Spain, Germany, Poland, Lithuania, Finland, Sweden, and Norway all promptly declared war on Russia. Nothing had yet happened, though, with the leadership of all these countries hoping that Trump would honour his alliance.

There was no reaction from the United States for hours. Trump had a press conference scheduled for 5 p.m., and what Trump said would be pivotal, with everybody acutely aware of the recently formed NWA. This was a huge conflict of interest for the United States, if not for the president. People still hoped, despite everything, that Trump would do the right thing and stand by his country's oldest friend.

The cabinet could do nothing, but all politeness had gone out the window.

"They are attacking our oldest ally," stated James Harrison, the Secretary of Defence. "We must help the UK."

"But the NWA," stated John Whittaker, the Secretary of State.

"To hell with the NWA, and to hell with you, you fat evil waste of skin," Harrison spat. "You know they call you Goering when you're not around? After another evil fat Nazi prick!"

"Mr President, surely this lack of civility will not get us anyw…"

"For now, we do nothing," the president said, cutting off Whittaker. "The UK are holding their own, and I do not want this to escalate into a world war," he added, thinking only of the tape and keeping it from ever seeing the light of day.

"I agree, Mr President," stated Robert Langley, the White House Chief of Staff, thinking only about his career.

"Look, I agree with James," the Secretary of Homeland Security, Michael Grant, stated. "James, being abusive is not the way to go, so let's please keep this civil," he added.

Harrison just sat sideways with his legs crossed, right hand cradling his forehead, shaking his head.

"All of our major allies have declared war on Russia. If we do not defend the UK, we potentially could be at war with all of our old allies. I just do not understand it. I mean, are the rumours true? You know – is he controlling you with an embarrassing tape?" asked Grant.

Trump was looking out onto the South Lawn and turned slowly. "Get him out," he ordered his agents.

The two agents spoke into their wrists, and two more came through the door. They grabbed Grant. Harrison looked outraged, ready to say more.

Trump saw this. "Get him out too."

They grabbed Harrison. Both men submitted and left voluntarily without being dragged out.

"This is not about your pride, Mr President," Harrison stated as he was marched out of the door.

Grant cursed the president under his breath and glared at him.

"You're fired," the president stated with a grin.

Whittaker also smirked, knowing the potential for unbridled power he could be elevated to as the world realigned itself.

The door opened again, and in walked David Caldwell, the Director of Infectious Diseases, Nathaniel Brooks, the Whitehouse Chief Science Officer, Sophia Mitchell, the Director of the CIA, and Andrew Sullivan, the Director of National Intelligence. None of them was privy to the exact exchange in the Oval Office, but they knew exactly what was going on. Trump had done nothing, and the only halfway decent cabinet members were trying to appeal to his non-existent humanity. This was confirmed when they had seen the expelled members escorted from the room moments earlier. They all nodded to Lucas Thompson, the Chairman of the Joint Chiefs, who was already aware of their news.

"Have a seat," said Trump.

They all awkwardly sat down but really wanted to be standing.

"Unfortunately, with this latest news, the situation is getting worse," said Mitchell. "We have unconfirmed reports of massive civil unrest in the United Kingdom, a lot more than expected," she continued.

Even during this serious meeting, the president's concentration was wandering, and they were losing the demented old narcissist.

"President Trump, sir!" Sullivan said in a significantly raised voice as he took over, reading the room.

The president looked angry, but they had his attention again for now.

Sullivan continued, "What we mean by a lot more civil unrest than expected is that there are widespread reports of random violence, where people suddenly and inexplicably are killing their family and friends and random strangers. It also looks like they are overwhelming Russian troops."

No reaction from Trump.

Mitchell took over again: "President Trump, sir!" she said as they started losing the cretin again. This did not appear to surprise him at all, although they knew better. "The people committing this random violence appear to be impervious to pain, with almost superhuman strength."

Trump did not give a shit. He was the one to decide what got done, and as far as he was concerned, the man with the tape could do whatever he liked.

Lucas Thompson stood up in an obvious act of defiance to Trump's show of domination over his staff. Trump looked Thompson up and down with contempt but chose not to challenge him. His attention was wandering again.

"President Trump, sir!" said Thompson.

He nodded to Brooks, who had never been in this room before but could not believe the farcical scenario playing out before him. "We believe the Russians have deployed a nerve agent which hyperstimulates the fight-or-flight response in human beings. It attacks the amygdala by hyperstimulation, with high affinity and efficacy for the adrenergic receptors of this area of the brain. The hyperstimulation is constant and non-stop, diverting blood flow from the frontal lobe of the brain, causing memory impairment and loss of reason. This can explain the super strength as well as the ability to block pain signalling."

Brooks continued after a brief pause. "It affects ten per cent of the population, which is more than enough to cripple your enemy. It can be metabolised, but not before the affected individual dies from starvation and/or dehydration as they have no urge to eat, not to mention the consequences of their own violent actions before that."

They all knew they had lost Trump, and Brooks

looked defeated. This in-depth explanation was for everyone else in the room, not Trump.

"President Trump, sir!" Mitchell said as she brought the president back from his demented daydreaming once again. "The Russians have attacked the UK with a highly pot... no, a very strong poison, causing them to kill each other."

Trump smiled inwardly. *Well played to you, the man with the tape,* he thought.

Mitchell nodded to Brooks again and he took a deep breath. "We made it. It is a short chain peptide we called STN-666 due to the effect it had on the death row inmates we experimented with. We do not know how the Russians got it."

Steven Miller, remaining silent throughout, caught Trump's eye, and they smirked at each other. No one noticed.

"And for the worst part," said Caldwell, speaking for the first time. He took a deep breath before continuing. "They have added their own extra piece of horror to the equation. They have created an mRNA which codes for the peptide and are delivering it within a viral vector, essentially a hollowed-out cold virus. Also inside this vector is reverse transcriptase, which converts the mRNA to DNA and integrase, which integrates the DNA into the genome of the individual. This causes the host to essentially produce an unlimited amount of STN-666. The changes within the hosts are permanent, meaning their blood becomes a reservoir. This is all theory, and we have no reports on the real-life effects on the affected individuals, but something tells me we will know it when we see it. It is possible that the individual will regain their memory or faculties due to the more chronic nature of the

STN-666 exposure. They could still be impervious to pain and have a lot of strength, but at the same time, they will probably want to see the world burn. The only piece of good news is that this delivery method is inherently unstable, and will therefore more than likely only affect a tiny subset of already susceptible individuals."

"What are we going to do, President Trump, sir?!" asked Thompson, not expecting a real answer.

Trump had a hankering for a milkshake. "I will speak at the press conference at 5 p.m. Do not bother me until then." Trump took out his phone and quickly logged on to Truth Central as he left the room.

Thompson, Mitchell and Sullivan looked at each other knowingly. As soon as it was known that Trump would betray the UK and side with Russia, immediate action would be taken. Enough was enough. On board were General Grace Anderson, the Chief of Staff of the Army, as well as their equivalents in the Navy and Airforce, Admiral Laura Evans and General Benjamin Parker.

White House North Lawn, 5 p.m. on day one.

"Ladies and gentlemen, the president will speak for a few minutes, updating you on the situation as it has unfolded, then he will take questions for a few minutes afterwards." Tomy Lahren's dead eyes regarded the press seated before her in the way a doctor might while thinking their life would be so much easier if not for the patients.

Special Agent Stefan Nowak of the United States Secret Service watched the crowd from the stage, as well as everywhere else he could see. His whole family were right-wing Trump supporters, but he was a traditional Republican. He tried to maintain a professional outlook. In his mind, he was happy to tolerate Trump's shortcomings. Something had been pecking at his subconscious since Trump's re-election and the brutal implementation of Project 2025, but his job was protecting the head of the Executive Branch, no matter his opinion of the person. He was proud of his professionalism and ability to compartmentalise his opinions in order to do his job without prejudice.

This was especially important now, considering his wife and eight-year-old daughter were now in London. His wife had always wanted to see England, and this was the trip of a lifetime, but his leave had been cancelled at the last minute due to rising global tensions. He came to terms with this a lot quicker than his wife, as it was what he had signed up for. It should never come as a surprise. He had convinced his wife to go anyway, although this was not easy. They lived paycheck to paycheck, like most Americans, and in the absence of a refund, they did not know if and when they could afford to pay for another trip like this in the foreseeable future.

Besides, he could enjoy it in real time with her with the advent of affordable, advanced VR technology, although it could never be as good as actually being with her. Although the thermonuclear weapon had not destroyed all of London, like all of the British Isles, it was a communication dead zone, and the detonation was, by far, not the most disturbing news that was coming from that part of the world. He gained some comfort from the fact that that his wife was an ex-Army Ranger and could handle herself. He was grateful to the president for not escalating tensions and tried to ignore those who asserted that his motives were not as virtuous as they seemed on the surface.

Trump started to speak.

"Ladiesh and gentlemen, I know you have all been worried about the advents. Let me assure you, I have been working tirelesishly with my cabinet, advisers and generals about how we can revolve the shituation. It is just shimply, oh, but he was there and he was strong. And other things too. I am – WE ARE doing a tremendous and also phenomenal diplomatic, believe me. Just like with the China virus. And the election of 2020 being rigged and stolen by the big, massive nighttime dumps. And they tried to give me the virus and other things. I can tell you the world is lucky I am the president again instead of Sleepy Joe, who would be doing nothing in his bunker. I have to commend my friend Vladimir Putin on his tremendous restraint, as most of Moscow is gone in a swift and swifin sweeping like nothing anyone has ever seen, but only a small part of London. And Putin says it was Ukrainian terrorists. He was so very strong. Very stong and tough in his denial. The English government has caused untold loss of life in Moscow. If you look at the numbers, five million people in Moscow are dead and only two million English people ..."

Stefan did not realise his jaw was hanging open. He felt like the moronic nonsense he had just heard had crossed a line and probably given him cancer. The pecking had finally reached his conscience. He closed his dry mouth and swallowed what felt like a brick. Not only was Trump going to do nothing, but he was going to side with the Russians, who had struck first against America's oldest ally. At that point, he had absolutely no doubt that Putin was blackmailing him, as even Trump could not possibly believe this.

"We just want to let Russia know we stand with them

and the millions of dead and suffering in Mosc..." Trump stopped speaking, and an instant later, the unmistakable sound of a firearm being discharged via suppressor could be heard. All sensation below Trump's neck was gone as he saw the podium come up to greet his chin, snapping his head back. Trump was now a heap of lard on the ground, not moving.

Stefan saw his shot land, right through Trump's windpipe and out the back of his neck. Stefan had wanted a clean headshot, though. He dropped his gun and braced himself. He heard shooting, but no bullets hit him. When he saw what was going on, he could not believe his eyes. All the journalists on the lawn scattered, running to safety. Secret Service agents were firing on the M1 Abrams tanks and Hummers outside the gate on both sides.

It would appear the instant before he had lifted his gun to fire, everyone else with guns saw the tanks come into view. When they heard the shot and the president falling an instant after seeing the tanks, they started firing on the tanks. The shots were ricocheting harmlessly off the military vehicles' armour when shouts of "HOLD YOUR FIRE!" rang out among the Secret Service ranks.

Stefan could see a presidential SUV-limo hybrid speeding away from the scene, and Trump was no longer behind the podium. Silence. The military vehicles had come to a stop and everybody just waited.

The familiar squawk of feedback was heard as a loudspeaker was turned on. "PLEASE PUT DOWN YOUR WEAPONS." It was a gruff, standard-issue military male voice.

All the special agents looked at each other, knowing they were outgunned and it was pointless to engage military hardware like that with small-arms fire.

Another voice came on the speaker.

"Men, the president has betrayed our oldest ally and sided with our oldest enemy." It was Victor Chilenko, Democratic Speaker of the House of Representatives.

"You killed the president!!" A shout rang out from a special agent on the other side of the podium, weapon still drawn.

"NO, WE DID NOT, THAT CAME FROM ONE OF YOUR OWN."

They all looked at each other but were robbed of the chance to think when they heard the familiar sound of their own uniformed division in four of their current armoured security vehicle of choice, the M1117, all of which quickly parked sideways in front of the podium, back-to-back. The agents all took cover behind the ASVs, including Stefan. These were facing the vehicles on Pennsylvania Avenue side on.

Stefan did not know what to do other than to follow his colleagues to the sides of the vehicles facing towards the White House. There, they received body armour, helmets, M4A1 assault rifles, ammo and hand grenades. Shit was getting serious.

Those men already kitted up quickly took up defensive positions around the ASVs, and with their own loudspeaker, one of the special agents calmly said, "We are here to defend the Executive Branch. Why have you taken up arms against your government?"

"Did you not hear? The president blatantly betrayed our oldest ally for spurious reasons. All of our other allies are on the verge of declaring war against us."

"The president gave his reasons. The UK overreacted when they ..."

"Are you saying the UK overreacted to an unprovoked thermonuclear attack?"

"Well, the death toll is greater in Russia!"

A large white canvas screen was quickly erected above the tanks. A video was projected onto the screen, showing Trump sitting on a chair in a hotel bedroom as staff draped plastic sheet wrap over the queen-size luxury bed. When they left, he started to take off his suit. His entire naked body was blurred out, but that did not matter. He then lay supine upon the plastic sheet while two beautiful women entered the room. They were apprehensive but probably paid a lot of money, so they proceeded to undress. They were blurred out as well, but it showed them getting onto the bed, and one of them began to squat over him.

One squatted above his head. A special agent shouted, "DEEP FAKE!! FAKE NEWS!!!" and fired an RPG at the army Humvee. The detonation caused serious damage, but it sped away, only to be replaced by another, this time with a roof mounted M240B, which quickly made short work of the agent with the RPG. Automatic machine-gun fire erupted from the side of the tank, and everyone else took this as their cue to engage. A few special agents tried to surrender, but their own men mowed them down. The turret of the tank started to rotate towards the ASVs.

Adam watched the ensuing chaos on a rooftop two miles away though his brother's M22 binoculars. "Good, I think the orange pig bastard is dead," Adam said to his brother Doug. "We have to get to England. Not only is Professor Cawl in danger, but if we can somehow stop the Russians getting hold of this technology, then I have to help. There's nothing that I can do about it, but if they do get it, I'll regret not trying, if I'm alive to do so. Also, what else is there for me to do, start a goddamn book club?"

"There's a Douglas C47 Skytrain going to RAF Lakenheath in Norfolk, England from Fort Bragg tomorrow morning, wheels up at 8 a.m.," said Doug.

"That's a five-hour drive, so we need to replace the plates on the Charger."

"You leave that to me. Meanwhile, that hippie van in the parking lot is not going to steal itself, nor will the plates switch themselves."

"What? Why?!"

"Well, one of us needs to be in a position to help the other if things go south, plus they are looking for you, but the last place they will look is in a hippie van driven by a shaven-headed, bearded man."

Adam looked at his brother in disbelief as he got a fake beard, a tie-dyed T-shirt and a bald cap out of his bag. "I understand," he said, although Doug's smile indicated he was going to enjoy this.

Chapter Ten

Hotel, Reception, Helps

After violating rules of parking and where to drive, rules which now were completely worthless, Greg and Tim pulled up beside the shed with only around six feet between the driver's side door and the shed door.

"Keep your dick out," Greg whispered.

Tim pinched the bridge of his nose and closed his eyes. "What you mean is keep dick! Jesus, I thought I was naïve! Were you actually born yesterday?"

Greg looked at him, defeated.

Tim took a deep breath and just said, "Sorry, Greg, stressful situation."

Greg just looked away and slowly nodded. "Right, gotcha." He slowly got out, approached the door and hesitated, trying to remember the agreed code. Then he knocked - *knock knock knock - knock - knock knock knock knock*. He heard the latch disengaging. The door opened, and a hand pulled him in, then a head looked out and beckoned Tim in urgently. Not wanting to risk getting out of his own door, he climbed across to the driver's side and disengaged the handbrake, allowing the truck to roll down the short and gentle incline before coming to a stop.

He flew in the shed door. He was getting that feeling; he needed to eat soon. The door was pulled shut after half a second, and the deadbolt was engaged a quarter of a second after that. They were greeted with many smartphone torches in their faces. It was almost completely dark in the shed, the only source of light previously being the single window. It was dusk outside. Greg instinctively used his still intact hand to cover his cheek, and they both closed their eyes against the onslaught of light.

"Stop shining those in our faces!!!" Tim shout-whispered.

They all complied.

A terrified male voice asked, "Where's Ethan?"

Greg motioned towards the door. "Outside," he said calmly. He was swaying now.

"Come and sit down now, my love," a female middle-aged voice invited.

Their eyes had adjusted to the very minimal light in the shed, and Greg saw a hand waving him over. He went over and sat down, and a thick blanket was draped over his shoulder. Only then did he realise he had been shivering.

Tim said to them all, "We both need something to eat. I'm diabetic, and I'm worried about him going into shock. He also lost the ring finger on his left hand."

In normal times, people would have gone to the canteen for lunch, but now, if going out for the day, they brought what they had. Besides, the canteen had had to shut down because of major problems with the supply chain.

Almost everyone had a packed lunch with them, including Tim, except he had left this in the truck.

"Where's your bag?" someone asked Greg.

"I don't know. It's blue with yellow bars." Greg sounded articulate but weak.

"Found it!" an elderly man said.

Greg handed Tim two of his four sandwiches and a packet of prawn cocktail crisps. Tim hesitated. "It's okay, my man," Greg said.

Every 'S' from Greg was now a whistle, which made Tim wince. After everyone had finished their food, with

Greg holding a fist to his cheek the whole time, Tim provided them with the entire story since they had left.

Greg then added, "Ethan said three words just before he died, but I can't remember them. Shit!!! What were they? It didn't make any sense ..."

"Take a long, slow, deep breath. Visualise," Tim said.

Greg took a long, slow, deep breath through his nose and closed his eyes. He repeated Ethan's dying words: "Hotel, reception, helps."

"What Three Words!!" someone, possibly an elderly gentleman, excitedly spoke up.

Tim sighed inwardly. *Not the time for demented babbling,* he thought. He saw a phone light up and coming towards him.

"It's an app," the old man said. "I'm Robert'.' He got to Tim and held up his screen, showing that it was an app.

"You can use your phone to search these three words, and you can use those words to navigate towards a specific grid reference. But you need the internet," the older lady looking after Greg stated.

Robert replied, "Yes, however, I have all maps relevant to Norwich and the surrounding area - the whole of Norfolk, in fact, downloaded on my phone. If these words relate to a point anywhere in Norfolk, we can find it as long as the satellites still work. I'm assuming they still do."

Tim could see the man looked very happy with himself.

Tim could not help but think that elderly people were either complete luddites or experts in regard to smartphones – no in between. He really did want to punch every elderly person who proclaimed loudly that they had no phone or did not use the internet. Tommy expressed this very sentiment about elderly people who could have their prescriptions managed with ease if they just stopped being arseholes and just opened their minds about new technology and how it could make their life easier. But they wouldn't have it.

Robert put the words into the app. These words did in fact point to a location in Norfolk. Specifically, they pointed to a location two hundred feet away from where they were in the engine shed.

"Is that correct?" Tim asked.

Robert could only stare at his phone. "Yes, I believe it is," he replied.

Tim tapped the icon at the bottom left to look at the satellite view. "It's a field," Tim stated with a sigh.

"So?" Robert said defensively, the rug pulled out from under him. "It deserves a look. Just because it doesn't show anything from the satellite view, it doesn't mean there isn't something there. In fact, that may be the entire point."

"Makes perfect sense to me," a lady with a French accent said.

Tim could hear everyone murmuring in agreement.

"We should go at first light," Robert said.

Greg was feeling happy but was convinced he had shat himself and could not rest until he checked. "I'm sorry, I am not spending the night here," he lied. He did not really care where he was; the impromptu suppository had seen to that. He shifted where he sat, just to see if there was any wetness. No one had mentioned a smell. Still, he could not reassure himself.

"I agree," Tim said. "This place is a dirty shit-hole, and it's possible that we may be safer under cover of darkness, as long as we stay quiet."

Did that mean there was a smell, or was it just the

shed in general? Greg thought. He wanted to go out there himself and check, using the wipes. He tried to put it out of his mind and enjoy the temporarily blocked agony he could sense from his injuries. He put his hand up to his cheek and pushed in the food which had tried to make its way out of the hole.

Robert remained beside Tim, who could see in the top right corner that the old man's phone had 46% battery life remaining. In his jacket pocket, he had a mini power bank, good for two phone charges, as long the phone was not used. But right now, he was sure that in this shed, there were more than a few people whose phone battery was dead, or was about to die. And they would sure love to get their hands on his mediocre power bank. He decided not to mention it for now. "Can you turn the screen brightness all the way down?" Tim asked.

Robert went ahead and did it, and he already had a walking route, five minutes to the destination. Tim went to grab the phone, but Robert pulled it away. "I'm coming," he stated with authority. "I just lost family members in the most obscene, grotesque ways imaginable. All I have is the hope that the rest are out there, safe. If I stay here, my mind will break. Because never in a thousand years would I have imagined that what happened today, happened. Whoever was responsible for this, including whoever enabled it, who stood back and let it happen, I want to live to see them pay for this. I need to occupy my mind."

There was no argument against this. Tim squeezed his shoulder. "They will, Robert. They absolutely will."

Greg had managed to convince himself that he had not shat his pants, and that he had only thought so because he had self-violated no more than an hour before. Or maybe longer? But he was warmed up and had eaten so was feeling much better. He had already developed the bad habit of running his tongue along the edges of the gaping wound, which he'd started doing to pick out any deposited food.

Mary, who had been looking after him, saw him do this, causing her to search the shed for something, anything, she could use. She eventually managed to find some superglue, using the ambient light from her phone's screen. She had been a nurse during the Falklands War. In her opinion, this war had contributed to the worst PTSD profile of any conflict. Not because of the war itself, but the *desolation*. Sufferers had also had to deal with cynicism about their PTSD and the war itself, further compounding the problem. Most importantly, however, she knew the value of superglue in closing a wound.

Carefully, she applied the glue around the edge of the wound, periodically holding the wound closed. "Leave your tongue out of it, sweetheart," she had to gently remind him on several occasions. Luckily, it took pretty quickly, and she covered it with some electrical tape she had also found. It would do for now. She also applied glue to the finger stump, which she was unable to find anything to clean with. But the barrier would help with the pain. She creatively tore the electrical tape into strips, wrapping them around his hand in order to anchor the glue onto his stump.

She did not want him to go with the others to see what was going on with this grid reference, but he had earned the right to go with them if he wanted and did not seem mentally impaired. Someone had donated a woollen fleece and hat, which he gladly accepted. Three were going, and between them, they either already had warm clothing, or else someone else had donated it to them.

Tim asked, "Is everyone ready to go? Are your eyes adjusted to the darkness?"

No answer.

"Okay, the ..."

"WAIT!" someone whispered.

"I have a car. Could I go home now?" This question was met with more murmuring.

"Well, I suppose, it *seems* pretty clear out there," Robert replied.

"Does anyone not have a car with them? I don't," Tim said. Tim counted five 'I don'ts', but within seconds, the problem resolved itself, as four of the five were able to get lifts with others going in their general direction.

"I'll come with you, Tim," Mary said. "I don't have a car, and I'm up here from London on a day trip. The only relatives I have are elderly, but I'm not particularly close to them."

Nobody protested. Tim just gave a nod to Mary.

"Make sure you have your key in your hand," Greg warned the rest of them. "Those pieces of shit will sneak up on you."

A chorus of keys jangling could be heard.

"Please close your doors quietly as well and engage your central locking straight away. Do not unlock your doors until everyone is at their doors. Do not start any cars before everyone has got in, and then start your cars as synchronised as you can," Mary added.

A man who had not spoken up previously stated, "And for the love of God, *leave in an orderly fashion and take your time!*" The man sounded middle-aged, with a gruff, authoritative tone.

Mary guessed this was a Royal Marine veteran, with

that ever-present, oddly specific arrogance and toxic contempt for civilians.

"Everyone happy?" Robert asked, asserting himself by value of his contribution.

This question was met with silence.

"Well, you know what I mean."

This was met by a few nervous chuckles.

"Speak up if you need time," Mary said.

"Wait." A teenage boy spoke up, quiet up until this point. "The last person out, should they sound their horn to create a distraction on the way out? That would help you four to get where you need to go, as long as you do it quietly."

"That's an amazing idea! What's your name?" asked Tim.

"Ollie," the voice responded, noticeably more confident.

"You got a lift, sweetie?" asked Mary.

"Yes, I'm going to Norwich with the Taylor family."

"Well, Taylor family, hold onto this one," Greg said, now hissing with each 'S'.

Tim preferred that to the whistling.

"We will," a soft and warm female voice said.

"Everyone stay close to whoever you are travelling with and hold hands. And DON'T run. Keep hold of each other's hands until you get to your cars," Robert said.

Shuffling and murmuring could be heard in the dark.

"Now, is everyone ready?" Tim asked.

No response. He took that as a yes, and slowly he undid the latch yet again.

A hand grasped his shoulder. "Window," Mary whispered.

Tim looked outside, and in the overcast gloom, he saw 'people' moving around outside. Their movements were erratic, randomly twitching here and there. They circled the bodies of the dead, sniffing the bodies and the air.

Tim put a hand up behind him in the universal signal of *quiet*. "If they're trying to sniff us out, I'm guessing we're protected by the oily stench," Tim whispered.

"They must have heard a commotion," Mary said.

"But from how far, though?" Greg asked rhetorically.

"Human hearing is not that advanced," Robert said.

Tim saw from the window that a few seemed to have given up and were jerking towards the main entrance, from where he assumed they had originally come. Tim could see that one of them, a male, had a complete break in the left humerus. Dragging behind him was an ankle pointing in the wrong direction by 90 degrees. This would have been unbearably painful for a normal person. "That one looks like my goddamn brother!" Tim said.

Tim shrugged this off, but he was disturbed. It was clear that death was the only thing that could stop them, as if he did not already know that. This was not a high-octane situation, though, in which adrenaline could temporarily mask pain. The arm had a complete break, and a night stroll does not need adrenaline. Ten EpiPens would not mask the pain from such injuries. Tim again had to dismiss the notion that the one with the ankle and upper arm injuries looked like his brother. Even if it was him, he was beyond help.

The four in the delegation peered out of the window. It was almost completely dark now, but they observed the remainder of the affected follow the limping, broken individual towards the main entrance, seemingly satisfied that there were no unaffected people around. Tim's hand went back to the latch and slowly lifted it. He pulled the door open a little, expecting to draw in fresh night air. But he was hit with the dirty smell of unwashed feet. It was *disgusting*. Something was wrong. *One problem at a time*, he told himself. There was no way nobody else noticed this, but nobody reacted as they went past him to leave slowly, each group of travellers holding each other's hands and exiting the shed silently. Their faces told him they noticed the smell. When all of them had left, he eventually realised he could only make out vague moving shadows. *Good.* The four who remained left the shed slowly and sat by a bush near the exit road.

He heard a succession of car doors closing softly and locks engaging. Then ignition sounds as most cars started. Most. They could hear an ignition turning over but no catching. The other cars started to leave in an orderly fashion.

They then heard a door opening as a 40-something entitled sounding woman with an American accent raced to the car closest to the one that would not start and slammed her hand onto it. The bright headlights obscured the view. "Let me in!" she demanded, as loud as if there were no monsters lurking in the dark.

"No more room!" a male voice replied in an angry whisper before they started moving.

"Asshole limeys!"

Tim pinched between his eyes. There was nothing he could do.

"Over here!" a female called to her.

The sound of running on the gravel could be heard. But not one person. At least ten. Then the American lady screamed in pain, and the scream slowly became more blood curdling, then a gurgling moan. The four of them, from near the shed, could only see headlights flicker as the affected ran back and forth past them. The last car pulled off but drove erratically. As this car got closer,

Tim and his companions saw a battle raging in the rear seat, with the internal lights on due to the rear door being open.

An upper body was squirming and struggling and snapping at the foot of a female repeatedly kicking its head. A male, also in the back seat, was raining punches down on the invader's face, neck and body, to no effect. Someone else seemed to be stabbing it. The BMW swerved and hit one of the trees lining the road to the car park, and instantly, a continuous horn rang out. And a sound that was like a babbling brook. They could see the smoke coming from the engine, which was still running. The head of the front seat passenger rested limply against the airbags. The driver's head was resting on the steering wheel, the airbag seeming to have failed. The battle continued to rage in the back seat.

After a minute, they could see that the smoke billowing out from under the bonnet was now black and accompanied by flame. The leaking petrol was soon ignited and whooshed from under the car. The driver seemed to regain consciousness. The screams started. Then an explosion thirty seconds later as the car lifted two feet in the air. At least the screams stopped. By the light of the flame, they could see that at least forty of the affected had gathered around the fire, watching the flames, captivated. Their eyes were dark, and their mouths hung open. One of them was pregnant. Whether the others had seen this or not, Tim did not care to point it out.

"They're not trying to get to those inside. It's the fire. They're transfixed," Robert whispered.

One of them snapped their neck to look in their direction. All four of them saw this and froze. Nobody whispered anything more. Slowly, the affected lady turned back to look at the fire. Robert took point and started moving slowly, keeping low to the ground. He could almost hear his knees screaming in agony with every step as he walked in a crouched position, almost afraid that the screams of his knees could give them away. Together, keeping an eye on the horde, they crossed the exit road and made their way out to the main road. After this, they crossed a wooden stile and entered a field. Tim was impressed that Google Maps included the stile in the walking route.

They were now in the field, looking up a slight incline towards the exit road they had been on. There were a few more affected walking slowly towards the fire, which was dying down.

"Just sodding great," Greg hissed. "All this over a car that wouldn't start the first time, and a *goddamn Karen*!"

"Looks like they have a weakness," Robert said.

"At least in *The Walking Dead*, they walked into the fire. They're just gathering now," Mary said.

"Unless something lucky happens, this 'weakness' will soon become a strength," Tim said, confirming Mary's assertion.

"We'll be left with a shit tonne once the fire burns out," Greg said, stating the obvious with real fear in his voice. He was sobering up.

With the fire dying down, more of the affected started to leave, into the dark night.

Robert showed the others his phone. They were right on top of the grid reference they were looking for. "Whatever we're looking for, it's around here. Let's find it quickly," he said.

The other three snapped out of their dread-filled trances.

Tim screamed inwardly in frustration at the absurdity of trying to look for something in the dark without knowing what he was supposed to be looking for, silently and without a torch. He was on his hands and knees, crawling aimlessly around the field, sweeping the earth on a dark, cold and empty winter night. On crawling forwards, his wrist painfully impacted a small metal handle. He let out a *yip* in pain. He looked up and saw many faces of those ex-humans still gathered around the dying fire, though some had started to leave. *And many more unseen.* He panicked and started pulling at the handle, but it would not budge.

Robert angrily pushed him over. "You are standing on the door, dickhead!" he said at full volume.

Clearly, keeping quiet now was pointless. "I found it, you miserable old shit!"

"Both of you, STOP!" Mary sternly warned.

He was starting to dislike Robert. Robert started pulling the handle, but the door, which appeared circular, only came up an inch or two. In a show of dominance, Tim pulled with both hands and all his might but only managed to raise it one foot or so. The other three got their hands under the door, and they were all able to lift it just enough for one person to go through.

"Okay," Mary said. "Robert, you first. You're the oldest and most feeble. Sorry, I'm just being pragmatic. Also, now would be a good time to turn on your phone lights."

Robert let go of the door, which did not seem to make much difference in the weight. He shone the light and saw a dark tunnel which had a single ladder, around five feet wide, stretching partway around the circumference of the tunnel. So he started to climb down. To his pleasant surprise, the bars were warm, but not too warm. It felt good in contrast to the winter night on his arthritic fingers. He shone his light down again and could see that this tunnel led to a bigger room. The other two started climbing down, and Greg, still the strongest, had manoeuvred around the door and was holding it open with his shoulders while standing at the top rung. He soon started shaking; there was not much time.

Greg slowly and shakily went down one rung and then the other. With only six inches or so to go, Mary and Tim had cleared their heads of the top.

"Okay, Greg, on three, pull yoursel…" Tim started to say.

With Greg's hands now on the top rung, a hand shot in and grabbed his left forearm and pulled it out. This caused Greg to instantly let go of the ladder. The rest of his body started to fall, and the door fell full force on his forearm. His entire weight was supported by this arm. Fingers appeared under the door, pulling it up. Greg's forearm snapped under his weight. This caused him to fall into the tunnel, leaving half of his forearm behind. He landed painfully at the bottom, a fall of around twenty feet. The arm was swiftly pulled away, the door dropping onto their fingers, which had lost their leverage. Bones were heard snapping, but there were no screams of pain.

Tim grabbed the locking wheel in the middle of the underside of the door. From the opposite side, Mary helped him turn the wheel clockwise. But it met resistance due to the fingers. They forced it as hard as they could until more snapping could be heard and the resistance gave way. This caused a series of lights to flicker on in the tunnel. There was banging on the door, but they all knew they were safe from that crowd of hellspawn.

They were not getting in. The tunnel was completely illuminated and the air smelt … fresh – no odour, just a nice, agreeable humidity level. Tim breathed it in deep and started to descend. About ten feet down, the tunnel was cut in half and opened into a *huge* room, ten feet or so high. It was a Portakabin. The biggest Portakabin Tim had ever seen. Buried. One of the four walls was entirely racked with guns of all kinds, including revolvers, assault rifles, automatic weapons, sniper rifles and even rocket launchers and anti-tank weapons. An actual machine gun was ceremoniously racked in the centre.

Along the floor that met with the wall was enough ammunition to take over the world. Around ten huge boxes were filled with individual sniper rounds, machine gun belts, grenades, magazines of different kinds, bump stocks, and what Tim guessed were stun grenades. All of the walls had a width of around a hundred feet.

On another wall was a window. No, not a window. A screen. In the middle of the wall, taking up roughly half of it, was a screen, which went back and forth from tropical fish in a crystal clear sea, then an alpine meadow, then a remote temperate forest. All the places you could imagine. At the bottom, the screen showed an icon that the sound was muted, and capital letters beside it read 'PLEASE SELECT LOCATION'.

"Bugger me," Tim said.

Below this screen were four brand new and very long garden sheds. Inside each one was a king size bed and a private bathroom with a shower and sink.

Tim was trying to understand where the water came from, but his best guess was from maybe a huge rainwater cistern nearby, or a large tank, and the waste would feed into a septic tank. With regard to the electricity, he instantly thought of the huge combined wind and solar farm around three miles away at Trissingam Broad. Did they tap into it? They were on a slight incline; was there an underground river for geothermal energy and water? Was it maybe a combination of all of those things? There was no way to know for sure.

On the third wall were endless shelves of clothing and medication, with nonperishables and cleaning products on the fourth wall.

"I hope there's a tin opener here," Mary said to Tim.

She was in the middle of the subterranean Portakabin, which looked like a central hub. There was a big screen showing two high resolution CCTV feeds above a circular office desk. One was showing inside the Portakabin, and the other showed the door in the middle of the field from outside, the camera presumably fixed to a tree. It was a thermal imaging camera. He could see the affected walking back and forth, jerking around in frustration and randomly attacking each other. They were all brightly lit up. They were very much alive. This was not the walking dead type.

Three ergonomic office chairs sat empty. What looked like recently completed laminate flooring covered the entire room, with off-white wallpaper and a white-painted ceiling.

Tim decided that he would have a proper look around in a bit. He went to Mary, who was applying superglue to Greg's left arm stump. Mary looked at Tim, who handed her another pregabalin, tramadol and Phenergan. He gave all the flucloxacillin capsules to her as well. Greg was delirious, drifting in and out of consciousness, and going into shock. Again.

"You're not going to be able to give those to him by mouth," Tim said.

Mary understood but was no stranger to the rectal mode of administration, and it didn't faze her. Then Tim threw her the wipes he still had, and Mary did what she had to do. After a couple of minutes, Greg melted in Mary's arms and started snoring softly.

"I'll stay here with him. You two, please find me anything possible to keep him warm and comfortable," Mary said. She manoeuvred Greg so that he was lying on his side, with his head on her lap, to stop him aspirating if he vomited. She saw a yellow pool spreading from his crotch onto the concrete floor, and before long, this pool was touching her. It smelt *bad*. Robert and Tim covered their noses.

Robert found Flash bleach spray and kitchen towels, and a pair of black sweatpants he guessed were Greg's size.

"Best take him to one of the sheds," said Robert.

Mary nodded to Robert and moved Greg as gently as she could to another dry area. Tim was able to neutralise the odour with bleach, and under the blanket, she removed Greg's trousers and underwear. She wiped around Greg's nether regions quickly and expertly dressed him in the black sweatpants that Robert had found. Tim also bleached the articles of clothing and kicked them away under the curved conference desk.

"Do you get the feeling there were supposed to be people here?" Robert pointed out.

Chapter Eleven

Kaitlin and The Wasters

Kaitlin did not know what to do. No electricity, no phone signal, no internet. The water seemed to be running, and she had already filled up every bottle of every kind she could find, even those retrieved from the recycle bin. At least she did not have to worry about water and food, with a functioning tin opener and different types of canned food in abundance in the house.

The previous night had been terrifying. She had heard explosions and gunfire a few miles away. She had heard two types of screaming, and these were really close, less than half a mile away. Maniacal screaming of the insane and screams of pain and terror. She was frozen to the spot hearing the sounds, with the pets surrounding her in a protective phalanx. She decided that this was not good enough and she needed a plan of action to hide quickly.

She had scoped out the attic above the upstairs bathroom, which she could reach with a stepladder. It was cramped, but she didn't think anyone would look for her there. She would need to take the stepladder with her as a stepladder sitting underneath the roof hatch would make her location obvious to any intruder. She had practised the whole manoeuvre many times now, and if she camped out in the bedroom adjacent to the bathroom, she could do the whole thing silently in fifteen seconds. She had also practised in the dark.

She had not known whether to stay put or go looking for her family but decided to stay put for now and wait. Something had changed in all her pets. Maia was friendly but silent and not at all hyper. Jesse and Violet were on the windowsills at each side of the bedroom, keeping watch like sentries. With a look, either one would beckon Akasha to take over if they wanted a rest on the bed, and they rotated shifts this way. Maia just stayed by Kaitlin's side, giving her the abundance of body heat she needed in the freezing January temperatures.

There was a wet nose on her face, nudging every three or four seconds, a soft furry paw tapping her cheek. She began to wake up on the bed, not remembering falling asleep whilst mulling over her options. The pets were warning her. BANG! BANG! BANG! It was the front door, on the other side of the house. Then a voice. *Check if it's bloody open, you stupid retard, ha ha ha.* The unmistakable stunted drawl of the addicted. Tommy had pointed it out to her when she saw him giving methadone to a patient while they spoke gravelly gibberish in the entitled belief that the world owed them something.

It's locked!

I'm just saying check first, ashhaa weakling like you couldn't take this door down, mate!

SHUT IT, YOU ARSEHOLE!!!

NO, YOU SHUT IT!!! Ya faggy spaassst…ard.

Hmmm … Spastard, Kaitlin thought. She liked it. She could hear that the first man to speak was clearer, but not by much, and sounded like he had been drinking.

Bugger me, mate, I'm clucking bad, innit, I hope they have something in there to take the edge off – d'ya know what I mean?

Well ven, letshh try round the back, ya faggot.

Ya' the faggot! Ya take it, din't ya mate!

Wellsshh, you like to push it back! Esshheshially if tha's some chicken powda in it for ya, innit?

Well, you swallow fa' quaaaf mate, don't yaaa.

As the voices faded, Kaitlin snapped out of her frozen

trance when she remembered she had left the back door open for Maia to do her business. She took a few deep breaths at the sound of them walking around the side of the house, shouting at each other unintelligibly, with the drunk man singing and whistling a tune she did not recognise. All three cats and Maia silently darted downstairs, and before she knew it, she was all the way up the stepladder and opening the hatch. She eased herself backwards and silently lifted the stepladder in with her, collapsed it, closed the hatch and listened.

Her arms were burning with lactic acid, trembling, and were starting to feel like dead weight when she realised she had not breathed in thirty seconds. She emptied her lungs and breathed in deeply as she felt the oxygen debt get repaid. She forced herself to breathe slowly and silently or she would be heard. When her breathing slowed, she still had to convince herself logically that there was no way her heartbeat could be heard.

What the hell was that, mate?? Give me the bastard torch, innit!

She heard the inebriated man clearly from the back garden.

I can't see anything, fo' fack sake, mate!

Well, ya' cluckiiin, mate! I saw shadows moving from the 'ouse to the gawwden, innit.

Shit, man, that's creepy. I can see eight glowin' eyes at the back of the garden, mate.

Give me the bastard torch, you junkie, mate, innit.

Yeah, probably just cats, bro, don't worry about it.

But they came from the 'ouse and one of the sets of eyes is a different colo…

Shut … shut up and get into the house!

Kaitlin could hear everything, including the fact that

the voices seemed suddenly clearer, more focused. The voices became muffled once they had entered the house. They went silent as she realised the sound of gunfire and repeated small explosions had started up again in the distance. She heard English accents, automatic weapon fire, then laughing. She refocused back inside the house. She heard the stairs to the small hallway between the bedroom and bathroom creaking as someone tentatively climbed them. She could see little glimpses of torchlight coming through the tiny spaces between the hatch and the ceiling and hear the nasally wheezing of the intruder.

He was in the bathroom, looking for something. The medicine cabinet opened, and he whispered an audible *bugger*. It was obvious now that they did not seem to be looking for someone to harm, just wanting to get their fix. This would probably change if they found her, though. The man made a desperate whining sound of someone at their wits' end. She heard him enter the bedroom, followed by the sounds of someone turning the place upside down, wheezing with desperation.

"Found myself a nice bottle of rosé, you find anything?" the other man shouted mockingly from downstairs.

"Piss off, you twat!" he wheezed. But then, "My lucky bastard day!" He joyously rattled a plastic bottle full of tablets and capsules that Tommy had hidden in case he lost any of the medication prescribed to him.

"Quiet!" the other man shouted from downstairs. "Someone's coming!"

Banging on the front door. Not loud knocking but banging, then gunfire. She heard the door splinter as she heard what sounded like several men hurriedly entering the house. She heard them shuffling through the hallway, into the kitchen, and then the living room, where they threw something onto the couch. She heard a wet gurgling sound, most likely another person they had carried, and she could hear them talking. She could not believe it.

"Chertovy angliyskiy ublyudki! My sdalis'!"

Another man cursed loudly and could be heard trashing the room. "Oni chertovski mertvy. Pervyy shussoff, kotoryy my poluchim, my uvidim, kak stradayet anglichanin."

Kaitlin had dabbled in Russian in the first form a long time ago. But she could not remember much. She heard 'Englishman' and 'suffer'.

The first two men had gone very quiet. She heard hushed whispers coming from the bedroom; they were both in there now. The first two men sounded panicked, even when whispering, and she could hear only a few words, like 'make a run for it' and 'we're screwed' and then, 'Okay, okay, okay'. Then they went silent again. The wet gurgling had stopped. She could hear the other men talking in Russian, and they had calmed down.

Suddenly, she heard the two Russian men start running for the front door they had come through, shouting, "Come back here, Englishman! We want to be your friend!" and she heard a struggle going on outside, two British lowlifes against two Russian soldiers. She heard the struggle move back to the living room, with the first two men shouting obscenities at the Russian soldiers as they were thrown onto the other couch.

They audibly gasped and went silent as they registered the dead Russian soldier on the first couch. In broken English, one of the soldiers spoke. "See what your soldiers did to my friend when we try to surrender? You can thank your bastard cowardly soldiers for the pain we will make you feel tonight."

"Sergey, voz'mi dva stula iz kukhni."

Kaitlin heard chairs dragging on tile and then carpet.

"Teper' naydite chto-to, chtoby sderzhivat' ikh."

She heard the sounds of searching and then the sound of duct tape being applied. Kaitlin could not let this happen.

"Anatoliy, ya idu za sigaretoy, ya vykhozhu na ulitsu dlya mochi."

She heard one of the men go outside and light up a cigarette as he started urinating against the wall, softly singing in Russian.

Then she just heard an 'eek' sound. The other soldier seemed to hear it too. She heard his footsteps go towards the back door, then she was removing the roof hatch and silently lowering herself first to the edge of the bath, then the floor. It was then that she heard the second Russian soldier screaming his native language into the darkness and shooting at nothing. The two duct-taped men started screaming for help at the sound of gunshots. Kaitlin entered the living room, and the two men gasped as they saw her. She put her fingers to her lips and they just stopped. The soldier was still outside screaming into the darkness and firing his weapon. She started to try and undo the duct tape. There was a gun in the house, but she did not know how to fire it; maybe one of the restrained men did. She had managed to make a start undoing the duct tape when the men looked towards the doorway. She turned and saw a huge soldier standing in the doorway, pointing his gun at her.

"Hello, pretty English lady." He was smiling as he walked slowly towards her, relishing the moment.

She caught furtive movement behind the soldier but kept her eyes locked on his. She could not believe what was happening. He looked like he was just about to speak again when he let out a shriek of pain. Jesse had bitten down with all his strength into the soldier's lower calf muscle. Just as the soldier was reacting to this, Kaitlin noticed that Kash had climbed onto the man's shoulder. Violet jumped and dug her claws into his inner thigh, holding her in place. Jesse was latched on to his opposite lower leg and biting repeatedly.

Violet sank her teeth into the man's crotch, and he screamed with pain and anguish; Kaitlin never even knew a man could make a sound like that. Kash was latched on and repeatedly biting around his face and neck. He dropped to his knees, and that was Kaitlin's cue. She remembered what Tommy had said to her many times when he talked about unwanted attention or encountering dangerous men. 'Do not poke, GOUGE!' She followed his advice and lunged at the man, four fingers on each hand driving into each of the man's orbital sockets as his screams went up another notch. When her fingers sank in and would not go further, she curled them inward and pulled back.

The gore that burst forth from this man's face onto hers was unimaginable, and in an instant, she threw up. Now the thing that made her want to vomit was covered in vomit, and she pushed the soldier's head away from her. When she looked at what was in her hands, she flung the contents away and wiped her hands on the carpet. The cats were still all over this man even though he was completely incapacitated. Her head was spinning, all stomach contents expended, when she heard the men in the chairs, their voices getting louder and louder, coming from far away even though they were right beside her.

They were motioning to a pair of scissors on the coffee table. Her head still spinning, she used the scissors to free the two men. She could tell the alcoholic from the junkie straight away, but the alcoholic was now completely sober. He took the soldier's gun and shot him in the head, the cats getting scared and scattering in three different directions like a cat-fail YouTube video. Kaitlin's head was clearing, but she felt the urge to go outside and get fresh air. A few feet from the back door, the other soldier was very dead indeed, his throat ripped out. She saw the yellow eyes moving towards her, and before she knew it, Maia was before her, more excited and glad to see her than she had ever been.

There was blood and gore all around Maia's muzzle, and it dawned on Kaitlin that her beloved pets had saved her. Inside, the two English men were petting all three cats as they turned on the charm. They were also grateful, even though they knew it was not them the pets had been trying to save.

Kaitlin went inside with Maia. She stood and looked at the two men in silence before saying, "I'm Kaitlin, this is Maia, and they are Jesse, Violet and Akasha."

The two men laughed a laugh of pure relief and disbelief at the absurdity of the situation.

The junkie wheezed and said, "I'm Keith, this is Kevin." He had Tommy's prescription medicines in his hand and popped the bottle. He looked at the contents, wide-eyed. "This *is* my lucky night. Got any water?"

Kaitlin laughed and got him a glass from the still flowing mains. "We can't stay here," Kaitlin said. "We need to get somewhere safe, and also, we need to find out what's going on."

The two men nodded at the dead Russian soldier in the kitchen. "Well, now you know a bit more than what you did half an hour ago!"

Chapter Twelve

Archer the Bastard

Archer

Archer was gradually becoming conscious again, being rebirthed into a world of unimaginable agony. He slowly lifted his right arm to the side of his head, the arm feeling like he had spent three days repeatedly punching a tree. But it seemed to be functional. He could feel a flap his torn scalp had created, which covered his possibly broken skull, but all he could feel was an inflamed mess, and he decided not to investigate the area any further. The pain was intensifying and beginning to concentrate on certain areas of his anatomy, but he could not focus on any one part of his body to determine the causes.

He tried to lift his left arm and up came half his humerus from his shoulder. The rest of the arm was hanging at an impossible angle by skin and tendon. Half an inch of white bone was protruding from his skin. *No no no no no no no...* was all he could think. He lifted himself into a seated position with his good arm and saw his right foot pointing 90 degrees in the wrong direction. Then he saw the girl: not ten feet from him on her back, obviously dead, mid-20s, throat ripped out and still white-knuckling a rock with a fresh bloody stain on it. Then he realised he could taste copper in his mouth. Oh God, no.

He tentatively lifted up his shirt with his right arm to reveal nothing but the variable colours of different stages of bruising. *What the hell happened?* All he remembered was walking back from a studio session in Sheringham with his best friend Simon, the far-off explosion, the low flying planes, the look of terror on Simon's face, and then nothing but unremembered nightmares still receding into his subconscious to stay forever. He was dehydrated. He was *starving*. He felt completely and utterly helpless, and this brief interlude of pain was borrowed time.

He gradually became aware that the sun was about to set, but bright artificial light was hurtling towards him. The vehicle stopped a couple of metres from him, and he had absolutely no strength to get out of the way. Another artificial light was now directly on his face, causing him to squint.

"Let me see your sodding eyes or I will finish you off right now!"

He opened his eyes to see a woman, mid-20s, holding a sledgehammer in one hand and a torch in the other.

"He's cool; his pupils are pin pricks."

"But look at the bloody girl! It's obvious he killed her."

"I know, but he won't even remember. It looks like it's out of his system."

"Well, get him in. They'll be after us."

Who? Archer thought. *Who is after them?*

Another woman was in the car, which seemed to be some kind of four-wheel drive.

Archer must have been very light, as the woman scooped him up and set him gently in the back seat. He felt a pin prick in his arm as a cannula was inserted.

"Hold it up, Clarette!"

"Okay, but hurry the hell up! You realise that they will do more than just kill us, right?"

"Fine! I'll be as quick as I can, but he needs fluids."

Archer felt something cold and wet in his mouth. An ice cube.

"Just swirl this in your mouth, mate. You're going to be fine. I'm going to set the bone in your arm – this will hurt."

Archer felt his pain spike slightly, but it was over quickly, and he had not the energy to react.

He felt the girl tie a splint to his upper arm, heard the tearing of fabric, and felt a makeshift sling being fitted to hold his arm in place. The girl then set his foot, and obviously, she saw no point in telling him this time, but he realised when he felt blood rushing into his foot with unbearable pins and needles that it had been numb since he woke up.

"Open the case, Clarette. I need a vial of Cyclimorph, one of cefalexin, and a 1ml syringe and needle."

Archer heard rummaging and saw the girl injecting into a bag several times, which was being held aloft by the other girl.

He felt a warmth spread over his body, and then he was losing consciousness. He heard a muffled voice and banging in the boot of the car as the first girl belted him in place as best she could whilst he was lying on his back.

"Hurry up, Charlotte. I can hear engines. We cannot let them catch us."

Archer sensed movement before the warmth and happiness of the Cyclimorph overtook him.

"What is going on with his head?" asked Clarette.

"Well, it looks like there might be a fracture, but the skull's integrity is intact. We can deal with it later."

Charlotte was amazed that the Russian paratrooper's head was in one piece after she had struck him with her sledgehammer. Even more miraculously, the paratrooper had regained consciousness and lucidity whilst she was speeding away, shouting English and Russian obscenities at her. She had originally parked the car and gone into a grove of trees for cover, trying to calm down and decide what to do next. The paratrooper had randomly landed near her, outside the treeline of the tiny grove, in a grazing field. She had assumed he was a straggler, as there were only the sounds of birds and no sign in this little grove that anything was wrong. Nor had she seen any military hardware.

When he was out cold, she had confiscated all the guns she could find, cut his harness off with a Stanley knife she had taken from work, bound him with electrical tape she had found in the 4 x 4 she had stolen, and stuffed him into the boot. She had confiscated a big gun and a small one, neither of which she knew how to use, but found the safety catch of each, both of which were already on, and put them in the passenger footwell. She would figure out how to use them later. She was speeding, however, because it hadn't taken long before she heard ominous, urgent engine noises. And not like normal engine noises, but terrifying engine noises which she could only assume were of military origin.

Clarette had been numb to what was happening, silently weeping in the passenger seat, but Charlotte did not blame her. Everybody was handling this differently, and this situation was utterly terrifying and completely unexpected. Clarette had eventually ended up sleeping after taking a Valium from the destroyed Red Cross mobile hospital they had scavenged through. If the invaders had destroyed this on purpose, based on their historical track record and what Charlotte had done, it was not an option to get caught alive.

She knew that paratroopers were special forces and were privy to more information than the average soldier, so the engines she had heard were probably to rescue the paratrooper before anyone could get any information. She was just a civilian and not someone to start torturing another person easily, but they did not know that.

The engine noises had eventually faded as she sped away from Bradwell in Great Yarmouth, hugging the coastline and making random turns in the countryside to evade capture. When there was only a quarter of a tank left and the sun started to set, they had found the broken but alive boy on the road near Sheringham. She treated him using knowledge she had gained in the prison service, her current job, and also from TV, somewhat successfully. The boy was lying on his side in the back seat, using their coats as a pillow, and she kept looking in the rear-view mirror to see his chest rising and falling. Clarette was holding the IV bag scavenged from the mobile Red Cross hospital and was awake and lucid.

Clarette was now very quiet but was completely compliant with everything Charlotte had said to do. She had obviously decided to put all of her trust in Charlotte. She had heard those god-awful engines again when they stopped to pick up the broken boy, but they were not necessarily coming after them at this point.

"There!" Clarette said. She pointed to a farmhouse about half a mile from the main road. In the dying light, the only thing that could be made out was an empty garage with an open door. "Good enough!" said Charlotte as she turned onto the single-lane track leading to the farmhouse.

They approached slowly, and although they could not tell for sure, it looked completely abandoned. Even the front door was open. Charlotte drove into the garage and turned the engine off. Clarette then jumped out of the passenger seat and pulled the dangling rope to close the garage door.

A short while later

Archer woke up on an extremely comfortable couch. He

felt heavily opiated but did not mind as he could also, on a deeper level, sense the pain awaiting him when his body metabolised the opiate in his system. As well as the general pain, there were two points of stiffness, immobility and discomfort on his body: the left arm and right ankle. He also felt a deep throbbing in his head. He shifted himself to a seated position as best he could and saw a glass of water beside him on a side table. He grabbed it and downed it in one. There were also blackcurrant soothers. He took one and just sucked on it. After the bad taste in his mouth and its dryness, it was ecstasy. Then he was able to make out a man looking at him, sitting on a kitchen chair in the room.

Archer registered that the room was in total darkness, and in the moonlight from the window, he slowly made out more detail of the man staring at him: he was wrapped around the chair with a comically excessive amount of electrical tape, as well as having some over his mouth. Despite the man's terrified expression, Archer let out a chuckle as he remembered the episode of *Bottom* where Rik and Eddie had taped burglars to the roof.

There was frantic whispering in the room next door the whole time.

"Hello?" he said.

"He's awake!!!"

The whispering stopped as Clarette and Charlotte came into the room. They all introduced themselves.

Charlotte just said, "Know anything about guns?"

Clarette just said, "Know anything about getting information out of a Russian paratrooper?"

They both burst out laughing, and in Archer's opiated state, he laughed along with them. "This is ludicrous," he said.

Two days later

Archer was in bad shape. He was only alive because the girl whose throat he had torn out had brained him with a good-sized rock. Right now, circling on the edges of consciousness, was PTSD, guilt, regret and rage with no discernible target. Basically, all of the negative emotions that existed. His subconscious was kindly protecting him from the full force of the mental trauma. If he lived long enough for his injuries to fully heal and the world around him eventually went back to normal, which he doubted, then he would inflict a living hell upon himself. He knew this was in store for him, and therefore, he knew he did not want to live through this, assuming that normal times were ever to exist again.

He knew he had torn out that poor girl's throat, but the worst part was that he did not remember anything of his homicidal rampage. He wanted to die before normal times ever resumed, but he would dedicate the remainder of his life to trying to offset the awful shit that he had done, even if he could not remember it. He knew that if all his actions were altruistic, this would pretty much guarantee that he would not live through this wasteland.

He was on a bed in what looked like a guest room, and propped up against the bedside table was a hard oak walking stick, which could easily double as a very effective blunt weapon. On the bedside table, there was a cup of water and a measuring cup with pills with a handwritten note that said, 'Please take this as soon as you wake'.

He did not question this and necked the pills, washing them down with the full glass of water. He lay back down and contorted for half an hour. As the medication hit his bloodstream and the pain faded to tolerable levels, he became aware of a very bad smell and screaming coming from somewhere in the building. He could hear, in broken English, nonsensical insults lost in translation and a female voice laughing and issuing threats. He listened for a few minutes.

"I bitch a dog, you English whore! I arsehole a mother whore and eat dog, I not wash dick, he like our mother and is shitting!"

"You are going to die, you low-life Russian scumbag. You've been sitting in your own shit for two days. Soon you'll go septic. You probably have blood clots in your legs, just waiting for you to stand up. If you tell us what we want to know, you may stand a chance of keeping the skin around your arse cheeks!"

"My family eats dogs and horses, I am a twat! Your mother she is nice not the shit!"

Clarette shrieked with amusement at this supposed insult.

Archer then heard a hissing sound followed by a scream of hopeless pain.

"News is scarce in Russian, but from what I hear, you lot are having your arses handed to you."

The Russian responded to this with a half laugh, half whimper. "I do not care, I hate Russia, I hate Putin, I do not belong anywhere. My heart beats, but my life, it is over! No matter what you do to me, worse will be done to my family now I am taken prisoner!"

Archer put the hard oak stick under his right arm like a crutch. His left humerus and his right foot were still heavily splinted and bandaged. He hobbled out of the room, putting all his weight on his left foot, and made his way towards the screaming and shouting. In the main living room sat the Russian in the same place as before, with a brown puddle forming under him. To Archer, the smell resembled that of a nursing home. Clarette held a poker which was red hot, taken from the fire they had started in the hearth. There was a pile of dried wood next to the fire.

"Despite the fact he clearly does not value his own life, I'm pretty sure that if he knew something, he would say something, just to make the pain stop," Archer said.

Charlotte entered the room from the kitchen.

"He knows something," Clarette responded.

"I'll tell you what," Charlotte said, addressing the soldier. "You give us something, anything at all, she will kill you quickly."

The soldier simply said, "We die so Putin can live. You had better pray he not find youth fountain."

With that, Charlotte nodded to Clarette, who drove the still red-hot poker down his throat, right to the hilt. The Russian screamed and gurgled for a solid three minutes as well as he could and was still.

"I think that was quick enough."

Archer almost fell when he tripped over something sticking out of the floor. He looked down and saw a metal ring. Clarette grabbed it and pulled it open. They could see a flight of stairs and darkness.

Suddenly, they all became aware of a light so bright, it was the only thing they could see. Archer held his hand up in front of his face and saw all the intricate bones of his wrist and hand. He knew what this was instantly. They all instinctually closed their eyes quickly, but Clarette had been looking directly at the source. Her corneas melted, sealing her eyes shut. The light started to fade after around five seconds, and Archer heard Clarette screaming.

Everything around them was smoking ever so slightly, and he could feel the air around him get hotter and hotter. Charlotte ran towards Archer and threw him over her shoulder. She brought him down the steep stairs, going around twenty feet below the surface, and gently laid him on the floor. The battery-powered fluorescent lighting flickered on. They both sighed in relief at the cool but slightly musty air. She ran back up the stairs to get Clarette, who was feeling around her, calling Charlotte's name.

Clarette's skin was reddening and lesions were showing. It was like being hit with a blast of hot air when opening an oven, but Charlotte ran over and grabbed her by the wrist. She also grabbed all of the supplies from a table in the corner of the room and flung the bags down the stairs. She was roughly pulling Clarette into the hole and down the stairway, but she felt resistance behind her. The soldier was still alive. The tape holding him to the chair had melted. He had used the opportunity to drive his service knife up through Clarette's chin.

He was making bestial noises and could not speak due to the poker down his throat. The knife exited from Clarette's mouth. The soldier pulled out the knife and blood burst out from the opened chin, but there was no arterial or venous pumping. She pulled her friend down the stairs as the Russian continued his unique noise of screaming in pain with a poker rammed down his throat.

Chapter Thirteen

Ginny and Jane Are Late to the Party

Apocalypse Rave

Neither Ginny nor Jane was able to give any information to the other and could only speculate. Ginny was going to try and go home but happened to remember a years' old conversation the family had had about the possibility of things going wrong in the world and where everyone would meet if they were separate and not able to contact each other. It was Tommy's parents' house when they had lived in Northern Ireland, but now it was the university. She hoped everyone else remembered the conversation and took it seriously.

As Jane and Ginny drove, it got dark, and soon after this, over the crest of a hill, they saw flashing lights and heard a pounding bass. There was also the cacophony of the drunk and merry. Not necessarily threatening, but Jane had a bad feeling.

"STOP!" she shouted suddenly.

Ginny slammed on the brakes, startled. "What are yo…"

Jane cut her off. "THERE!" she shouted again. She pointed to a lay-by on the other side of the road, the enclosed-by-trees type of lay-by popular with doggers, although she did not think there was much of a chance of running into them.

Jane was absolutely terrified, so Ginny took her seriously. She pulled in.

"Kill the lights," Jane said, much calmer now. Jane knew she needed to explain. "Since I was ten, I've felt like this on two other occasions. Both of those times, within a short period of time but not immediately, something awful happened. Don't get me wrong, other awful things have happened not preceded by this feeling. But when I have this gut-wrenching sense of dread, something WILL happen. It made sense to me that we hide until whatever is going to happen is over."

"Exactly what awful things are we talking about?"

"It doesn't matter at this point. I'll tell you when I'm ready. I really recommend you humour me on this one."

Ginny understood. She had had her own fair share of trauma that she would not necessarily want to share with strangers, especially in a high tension situation such as this. Ginny did not want to engage with a crowd at this point and saw no reason not to go along with Jane on this one.

The apocalypse rave continued on until the early hours. Neither Jane nor Ginny was in any mood for sleeping. Neither felt safe enough to do so, and their adrenaline release was not slowing down. Both passed the time talking about their lives but still keeping it light and surface only. Ginny told stories to Jane about her kids, like the time her musical genius son impressed a crowd of people by mastering the drums to the beat of the song 'Gay Bar' despite only having learnt guitar at that point.

At that point, everything hit Ginny at once, like a brick to the head. She welled up with tears. "I don't know if he's dead or alive, nor anyone else in my family. Will I ever see any of them again?"

"I don't know," Jane said flatly, having no kids of her own and a family which consisted only of complete bastards. She had fallen in love before, but it was not long until that love was betrayed, when she stumbled upon things on her boyfriend's laptop which could not be unseen. The shame and betrayal she had felt as he was led out of the house in handcuffs had ruined her mental health and led her to where she was now.

To think that he enjoyed that sort of thing, whilst seeming to be all of her dreams come true at the same time, almost broke her. It was a mystery how people could ever really know a person, let alone trust them.

"Look, all I know is that it's not useful to you to think this way now," Jane said. "You must assume that they're all still alive. Despite everything, the majority of the country is still alive. We just don't know for how long, as every single person's risk factor for death just went up a hundredfold."

Ginny thought about this for a second and said, "You're absolutely right; these tears are useless t..." Ginny could not finish her sentence because the music stopped suddenly and the screaming started.

Both Ginny and Jane recognised the sound of the other type of screaming, the same type Jane's friends had emitted as they turned feral. It was obvious what had happened. But it sounded like a lot of them, not just 5 or 6 as they had dealt with previously. They then heard the unmistakable sound of automatic gunfire and the whooping from who they assumed to be those firing the weapons. They heard a whoop cut short by the other type of screaming. It sounded like the feral people were overwhelming the ones with the guns, having no regard for their own lives. Everything died down to complete silence, and all that could be heard was talking and laughing by a very small group of individuals. Individuals they assumed were lucky enough to survive the confrontation.

They heard music, but it wasn't rave, just the standard

pop you hear on the radio, a lot lower in volume, just background music. Ginny took the biggest knife out of the rucksack and clutched it. They heard some men getting into a truck and driving away, in the opposite direction from which Ginny and Jane had come. Then silence.

A short while later

Tap tap tap. TAP TAP TAP TAP … Ginny snapped awake, and dread sank in her gut. She could not remember falling asleep, but it was now what appeared to be dawn. It was light outside but not just like any day. The sky looked like a badly sprained ankle. Yellow, black, brown, scarlet. Hellish.

"Roll the window down," said a calm voice.

She looked outside and laid her eyes on a middle-aged man in some sort of military type uniform. But it was not real. It looked fake, as if it was thrown together from military surplus equipment by an unemployable man whose time it now was to shine. He was holding an AR15. That was real. Ginny recognised it due to all the publicity from American school shootings. Pretty much everyone now knew what they looked like.

She looked past the man and saw another man, an ageing biker type, covered in tattoos. He was holding a gun, a small revolver, against Jane's head. A scared-looking teenage boy stood off to the side. He had no weapons. Ginny rolled the window down.

"Have you got any food or water?" he asked in a demanding tone.

"Yes, in my backpack, but it's not wa…"

"Shut up. Give the backpack to me," he said, strangely

calm this time.

"Look, just listen to me, that is not w…"

"SHUT UP!!!" He was losing his cool now but fighting to keep it.

The biker man cocked the revolver.

"DAD!" the teenager shouted.

"SHUT UP, STEVE! Now YOU give me your sodding backpack with the water. I am more thirsty than I have ever been, and that water is probably freezing cold. So give it to me. NOW!"

Ginny threw her hands up. She had tried. Any further protest would get Jane killed. She gave him the backpack, and the first thing he did was take the bottle out. He held it aloft, savouring the imminent quenching of his thirst. Jane knew what was in there and was readying herself to act fast. He would get one third, his son and his father a third each. But he was going to go first.

He pulled open the spill-proof cap, put it to his mouth, not giving himself a chance to even smell the noxious fumes that would have been released. He gulped down around three mouthfuls before it appeared to register on his face what he had just put inside his body. It was too late. He dropped the AR15 and fell to his knees, making a wet, gurgling, moaning noise of agony. He clutched his throat as he foamed at the mouth, and the red foam spilled chunks of gore from his mouth as he lay on his side, contorting and reaching an arm out towards Ginny. All over the driver's side of the car, she could see blood and gore, all from the man's mouth as the acid ate mercilessly at his insides slowly and painfully.

Jane tried to grab the gun, but the old man pulled it back and punched her square in the face. She was on the ground as he took aim, but something splashed in his face. The gun went off, but the bullet hit the dirt right by Jane's head. The old man dropped the gun, put his hand to his face and started screaming in agony. She then saw the young boy the man had called Steve standing with the bottle in both hands, still aiming it at his grandfather. He simply said, "I've always hated them both, but whatever situation we're in, this has brought out the absolute worst in them. I wasn't going to watch as they killed you both. Not going to happen."

Ginny had grabbed the AR15 and Jane the handgun. The first man was still on the ground, contorting silently, with his eyes bulging out of their sockets. The second man was screaming in pain, hurling threats and abuse as Jane raised the handgun. Ginny raised the AR15, even though she had never fired a gun before, but she knew to let her shoulder absorb the recoil.

"NO!" Steve shouted. "Let them suffer. Neither deserves to be put out of their misery. If I told you how much pain they put people though, even before this all happened, you would understand. Let them suffer."

"Okay," Ginny said. "But I can't watch this. We're out of here."

Jane nodded and they both jumped into the car. Ginny started the engine.

"WAIT!" Steve shouted. "Please let me come with you!"

Jane and Ginny looked at each other. Jane nodded and Ginny motioned for him to get in. He did, and she peeled out of there as quickly as she could. As they rounded the crest of the hill, an apocalyptic scene greeted them. Bodies strewn all over the road. Some looked normal, but they had grotesque injuries – ripped-out throats or disembowelment.

Some of them were dressed as though they had been

raving, and there was a full set of decks and speakers hooked up to numerous car batteries. The affected still looked animalistic, even in death, with teeth bared in eternal snarls and black eyes completely open. They were full of bullet holes and contorted like dead spiders. They were terrifying in the way a scorpion might sting, even in death.

"What happened here?" Ginny asked.

"You do *not* want to know," Steve said.

Jane cocked the revolver. "We *do* want to know."

"My dad and a few friends of his and my grandfather thought it would be funny to get as many of the cacodemons chasing us ..."

"Demons?" Ginny and Jane said in unison.

"Well, not demons, literally, but it seemed like a good descriptive term. They were able to get around 20 of those things to chase us, and they revelled in the fact that they had led them to this apocalypse party. They thought it was hilarious as the demons slaughtered the ravers. That is, until the demons decided to turn on us, and only myself, my dad and my grandfather and two others were left. Then when our backs were turned, the other two piled into the truck we'd come in and abandoned us. The guns they had, the demons were able to bend and break them with their bare hands."

Ginny and Jane looked at each other, disgusted by Steve's story.

"So what else did your wonderful father do?" Jane asked.

"Well, I could go on about that all day. But I grew up with him abusing my mother, and when she finally found the nerve to leave him, all this happened. I was barricaded at home, and he turned up, seemingly ready to make amends. But no, my arsehole grandfather shot her in the head, and they took me."

"Thank you for what you did, Steve," Jane said.

"Yes, thank you," Ginny said.

"Now we both have no family to find, but Ginny does, and we are going to help her find them."

"Sounds like a plan to me. Thanks so much for taking me in after my twat dad's behaviour!'

Chapter Fourteen

The Rightful Owners

Before anyone could say anything, they heard automatic- or machine-gun fire above. They listened as a heavy vehicle seemed to circle around the entrance. After around three minutes, it stopped. And then the phone rang. The phone that no one had clocked yet.

"Help me carry him to bed," Mary instructed.

Within half a minute, they had placed Greg gently on the nearest bed, on his side. The phone had stopped ringing. They went back to the central hub and stood around the phone in silence for another fifteen seconds. Predictably, they all jumped when it rang again.

It was just a standard portable landline between two computers and flashed blue when ringing. Just a gimmick.

Robert picked it up. "H... h.... hello?" he said sheepishly.

"Hey, Ethan, it's the colonel. We got rid of the ghouls up above, but it's only temporary. The noise will no doubt attract more. I'll tell you, Ethan, I am glad you talked me into investing in this. I would be totally screwed now if I hadn't, eh?"

Robert noted the voice seemed almost worn out after years of screaming. It was a friendly tone, but something told Robert that could change in an instant.

"P... pe... Ethan's not here." The stress of the situation seemed to trigger a stutter in Robert.

The man at the other end of the line went silent for a good fifteen seconds, and Robert could almost hear the cogs turning inside the colonel's head.

"Please explain." The voice was even softer now. Not threatening, but very assertive.

Tim reached out to the phone, and Robert gladly gave

it to him, feeling vulnerable having given away what was, in his mind, a weakness.

"Hey, Colonel, I'm Tim, and I am here with three other people ..." Tim relayed the entire sequence of events to the colonel.

The colonel patiently listened without interruption. His voice now returned to its original tone; he had no reason not to believe them. "Sounds like you're in bad shape. So the ghouls inflicted mortal injury on Ethan, and his last words were the grid reference to that place?"

Tim could hear explosions in the background. Artillery fire. He could tell there were two distinct sounding explosions, even over the phone. "Well, yeah. He was killed by ... the ghouls? Is that what you're calling them? Is that the Russians you're fighting?"

"Yes, and yes. How did you know it was the Russians?"

"I heard snippets of info on a car radio. Are we winning?"

"Yes, for now. But that orange arsehole Donald Trump refuses to get involved, not for any good reason. We're afraid America will turn on us and pick the NWA over us. All other NATO members have invoked Article 5, except Latvia. I understand why, but they wouldn't be of much use to us. Anyway, it sounds like you're in bad shape. My men are trained; they'll look after you. We have a medic up here as well."

So much information. So many questions to ask. It made Tim's head hurt. He was utterly horrified about what was going on. He could almost handle the knowledge that the Russians were invading, but *America not having our back*? He felt nauseous.

"Hello?" the colonel said.

"Yes, sorry. I just cannot believe America is actually betraying us. I utterly despise and *hate* Donald Trump."

"You won't get any argument from me," the colonel said. "Look, mate, I paid a lot of money to build the shelter you're in. It's supposed to be for Ethan, my men, and our families."

"Where are your families?"

"Dead, missing, or unknown. You're talking on a satellite phone. We didn't expect the communication infrastructure to collapse so catastrophically, even though we prepared for it. I think it's partly due to cyber warfare. Down there, we have advanced communications systems, which means that we have much more chance of making contact with our families."

Tim was starting to like the colonel; he seemed genuine.

"Will you please let us in?" the colonel asked with urgency.

"Are there more ghouls on the way?" Tim asked.

"We can hear them. We can hide in the APC, but we have nothing with us. No food, water, etc."

Silence.

"How long have you been down there?" the colonel asked.

"Forty-five minutes," said Tim.

The colonel laughed benignly. "So you haven't had a chance to explore?"

More silence.

"That's okay, I can show you around when you let us down."

Tim thought he heard a faint giggling. He dismissed it as his own stress and tiredness and the need for sugar. *Oh, shit.* His head was swimming. He handed the phone to Robert and sat down. Mary brought some more Glucogel to Tim. He gulped it down with relief.

"Robert, honey, can I please have the phone?"

He handed it to her with relief, like it was old roadkill.

"Hello, hello, mate, where did you go?"

"This is Mary. Hello, Colonel," she said with warmth.

"Oh, hi, Mary. What happened to my mate? I didn't get his name."

"Tim is diabetic, with his sugar running low. This is all too much for him. He's injured too, although not as bad as Greg."

"Hi, Mary, I am Colonel Henry George Brown of the Royal Tank Regiment. Lovely to meet you. There's enough room down there for us all. Can you let us in?"

This was a tough decision.

"Okay," said Mary. "We'll come up and let you in. I used to be a nurse in the Falklands. The soldiers who fought in that war were amazing people, underappreciated. I hope you are good people too."

"We are, and it sounds like we'll have no end of stories to regale each other with. I was in Afghanistan and Iraq. All my men have been in one or both. You'll be in good company."

"Okay. I'm coming up. I'll see you soon, Colonel."

"Thank you, Mary. See you soon. You can call me Henry."

Mary went to hang up, but then she heard faint whispering and sniggering. She put the phone back to her ear. Just before the colonel hung up, she clearly heard the whispered words, *stupid idiots*. Mary threw the phone and handset at the wall. "Now let's see who's a stupid idiot," Mary said in a devastated tone, a sob in her voice. She had wanted so badly to trust them. She wanted to keep members of the armed forces on a pedestal. But some were animals and dangerous narcissists. They were not coming down here.

Robert and Tim, who was now alert again, just looked at her.

"That escalated on a dime!" Robert said amusedly.

"Well, someone needs to learn to hang up the phone before they reveal their true intentions."

"Which were?"

"Not good," was all Mary would say.

Within a few minutes, the banging started.

"I pray that it holds," Mary said. "Whatever their plans were before, we can expect much worse if they get through that door. Can one of you please find a saline IV drip, cannula, tape and stand? We need to make sure Greg is hydrated."

Within a few minutes, Tim returned with her requested items. The saline he had found in a fridge.

"There are nine more in there," he said.

Mary went to the shed, and using her vast experience, had the saline drip set up in forty seconds. She went to the central hub with Tim and Robert.

"We're happy you are here, Mary. Thank you," Robert said.

Tim nodded in agreement. With his medical condition, and seeing Mary in action, he felt very reassured. The banging was unceasing. There were some muffled screams of rage, then screams of pain. The banging stopped, closely followed by machine-gun fire.

They decided to explore the huge room to take their minds off what was happening thirty feet above their heads. Tim could see individual black leather recliners arranged in a circle around an antique coffee table, and on this sat many different unopened brands of cigarettes and cigars, rolling tobacco, skins, filters and a cigar cutter, with a few lighters and a few unopened vape pens.

There were three clear bags, two of which held white powder. On each bag, there was a single letter written in permanent marker: C and M. The third bag did not need a label. It was green.

Robert grabbed the bag, put it to his nose and sniffed deeply, filling up his lungs with that all too familiar smell he clearly loved. "It's been so long. I have missed this so badly."

Under the coffee table, Robert found a mini pharmacy. It had generic diazepam, zopiclone, Concerta, pregabalin, Zomorph, tapentadol, cyclizine, sildenafil and tramadol. On the bottom shelf were EpiPens, Jext, syringes and needles, adrenaline ampoules, and salbutamol and Clenil Modulite inhalers.

"Something tells me the majority of this was to be used recreationally," Tim said.

The 'window' on the far wall now showed a mighty, violent waterfall with a rainbow caused by the droplets.

Further down, near where the gun wall met the row of sheds, there was a fifty-inch Samsung television, with twelve seats facing it. Underneath was a DVD player and a shelf full of movies dating back to at least the 1940s: *North by Northwest*, *It's a Wonderful Life*, *Trains, Planes and Automobiles*, *Serpico*, *Goodfellas*, *Casino*, *Chitty Chitty Bang Bang*.

Robert looked behind him at the screen on the wall, transfixed by the crystal-clear display, which showed a city skyline under a full moon, then a remote mountain under the Milky Way galaxy.

"Do you think we should have let them down?" Robert said, hoping Tim would say something to somehow alleviate his guilt.

"No. There's a good chance their families are dead

anyway. And they would not have shared an inch of space or any resources with us. If we had let them down, we'd be dead by now. We got lucky. Besides, Ethan himself wanted us to be here. I trust Mary's judgement. And also … screw 'em, I hate squaddies anyway."

Robert rubbed his chin. "You have a point," he responded. He had no hate for squaddies, but he did not feel an obligation to them.

Mary remained silent, contemplating the fact that she had almost made a terrible error of judgement which would have got all four of them killed.

When they got closer to the wall of clothing and medicines, they saw cheap-looking closets, and on looking inside, they found many other items of thermal clothing and military surplus gear as well as all green pop-up tents, sleeping bags, camping stoves, fire extinguishers, powerful torches, batteries, power banks, and a few solar-powered satellite phones.

"It looks like this required decades of preparation," Tim said. "I don't know about you, but this place is catered to all of my needs."

Stored in random boxes all over the room were various electronics and game systems, televisions, etc. Raw building materials were also scattered everywhere. This was a work in progress.

"It looks like it's been updated regularly over time, a fluid project. I think maybe they were planning on sectioning this big room into smaller rooms, with each section having a particular purpose."

"Yes," Mary said. "This place is too big and white and sterile, but the basic survival necessities have been taken care of. It looks like they haven't finished with aesthetics and comfort. I shouldn't complain. We're very lucky."

They spied things from across the room which needed no further investigation for now: washing machines and dryers, exercise equipment, chest freezers.

They all went to the first shed to check on Greg, who was sleeping soundly on his side. Robert tapped Tim's shoulder and pointed to a brass plate on the wall opposite the bed which simply said, 'Ken and Barbie'. Robert was not sure what to do, so he knocked on the wall next to the plate.

"Hello? Ken? Barbie? Is anyone there?" He looked at Tim and gave a playful wink.

Tim smiled for the first time in this long, long day. Nobody responded, so after a couple of minutes, Robert tentatively prodded at the wood around the plate until he heard a click. A hidden door opened a few inches. Robert looked at Tim, confused and surprised. The door was from roof to floor, with the edges cleverly hidden between wooden slats.

Robert pulled the door open all the way and saw a man and woman naked and sitting beside each other on wooden chairs. He pushed the door closed again, eyes wide. "Sorry! Sorry! Sorry!" Robert said with fear in his voice.

Tim was getting impatient, so he pushed the door all the way open again. Tim then let out a laugh when he saw what lay before him. Robert was having difficulty processing what he saw.

"RealDolls!" Tim exclaimed.

"But they look *so* … real!" Robert said.

"Yes, that's the whole point. That's why they're called 'RealDolls'. They look like extremely attractive humans. You bang them." Tim was laughing again, more at how confused Robert was. "Look at the shelves beside the bed; they're for cleaning out the 'cavities'."

Robert was getting it now. "This is disgusting." he said.

Tim let out a chuckle and replied, "They offer unconditional love too. Well, I suppose the only condition is that you clean out the cavities when you're done."

Robert blushed. Tim knew they both were going to bang one or both of them at some point. A sharp intake of breath came from Mary. She had entered the shed without them knowing. She just stood there, her hands covering her mouth in shock but her eyes smiling. Suddenly, Tim had an idea and ran to the next shed to look at the same wall. Mary and Robert followed. 'Haru and Aya', it said. Third shed: 'Imani and Adissa'. Fourth shed: 'Rafael and Sofia'. Now, they just looked at each other awkwardly. They knew that all of them would make use of the dolls, given enough time.

Chapter Fifteen

Moloch

The sexless creature, made masculine and named Moloch when it had crawled through the hole to this world, walked silently down the deserted A47. It was early in the morning, just as the brown fallout clouds were starting to show. The smell of unwashed feet hung in the air. Moloch was enjoying making humanity's second attempt at civilization suffer and decay for as long as possible before ultimately destroying it.

The first time around, Moloch had revelled in the human civilization's quick annihilation. They had such a perfect world, almost free from suffering and injustice. Their gene pool was rich and varied, but they were crippled with guilt and regret. Moloch had been their worst mistake, born of this guilt and fear. It was too easy for him.

Moloch came from a world of sentient parasites. There was no love, no happiness. Only power. Only misery. This second attempt at advanced civilization by humanity had a genetic bottleneck to contend with. It bore a little more of a resemblance to Moloch's home world. As the millennia passed by, he had enjoyed watching as a broken race tried to rise again. Moloch and various others the world over did everything they could to corrupt mankind without slowing its progress. He had not felt the need to interfere in higher powers for the sake of the destruction of this human civilization until recently.

Where Moloch had come from, hatred, jealousy and rage were the only motivators. Moloch hated humanity and was jealous of this beautiful world they lived in. He felt utter despair at never being a part of it. He was too corrupted, too broken. Moloch's appearance reflected what he was on the inside: grotesque and deformed. He was not able to hide this appearance from humans 100% of the time.

The stories were passed around the campfire over many thousands of years. These stories included that of the Nephilim, angels, goblins, demons, ghouls, wendigo, vampires, werewolves, faerie, witches, and leprechauns, as well as many others. There were many more like Moloch, but they kept away from each other, and over time, they had carved up the world into their very own principalities. He was a demon, only in the sense that sightings of him and others in their true form had woven the narrative over many millennia. Some like Moloch imparted knowledge of their home world to humans, gaslighting to instil a fear of ending up there. This was beautifully woven into the Christian narrative so their leadership could count on the subservience of the poor and ignorant masses.

Sometimes, a warrior from the past had interfered with the evildoings of the Echthroi, and sometimes, they had been successful. This warrior was not more powerful, but very elusive, and sought to make the Echthroi's goals difficult to achieve, to the point where it was not worth the effort. Soon, they would not need to hide themselves anymore. And maybe the ancient warrior could be caught and dealt with. Despite the first civilization being destroyed and largely forgotten, humans had, in their racial subconscious memory, a fear of the end times and the supernatural entities responsible for corrupting the hearts of all men and women.

Whenever Moloch revealed himself to an individual deliberately, it was generally the last thing that person ever saw. Most of the time. Sometimes he would appear in his true form to those who were already mentally very vulnerable, causing them to fall into a chasm of deliration. Very entertaining to Moloch.

The technology, indistinguishable from magic, that had allowed Moloch and the other Echthroi to enter this world, was the only thing that could banish them again, and the scientists of old knew this. That was another factor in Moloch's desire to end their first civilization quickly. The new, tainted civilization did not even know for sure that the Echthroi existed, never mind knowing how to destroy them.

The same technology in the new civilization, which was the ability to manipulate the building blocks of the universe to do the users' bidding, was in its infancy. Not only could this technology banish Moloch, but it could theoretically allow the user to take him apart at the molecular level. While this technology existed, even at this early stage, it posed a threat, and Moloch could not allow an individual human to wield more power than him. It did not matter to Moloch whether the technology fell into good hands or evil hands. Even if it did end up in good hands, the power would just corrupt anyway.

The nature and inner workings of this technology needed to be known by Moloch before it was destroyed, for the sake of curiosity and pragmatism. The knowledge might come in useful one day, especially if he was the only one who possessed it. Moloch was heading to the university, as he had learned that whatever had been documented of this technology was intentionally left incomplete by the professor. Nothing ultimately came of the theft of the professor's research notes.

The information they had was not a threat for now.

Moloch had planned to use whatever tools were at his disposal to obtain this missing information. Maybe showing his true form to the professor would be enough. But there were plenty of ways to extract this information. What Moloch also did not want was for a gate to be reopened to allow more of his kind to come through. He was not willing to share humanity's torment any more than he already had to.

Moloch could shapeshift, but frustratingly, could only maintain a shift for ten or so minutes. Others of his kind were able to shift for much longer, and because of that, their influence on those around them was profoundly negative. They would shapeshift and murder the spouse of the person they were mimicking, framing them for murder. Moloch had an arguably more powerful ability. Depending on the person, he could influence them in a negative manner by controlling the mind directly. Unfortunately, very few people were susceptible to this level of manipulation, and even then, it would only be for a matter of seconds. This would generally only be good for a brief act of extreme violence, and intricate tasks were not possible.

He could also manipulate subconsciously by suggestion. He could cause havoc by simply transmitting raw hatred into a single persons' mind or into an entire mob. How well this could be done would depend on Moloch's proximity to people and on their susceptibility. For some folks, their minds would be like fortresses. If this were the case in an important individual, then Moloch could psychically manipulate someone close to and trusted by that individual.

For some, it could be actual voices in a person's mind, but this quickly led to mental ruin. These people were dismissed as crazy more often than not, and medication would close the door he had used to gain entry into a person's mind – not practical and only really done for entertainment. The subtle subconscious manipulation approach was the best method, and for sociopathic people especially, this was highly effective.

Sometimes, all it required would be just a little nudge, just as recently, when Putin had decided on the execution of Operation Red Claw. Putin was led to believe this had been entirely his decision, unaware of the subconscious manipulation. Moloch did not need to spend more than an hour at the right time in the sewer underneath the Kremlin.

An armoured personnel carrier full of Russian soldiers was coming toward him in the distance, so Moloch concentrated his power to morph into a beautiful, flawless-looking teenage female, something he would be unable to do for more than ten minutes at a time before running out of energy and morphing back. He knew that Russian soldiers were the worst of the worst, and he thoroughly enjoyed setting very real honey traps for them. He always needed to find clothes after morphing, but not this time.

He finished the transition just as the APC came into view, and it slowed down behind the naked girl. The girl turned around, making sure to look terrified and helpless, trying to cover up using her hands. Millennia of practice had allowed Moloch to perfect the technique of looking afraid. The APC went up ahead about twenty feet. The terrified, naked girl stopped walking, and the APC also stopped. As the APC opened its back doors, the girl looked even more scared and started to slowly back away.

In the APC were about ten men aged from 18 to 50.

The youngest looked scared, but the older, obviously more high-ranking men, based on their uniforms, simply leered. The driver also got out. They were clearly under the influence of *something*, maybe several narcotics. This would be so easy. These men started approaching her, still leering. One was drinking vodka straight out of the bottle, and they were passing the bottle around. Two more were smoking fat cigars, and another appeared to sniff a white powder off his knuckle. He was not leering, just looking at her with predatory hatred in his eyes, only one thing on his overstimulated mind.

"Where are your clothes, pretty English lady? Is it laundry day?" the middle-aged officer holding the vodka bottle said.

The rest started laughing as the girl screamed and started running, falling on purpose after a few steps. They grabbed her and pulled her kicking and screaming into the APC as she pleaded with them to stop and leave her alone. They threw her on the floor, closed the door and surrounded her, whilst the young conscripted men watched.

The vodka swilling officer pointed at one of them and shouted, "Maksim, do you now want to become a man so we don't call you a virgin anymore?"

They all laughed again while Maksim cowered in the corner. But the officer's face darkened as he passed on the vodka again.

"Maksim, you come here NOW!!" he screamed. "And take your clothes off!"

All went silent as Maksim approached, looking horrified at what they were ordering him to do. The fist-bumping, highest-ranking officer was glaring at Maksim and at the officer who had given the rape order to the young soldier. He was already visibly aroused, clenching his jaw and tightening his fist over and over again. He suddenly moved forwards and punched the officer who had given the order, wasting no time in undressing his own lower half. Maksim was off the hook for now.

The girl screamed, "Please don't do this, I beg you! Please let me go. I won't say anything!"

"We do not care," another officer stated. "No one will listen to you anyway, you stupid girl."

The punched officer was nursing his jaw but did not look like he was about to retaliate. The other men started holding her down for the fist bumper, obviously being the highest-ranking officer, as if this was not already clear.

"What will your wife say, Sergei?" the other men mocked and laughed.

"To hell with that ugly witch," he responded as he put his hand around the girl's throat.

"Don't worry, he is gentle," another man said, and they all laughed again.

The girl was looking into Sergei's eyes and was pleading with him directly to stop.

Suddenly, a vague ripple passed through the girl's body and she started smiling. Sergei looked confused as he took his hand from her throat.

She started laughing, a human voice at first, which became deep, ancient and guttural very quickly. "Please don't hurt me," the voice said as the volume of the menacing laughter increased. A primaeval, subconscious memory had been revived. They all gave each other a knowing look as each one's individual reptilian instincts told them what was to come. Sergei emptied his sidearm into the girl's head at point blank range, even though he knew deep down it was futile. Each shot in the enclosed space was like a screwdriver in the ears of each soldier. But that was the least of their worries.

The girl appeared to fall back dead as Sergei, still naked from the waist down, kept his empty gun trained on her head. He felt something rough, hairy and cold brush against his thigh. Maksim and a few others saw that the skin of the girl's right hand was changing colour from pale white to a dirty, mottled brownish blue, with patches of coarse black hair and what could only be described as scales. But it was not finished. Not only was the discolouration travelling up her arm, but dirty brown long, sharp claws were growing from the three-fingered hand.

Just as Sergei felt the cold rough thing clasp his member, the girl smiled again as her head wounds inexplicably healed, but the healed flesh looked nothing like before. He could smell rotting eggs, and he looked around to see that so could his men, all holding their noses, some crying. The claw started to pull, and Moloch kept pulling. Slowly but not in a good way. And it did not stop. Sergei knew his time was up and that if there was an afterlife, he would rot in hell and his wife would throw a party. His traumatised adult children would happily attend, especially if they knew how he had died.

"It's your turn to beg for mercy, Sergei," the horrible voice rasped. The change continued slowly, and Maksim snapped out of his terrified trance. He grabbed the axe on the wall of the APC, barging past the demon thing on the floor as well as his 'colleagues', to whom he owed less than nothing. He reached for the door, opened it, and flew out the back in one fluid movement. Without wasting time, he barred shut the door with the axe and sprinted off down the dual carriageway into the hellish morning.

He heard Sergei screaming just before all of the others

started screaming in unison as more shots were fired off uselessly in a vain attempt to save their own lives. A deep, gravelly and evil voice seemingly from inside his own head said, "Maybe we will meet again, Maksim. Make sure you stay pure, my little virgin." Then the nauseating cackle of ancient, evil laughter thankfully faded. Maksim did not stop running.

Chapter Sixteen

Story Time with the Professor

Ginny, Jane and Steve used the sound of Professor Cawl's voice to find the hidden entrance to the fallout shelter. Ginny had had no clue this place even existed, despite many years studying at UEA. The chances of stumbling upon this hidden entrance were next to zero, never mind recognising it as such. It could only be locked and unlocked from the inside using a hatch, similar to the wheel on a submarine door.

Once the three were in, a good thirty feet down, they were impressed by the size of the bunker and the books and computer equipment it contained, as well as the control terminal. They were not so impressed by the unshowered-man smell and general untidiness. However, it was not a *dirty* mess, so to speak. They all turned around to regard the out-of-breath late-middle-aged man as he finished descending the fixed ladder from the entrance.

He quickly regained his breath, but it was obvious this man was on borrowed time. He was very sick, although it was not obvious what he was suffering from. Despite this, it did not look like he would die at any second. Once he was done composing himself, he began to speak.

"You have no idea how important it is that you've arrived here now." He could only speak in short sentences before breathlessness took over and he had to compose himself again.

"How so?" Jane asked. "Also, why are you sick? What's wrong with you?"

He laughed. "Oh, the irony. This place was supposed to protect from radiation. I guess if the bomb is far away enough, in the fresh air outside, you're exposed to much less rads than in a fallout shelter. If I had found out sooner or if the bomb had been much closer, I would have known to switch to the air recycling and filtration system. But as it stands, my exposure to the radiation from the air outside built up insidiously in this stuffy and stagnant environment until it was too late. Don't worry. I switched it on well before you came in."

"What bloody bomb?" Jane said. "A nuclear bomb?!"

Ginny put her head in her hands.

Steve interlocked his fingers behind his head and did a full 360, in a 'this *cannot* be happening' gesture.

"A hydrogen bomb, to be exact. Russian. Detonated over Westminster."

"Why?" Ginny and Jane said in unison.

"They want something. Don't worry, Moscow is completely gone. It's nothing short of a miracle that it hasn't escalated further. The very last thing I saw from the outside world was Donald Trump holding a press conference, basically saying he is doing nothing in order to avoid that escalation. Obviously, Putin has something on him, and this is his biggest motivational factor. I always suspected this. There seemed to be some commotion in the background, and the press conference got cut off."

"Please tell us why it's so important that we came here at this time," Ginny said. Might as well be pragmatic; there was piss-all she could do about anything the professor had just told her.

"I have information that could potentially destroy the world, and/or restore it." He paused again to catch his breath.

Jane was about to speak, and he put up his hand.

Steve just stared open-mouthed into the corner. They all left the youngster to process the information he had been hit with. Cawl moved between Ginny and Jane and lifted a tattered and dog-eared notebook from his desk, covered in books about quantum physics and string theory.

"I have a prototype, but it is utterly useless." He laughed, which caused a horrible wheeze and coughing.

Ginny and Jane just waited; they were intrigued. Steve was gradually returning to the room.

"This book will allow you to build a prototype, but that's all. It's impressive in what it can do but has no practical purposes."

"What can it do?" Ginny asked.

"What can it not do? Theoretically, there's nothing it cannot do. With a few equations added in and a few tweaks of the existing equations here and there, as well as removing some red herrings that may lead you up the garden path, then a technology could exist that could do anything. If I so decide, I might just take that data to the grave with me. There's nothing so far that has convinced me that mankind deserves or needs this technology. It could do so much good, but it could destroy everything. I am pretty much convinced it would at this point."

"Let me guess; this is nanotechnology based, working on the principles of quantum theory, and the issues are related to stability and optimisation of energy consumption," Ginny stated.

"How on earth did you guess that?"

"I can see the books all over your desk, plus the term 'utterly useless' generally denotes that something uses up too much energy for too little reward. That, and I have a science background. Not as hardcore as yours, but still, I know enough to have a rudimentary understanding."

"I understand why you would be tempted to take this to your grave," Jane said. "Anyone who had control of this would have absolute power, and this situation would only be made worse if this technology were able to wrest control from that person, effectively controlling itself. It's anyone's guess what its agenda would be at that point. But something tells me that this agenda would not be to nurture and protect humanity."

"See what I mean about why it is so important that the three of you turned up here now?"

Ginny and Jane looked at each other with a mutual understanding.

"The worst is already happening," stated Steve. "Nothing to lose now by giving it a try."

"Is it possible that your technology is what the Russians want?" Jane asked.

The professor sighed. "The Russians were looking for something here before they gave up and left. I had a PhD student, American. He disappeared. I don't want to believe he betrayed me. Can you now see this is *all* my fault? The technology only exists in theory, inside my head, and look at all the destruction it's already caused!!"

"I find it very hard to disagree with that. It would appear that this knowledge was pursued blind to the possible consequences of gaining that knowledge," Steve angrily asserted.

"That's why I believed the best possible thing I could do would be to never reveal this knowledge. But I never thought it would be this coveted, when the technology is essentially in its infancy."

"Good point," Jane said. She looked to Steve and back to Cawl. "But that ship has sailed. You should never even have pursued it in the first place, but that is not human nature, I suppose. I can't fault you for that. And how were you supposed to know your student would betray you? And what if the practical application of all this knowledge is the only thing that could undo this destruction, especially if it escalates?" she asked.

"What about all the points of no return that humanity has crossed?" Ginny asked rhetorically. "What if this is the only thing that could redeem humanity's terrible mistakes, saving the planet *and* humanity? Do you not believe in redemption?"

"That is the best-case scenario, not to mention raising the question of whether or not humanity deserves such redemption. We would be even more out of control with the existence of this technology, knowing we as a race or as individuals could do whatever we liked. We would degenerate as a race, becoming even more evil and reckless." He drew a raggedy breath in and out, closed his eyes, and continued. "That being said, I have changed my mind about taking my knowledge to the grave. I can see you three are good people, and although I don't expect you to understand the science behind this – no offence – it is obvious that you understand how it would work, the dangers of its use and the endless ethical implications. I am passing responsibility to you as to whether this breakthrough should see the light of day. I still haven't decided, and being dead will severely impede my ability to mull it over some more. So now, you must decide."

Ginny, Jane and Steve looked overwhelmed by his speech, looking at each other in vain for answers.

Cawl could see this. "How about a hot drink and some comfort food? I need you to think this through with a clear head, so please get some sleep. I have a bathroom but no shower – you can use baby wipes."

"I can see someone on the screen walking past the sports park," Ginny said.

"Adam!" the professor said. "He's come back to me!" Cawl made his way to the stairs.

"STOP!" Jane shouted. "Do not open that hatch. Ginny, do you remember I told you about the feelings I get? Well, this is the strongest I have ever felt it. Not only that, but I feel fear reaching through that screen down to the darkest recesses of my mind."

"Well, I believe you, and I can feel it too," Ginny said. "Something is wrong here. Look at the way 'Adam' is moving. It's very subtle, but do you see the little twitches and tics? I know people suffer from this sort of thing, but it's like the tics and twitches are fighting off something."

Steve did not question his new friends.

"Do you feel it, Professor?" Jane asked.

But they could see daylight pouring down the ladder as the creaking of metal signified the hatch being opened. "Over here!!!!" they heard the professor shout.

Just then, Ginny saw an unnatural smile spread across Adam's face. Anybody would have been able to see the malevolence emanating from this thing.

As it started to walk towards the open hatch, it started *changing*. Jane realised Steve had gone up the steps but was lying in a heap at the bottom; the professor had kicked him off the ladder. Adrenaline pumping, Jane went up the steps in one swift movement, grabbed the professor by the testicles and squeezed and pulled. He let go of the ladder, but there was nowhere for him to go. She was under him at the bottom now, and he was using the situation to his advantage, not letting her get up. Ginny went up the steps as fast as she could. She looked out, and no further than thirty feet away, the creature was headed for the hatch, walking fast.

She froze as she tried to process the horror of this creature's appearance. She snapped out of it quickly, pulled the hatch shut, and locked it just as the creature was upon her. A preternatural, guttural and ancient scream of pain pierced the air above, and Ginny realised the hatch had amputated two of the creatures fingers. Like the rest of it, they were brown and mottled with a bluish undertone, almost like all the skin diseases a person could possibly have. And they were wet with a dark liquid oozing from them, as from an infected wound struggling to heal. And they *stank*. They obviously were made of or exuding sulphurous compounds.

*

Cawl was now off Jane, in the prone position, hands covering his face as he wept audibly. "I thought it was Adam. I miss him so much. That thing knew what Adam looked like, knew that I missed him."

"The implications of that are terrifying. Can it get into our heads? That thing basically fitted the description of a demon from biblical hell."

"It wants this technology to use or else destroy all traces because it is a threat. Look at these."

Ginny showed the professor and Jane the severed fingers.

They recoiled in disgust.

"I think if there is even a remote possibility that this thing could be destroyed by this technology, then this further reinforces the need to give you the missing information," Cawl stated as he composed himself.

"How does it know that this technology could destroy it, if that were the case?" Jane said.

"Well, maybe it's a stretch, but do you know how long human beings have existed on this earth?" the professor asked.

"Quarter of a million years? Ginny said.

"More like two hundred thousand," Jane said.

"Bang on. That is 194,000 years of unrecorded history. Is it really such a stretch that this technology was in fact discovered and used by an ancient advanced human civilisation there is next to no trace of? Is it also such a stretch to think that this technology was what brought forth this creature? Something must have gone very wrong if that were the case. I think it would therefore be safe to assume that this technology could be the only thing that could destroy it or send it back where it came from."

"It's all conjecture, but what you're saying makes perfect sense," Ginny said.

Jane and Steve nodded in agreement. Steve had a cut above his right eye and was glaring at Cawl.

Cawl did not tell them he could hear Adam's voice in his head, begging to be let in. He knew it could not possibly be real as he observed on the CCTV the creature's fingers growing back.

"Does the creature know it's on CCTV?" Ginny asked.

"No, I don't think so. And that's encouraging," Cawl replied.

"There is a limit to its intelligence, then," Steve added.

"The thing is banging at the hatch of the bunker to get in," Steve said.

They all heard it and were trying to ignore it.

"Obviously, it's extremely strong, but it looks like

both its strength and intelligence is limited," Ginny said.

It stopped after a few minutes, when the creature realised the futility.

The foul-smelling fingers would not flush away, and they seemed to be morphing into something. They put them in a concentrated bleach solution in the basin, which did nothing but make them smell worse. They were gathered around the sink observing the fingers, which started to change into two miniature humanoid shapes after the bleach solution was emptied out.

"Noooo …" Steve said.

They could only stare, transfixed.

"I have an idea," said Ginny as she rushed to get her bag.

Ginny brought over the 100% ethanol she had pilfered from her lab. She used two sporks to lift the two disgusting masses out of the washbasin and rinsed them with water. After returning them to the basin, Ginny poured the 100% ethanol onto the severed digits. They bubbled and popped under the surface as everyone held their noses, anticipating an even worse smell.

The ethanol clearly caused harm, but the masses were still moving towards their final goal – tiny humanoids – just more slowly now.

"How much did you put in?" Cawl asked.

"One litre," Ginny replied. She thought for a second. "I'm going to add another 430 millilitres of water," she added.

"Why?" asked Jane.

"Because that would make it a seventy per cent solution. Optimum for killing bacteria," Cawl replied.

"Yes, but devil fingers soon to become tiny sentient demons are not bacteria!" Jane said incredulously, without a scientific background to draw on.

"You got a better idea?" retorted Cawl.

Jane was visibly annoyed. Ginny used the original container to measure out 430 ml of tap water, then added it to the bubbling black liquid. There was a low-pitched screeching sound which sounded like it came from the depths of hell and made them all instantly nauseous. But this died away, and what was left was an odourless black mass. This did flush. Jane realised that while they all had their part to play, she had no knowledge of science and could not contribute in a situation such as this.

For a few hours, they chatted, ate, drank some tea and coffee, and then freshened up. They were all very disturbed by the thing outside; it shattered all of their belief systems, so they simply talked about their lives and experiences, good and bad. It turned out the professor had toothpaste. This was a relief. The two women and Steve were getting concerned that they had not brushed their teeth for a couple of days, and their teeth were hurting.

Eventually, Cawl slowly stood up and said, "Time to get to work. Okay, I'm going to write down all of the missing equations, corrections and distractions. You don't have to understand it. I want you all to memorise every last thing I write down, and once you've done this, I'll destroy what I've written.

"What you will memorise is nothing without the notes, and vice versa. You must all guard this notebook with your lives. There's a government facility in Scotland I must direct you to. It's not on any maps, but it's there. You have to try to get there. What I don't know is whether or not you'll be taken seriously or even if there's anyone there. And I can't go. I know I wouldn't survive the journey.

"There's a good friend of mine based at Hull University who knows of my research but not the missing info. First, you need to look for him in Hull. He's unmarried without children, so he may be at his office at the university. Look there first. I'll write down his home address just in case. If he's there, convince him to go with you to Scotland. He's multidisciplinary and will be able to use and understand the knowledge you will memorise.

"But all the equipment is in the hidden lab, and some of the resident scientific staff will probably be there, as it is essentially a well-stocked survival bunker. You'll need them too. As far as he and they are concerned, right now, the research has hit a dead end."

"Who is this guy?" Ginny asked.

"Professor Hussof Khuntz."

Jane laughed. "House of whats?!"

Cawl rolled his eyes, having heard this before. He spelled the name on his whiteboard, rubbing off some equations. Steve smiled in amusement for the first time in days.

Then an explosion rang out, louder than any of them had ever heard; it was almost unbearable, even in the soundproof bunker. Despite the unfamiliar sound, they all knew what it was. The CCTV screens had gone completely white, then black, then static.

"Looks like things have escalated," Jane said.

Steve looked terrified, but the others had been expecting it. Following the explosion, there were a few minutes of rumbling, increasing in intensity, causing various items to fall off shelves and counters. Things clattered and smashed, but it soon died down. It was obvious that the closest detonation was at least 100 km away, although they could hear others.

The creature outside was still the uppermost thing on their minds, though.

Steve spoke. "More bombs, then?"

"Yup," Jane replied.

"You think there are more of those creatures out there?" Steve asked.

"WAIT!" Ginny snapped.

"What is it?" Cawl asked.

She ignored everyone.

"Ginny, what are you …"

Ginny cut Jane off. "57,000, 58,000, 59,000, 60,000." Ginny raised a finger. "1,000, 2,000, 3000 …" Ten minutes and ten fingers later, she closed her fists and started again.

Then, thirty seconds into the twelfth minute, they felt a whooshing overhead. Everything was thrown to the right a few inches, almost causing them to fall. A few more items crashed to the floor.

"Twelve minutes. The nearest detonation was about 160 miles away," Ginny said.

"Birmingham," said Steve. "I'm good at geography."

"Why so far away?" Jane asked, already knowing the answer. For now, this seemed like a partial exchange.

"Putin hasn't lost hope of attaining the fountain of youth," said Cawl. He then randomly pointed at an item which had previously gone unnoticed. "That's a telegraph machine. Beside it is the alphabet, with random dots and dashes beside each letter. Steve, can you please tell the world of that creature's weaknesses? If anyone is listening?"

Chapter Seventeen

Tim and the Gang

Very temporary comfort

A few hours later, Mary, Tim and Robert sat exhausted on the extremely comfortable recliners around the coffee table. They had all showered, and there were plenty of clothes to fit all of them in the closets. They had gone for tracksuit bottoms and black hoodies. They all had on the extremely comfortable heat holders as well, so they felt as happy as they possibly could have, given the circumstances.

"It must have taken *years* to build this, at least a decade," Robert said as he happily devoured his chicken Meal, Ready to Eat (MRE).

"How did all this stay under the radar?" Mary asked, not expecting any good answer.

"All I know is that we were extremely lucky. The people who paid for this are either infected, dead, cut off or pissed off, apart from our friend up there," Tim said.

"If they are pissed off, we should be worried," Mary said, saying what they were all thinking.

Then fighting was heard above. Muffled, but Mary knew it all too well. Artillery bombardment, which up close, caused shellshock, later contributing to PTSD. They could hear shouting, but they could not discern the language being used.

Four hours later, Greg was awake and alert, and Mary updated him on all that had happened. A couple of hours before, Mary had taken advantage of Greg's unconsciousness to properly clean and stitch up his open wounds after carefully removing the superglue with acetone. The shelves had an abundance of everything that was needed.

The stitches were dissolvable, so they would not need to be removed.

Greg took well the news that he had lost his left forearm, even joking that he was glad it was the one that had already lost the middle finger. But this was normal. Both good news and bad news took time to sink in, as the human brain was not able to immediately appreciate the implications of either.

"What is that noise?" Greg said in a weak voice.

"War. Happening right above us. Based on the information that we have, we're fighting the Russians. But that's what we know. It started about four hours ago and has gone up and down in volume since. Robert and Tim are asleep in the beds next door." Mary giggled.

Greg looked at her, amused as she put her head down and her hand over her mouth.

She looked up, seemingly glad she was still able to laugh. "I hope you like RealDolls," she said.

"Real dolls?" Greg asked inquisitively.

"Hey, guys, come over here!" They heard the voice of Robert from somewhere inside the Portakabin.

"Stay here," Mary said to Greg.

Robert must have woken up and gone exploring, undetected. Only Mary came, as Tim could not be awoken from his deep sleep.

When she got to Robert, he was carefully removing an antiquated-looking piece of equipment from what looked like a bedside cupboard which had been tucked away inconspicuously behind other furniture near the middle of the gun wall.

"It's a CB radio. You know, the very worst thing in the situation we're in is that when we really, really need the news, we can't get it. Not official news like with the BBC, but from other people. CB stands for 'citizens' band'."

"But aren't all communications affected?" Mary asked.

"Not necessarily. Radio signals are harnessed, but mobile phone signals are created. Official radio stations may not be broadcasting for a variety of reasons, but the signal is still there. My best guess is that a lot of equipment is damaged or destroyed due to the electromagnetic pulse from the bomb, but that would be localised. Or people abandoned the stations to seek out their loved ones."

"Can you use it?"

"Yes, I can, but I need some time. Hopefully, I can establish communication with someone who knows something." Robert turned it on and started to look it over and tinker with it.

Mary then became overcome with the type of exhaustion she had only ever felt in the field. She went to get water, medicines and MREs for Greg. She left them on his bedside table and kissed him on the head. He gave a weak, tired smile. Then she went to her shed, collapsed into her allocated bed and blacked out.

When she got up, both Tim and Robert were in Greg's room. All three had an open pack of MRE nearby. They really seemed to like them. There was an unopened meal on the bed next to Greg, which he handed to her. Beef.

"Okay, buddy, over and out," Robert said in a flat tone into the receiver. The others wished goodbye to the person on the other end in an equally flat but appreciative tone. The CB radio had been moved into Greg's room and was resting on a table. They were quiet. Robert did not look at her, just stared ahead, processing the information imparted to him.

Greg seemed in good spirits, but that was probably the Cyclimorph and pregabalin in his system.

Tim looked at her as he processed the reality of the

situation. "It looks like Donald Trump has been assassinated, probably because he took no action," he said.

"Action against what?" Mary asked.

Everyone went quiet again.

"A thermonuclear warhead was airburst over Westminster by the Russians," Tim answered.

Mary just let her jaw drop.

Tim continued, "It looked like he was going to choose the NWA instead of the UK. We were right, Russia did launch a full-scale invasion of the UK without any fear of repercussions from the US. But now there's a new president, and they've ordered Russia to withdraw completely or face the consequences. Although this is technically good news, it really isn't, as I'm sure you can imagine."

"There is some actual good news," Greg said, smiling as he ferociously devoured the MRE. "The Russians are so unbelievably stupid that they keep becoming Jeffries and getting overrun by them."

"The … what?" Mary gave a nervous laugh.

"The ones that disfigured my face. They are the Jeffries." He gave a belly laugh, and his bloodshot eyes gave away his inebriated state.

Mary figured out pretty quickly why they called them Jeffries. They were terrifying – what better way to make them seem less scary?

"Anyway, they created the Jeffries using some nerve agent and didn't consider how to protect themselves. That's what we're up against," Robert scoffed.

Tim interjected, "Two hydrogen bombs have been airburst already, in London and Moscow. A nuclear war has started. Neither side will likely back down. There's a rumour that Putin has some sort of cancer that is not treatable. But that's just a rumour."

There was a pause, and then Robert spoke. "There's nothing we can do, nowhere to go, for now. We just have to hope for the best. But at least we have some information."

Greg got a large-size mint Aero bar seemingly from nowhere, and he closed his eyes in ecstasy after taking the first bite.

Robert produced a massive joint and ran it under his nose, taking a deep sniff. "My Camberwell carrot", he said. He looked at it lovingly before lighting it up. He took a long draw, and his mind returned to a different life, lived long ago. He passed it to Tim on his left-hand side and lifted a remote. He held it up and hit a button. Then they all heard, in crystal clear sound, *It a go bun (give me the music, make me jump and prance).*

Two days later

Tim was sitting upright in his bed enjoying the filtered air, thinking of the people who had built this underground lair and what they would do to him and his new friends if they were still alive and if they ever got their hands on them. The sound of exploding artillery from above and the sound of Jeffries and normal humans shouting and screaming could still be heard. It was muffled but constant and still audible through twenty feet of earth. All he could imagine was how the soldiers would torture them if they got the chance. In his right hand, he twirled a fully loaded Beretta 21A Bobcat with the safety off. All morning, he had been vaping his now-green vape liquid, in which he had dissolved THC crystals ground down from the high-quality weed available to them.

All it was doing was making him more paranoid, but

that was offset by taking 5 mg of diamorphine orally using lyophilisate taken out of an IV ampoule. He was feeling pretty relaxed now, spinning the bag of ketamine powder in his left hand. He looked into the eyes of his next temptation across the room, thinking of how creepy it was being this close to life, but … not. He aimed the Beretta at Barbie and shot at her face. Tim's hand flew back with the recoil and the gun smacked against his forehead. "SHIT!!!"

"Are you okay, mate?" Robert shouted through the door.

"Yes!!! I am bloody well alright!!!"

"Can I come in??"

Mary's voice soothed him. He did not answer, and she slowly opened the door. There were fragments of silicone and plastic and twisted pieces of metal all over the room as well as a headless Barbie. Mary could see where the bullet had lodged itself in the wall at an angle a foot or so over the headless RealDoll.

"She was creeping me out. I'm already creeped out. I don't know what to do, what to say, what to feel, and this shit is not helping!" Tim threw the bag of white powder across the room. He drew a sharp intake of breath, sobbing noticeably. A single tear rolled down his cheek, his face contorted in anguish. He put the gun against his head. "Maybe this will help. I can't go on feeling like this if I don't exist!" He was doing everything he could do to not break down completely, fearing if he did, he would go completely mad and never come back from that, that the resulting insanity would render him incapable of even taking his own life.

Mary softly put her hand on his, with her other hand taking the barrel and slowly pointing it at the back wall. He did not resist when she gently clicked the safety on and took the gun out of his hand. She put it on the end of the bed, out of his reach, making a mental note to do everything she could to keep him away from guns. She sat down beside him.

"I let my family down. I only caused them pain and suffering and I've alienated my brothers and sister. Now I don't know if I'll ever see them again to say sorry. I just want my mum to put her arms around me and feel her warmth and softness, to protect me from this god-awful world, which by the sounds of it, is only getting worse."

"Will I do?" Mary asked.

He looked up at her, his eyes bloodshot and full of anger and regret turned inward. "What do you mean?" he asked through another deep breath, full of sobs. He closed his eyes. Tears ran down from each eye.

She put her hand gently on his cheek and he leaned into it. Then she gently pulled him closer to her, resting his head on her shoulder. She leaned her head onto his, a comforting pressure between her hand and head. "Just let it go!" she whispered softly.

With this, he put his arms around her, submitting completely to her offer of comfort. Then he stopped holding back and let go. He cried. Tears streamed from his face onto her blouse, but she did not care. His sobs were more violent now. "I'm so, so sorry, Mum!"

She knew he had not gone mad; she was just an outlet for his guilt and remorse. She had heard the other two arrive at the doorway. They had been watching a movie called *Frequency*, causing them all to feel a little emotional. She could not see them, but she knew they were teetering. She could hear them whispering to each other. They were trying to keep the noise to a minimum, but these whispers were shaky and racked with sobbing as they wrestled with their own demons of regret. Regret of not appreciating their loved ones, of taking them for granted.

And fear. Real fear for themselves and the suffering of humanity above their heads. Of what came next. Tim looked up, and Robert had his head down, face contorted in wretched misery, tears dripping from his hand and down his face. Greg just stood there, looking completely and utterly lost, eyes wide with uncertainty, fear, and mental trauma from his injuries. Both Mary and Tim put their hands out towards them and shifted round to make room. Robert and Greg did not hesitate. Soon it became a four-way comfort hug, and they held each other tight. Mary, Robert and Tim were all letting go, all crying in their own way, making their own individual sounds without judgement from the others. Greg just closed his eyes. He was numb, but he knew the juggernaut of reality was hurtling towards him, and in time, it would hit him hard, but not yet. Still, though, he needed this, to feel the warmth and pressure of platonic, genuine human contact with those he trusted.

If anyone had stumbled upon this scene, they would have run away very fast, but circumstances were far from normal. After five minutes or so, they were spent emotionally but enjoyed the euphoria that followed pouring out all of the negative emotions they had. This was healthy; this was wholesome. Tim could not remember the last time he had felt such relief. He swore to himself at this moment that he would be good to them and do everything he could to protect them, especially Mary. Greg was sitting on the bed with his head buried in his remaining hand, his fingers subconsciously running up and down his fresh scar.

Mary rubbed her hand up and down Greg's back, and Tim

squeezed his shoulder.

"When it comes, we will be here, won't we?" Mary said.

The other two nodded in agreement.

"We'll be here for you," Robert stated in an honest, genuine and comforting fashion.

Tim looked up, confused. The mechanised vehicles were on the move, and the shelling had stopped. They heard panicked shouting and then metal on metal banging on the entry door above. They could hear someone screaming at the top of their lungs but only heard the last two words –"...*ing bastards*!" They could all fill in the blanks. Then they heard that creepy, familiar noise: an air raid siren. A sound they had only heard in countless movies but never in real life. They were able to keep abreast of events through various individuals via CB radio. There were some gaps in the sequence of events. They knew Trump had been shot but not of his ultimate fate.

The most important fact they did know was that the new US government had demanded that Putin remove his invasion force from the UK in its entirety and/or order the surrender of these troops. If he did not do this by a certain date or time, he would face the consequences, and they were not sure exactly, but it was looking like that deadline had passed.

"It looks like the ego and hubris of Putin won't allow him to comply with the ultimatum. He doesn't care. If he's dying, he'll gladly see the earth burn rather than submit," Tim said.

"This is really happening, isn't it?" Mary asked rhetorically.

Robert and Greg had nothing to add.

Then everything went dark.

Chapter Eighteen

The Road to Nowhere

Kaitlin, along with Keith and Kevin, followed by the three cats and dog, had slowly made their way along the other side of the hedges to Sawyers Lane. A few cars had driven past, and each time, they hunkered down. Their progress was painfully slow after their close call with the Russian soldiers. They did not want to run into anymore.

Kevin was an ex-Royal Marine, and although the three AK74-M assault rifles taken from the dead soldiers were not what he was used to, he was able to figure out how to use them quickly enough and had given Kaitlin and Keith a crash course. The two men had sobered up remarkably quickly, even though Keith was happily popping pills and Kevin was taking swigs from the wine and the Johnnie Walker whisky he had found in Archer's bedroom.

They seem like good guys, but it may become a problem, and soon, if they run out, Kaitlin thought. But one problem at a time.

Once they had got to the B1172 London Road, some cars drove by, with screaming people shouting all manners of crazy, nonsensical things out of the windows. It was completely unknown who or what they could come across, so they had to stay out of sight, but progress was slow during daytime. The first night, they pitched two tents behind a thick hedge, as it had taken all day to get through Sawyers Lane to the B1172, and they were all completely drained. They seemed to have done a good job staying out of sight so far. The sounds of artillery and screaming never really went away but stayed at a safe distance.

Maia was constantly scanning the horizon and huffed a few times at what was unseen, but she lost interest quickly. She did not respond to petting and was not her usual self. She was in full protective mode and would not snap out of it, electing to 'sleep' outside the tent in the dead of winter, obviously shivering. Kaitlin put a thick blanket over her and went into the tent. The cats stayed out of their sight but were following them, with little glimpses of cat-shaped shadows in the gloom. Kaitlin was still in disbelief at what they did to protect them.

It was still unbelievable that such a sweet dog could just rip out the throat of a soldier, but the cats... Knowing they were keeping guard on the periphery with their super senses, and what they had shown themselves to be capable of, was a huge comfort to all of them. Kevin and Keith were to sleep in shifts, and everyone was to be on the move by 6.30 a.m. The destination was UEA. It would be even harder to move unseen once they reached the A15, and God only knew what was waiting to greet them on the way. Kaitlin got to sleep through for saving them both from a slow and painful death. Despite never having fired a gun before, she clutched it close while she slept and thanked God she did not snore.

She blinked at 11 p.m., and in an instant, was awoken by the silent vibration at 5 a.m. She crawled out of the sleeping bag fully clothed, put on her DM boots and got out of the tent. Keith was snoring softly in the other tent, while Kevin stayed outside, head dropping frequently with each microsleep, rifle on the ground and white-knuckling the neck of the half-full bottle of Johnnie Walker while it hovered around his mouth.

Kaitlin walked over and took it out of his hand, taking an entire mouthful. She quickly felt warm all over and very relaxed. She handed it back to Kevin. "Time to go," she said.

Kevin snapped awake and unzipped the tent where Keith was. "Get up, faggot!" he shouted to Keith.

He took a swig of the whisky and smiled a typical drunken leer at Kaitlin. He took a long sniff of the drink while standing up, stretching and making a weird noise. Kaitlin assumed this helped him wake up.

Keith's head poked out of the tent entrance, and with his extremely bloodshot eyes, he looked around confused, then looked at Kaitlin confused. His hand came up to his face as he remembered the situation they were in and went back into the tent. She heard the sound of tablets and capsules rattling in a plastic container. Keith was making a subconscious growling sound at the back of his throat before a long sniff and a satisfied groaning was heard.

"Guess you don't need water to wash that down with, dickhead. Ha ha!" Kevin said.

Kaitlin laughed loudly, but she wondered if they were this much fun during forced sobriety.

Ten minutes later, everything was packed up. Maia showed up out of nowhere, fresh blood on her maw. Kaitlin had no idea whether or not it was animal or human, and she did not care. For a brief ten seconds, she greeted her like she always did before turning back to sentry mode. This reassured Kaitlin greatly. After briefly sharing a couple of cold cans of Heinz sausage and baked beans, they were ready to go. They all used two Stargate night-vision monoculars taken from the soldiers to scan the horizon.

Kaitlin was just going to put them down when she noticed a strange sight in a random field about a mile away. "Kevin, you need to see this," she said.

The heat signatures showed a group of three to four

people. Adults, possibly of both sexes, but she was not sure. They were crouched behind a hedge separating two fields. On the other side of the hedge, she was not sure what she was looking at. A group of about twenty people following another person, headed in this direction. This was encouraging. Survivors banding together? Safety in numbers? It sure as hell beat their current situation hands down. Then her heart sank. Why were those people hiding? Just then, the lead figure stopped and moved his head towards the hiding figures. One of those hiding had their hand clamped over their mouth.

The rest of the figures stopped suddenly as well. Kaitlin could hear faint howls in the distance, with a slight delay before they visibly appeared to be whooping and screaming. They were all very animated but stayed in place. The lead figure remained still and just started walking slowly towards the hidden figures.

"What's going on?" Keith looked happy as his morning withdrawal was replaced by the familiar warm feeling.

She heard the sound of electrical tape being pulled off the roll. Kaitlin's open bag was beside Kevin. She watched him use the electrical tape to stick the Stargate to the AK74-M to use as a scope. She thanked her past self for electing to bring it. He came over to her and did the same with her rifle and monocular.

"Are you expecting me to do what I think you are? I've never done this before."

"It's okay, just do your best. The air's still this morning." He flicked the safety off and changed both rifles to single shot, showing Kaitlin exactly how to do that.

"Now, there's more to sniping than just lining up the target with the centre, and the scope isn't calibrated with the gun. Just place the butt against your shoulder for the recoil, and when you fire, you squeeze the trigger slowly after a long, slow, deep breath out."

"Well, it's always nice to try new things."

They all laughed, followed by a gurgling wheeze from Keith.

Kevin took a sip of the Johnnie Walker and said, "Don't do drugs, kids, just become an alcoholic like me!"

"And me, very soon," said Kaitlin.

They both got into their positions at the edge of the field, lying supine not being an option due to the topography. Keith pulled a badly rolled joint out of nowhere and struggled to light it. Kaitlin just looked at him, and he shrugged his shoulders.

"Got a rifle but no monocular!" He cherished the joint lovingly as if it was his last.

Kevin and Kaitlin observed the scene as all the 'people' in the field advanced on the terrified, no-longer-hidden people. Obviously, they had decided running for it was not an option at this point. Kevin lined up the centre at the lead figure's head and followed his training. They were to fire simultaneously at the lead figure's head on the count of three, and so they did. The shots rang out. Someone about four feet behind the main figure, two feet closer to Kevin, collapsed as a bullet hit their lower leg. No shouts of pain could be heard, but the figure could not get up. Only one shot landed, and it was probably Kevin's. All of the people remained in place, including the leader, as they tried to ascertain where the shots had come from.

With the leader still in place, Kevin aimed the centre at the equivalent mirror-image distance to where the first shot landed, up and to the left. He fired. The leader's shoulder snapped back as his right arm flopped uselessly. The leader just stood there looking down at his arm. With his other arm, he lifted it up, and it flopped down lifelessly. Kevin realised the followers were advancing on him. Calmly, he grabbed one of them, lifting them up by the throat, and literally snapped the follower's neck at a right angle. Another follower bit into his neck, the leader reacting by throwing the follower into the field where the people were hiding.

But they were not there anymore. They were climbing a gate at the opposite side of the field. The second-to-last helped the last one over the gate, and they kept on running. When Kevin looked back, he could see about half of the followers on top of the leader, seemingly tearing him apart. A few followers were flung lifelessly from the pile, but eventually, they got the better of him. Only then did Kevin realise the other half of the followers were sprinting in the direction of the gunfire, *their* direction.

"SWITCH TO AUTOMATIC!!!" Kevin shouted, and Kaitlin did what she was told.

Keith sat calmly on a nearby rock, lovingly puffing on what he thought was his last joint.

"GET OVER HERE, DICKHEAD!!" Kevin shouted.

Keith sauntered over in a half-defiant, half-compliant manner. Kevin grabbed the joint, which was on the verge of falling apart, and took a long, slow draw.

"Oh, to hell with it!" said Kaitlin, and Kevin gladly handed her the soon to be ex-joint. "It's a really bad idea smoking something which will get us paranoid, in the middle of the countryside, in the dark, with around ten maniacs sprinting at us," she said as she took a long, slow draw.

"What's in this?" Kevin asked as it seemed to dawn on both Kevin and Kaitlin at the same time that this was more than just weed.

"Crack. A whole shitload of crack. Now I have no crack left."

Kaitlin and Kevin felt their alertness go to maximum as a shard of pure energy and strength surged through them. Kaitlin had never felt this alive. And powerful.

"You didn't ask," Keith said as he opened a tramadol capsule and a pregabalin onto the back of his index finger and took a long sniff. He grabbed his rifle and switched to full automatic. "This is a great time to be wasted."

Half a mile away, they were sprinting full speed. Kaitlin felt the opposite of what she expected. There was no fear, just focus. All three of them knew without saying anything that it was a case of taking as many down as possible. They could now only just about make out the sprinting menaces in the pre-dawn, murky-brown radioactive morning light. They backed away from the hedge about two hundred feet. They had two extra magazines between the three of them, and these were held by Kaitlin and Kevin. Kevin had also instructed Kaitlin and Keith on how to change a magazine earlier, if Keith's scrambled brain could recall it. That is why he did not get a spare.

"SHORT, CONTROLLED BURSTS!" Kevin reminded them.

The closer they get, the more accurate the shot.

"Choose targets relative to where we are in relation to each other. Good luck."

All three of them were too wasted to be afraid.

"I'm not expecting you to be much help, Keith. Just don't shoot either of us," Kevin said.

Keith's body did not know whether to sleep for fourteen hours or climb a mountain. He just stood and swayed, waiting for these humanoid things to spill over the hedge.

Ten minutes later

Kaitlin came to when Kevin grabbed her arm. She held the butt of the gun towards the ground, and below her was a pitiful sight. A middle-aged lady dressed in middle-aged lady clothes was on the ground, and Kaitlin could barely make out any skull from what remained of her head. Around ten bodies lay strewn across the field. Kaitlin had a huge bite on her forearm, with clearly visible bone, and Kevin had had his cheek torn open.

She heard a familiar, raspy voice.

"Help me, help me, help me …"

Kaitlin and Kevin approached Keith, who had a bullet wound on his foot.

Keith shouted, "I've been shot!!"

Kaitlin and Keith instantly brought up their guns and scanned the horizon.

"Don't worry, it was me!"

Kaitlin and Kevin laughed loudly.

"It was not my fault!!! He rammed into me as I was shooting at him and that made me point the gun at my feet!"

"Yes, it's not your fault," said Kevin, still laughing.

"Really?" Keith said.

"No, you shot yourself, dipshit – it's your fault. I'm just glad you didn't shoot either one of us!"

"Whatever, you twat. Give me that sodding Johnnie Walker!"

Kevin did not have the heart to refuse it.

He handed him the whisky and took a closer look at the foot using his phone torch. The battery was at 3%. "It's not gushing. Your foot's destroyed, but you'll live," Kevin said.

"Or maybe not, considering none of us have access to basic healthcare and our wounds are pretty bad," Kaitlin corrected.

They all pondered this in silence and gradually became aware of a stationary car a few hundred feet away on the road, flashing its full beams. Kevin flashed using his phone light a couple of times before his phone died. But it was enough. The car slowly approached them. It looked like a Peugeot 207.

Kaitlin slowly made out the number plate. "Tommy???" she thought out loud.

They both looked at her.

Chapter Nineteen:

Anything Is Better Than Being a Pharmacist

They had to leave the Stratton River pharmacy. There were more and more people trying to gain entrance, either for shelter or drugs. Not all of them were unaffected by the toxin. Eventually, someone would get in. They waited until it was relatively quiet, opened the shutters, and sprinted to Tommy's car. They had no choice but to use the car, with headlights attracting all manner of dangerous humans and even more dangerous subhumans. Unless they were to walk. In the dark. In January. With roving bands of cannibalistic maniacs they could not see. Without streetlights. No. Honestly, they had no idea if they had made the right choice about when to travel and how. This was an unexpected, unfamiliar situation, to say the least.

Tommy was extremely lucky to be in an area of low population density, easily finding a tiny petrol station on the backroads with an open door, no one around and shelves not completely empty. He got some bread and canned goods without incident, but there was nothing else. He guessed that people were less likely to storm shops with worldwide supply-chain problems. This had caused people like Tommy and Ginny to add to the empty shelf problem by hoarding nonperishable goods. If anywhere were to be looted for food, houses would be more lucrative than shops.

Suzanne elected to be in the boot. Tommy could not risk having her beside him if she kicked off, as the toxin was not yet out of her system. When the effects of the toxin took over, it was sudden, although after each sedation, its effects were lesser in intensity. They were both encouraged by this, when Suzanne was not trying to eat him. She was to knock twice, knock once, then twice again if she was in her right mind and if being in the boot got too much for her. Tommy had the sedative injections in the passenger seat, ready to use.

The journey to the university was the correct option based on prior agreements with his family, but Tommy decided to check home first, as it was not much of a detour and the journey was via the middle of nowhere. He was glad to be out of there, and he was right about the journey being uneventful. Almost. As he was getting to the Sawyer's, Suzanne started going apeshit in the boot. Not the agreed knocks, and he did not want to grapple with her right now. He might not get so lucky this time. He really did not know when it would be a good time.

He felt the pain of many pulled muscles from tackling Suzanne and was mouth breathing more than ever. Little air was getting through his atopic nostrils at the best of times, especially with a badly broken nose crusted with dried blood. The bleeding had finally stopped after about eight hours. He did not want to touch it because of the pain and was not looking forward to looking in a mirror. He guessed he had gone from mediocre to grotesque.

The Concerta XL tablets took the edge off the whole thing. Every cloud has its silver lining; there were many drugs he was very curious about, and he was now free to try whatever he liked at his leisure. Concerta, or its generic, methylphenidate, were at the top of that list. He had wasted no time satisfying this curiosity and was not disappointed. He was looking forward to trying tapentadol and then maybe valproic acid. The Cyclimorph and diazepam injections were exclusively for Suzanne. He was also intending to use trial and error on his own terms to see which inhaler worked best for his asthma, now he did not have to see a GP. Tommy did not like GP visits at all.

He was able to pick up some news from the radio, little snippets. It would appear that Russia had attacked the UK with only one nuclear strike. What was America doing? It would explain the brown clouds and the sepia sky, and the vague feeling of nausea that would not go away. He could not smell anything but could *taste* something unpleasant in the air. *Fran... declared war... Austral... dec... war.* Lots of war declarations. Tommy hated Trump and fully expected him to adhere to the NWA and turn his back on England. He kept trying the radio. *Th... wor... wait... Ameri... new pres... Russ... ultimatum... Trump in critical con...* Oh, no. In between the snippets, the familiar jarring, discordant sound had no use other than to fill listeners with dread. *So, end of the world then*, Tommy thought drily.

He got out of the car after parking in the Sawyer's driveway and left Suzanne to it in the boot. He hoped the boot held. Tommy, torch in hand, walked around to the back like he always did. Outside on the old patio lay a fully kitted-up soldier in fatigues he thought he recognised as Russian. So Russia had invaded the UK. Great. *We are so screwed*, he thought. The soldier was obviously dead, his throat ripped out, completely gone. This looked like an animal-inflicted wound, but it did not look like any of him had been eaten.

He cautiously shone the torch through the back door, and there lay a soldier in what was obviously an officer's uniform. This guy was even more dead than the other. No eyes. Cuts and tears in his flesh all over, with a single bullet wound in his chest. Tommy could only think of extreme prejudice as he regarded this very dead man. He wondered if their obvious enemy was his friend. Nothing was different in the rest of the house, other than the nonperishable food was gone, only the shit stuff left. The reserve medication was gone. He did not care; it was dwarfed in quantity by what he had taken from the Stratton River pharmacy.

He felt very alert, warm and strong, ready for everything. He did not feel depressed. Previously, he had known that depression was at least partially caused by the fact that humans focused on long-term rather than daily survival. He felt very calm about the fact that he might not live through the next hour. When there was something to actually panic about, there was no panic. One of many contradictions in the human psyche. He just let go of everything, and warmth replaced the interminable feeling of dread in the pit of his stomach which had plagued his entire, tortured life.

He would try to survive and he would try to find his family, but there was no risk of losing his job or living for years in a wheelchair paralysed from the neck down. Just delightful oblivion was the worst thing that could occur. Before, a perceived error that might have happened at work that could have cost him his job would pop randomly into Tommy's head, and his mind would go haywire. It was guaranteed that after nine seconds, he was imagining sleeping on the streets and giving his pets up for adoption. He laughed out loud at how stupid it was to be terrified of losing the thing he hated the most. *Where are my pets?* He wondered. He most definitely did not hate them.

He was free of that terrible job. *To hell with that job*. It looked now like getting old was not going to be a problem either. Tommy dreaded getting old and was hoping to die by the time he was sixty. In his job every day, all he saw was old people who lived in the community and had no quality of life, all bent out of shape, lonely, mentally ill, with deteriorated nervous systems. It was either that option or living in a care home, out of his mind and getting abused by people recruited from the bottom of the barrel. No, thank you.

He did not believe in heaven or hell, but due to his Catholic upbringing, it would be preferable if he had just enough time before death for the Lord's Prayer, just in case. Any form of living forever would be horrible, but if he had to go somewhere, Tommy would choose heaven and take it from there. Maybe God would give him oblivion if he asked nicely. But surely no one would listen to him in hell.

Ironically, the irrational fear of hell was the only thing that had saved him from committing suicide many times. Tommy was convinced he would have done it in a moment of madness at some point if not for this fear. These days, up until recently, the thoughts of suicide were an idle, non-dramatic process brought about by that constant worry of his worst fears coming true, which caused the aforementioned dread.

Tommy often asked Ginny if she thought he would give his life to protect hers. Her answer would always be along the lines of *Yes, but only because you will see it as a chance to die, and that if you do so heroically, you won't go to hell.* He could never disagree with this. He had been reciting the Lord's Prayer in his head every hour or so since leaving the pharmacy, but logic dictated that the closer to death, the better. Only a maximum of one hour of sinning by existing, like in the stupid bloody Bible.

Tommy accepted the fact that the Catholic dogma of

his childhood could probably precipitate insanity at some point but … whatever. Going insane was not something he worried about now but had been before all this happened. He had had glimpses of insanity before, such as hearing snippets of conversations about him, familiar voices that he could not specifically identify. Always in the bathroom, for some reason.

There were also the convergers. On a daily basis, whenever he was walking in a particular direction, there always seemed to be an individual who would appear out of nowhere, walking with assertive purpose to the same exact point in space and time as Tommy. Like a game of chicken played at an angle. This would always initiate a mind game where someone had to change pace or direction to avoid a collision. Yeah, these things happen, but in Tommy's perception, it always seemed to be done with intent by the other party involved. It happened way too often, and it messed with his head and pissed him off.

Never mind the fact that most of the time when he looked at a digital clock, it was on the minute. Despite all of this, Tommy was sane in normal times. But these times were far from normal, and insanity may very well have been the new normal. Insanity might help him to live just that little bit longer. Because only now did he seem to want that. Well, there was nothing else for it but to drive to the B1172 and head to the university. Maybe he had the strength to tackle Suzanne because of the Concerta, but that had to be an illusion. He approached the car, where Suzanne was still pounding, but it sounded weak, and she appeared to be crying. Maybe the toxin was finally out of her system? *No, let's put it off a bit longer*, he thought.

He placed a 10 mg Medikinet on the dashboard as he

sat in the driver's seat, one leg out the door. The banging intensified once she realised he was in the car. He slammed the bottom of a plastic glass on the pill. He put as much as possible of the powder on his knuckle and snorted it all in. He rolled up a cigarette from paraphernalia found in Tim's room, lit it, and breathed it in – the beautiful, disgusting, vile, lovely taste he had not had in ten years. He coughed like an emphysema tramp for ten seconds and started laughing. "TO HELL WITH VAPING! YEEEOOOOW!!." he screamed.

Suzanne's reaction was to scream louder and bang harder.

"SHUT THE HELL UP, YOU TWAT!!!!" he screamed as loud as he could.

"Who's there?"

He heard the thick Norfolk accent a couple of hundred feet away. "SANTA CLAUS!" Tommy shouted and then laughed some more. He could hear someone approaching the car from the backroad. "LEAVE ME ALONE!" he shouted as a torch was shone at him from the end of the driveway.

"Well, you are being quite loud, and it's la…"

Just then, *pop pop pop pop pop pop pop pop*. Gunfire. Automatic gunfire from the direction he was intending to go in. The old farmer took the flashlight out of Tommy's face and took off running.

Chapter Twenty

Don't Shoot the Devil in the Back

Adam returns to the professor

Bang bang bang. Bang. Bang bang. Bang. Ginny, Jane and Steve had been hearing that rhythmic, metal-on-metal collision for around 45 minutes now. The exact same every time, with a gap of a few seconds to a few minutes.

"Why does that thing think we'll suddenly decide to let it in now, after all this time?" Ginny asked rhetorically.

"I don't know, but it seems curious that the bangs are a coded knock, each series of bangs identical to the last," Steve replied.

They both looked at Jane quizzically.

Jane answered the question they had not asked. "It's gone," she said.

"What's gone?" Ginny replied, seeking clarity.

"That feeling. It doesn't matter, though, I think it's a stretch to say that the feeling is accurate a hundred per cent of the time. But I do feel like the danger has passed, for now."

She knotted up the tenth 70% proof ethanol water balloon and guessed there was enough ethanol to make about fifteen more. They had found the water balloons tucked mysteriously away at the back of a drawer whilst looking for cigarettes, and Steve was still proud of his idea, in his mind making him worthy of being part of the group. They all went quiet again. It had been two days since the white flash had turned the CCTV feeds into white noise and the concussive blast had made them all fear being buried alive. Steve had kept them engaged in playing *Halo* on the Xbox as well as *Call of Duty* on the

PlayStation 3.

Ginny had returned the favour by introducing him to the vintage Sega Mega Drive console and the games included: *Sonic the Hedgehog* and *Altered Beast*. After he claimed that *Altered Beast* was a 'piece of shit', Ginny laughed with a tear in her eye when she realised that her long-dead brother had expressed the same sentiment. Ginny and Jane played the newer consoles and Steve the oldest, as the vintage games' simpler layout was a novelty for him. When they had asked the professor why he had all these gaming consoles, he said that although gaming didn't appeal to him now, what was even less appealing was deciding to peel himself like an orange once the boredom set in.

Suddenly the professor, after hours of shallow breathing and various states of delirium, drew in a sharp, wheezy rattle. He was fully conscious, if confused, just saying over and over, "It's our code. Our code! Adam! Adam!" *Bang bang bang. Bang. Bang bang.* "Please let him in! Pleeeease!! I have to see him one more time!!" As if to answer the question all three of them had, the professor looked at each one in succession. "Nobody else knooooowwwws! Pleeeeeease!" He was crying.

"Okay!" Steve said, not able to listen to the old man's pleading any longer. "Ginny, Jane, I'll need a few balloons."

Ginny nodded to Jane, who placed four balloons in Steve's backpack. He went to the ladder, climbed up and unlocked the trapdoor. Before opening it, he took a balloon from his backpack and held it in his hand. He hooked the arm holding the balloon around a rung in the ladder and awkwardly pushed the door open with his other hand. He quickly unhooked his arm, ready to throw the balloon. Above him were two men in full white hazmat suits. Steve saw a brown chaotic sky in the background. There was a smell of burnt hair and unwashed feet as well as faint hints of other bad smells which made him gag.

"We're looking for Professor Cawl," one of the men shouted.

"Is he in there?" the other man shouted with urgency. "We do not pose a threat to you, but I'm getting a feeling something is watching us."

That instant, Jane felt a shudder of pure fear engulf her. "IT'S BACK! HURRY UP AND GET THAT DOOR CLOSED!"

Steve was still gagging, but he said urgently to the men, "Get down here and close the door NOW!" He climbed down, dry heaving.

One of the men hurried down the ladder, followed by the other one. When the second man at the top reached for the door to close it, he could see the thing that was watching them come into view. He did not know what he was looking at, but it was immeasurably worse than anything the best horror writer's imagination could conjure. He planted his feet on the ladder and pushed his back against the wall so that his hands were free and he had a good angle. He grabbed the AR-15 which was slung over his shoulder and unloaded the full clip into whatever this thing was. This only resulted in it staggering back a few feet. It shrugged off the bullets and then came at him, with eyes full of ancient hatred.

Adam closed his eyes. He would not be able to reload quickly enough.

"ADAM!" His brother handed him a full water balloon. "THROW IT!"

Adam took a second or two to register. He could not

see how a water balloon could help him, but as the creature was almost upon him, Adam smashed the balloon point-blank into the creature's face, exploding its contents over the creature's head and Adam's hand.

He registered the smell of ethanol followed by the stronger smell of sulphur and the sound of sizzling. The creature fell backwards, screeching in pain. There were no words in the English language to fully do justice to that sound. Adam knew what he saw. This thing was a *demon*. His brother handed him another balloon just as the creature was starting to rise again. The creature's face was melting, with bits falling to the ground. It looked like steam was also rising from the demon's face. The screeching was dying down but still almost unbearable. He flung the second water balloon at the demon's face, but it tried to dodge it, causing the balloon to impact and explode over the demon's shoulder, chest and abdomen. The screech was at full volume again. He heard aeons of suffering and misery. This thing was *old*.

Just as the smell of sulphur hit Adam for the second time, fully fresh again, he pulled the hatch closed before the demon could heal and rise up again. He locked it using the wheel and also engaged the backup bolt. He climbed down the ladder and looked around him. The professor. He could hear the breath rattle and wheeze and made a beeline for him. He took off the hazmat gear, and his brother followed suit. Adam took the professor's hand in both of his and just looked at him. Cawl could barely speak at this point, and he just looked up lovingly at Adam.

"I am so sorry. I betrayed your trust, Professor. Please forgive me."

Cawl slowly nodded and lifted his other hand so they

were holding each other's hands. "Please look after them. You are now the only hope the world has left."

Hope was hard to feel right now with a brown shitty sky and demonic entities creeping around in the dark. *And the smell ... gym socks*? Adam could feel what little strength the professor had in his arms ebb away. His eyes glazed over, and he was gone. A tear rolled down Adam's cheek. He closed his eyes, and his brother put a hand on his shoulder.

"Dude, he forgave you. In fact, he wasn't even angry in the first place. He just wanted to see you again."

"I know, it's like he was hanging on just for me. How the hell can I do anything now if he can't give me the unwritten information? That was the whole goddamn point. We only narrowly landed just in time at Tarn Scrubs before the full exchange. Then we had to fight our way out of a bunker full of insane, murderous RAF staff and a countryside full of insane citizenry just to not get what we came for? Nothing can be done now. It's OVER!"

"No, it isn't," Ginny said.

Adam suddenly became aware of the other three. "He's relayed it all to us. We don't really understand it, but we sure as shit remember it."

"But wh... wha..." Adam tried to ask them.

"Right place, right time," Jane said, knowing what the question would be.

"He wants us to go to Scotland," Steve said.

"Why?" asked Adam.

"Some kind of facility," Ginny answered.

"Where?"

"We have to get to Argyll and Bute, to a mountain called Ben Cruachan. There's a facility built into the dam where this knowledge can be properly implemented. It has a particle accelerator, and most likely the staff and their families are there, as it doubles as a survival bunker," Ginny answered.

Adam looked at his brother. "In the agency, the Brits shared the existence of this location to us. Highly classified and only people with the correct security clearance knew of it. That would include me. And classified hardly matters anymore, does it?"

"So, you're Adam. He told us about you," Steve said. He nodded to the other man, who had an unsettling aura. "Who are you, sir?" he asked the man.

The man just looked at Steve like he was prey.

"This is my brother, Doug. I'm so sorry; looks can be deceiving."

At that, Doug's face broke into the warmest smile Steve had ever seen. Doug walked towards Steve and his hand shot out. Steve took Doug's hand and shook it. Doug had a gentle but sturdy grip. Steve made a mental note not to get on this guy's bad side, even in the smallest way, but at the same time, he trusted that Doug would be the type of individual to figure out a way to get around any dangerous situation unscathed.

Once they were all introduced, Ginny said, "We have enough food for around five weeks for all of us. The air filtration system should last four weeks if we're sensible with use of power. We're running off a massive diesel generator. But we were planning on leaving in a week with all the food we can carry."

Jane thought about sleeping arrangements. "If myself and Ginny share, all the boys can have a bed of their own. One of the beds is a futon, though."

She nodded towards the sofa, and they all realised the

problem. A decaying corpse.

Adam knew what everyone was thinking. "Well, it looks like we're feeding my beloved professor to Satan. If anyone has a better idea, I am all ears."

As if to agree with Adam, the lighting flickered and most of the lights went out, leaving only the ambient light of energy-saving lamps. The hum that no one had realised they were hearing also stopped. The air quickly went dead, and a sheen of sweat formed quickly on all their foreheads.

"The generators are pretty much done," said Doug, stating the obvious.

"We need to think of a plan, NOW," said Ginny, with a tremble in her voice.

Two days later

Moloch, the ancient interloper, was nearby, awaiting any opportunity that arose to gain the knowledge he desired and to end those who would use that knowledge to end him. He barely felt the piercing cold wind and was not bothered by the awful smell that hung in the air. The nature of his own genetics was such that both his resilience to damage and ability to repair any damage resulted in an indefinite lifespan. Radiation did more damage than it would to humans due to the complicated DNA, but it was nothing his repair mechanisms couldn't handle. Pretty much all reproduction had stopped in his own realm. There were no more genders. At one point, his own world had been similar to this one. A series of cataclysms, both natural and unnatural, had permanently damaged the environment and altered the very nature of life. Only the fittest and most hardy of life forms had survived, but at a terrible cost. Reproduction was seen only as a weakness to be exploited. Eventually, it stopped altogether in favour of immortal, hardy beings freed from this frailty.

Whatever they had attacked him with the last time the bunker door was open, it *hurt*. He had not ever experienced such pain, and this, coupled with the radiation, had drastically reduced healing time. The pain was gone and vision was back, but he had not healed completely. There were fleeting dark areas in his vision and what seemed to be scar tissue on his face and torso. He was more than a little troubled by this, which was why he held back when the hatch opened again. It opened for only a few seconds and out catapulted the elderly professor, who now lay unceremoniously sprawled on the tarmac.

He was hungry. Like he always was. He tentatively made his way towards the professor, saliva dribbling down his chest through the hole in his mouth which refused to heal. In a scene which would instantly ruin the mental health of any observer, he dislocated his jaw, causing his hateful eyes to bulge like they were going to burst. The inside of his mouth looked like the entrance to hell. With one bite, he decapitated the professor. His hunger and injured state caused him to ignore the fact that the corpse had been interfered with and its head was covered with a bandage.

Something he could easily digest. He bit down, expecting an explosion of flavour which did happen initially. What was inside the skull now should not have been there. Something did explode in his mouth, and what was initially a foul taste started to burn. Being as greedy as he was, he had already started to swallow. The burning snaked its way inside, destroying tissue and cells in its wake. The pain was building and building to the point of unbearable suffering. He could feel himself healing, but even the healed tissue was destroyed immediately due to the volume ingested.

He realised he was on his back and unable to move. As blackness started moving in from his peripheral vision, he saw the hatch open slowly and a face tentatively come into view. All he could manage was a baleful groan of frustration. A single limb reached out towards the face watching him from the hatch. He now started drifting in and out of consciousness but realised all the damage that could be done was done, and the healing started. Each time he regained consciousness, he felt stronger but still sensed that some of the internal damage was permanent. Three human males and two human females stood close, looking down at him.

When he felt strong enough to attempt to get up, he was pelted with projectiles containing the noxious substance. Without delay, one of the men emptied a cartridge of bullets point blank into his skull. Then before this wound could even start to heal, one of the women placed a projectile carefully on his ruined skull and stamped. He lost consciousness completely but not before he had understood that the nervous system tissue would be permanently corrupted.

"Get the food!! All the food you can!!!" Doug shouted. He regarded the splattering of organic matter on the tarmac. Being a former US ranger, he could withstand the pervasive smell of decay, the dirty brown sky, and the bleakness of the situation. But this corrupted mass had an aroma of its own, never intended for the human olfactory system. It sizzled and squelched, *angrily*, but it was somehow trying to put itself back together. "Adam, bring that jerrycan over here!"

Adam complied, knowing what his brother wanted to do.

"Is everything in the Hummer?" Doug asked.

"Most of it. Ginny! Jane! Steve! Is that your last run?"

All three gave a thumbs up as they headed for the Hummer.

Doug lifted his rifle and emptied another clip into the reassembling head. He then flung the last balloon at where a jawbone seemed to be reconstructing itself, and what had begun to heal was again dissolved. Some time had been bought. They both had their hands over their mouths as the offensive scent intensified with the fresh round of tissue destruction. Adam soaked the infernal roadkill with unleaded petrol syphoned a few days before by Doug on their journey to UEA. The smell of the petrol was like a breath of fresh air, and they were both able to uncover their faces. Doug noticed the ruined, liquified flesh flowing around his boot, depositing itself there. He struck a match and spat on the disgusting mess. Then he looked at his brother.

"You can't kill the devil," Adam said, wide-eyed.

"Well, clearly we can hurt him." Doug threw the match and the devil started burning.

Implausible and unmistakable screeches of pain started emanating from what was essentially a mass of inert, burning matter.

"Now would be a good time to run away, fast and for a considerable amount of time," Adam said.

Doug nodded, blessing himself before turning and running for the Humvee, Adam followed, with full knowledge that horrific PTSD awaited them both if they survived long enough. As they sped off, they observed the burning mass rippling as it healed, hatred inexplicably exuding from every fundamental particle of its existence. Jane felt violated, a violation of her very soul. Something from the creature had invaded and grabbed hold of her on a fundamental psychic level and was not going to let go easily. They all knew that eventually, this thing would catch up to them one way or another, and on this occasion, they had simply got lucky and borrowed some time. None of them would have a peaceful night's sleep for a long time, if ever again.

"Where are we going?" Doug eventually asked as they approached a sign on the dual carriageway: exit north, keep going to go south.

"North," Ginny and Jane said in unison.

"It's a long shot, but there's an address in Hull we must go to first, if it's still standing. There's a good chance that the Russians didn't bother to flatten Hull directly," Ginny said.

This garnered a chuckle from the three English people. Doug and Adam looked at each other, confused.

"I guess Hull is a shit-hole?" Adam asked.

They just continued to chuckle, but it was fleeting.

"Maybe it's gotten the remodelling it needs," Doug chimed in.

Jane caught Doug's eye in the rearview as she smiled. He gave her a warm smirk and her face involuntarily glowed in response. At the same time, Adam used the moment to turn around and steal a glance at Steve so he might have his suspicions confirmed. As Steve looked at Adam, he coyly looked away, then back again. Both Steve and Adam now had their suspicions confirmed, and both felt that familiar warm feeling of anticipation wash over them.

Ginny was oblivious and stared out of the window at the ash snow that had started to fall, thinking of her pets, her husband, her family, colleagues, anyone she had ever met, wondering if this ash had ever been part of them.

"Between all of us, we have all of the correct data and theory branded in our minds. We made sure of that. We even know where to go that has the equipment for that implementation to take place. But we need ..." Adam pinched his nose and closed his eyes. "Professor Hussoff Khuntz," he said wearily.

The others awaited an explanation.

Adam continued, "He was or is an expert at making snide and passive aggressive homophobic insults and remarks.

"An expert, in that he only ever said enough to fly under the radar and not get 'cancelled'. He always made sure he had plausible deniability. If I complained, I'd look paranoid. And I was never able to figure out if he even knew I was gay." He stole a look at Steve.

"So, why are we paying this delightful individual a visit?" asked Jane.

Ginny replied, "Well, according to Professor Cawl, they were both in competition with each other, since a falling out years back. The ironic thing is, if they had actually worked together, the technology we risked everything for in the hope that all this could be reversed might have been in widespread use by now. Of course, it's open to debate whether or not that would have been a good thing. We don't have Professor Cawl, but we carry his knowledge."

Adam had his head back, still pinching his nose. "You okay, bro?" Doug asked.

"Well, I can't remember any other time in my life where I had hoped so much for someone I hated so much to be alive and well and that I would see them again."

Doug nodded in understanding.

"He's a world-renowned particle physicist, and we need him," Ginny said.

"Well, he is a world-renowned multi-disciplinary physicist and biologist, but also a huge asshole," Adam replied sarcastically but then continued, "but I understand I need to focus on his positive qualities for the good of, well, everyone."

Ginny felt somewhat reassured and hopeful. There was a plan, however far-fetched it may be. She had been about to become a grandmother before all this, and any amount of hope would do. Jane rubbed Ginny's shoulder in a reassuring gesture, and Ginny sat back with her eyes closed. She turned her head towards the window, and a single sob welled up within her. The silent tears inevitably came and rolled down through her fingers and face. Steve looked at Ginny, then Jane, concerned.

Jane then said, "Steve, if we meet this charming German fellow, probably best to keep a low profile. Maybe the apocalypse has made him more homophobic. Hell, he might even be blaming it on you guys."

Adam started laughing, then Steve, and then Ginny. Sobbing laughs. Ginny turned, wiping her eyes and apologising.

Jane kissed her on the forehead. "For now, let's look after each other and hope for the best. It is the default, right? We've got weapons, food, and a fully fuelled tank. Most people don't have that."

Doug scoffed. Jane shot him a disapproving look and widened her eyes.

"That's the problem. You don't think that every person we meet is going to want to come with us or take what's ours?"

Jane just blinked and looked down, contemplating this bleak but completely accurate outlook.

Doug continued, "Look, we have to be realistic. We have to do what we need to do without asking anyone for help, as no one is doing anything out of the goodness of their hearts anymore, and that goes for us too. The rules of the game haven't changed; the game's just become harsher."

"I know what you mean. I found a Sega Mega Drive game called *Hellfire*, which I completed in easy mode, but I kept getting killed quickly in the difficult mode," Steve said.

They all looked at him.

Doug chuckled and shook his head. "I'll tell you one thing, boy. That has got to be the dumbest, most intelligent observation I have ever heard. Are we all on the same page th…"

Jane clutched her head. That familiar, baleful moan of pain and rage was building, and it seemed to echo inside her skull, killing off precious brain cells that were in its path. Just when she thought she would not be able to take it any longer, it abruptly stopped. She stole a look at her companions, who were all looking at her. It dawned on her that this was not a real sound but a psychic shard of pure rage cutting through her mind. It did not seem directed at her, though; the devil was more interested in healing itself than pursuing them, for now.

As if in realisation of this, Doug pushed down the accelerator to the absolute limit he could control. Right now, their sole focus was to keep as much distance as possible between them and the devil, who had a thirst for vengeance only their blood could quench. Ginny just thought of her husband, who loved horror movies. If this sequence of events had been the plot of any horror movie, even he would have been too afraid to watch it.

Chapter Twenty-One

Ken Makes a Noble Sacrifice

Uh-oh

When everything had gone dark, Tim and his group of survivors realised what had happened. Either the angry colonel had attacked the renewable energy source, the detonations or shockwaves had destroyed everything, or the sunlight was blocked. Or all of that. The lights came back on quickly when the diesel generators kicked in.

Tim knew the smell instantly and smiled. "YOU SILLY CHEAP BASTARDS!!!"

"Why would they penny pinch with red diesel?" Robert asked.

"Who knows?" replied Tim.

"How long have we got?" asked Mary.

The Tannoy came to life and announced, "PLEASE RESTORE RENEWABLE POWER SOURCE. GENERATORS NOW ACTIVE. THREE DAYS AT FULL CAPACITY UNTIL DIESEL IS EXHAUSTED."

"I know what's going on," said Tim. "Pancake land is not a good place for a fallout shelter. You can't use underground or overground hydropower, and you spend extra energy pumping out the groundwater. You can use renewables, but they are vulnerable as shit. And diesel is not exactly renewable."

"What if we can reduce the amount of diesel we're using?" asked Greg.

"Well, all the lighting is automatic, and it would take us more than three days to work out how to properly run things from the central terminal. Plus, we may need to sacrifice things like fresh water and air conditioning."

"OKAY," Tim said with authority. He knew he was the leader here and loved it, but he was sadly not the most intelligent. That was Greg. "Greg, get to the central terminal and find out how this place works."

"On it," said Greg.

"OKAY," Tim said again. "Us three. We gather all the nonperishable food like MREs, tinned goods, etc. And weapons. We need to take as many weapons as we can carry, as well as ammo, clothes, tents, anything we need. We don't have a choice but to leave. Whoever is waiting for us out there, they will not be offering free food and shelter. Even if they were, a good raping will most likely be on the cards."

"TIM!!" said Mary. "Rape is not a laughing matter!!"

"Yes, yes, it is," said Robert. "There is only one way to mentally handle the evil you see and the evil you know is in the world. And that is the blackest of humour."

Tim and Robert fist bumped.

"Well, when you're right, you're right." said Mary, shrugging her shoulders.

In two hours, they had gathered everything together and figured out who was carrying what, as well as heavier items they would carry in shifts. Tim had always wanted a gun, and endless hours on YouTube watching tutorials on how to use various guns was paying dividends. Otherwise, no one would have thought of taking gun oil and barrel brushes. Tim realised he was coming to life. He did wonder how his brothers and sister were doing.

At the end of the first day, they had dressed Ken the doll in street clothes.

Above ground

Colonel Henry George Brown of the Royal Tank Regiment

waited with what remained of his men. He was nursing a deep laceration in his neck and a second degree burn on the left side of his face. All around were the corpses of the infected, Russian soldiers, and infected Russian soldiers. He had realised pretty quickly that if you did not kill them straight away with a bullet to the head or heart, yes, they would die but would still be deadly until they bled out. Accurate shots took time, something a person did not have when being swarmed.

Half of his men were gone. The infected ones had identified a leader of sorts, who directed them. This leader had normal eyes, and they showed an articulate malevolence, unlike his black-eyed, animalistic subordinates. When a 7.62 mm round from the coaxial L94A1 chain gun on the Challenger 2 had hit the leader on the leg, he had gone down not from pain but because the round had removed the leg. He was not in pain, clearly.

When his horde knew he was injured, they had swarmed him. On his back, he had dispatched at least ten of them. The tank gunner had then fired several L30A1 120 mm rounds at the infected cluster, finally getting rid of them.

The colonel had sent several of his men in a commandeered car to take out the wind turbines and solar panels a mile away. He had seen and heard the claymores going off, and he knew the bastards down below would show themselves eventually. They had no choice now the power source was gone.

The burns on his face had become infected. He had also heard automatic gunfire and screaming in the aftermath of the explosion. He had to get down to the shelter for safety and medical treatment, even if there was no power after a few days. He stayed quiet, as did his remaining men (under strict orders to do so) and waited and watched from the tank driver's hole. The chain gun was loaded and aimed for the door to his desired (and deserved) subterranean sanctuary.

An entire day after the power sources had been destroyed, he was smoking another joint to stave off despair and deal with the pain. He and his men had used up the last of their rations 12 hours ago, and all he could think about were things like fruit pastels, Sensations, Jelly Babies, all of that. Now that he could not have that stuff, he looked at the joint with resentment. Overwhelming despair was setting in. *Creeeaaakk* ... they all tensed, and Colonel Brown threw away the almost finished joint.

His machine gunner rested his finger on the trigger. It was itching. The wheel was turning. *Clunk*. It was unlocked. After yet another eternity, the door opened but only slightly. It was being opened slowly with some sort of stick or plank. A head showed itself. And then eyes. The eyes were dead, though. Uncanny valley dead.

"Ken??" the colonel said incredulously.

This was his gunner's cue to light up the door. Foam and silicone flew everywhere, and the door slammed shut. He ran for the door and pulled but felt a slight tremor, which made him hesitate.

"How the hell did they ... RUN!!!!"

He ran, but it was too late. In all four corners of the area covering the shelter, L111A1 12.7 mm (.50) heavy machine guns burst out of the ground, all pointed towards the centre. A system meant to protect him was being used against him, and he could not believe they had figured it out.

As they rose, pins were pulled out of the mechanisms,

preventing galvanised metal-wire ropes from tightening against the triggers. He was out of the line of initial fire but guessed they had also figured out how to activate the integrated claymore network under their feet.

All he could think of to say was "FUUUUU…" He did not even get to finish that word.

Chapter Twenty-Two

To The Fouyers

Well, no Kaitlin, no Ginny, just two dead foreign soldiers round the back. There was no option but to keep on going. He tried to tune out the banging and screaming in the boot and was just glad it was holding. He inched painfully down Fouyer's Lane, with the headlights off now he was able to navigate visually in the disgusting early dawn light. Quite the uneventful journey, apart from there being rabbits literally covering the fields, darting back and forth. It did not look natural, though. They appeared to be freaking out, panicking without knowing why. Above, he could make out birds of all kinds completely filling the sky, flying ever so silently. No dawn chorus. Just a quiet hellscape where no rabbit seemed to know what was happening.

He turned on the radio again. It went from static to discordant screeching to fragments of serious sounding announcers. *New pres... vic... Chilen... Russ... deadli... Dec... WAR.* He perceived that last word as being louder than it was, possibly because the signal strengthened, but it was the only complete word he heard. It made Tommy's arse pucker. A wave of exhaustion went through his body. He was perceiving dark shadows in the corner of his vision, which would run away when he tried to look directly at them. He could also hear members of his extended family back home saying his name. This was nothing new as this always happened when he was tired. With the stimulants, though, it was more *vivid.*

He went even slower around the final bend, and what he saw looked like a last stand made by a few people against these hyper-athletic humanoid things affected by the agent. They seemed to know what they were doing. They were doing their best to make sure not one bullet went to waste. One of them was firing on one of those things when it got really close and slammed into the shooter, causing him to shoot himself in the lower leg or foot. He yelped in pain. Luckily, the thing had caught enough bullets to die, so the man crawled out from under it, moaning in pain.

There were only three subhumans left when the bullets appeared to be expended. The bloke took care of two of them with the butt of the gun, and the girl did in the same way, but she seemed to get carried away, smashing the butt down angrily long after the need had passed. Hold on a second. *Kaitlin*? He moved forwards slowly to about two hundred feet away. He made sure the doors were locked. He was ready to press the button to open the boot and use Suzanne to his advantage. Although this person seemed to bear a resemblance to Kaitlin, she certainly was not acting like her.

When the action had ended, he flashed his headlights twice, this still being an obvious way of getting attention on this slowly brightening morning. From what he could see so far, he wished it had just stayed dark so he could not see the brown radioactive hellscape. Tommy wondered if he was one of those people who were more resistant to radioactivity than others. He only wondered, not hoped.

After a few seconds, he saw a double flash from what appeared to be a mobile phone torch. He inched forwards some more and saw that it was Kaitlin. Everything seemed different about her, especially her gait. He put down his passenger-side window in time to hear her saying his name. That was enough for him to stop the car and get out. Before he could say anything, he heard a familiar sound. His heart fluttered, and he felt a warmth in his stomach as the bell got louder. Then he heard that delightful trilling sound he had never thought he would hear again. The trilling took on a more excited tone as Violet closed the distance. He got down on one knee in preparation for the joyous reunion, all else temporarily forgotten. Kaitlin was beaming from ear to ear as she saw her stepdad turn to jelly.

Violet reached him and started repeatedly headbutting him, rubbing herself all over him and rolling around, showing her belly, not swiping as Tommy rubbed it gently. Jesse was there too, gently sniffing Tommy's left hand. It was an older and more dignified welcome as he patiently waited for that familiar full body caress, and he did not have to wait long. Tommy gradually became aware of Maia doing her little dance as though the ground was hot, yelping in anticipation but not wanting to get in Violet's way. Violet and Jesse suddenly looked at each other in a silent conveyance and ran off in opposite directions. Once Maia had done with her violent and clumsy welcome, her demeanour suddenly took on a serious tone, and she took off into the filthy morning. Then, finally, Akasha appeared. After a gentle, affectionate welcome, she also took off. Tommy did not understand why his pets were acting this way and could only speculate that the situation called for this behavioural change. He could ask questions later.

Tommy stood, and his attention redirected towards Kaitlin. As they suspiciously approached each other, he saw that her eyes were *fried*. There was something terrifyingly dangerous about them, but it was obvious she was not one of those things.

"Hold up," Kaitlin said. "What the heck is wrong with your eyes?"

Kaitlin did not swear, something which always frustrated Tommy. But it seemed that part of her, at least, was still there.

"Well, that's rich coming from someone whose eyes are the very embodiment of the abyss," Tommy replied. "You been taking drugs?" he asked.

"Well, yeah, but going by your eyes, you're a hypocrite. I have also been drinking," Kaitlin said.

Tommy had not drunk a drop of alcohol since 2010, when he had done a skydive from a hot air balloon at five in the morning after staying up all night drinking. Then he was almost murdered by a herd of angry, calving cows miles from where he was supposed to land, and he got stuck in the countryside for three hours: did not ruin the experience, only tainted it.

"You have anything I could drink? I'm flying quite high; I probably should reduce altitude," Tommy said.

Kaitlin smiled. "KEVIN! Get my stepdad some of that Johnnie Walker."

They both approached, and Kevin handed Tommy the bottle, hoping he would not take too much. Keith limped over thirty seconds later and handed Tommy a tub, simply saying, "Sorry, mate!" in a gravelly rasp.

Tommy did not care. "Keep it, mate, I got plenty of drugs to be getting on with. Besides, it looks like you need it."

Keith's eyes widened. "What have you got?" he asked.

"Well, everything," Tommy said.

Keith smiled, showing lots of missing and rotted teeth.

"Look, you can have whatever you like, mate, eh? Just don't smile at me. Again. Ever," Tommy said as he took a single huge swig from the bottle. Then he pushed it back into Kevin's chest. He winced as the whisky burned his throat, and he felt an unfamiliar fire inside him as it introduced itself into the drug melting pot that was Tommy's body.

Kaitlin and Kevin cackled uncontrollably as the smile disappeared from Keith's face.

"What happened to your face?" asked Keith. "I have never seen a face like that on a live person."

Now they were cackling at Tommy.

"Do you want any of my drugs or not?" Tommy asked mockingly.

They kept laughing, but Tommy found it funny too.

"Sorry, mate, but seriously, what happened to your face?"

Tommy just turned around and nodded to the boot of the car. Then they all became aware of the banging.

Kaitlin looked at Tommy with horror. "You have one of those things in there?" she asked.

"Yes," Tommy replied. "This is nothing compared to what she was like initially. I'm lucky to be alive. Good news is, the effects will wear off eventually, going by what I've seen. It seems more long-acting than any nervous system depressants ..."

"In English, mate," Kevin said.

"I mean things like benzos, morphine, etc.," Tommy clarified.

"Oooohhhhh," Keith and Kevin said in unison.

Tommy continued, "Anyway, nervous system depressants do reverse the effects, but only temporarily. I'm trying to dose her every time she turns, until she stops turning. This is a friend of mine; I worked with her." Tommy paused to make sure everyone was following.

No questions.

"I am wired, I feel good, I feel strong and fast. But I'm certain this is an illusion. I have taken *a lot* of drugs."

They all smiled at him.

"Why not? The world is ending," Keith said.

The other two nodded at the logic of this.

"Now, I am going to open the boot to SHUT THIS dickhead UP!!!" Tommy said, the outburst due to the presence of whisky in his blood.

The other three took a step back. Tommy put his hand up to his face.

"Nice friend," Kaitlin said.

Tommy dismissed her with a gesture and took a deep breath. "I need you to hold her down while I inject her with drugs to reverse the effects. I'm hoping this will be the last time I need to do this."

"Well, three of us, one of her," said Kevin.

"Please, look at my face. Do not underestimate her," Tommy said.

They were not taking this seriously. They would understand soon enough.

Besides, it looks like Mr Keith will have to sit this one out."

Keith was already sitting against the hedge, looking like he was going into shock.

The three of them stood at the back of the car as the day became more disgusting. In his hand, Tommy held a full 5 ml intramuscular injection of half-and-half Cyclimorph 50/10 mg/ml and diazepam 5 mg/ml. Therefore, he had 15 mg of diazepam, 125 mg of cyclizine, and 25 mg of morphine. They all took a deep breath as Tommy pulled the boot release switch. No weapons.

It took a full thirty seconds for them to get her to hold

still long enough for Tommy to slam the injection into the back of her thigh and plunge the contents into her muscle. The longest thirty seconds of their lives, it seemed to all of them. Kevin had a prominent bite mark, which broke the skin but was otherwise superficial. Kaitlin had banged her head on the gravelly road and was holding her head while blood seeped through her fingers.

But Suzanne was sitting upright on the ground. She was compos mentis, and she wiped away a tear and stood up. Everyone stepped back.

She knew why. "Roll me a cigarette," she said.

"You don't smoke," said Tommy.

"I also do not turn into a monster and try to kill everybody," she replied.

"Touché,'' replied Tommy. He had already started rolling it.

She lit the cigarette and grabbed a large bottle of water from the boot and drank greedily. She then went over to lean on the nearby gate to get some brief peace, despite the smell.

"First things first, you are all going on a course of both doxycycline and flucloxacillin, and a single dose of fluconazole for good measure. That one is the ladies' thrush capsule. But don't worry, it fixes and prevents other fungal infections."

"Better give Keith that last one ASAP; he is an aggravating twat," Kevin said.

All Keith could do was swallow with difficulty with his dried-out mouth and throat and slowly raise his middle finger. Tommy was not a nurse but decided to do his best to tend to their wounds.

He gently took off Keith's shoe and sock. The smell did not do much to add to the one already in the air. The bullet had made a clean hole through the fleshy part of the foot between the third and fourth metatarsals. He cleaned around it with sterile wipes taken from the pharmacy. Tommy rinsed the wound and poured some sterile Irripod wound irrigation through the hole. He applied an elastic self-fastening bandage with reasonable tightness and put a thermal sock over the foot. He gave Keith the other thermal sock for his other foot.

Then he gave the first doses of doxycycline, flucloxacillin and single fluconazole, which Keith swallowed with water. Tommy gave him the boxes, and Keith was responsible for finishing the rest of the antibiotic doses himself. He also gave him two 10 mg diazepam tablets for the shock, and Keith assured him he was tolerant enough to handle such a dose.

Another 45 minutes later, everyone had had their wounds cleaned and bandaged, with all the first doses administered and the rest given with instructions. Stitching would have been preferable, but it was too painful without a local anaesthetic. This would have to do for now. Hopefully, it was enough. Everyone stood around the car, including Suzanne, and they were all smoking a rolled cigarette each in contemplation. Tommy was almost certain he did not need to sedate Suzanne again. He was glad he had been reunited with Kaitlin and also glad she had met two guys who could be trusted and easily slotted into the 'scumbags but not evil' category.

"I managed to gain a little information from the intermittent radio signal. There appears to be a new president in America, and they've given a warning to Russia," Tommy stated.

Kevin and Kaitlin sighed in relief.

"Not so fast," Keith rasped slowly, looking close to

passing out. "Yesshhhs, all this could wery werrrvery well go away, but alshho, it may mean a shitload more nuclear bombs falling on our green and pleasshhant land."

Tommy thought about the birds and the rabbits. He also remembered the rumours of their landlord Edwin having a fallout shelter where he lived, five minutes from the Sawyers in a big house called 'The Fouyers'.

Like in a stellar nursery within a far-off nebula, as if the universe was listening, a blinding white light filled the sky in an instant as a tiny star was born. When the flash died down, a perfect ball of white light was left. The miniature sun's life was over in seconds as it faded to nothing, replaced by a blackened ball of fire turning in on itself as it went supernova. When the dark early morning suddenly became like a summer afternoon, Tommy had his back to the flash, as did Kaitlin. Kevin and Suzanne were facing it but averted their gaze in time. Keith's reaction time was not so quick, and he lay there, looking at the slowly fading light. His mouth hung open and he was drooling, a smile at the corner of his lips. Blood trickled from his burnt-out eye sockets.

They all became aware very quickly of the slowly building temperature, and it was almost pleasant. There before them was the mushroom cloud, a truly majestic sight. They all gazed at it in awe.

It was the most magnificent thing Tommy had ever seen. His best guess was that it was at least 150 km away. "The shock wave is on its way," he said calmly, the drugs in his system ensuring that panic was impossible. "The only way we don't die is *if* we can make it back to The Fouyers, *if* the rumours are true that Edwin has a fallout shelter there, *if* we can get in, and *if* it will protect us."

A single drop of perspiration trickled down Tommy's face. Everyone just stood there, in shock and awe at the beautiful sight, all with a sheen of perspiration forming on their foreheads.

Tommy got into the car and engaged the mechanism to get the top down. "Everybody get in, find something to hold on to, and do not let go."

Kevin looked at his utterly destroyed friend, who was no longer smiling. His face was contorted into what could only be described as an expression of pure emotional agony and regret, with his eyelids now shut tight over two gaping wounds that had once contained functioning eyes, blood tears streaming down his cheeks. Kevin got in Keith's face as Kaitlin positioned herself on the lap of the heavier Suzanne in the front passenger seat, with both front seats pushed as far forwards as possible to accommodate Kevin and Keith.

"DO YOU WANT TO LIVE? YES OR NO?" Kevin shouted at his friend.

Keith slowly nodded, and Kevin, adrenalin surging through his veins, effortlessly picked him up and draped him over his shoulders. He carried him the short distance to the car and roughly threw him onto the back seat. He jumped in after him, and wasting no time, Tommy tore off down the country lane towards his landlord Edwin's house, The Fouyers, in what seemed essentially a futile attempt to live beyond the next few minutes.

Against the backdrop of a heartbreakingly bleak morning, a huge black and grey wall with a height of around a hundred feet came into view for the disparate group of survivors. Stunning blue and red lightning arced across the wall, which stretched across the entire western horizon. The temperature was slowly becoming uncomfortable for all of them. Tommy, struggling to keep his eyes on the road and away from the magnificent sight, took a swig of whisky and blasted his face with the two-litre bottle of room-temperature water he was keeping in the pocket of the driver-side door. He passed it to the next person, who grabbed it, and they all did the same.

Kevin lifted Keith to an upright position. Keith was still whimpering, speaking quickly and incoherently.

"Hey, you big wet fanny, I'm giving you some water. Just try not to breathe it in, okay? *I need you.*"

Kaitlin snapped her head around as it became blatantly obvious that the 'alcoholic waster' was not Kevin's true form. Straightaway she faced forwards when she realised that *she liked him.* As a mate, though. Didn't matter now anyway. They all knew their chances of survival were low.

Passing their old family residence, they rounded the last bend before The Fouyers. Tommy clocked the farmer who had shouted at him earlier out in his garden, just staring at the beautiful land tsunami racing towards him, unobstructed by the flatness of the Norfolk countryside.

"Best view in the country!!" Tommy laughed as he inhaled the powder from a Shortec capsule deep into his lungs, somehow managing not to crash on this narrow country lane. Through the hedge, he could see the brake lights and headlights of a car parked on the driveway of The Fouyers. This did not matter as everyone grabbed what was important to them and were jumping out before Tommy could even stop. He did not forget to take his party bag with him and did not even engage the handbrake before leaping out, joining the rest and sprinting towards the driveway.

The Peugeot was drifting slowly towards the ditch on

the other side of the road, its back end sticking out. Tommy smiled as he caught himself thinking that might be dangerous to other motorists. He caught Suzanne looking at him in horror as he smiled, a far cry from the professional face he portrayed to the world. *Screw you,* he thought as his smile instantly vanished. Just before he reached the driveway, Kevin handed him the other AK74-M, now useless to Keith, who was slung over Kevin's shoulder, muttering complete nonsense.

For some reason, it reminded Tommy of trying to manually search all FM wavelengths for the only station in a remote area, hearing words intermingled with static.

Kevin simply looked him in the eyes and said, "Figure it out; you've seen enough movies. It's ready, on single shot. I've turned off the safety."

As everyone gathered in the driveway, Tommy arrived last and locked eyes with Edwin, his landlord. He was standing outside of his still-running metallic-blue Lexus. Edwin was okay; he had never been a problem for Tommy, and they even had a good relationship, with Edwin reducing the rent by 30% in the initial COVID-19 crisis.

That was back when the governments of the world thought they could control this seemingly sentient and shape-shifting virus engaged in a war of attrition with humankind.

It took Edwin a few seconds to recognise Tommy, and he just said, "What are you doing here?"

Before anyone could reply, Edwin's demeanour changed as he realised why they were on his driveway. The change in demeanour caused something to uncoil in their stomachs. Kevin, as if he did not have another fully-grown man over his shoulder, instinctively raised his

Russian rifle as Edwin tapped the touchscreen on his smartphone. Under the pile of wood at the side of The Fouyers, where they had intended to look for the shelter, a metallic whirring preceded the rise of an enclosed, lighted platform as the pile of wood fell to both sides.

Chapter Twenty-Three

Ása-Þór, the Reawakening

When Batak Toba had erupted, the staff supervising the stasis of the old ones had abandoned their posts. This supervision was a redundant job managed by local, autonomous artificial intelligence and had not required human intervention even once. The facility was powered by geothermal energy, the source and the technology undiscovered by modern humans. It had an emergency backup which would last eighteen months should access to the geothermal energy be taken offline. In January 2026, Russia had attacked Paris with a single thermonuclear warhead detonated in the centre of Paris. Deep under the catacombs, the facility containing the old ones had lain undisturbed for almost eighty millennia. This bunker-busting thermonuclear warhead had not damaged the facility but had shifted its location and rotated it slightly. This had compromised the supply of geothermal energy and started the eighteen-month countdown.

Ása-Þór powered up, his stasis ending as the facility lost the hydrothermal power. Ása-Þór was the only old one who was completely synthetic, with the rest having integrated synthetic and biological nervous systems. Ása-Þór was the only one who had not put up a fight and had agreed to go into stasis. His mission was only to assist humans, and if he needed to go into stasis until they needed him again, then so be it. And he had done just that, but not before helping the humans subdue the other titans. He was super intelligent but without emotion or ego. Talos had been chosen to fight the Echthroi as he had not been built with the state-of-the-art EMP shields that the rest of them had. Clearly, knowledge of the nature of Ása-Þór had been forgotten in time, or he would have been chosen.

He observed the empty casket of Talos. Ása-Þór had been fed information of world events up to and including the artificial and premature eruption of Batak Toba caused by a deeply hurt and betrayed Talos. The other transparent caskets containing the titans of old had failed as the emergency power could not contain their artificial stasis, causing loss of pressure, and before melting, the ice had changed from amorphous to crystalline, destroying both the biological and synthetic components. Inside the caskets were the decomposing biological matter and ruined synthetic components. Ása-Þór was the last one. Ása-Þór had no idea how much time had passed since the betrayal of Talos, nor what had happened since then, but something big had obviously happened on the surface, an event of unimaginable destruction. People needed help.

Ironically, Ása-Þór looked the most human of all of the titans of old. A synthetic polymer which looked and felt like skin completely covered his body. He had long black hair and striking blue eyes, and was dressed in clothes just like the humans of the time wore. He was around seventy-five feet tall. He possessed only a sword of tungsten carbide, the same substance of which his endoskeleton was made. He did not know how to get out. He scanned the thickness of the walls of the facility and their composition, and he identified exactly where the weakest point was that he could access easily. He estimated that it would take three weeks to breach them and another week to get to the surface. He made his way to the optimum point he had identified with his scan and began to strike at the wall with his sword.

Somewhere in the Amazon Rainforest - one week later

Baphomet had not for a second taken seriously the band of barely surviving humans on some godforsaken island and the possibility that they might wipe him from existence or send him back. He had been here for many millennia, and if they had not figured out how to get rid of him by now, they never would, especially now that human infrastructure and society was destroyed and there were no signs things would ever get better.

He was dressed in a hooded cloak as the new witch doctor of an isolated tribe was directing the ceremony of sacrifice to bring back the sky and trees, both of which were now permanently and inexplicably barren. This tribe was one of the only ones to survive the firestorms. There was rarely any rain anymore, and what rain did fall was poisonous. The tribe was starving and would agree to anything Baphomet suggested, no matter how depraved. And they did. They believed his promises. If not, then all hope would be lost. They had nothing to hold on to other than the promises of the hooded monster.

The hooded monster never showed his face. Not out of shame but because he was too loathsome to allow the tribespeople to see him. Only the three-digit, clawed hand would appear, allowing them to feel just the right amount of fear. The clawed hand and the ancient, raspy voice directed them. Around twenty tribespeople, adult and child, man and woman, had been placed on racks, their wrists and ankles bound tight enough to cut off blood flow. These unfortunate people bore the marks of previous rounds of ceremonial torture in the lead-up to the ultimate sacrifice, which Baphomet gleefully made up as he went along. All were completely naked, but this tribe did not wear clothes anyway.

Baphomet slowly raised the three-clawed hand, which directed the tribespeople to begin turning the wheels of the racks. After a few turns, the unfortunate chosen began to cry out in pain. At this point, if the chosen were released, there would be no permanent damage. Baphomet wanted to savour this moment. The slower, the better. There was no joy to be had in rushing the good times.

Baphomet heard a sound behind him, and he turned and looked up, causing the hood to come down. The screams of all the tribespeople could be heard as they laid their eyes on the face and head below the hood. Up in the air, he saw a giant hand. This hand came down hard and flattened Baphomet. Then he was scooped up and taken.

Ása-Þór waited for Baphomet to regenerate. He then held him tight. He had taken Baphomet to the rim of Volcan Reventador. In the ancient language, he said, "Talos had the right idea. Your time has come. Be gone from this world, you evil parasite. I hope you will soon be in hell."

Baphomet did not show fear as he was hurled into the lava bowl.

Chapter Twenty-Four

Under The Fouyers

The unveiling

The platform resembled a large lift, like the ones used in hospitals for laundry, food and waste. Once it was all the way up, Edwin started backing away towards it.

"DONT!!!" screamed Kevin.

"You can allow us in, or we will take it from you," stated Suzanne calmly and menacingly.

It occurred to Kaitlin that they had become a roving gang of criminals all too quickly, not quite at the point where they would murder Edwin and take what he had. And what he had was a miracle. Edwin had saved them. But they would apologise later.

The heat was becoming unbearable, and the shockwave would be upon them in seconds. Small debris was landing all around them and upon them, and they could hear the metallic *clink* as the small sticks and stones landed on the Lexus and ruined the paintwork.

"Well, it'll probably be a write-off soon anyway. COME ON AND FOLLOW ME!" shouted Edwin, instantly switching off the unpleasant demeanour, which confused Kevin.

Kevin lowered the rifle but clutched the metal behind the trigger. He sprinted to the platform, and so did everyone else. They all piled in, and Edwin pressed the button on his smartphone again.

When they were halfway underground, Maia, Jesse, Violet and Akasha came out of nowhere and dived in, having been outpaced by Tommy's getaway-style driving. Everyone welcomed their sentries and protectors, with Kaitlin and Tommy being most relieved, although both had forgotten about the pets in their drug-addled and adrenaline-fuelled state. The electric juggernaut of death was only about ten kilometres away now, and as they were lowered down, they all just stared. They could make out details in grey and black mass. Buses, cars, charred limbs, road signs, trees: all fragmented and burnt remnants of the world that was now gone, the gift humanity had been given just once, with no second chances.

Once they had cleared ground level, they expected the platform to stop, but it kept going. The loud roar they could hear from overhead now faded into silence, an anticlimax they were all so relieved for. Then it stopped. Kevin had counted the seven seconds it took to clear one length of itself, and it was eight feet tall. They had been going down for roughly forty seconds, so almost six times its own length of eight feet. They were at least forty-five feet down, perhaps fifty.

A brief pause allowed Tommy to ask Edwin, "How?"

"I'm rich. Actually, I *was* rich. Cash can only be used now to heat the hearth, and until *very* recently, most money existed electronically, so that has simply ceased to exist."

"Thank you," said Tommy, sincerely.

Everyone else mumbled the same sentiment.

Edwin simply nodded.

Suzanne then asked, in her new monotone, which understandably alarmed Tommy, "So, you're saying what we're all thinking – we're done, we've destroyed our world, the only one we have."

Edwin simply bowed his head. "They shot Trump through the neck. He was in cahoots with Putin, some say unwillingly, that Putin had leverage. With no leverage over the new US president, the US took our side, and Russia refused to back down. You can fill in the blanks."

"Is he still alive?" asked Tommy.

"I assume you mean Trump. Yes, they have him stabilised. The bullet missed his large veins and arteries, as well as the oesophagus, but the bullet smashed his vertebrae and tore through his vocal cords."

Tommy smiled into his own abyss. "So, he's paralysed and can't talk." His mother had often told him he could always find something good in the worst things that can happen.

Then, like a washing machine spinning at maximum speed with a brick inside it, they heard the roar above them build for five seconds, then fade. After another few seconds, the whole compartment started vibrating at an extremely low wavelength that made everyone's ears ring. Once this was gone, Edwin pressed the touchscreen on his smartphone. The whole time in the lift, the temperature had been decreasing, and when the door started to open, filtered and conditioned air rushed in. Everyone took a deep breath, tasting what seemed like the best air they had ever breathed. As soon as the opening was wide enough for a single person, Edwin ran through the gap.

Kaitlin and Tommy calmly lifted their Russian rifles on Kevin's Cue. He gave the still babbling Keith to Suzanne. "Please look after him."

All three rifles were levelled at the slowly opening door. Once it had fully opened, the lights went out in the lift. The sight they were greeted with was confusing. The whole room had no straight corners or wall junctions or steps; all were curved in a design adopted by some hospitals in their aseptic preparation departments. This prevented the growth of unwanted bacteria, or any bacteria.

Tommy had learned about this in university and guessed that all the surfaces were made of an intrinsically antimicrobial material and were coated with methicillin. The area was not fully lit, but after their eyes adjusted, they could make out the details. The walls, floor and ceiling were an off-white colour. There were several doorways out of the room and a winding staircase on each side. Above, there was a gallery which went around the entire room. A doorway with curved edges had a stairway leading to the gallery on each wall. No sign of Edwin. They felt like sitting ducks. In the middle of the room were some very comfortable-looking black modern sofas with four corners, set a few feet down from the main floor and accessed by a small aseptic staircase.

The seating confused Tommy, as it was obviously not aseptic, although aseptic seating is pretty much impossible, and it was not a lab. All the couches faced what appeared to be the image of a crackling fire inside a 360 degree glass ball, which contributed to the ambient light. The only other lighting pointed upwards. The uplighting illuminated two structures near to each other on the far wall.

Kevin was peering through the Russian night-vision monocular still taped to the rifle, and horror spread across his face as he slowly turned to look at the others.

"Are they … cages?" Kaitlin said.

Due to the uplighting, the fronts of the cages were lit, but it was too gloomy to see inside.

They looked like they were not very big, about 6 foot by 3: only enough for a person to stand. Tommy fumbled in his bag for the strong headlamp he had used during a recent hiking trip. He found it, put it on, turned it on, and focused the strong beam on the cages. Then he understood the horror on Kevin's face, but what Tommy saw was worse. Two women, one in each cage, had their arms tied above their heads to the top of the cages. Each woman was only able to avoid hanging on their full weight by standing on their tiptoes, which itself was extremely painful. They were naked, clearly extremely underweight, and covered in cuts and bruises.

A man, not Edwin, appeared in the gallery up and to the right and aimed a revolver at the dark lift, only hoping to hit something, and emptied the gun at them. He was dressed in expensive clothes for lounging around in and was clearly not a firearms expert.

Kevin shot him in the gut, and the man went down behind the gallery. "BASTARD SHITHEADS!" Kevin screamed.

Suzanne was the only one who noticed that Keith had taken a bullet to his leg. He clearly did not notice it himself and continued like he was sleep-talking in a nightmare.

"He's been shot," Suzanne calmly stated. She put him down against the wall of the lift, and Tommy pointed his headlamp at the wound.

"Oh, Jesus Christ, Keith," Kevin said. "If you want to live, it's best not to get shot all the time, you DICKHEAD!"

Tommy let out a laugh at this but stopped quickly.

Kevin then became serious. "It's just a graze; no arteries have been hit. Anyway, Kaitlin and Tommy, you're with me. I'll move forwards and you cover behind me. You got another one of these?" Kevin asked, referring to the headlamp.

"Yes, upstairs. At home." Tommy laughed as he remembered he also had two torches in his bag.

Before Kevin could get angry, Tommy found the torches and showed them to Kevin.

Kaitlin was thinking at light speed and had her electrical tape out almost instantly to attach the two torches to hers and Tommy's gun barrels.

"You take the headlamp; you're on point," Tommy said to Kevin.

Kevin nodded and took it.

"You'll blind any scumbag if you shine the centre of the beam in their faces," Tommy emphasised.

Kevin smiled.

After the two torches were taped to Kaitlin and Tommy's guns, Kevin said to Suzanne, "Leave him here in the lift, he's comparatively safe here. Try to free those two girls. They're in a lot of pain."

"Okay," Suzanne confirmed, like it was going to be an easy task for her.

He turned to Tommy and Kaitlin. "Ready?"

No answer from either.

"Okay, then, let's go."

As soon as Kevin set foot outside the lift, Maia and the three cats shot out and went in different directions, swallowed up by the gloom.

"Thankfully, they don't need help to see in this gloom," Kaitlin stated.

Kevin spotted a balding, fat middle-aged man, also dressed in expensive clothes, coming out of a doorway with an AK-47, useless to him as Kevin shone the centre of the light at his face. Kevin kneecapped the man and shot his other knee before he hit the ground, still very much alive. They raced towards the man. Kevin grabbed the man's gun, which he had not even had the chance to fire, and threw the gun to Suzanne. He looked confused as he was about to give her a heads up of the throw, but the words froze in his mouth. Tommy saw Suzanne right in front of the cages, still as a rock. Without looking in their direction, her right hand shot out and grabbed the firearm.

This was too much to deal with right now as all three moved in formation towards a spiral staircase. As they went up the staircase, they heard the slow bending and snapping of steel as Suzanne took apart the cages with her bare hands. Tommy had his firearm pointed down the short but steep stairway and saw a hand lob a grenade up the stairs. It bounced off Tommy's knee painlessly and rolled back down the stairs and out of the doorway.

"OH, NO!!!" and running footsteps was all that Tommy heard before a concussive blast and a scream of pain. "Somehow I don't think these guys are special forces," Tommy said to the other two. He heard two pops as Kevin seemed to dispatch an unseen enemy.

Once above at the gallery, Kevin went straight for the gun of the man he'd taken out first. There was no ammo left in it, but Kevin was able to find three speed loaders in the man's jacket which he'd had no chance to use. He loaded the revolver and tucked it into his belt so it was covered by his shirt. He pocketed the other two speed loaders. Behind him, Kaitlin and Tommy were still in formation but looking confused at the lower level. Suzanne was on the couch with the two girls, all sitting upright, and both girls had big blankets around their shoulders. She was giving them both water, which they drank greedily.

Keith was at the opposite end, also covered in the same type of blanket, but he was in the foetal position, and the sound of his keening carried up to the gallery, a noise which they all tuned out. They looked over at the cages. On the floor were bent and snapped metal bars, around four of them. There was also an overweight elderly man decked out in golfing gear, prone and clearly breathing with Cheyne-Stokes respirations, probably due to him now having half a leg and no leg. The kneecapped man was lying on his back, motionless except for the autonomic rise and fall of his chest.

All three in formation laughed at the crippled men, because this idiot had not realised gravity would take the grenade back to him. Also, no compassion would be shown to these evil perverts. The two rescued girls looked up to all three, their eyes filled with tears of relief and the pain of what these guys had done to them.

"Don't worry, love, we'll take care of these scumbags and show no mercy, then get you taken care of. Can you tell us if there are any more entrances?"

One of the girls nodded. "I don't think it's working, though," she said meekly.

"How come?" asked Kaitlin.

The girl continued, "Both entrances make a lot of noise. There was a commotion at the other entrance a few weeks ago, and I haven't heard it since. In fact, this is the first time I've heard the one you came in."

"Watch the doors! Remember the formation!" Kevin barked at Kaitlin and Tommy.

They both felt stupid and angry with themselves but refocused to ensure the full 360-degree view was re-established.

"We should check it out anyway," stated Tommy.

"Agreed," said Kevin. He closed his eyes, took a deep breath, and swayed a little. He kept his eyes closed and put his arm out. "Gimme a fag and some JW, please."

Tommy was carrying the JW in the side pocket of his bag. Kaitlin took it out and gave it to Kevin. Kaitlin had the cigarettes and just lit one and put it in Kevin's mouth. Then, keeping an eye on what was going on around them, they all lit one each. Tommy declined the JW and decided against taking more drugs until he could relax properly, being starved of sleep and beginning to hallucinate.

The two girls looked at Suzanne, who smiled gently at them, but the smile was empty.

"I think these girls deserve a cigarette, don't you?" Kaitlin threw the cigarettes down, the lighter in the box.

The girl's eyes widened at the sight of the Marlboro Reds. They lit the cigarettes, and their eyes closed in bliss at the first drag. Kevin thought he would try something. He hurled the JW bottle, now just over half full, straight at Suzanne's head. As he predicted, the arm shot out and flawlessly caught the bottle.

"Thanks," Suzanne said flatly.

Kevin simply raised his eyebrow, now visibly reinvigorated. Tommy did the same with his backpack, but it was quite heavy and landed on the hapless, legless golfer's head. He groaned, showing he was not quite dead.

"You know what to do, Suzanne; give them what they need."

She looked at Tommy and nodded. They now had an unbreakable bond of trust after what they had gone through together.

"How many are left?" asked Kaitlin.

"Four," one of the girls said.

"Are they all this ridiculously stupid?" Tommy asked.

The girls looked at each other and smiled on hearing

this. Suzanne cleared her throat and calmly manoeuvred the AK-47 into the firing position, taking aim at the door leading to the other side of the gallery. A forehead slowly came into view from one of the upper doorways opposite them, presumably to have a look. Suzanne cleanly squeezed off a single shot, opening up the man's head and spraying the contents all over the clean off-white wall behind him before his eyes even came into view.

"Three stupid men!" one of the girls giggled.

Tommy detected an Eastern European accent. He realised now that Edwin was a people trafficker, and his stomach dropped. "Where's the other entrance?" he asked.

"The door nearest you," the other girl said. She was clearly black, but her skin colour was relatively light, perhaps mixed race. They all recognised the thick African accent, which only confirmed Tommy's theory. It was obvious now what Edwin was.

"Stay close," said Kevin, slightly slurred.

They went towards the door. This led to a long hallway which curved to the right, with doors on either side.

Opening the first door, they found only a furnace with embers still glowing. They all realised the implication but said nothing. The opposite room was a huge library. There were countless DVDs, all in chronological order by year and alphabetical within the year. All had a name written on the case in black permanent marker, and any names they did recognise were female. All but a few were foreign. Further back within the room were VHS tapes, and even Betamax. 1984 was the earliest year.

None of them said a word as they swept their lights around the room. Kaitlin started to cry.

"Okay, out!" Kevin said.

"Gladly," said Tommy. He gave Kaitlin a hug, and she sobbed a few times into his shirt, clearly trying to fight off her rage.

Kevin was impatient, but he understood. This was horrifying to him, but this was a thousand times worse for her, being female. He felt ashamed to be a man and wished he had not flung the JW to Suzanne. He took a long final draw of his cigarette and stamped it out. Tommy and Kaitlin took a draw too but were not finished. They left the room in formation and came to the third and final door.

Kevin opened the door slightly, standing to the side, and was met with three shots, none of which penetrated the door. "If you come out now, you will live, but you have five seconds," he slurred.

"Eat shit, you shit-eating *schweinhund!*" shouted a voice with a thick German accent.

Kaitlin had caught sight of a petrol can with a rag sticking out of it on a metal shelf alongside cleaning products, fly spray and a few other pressurised aerosol cans. This was a broom cupboard. "Have you got another lighter?" Kaitlin asked the others.

"No," Tommy said.

"Me neither," said Kevin.

Just then, the lighter from the cigarette pack which they had thrown to Suzanne sailed over the gallery balcony and through the open doorway, clattering to the ground ten feet away.

Tommy retrieved it for Kaitlin, ignoring the fact that there was no normal way Suzanne could have known they would need the lighter. Kaitlin reached through the door, grabbed the petrol can, and pulled it out. They heard another three shots and the man screaming at them in German interspersed with English insults they all knew and loved.

"Wait!" another voice called out. "I'm coming out. Please don't kill me!"

This voice was heavily accented, but the trio could not identify it. Another shot rang out, then the sound of a body as it crumpled to the ground. A gurgling sound could be heard.

"I will get at least one of you before you get to me!" the German guy screamed. His voice was filled with entitlement and psychotic rage, not only because he was screaming at them. This voice had been moulded over a lifetime.

Kaitlin took out the rag and screwed the one-foot nozzle onto the jerry can. She then opened the door a crack and poured the quarter-full can of what smelt like unleaded petrol out through the nozzle, which she used to hold open the door. The German piece of work seemed to realise what she was doing and started firing wildly at Kaitlin and screaming again, until all that could be heard was *click, click, click*.

"We could shoot him before he reloads," smiled Tommy.

"Yeah, I suppose we could," Kaitlin responded as she lit the rag. She threw it in and the petrol ignited. "I hope there are plenty of aerosols and flammable products in there," she said.

"Yes, a lot of old newspapers and A4 printer paper, not to mention a dead human body. That fat arsehole Admir will burn for a while, you hear that, Günter?" a voice said.

There was Edwin, who had come around the corner with a nasty-looking modern assault rifle.

"Edwin, please help me!" cried Günter.

"No, sorry." Edwin calmly stated. "Guns, now!" he ordered as the fire whooshed behind the now unopenable fire door.

The agonised screams began. The three felt ashamed as they dropped their firearms and kicked them over to him.

Edwin flung the three rifles over his shoulder, his hubris preventing him from searching any of them. Kevin hawked and spat green and yellow phlegm next to Edwin's boot. He had actually got changed into tactical gear. That offence earned Kevin a merciless blow to the sternum from the rifle's muzzle, causing him to collapse to his knees and start wheezing.

"He'll be fine. Well, he won't. But you know what I mean. Move!" He motioned back the way they had come.

As they walked, Kevin struggled to get a breath but was improving by the second.

Edwin screamed down the hallway, "I know there's one more of you. Drop your weapon and come up with your hands up!"

The Kalashnikov clattered onto the ground in front of them, lobbed over the balcony from the floor below. Edwin frowned in confusion and simply got a shrug from Kevin. Kevin still did not know what was going on with Suzanne.

"All three of you, have a seat on the floor, NOW!" Edwin ordered.

They complied.

Edwin slowly approached the doorway, shouting, "Get up here, you goddamn witch, or I kill the young girl, only because the other two don't seem to give a shit about living or dying!"

Kevin and Tommy looked at each other for a second, thinking this over. Eventually, each one just gave the other a shrug.

As Edwin moved in front of them towards the doorway, Kevin nonchalantly started moving his hand towards the revolver under his shirt. Edwin snapped his head back at them, Kevin hiding what he was doing very well, simply looking like he was uncomfortably changing position from sitting on a cold, hard floor. Edwin continued to approach the doorway of the corridor, ready to fire. Almost there. Kevin now had his hands on the butt of the revolver, ready to make his move, but he needn't have bothered. Just as Edwin's muzzle was within inches of the opening to the corridor, a hand shot out from around the doorway and grabbed the muzzle.

Kevin's heart sank as he realised the idiocy of this move. Suzanne still remained mostly out of sight just around the corner. Edwin yanked back, and the incredulity on his face was compounded when it would only move back a maximum of two inches. Edwin looked back, and Kevin was smiling, with a fully loaded revolver pointed right at him.

Edwin pulled back again and again. "LET GO, YOU TWAT!!"

Unsurprisingly, Suzanne held on. She kept the muzzle pointed at the same general area, away from everyone, to the top left of the main room. Edwin opened fire, emptying an entire clip in that direction, with Suzanne's hand barely moving. They heard the ricochet of a few of the bullets and a yelp of pain.

The two girls collectively gasped, the African woman shouting, "They shot him!!"

Kevin put his hand to his face, closed his eyes and

massaged his temples with his index finger. "AGAIN???" he shouted.

Tommy and Kaitlin tried not to laugh, the drugs possibly blocking their empathy circuits. Somehow, they knew it was not serious. At the same time, they heard the combined growl of both the canine and feline kind from the door off the opposite gallery. Then automatic fire. They could see the muzzle flashes from around the corner of the opposite hallway, seemingly identical to this one, then screaming and a cacophony of very aggressive feline and canine noises.

Kaitlin, already emotional, shed another tear at her best friends coming through for her again. Then a distinct canine yelp. The noises continued while Suzanne crept into view. Looking bored, she peeled her hand off the muzzle and looked at the second-degree burns. She rolled her eyes while her other hand shot out, firmly grabbing the dumbfounded Edwin's windpipe. She held it in a tight but not immediately lethal grip. He grabbed her arm but it felt like rebar. He tried punching and slapping the arm before quickly losing strength as he could not breathe. She cocked her head, looking at him, and then looked at the three in the hallway.

Suzanne moved him 90 degrees so they could see his now purple face. In those bulging eyes was a primal fear.

"Well, I can't speak for all here, obviously," Tommy said, putting a hand to his chest, "but I do love seeing the fear and pain in that slimeball's eyes."

"If I may interject, with my apologies to my friend Tommy here," Kevin said.

Tommy and Kevin smiled wickedly at each other.

Kevin continued, "I agree with my friend, and I'd like to add that I would like to see a lot more of this fear and pain, and I'd bet my life savings, if I had any, that those two traumatised young girls downstairs would concur with this assertion."

Suzanne dropped Edwin.

He lay on the ground, gasping for breath, but despite this, attempted to reach for one of the captured Russian rifles. Kevin shot him in the ankle, causing Edwin to attempt a squeal, but he could not, due to his traumatised windpipe. Needless to say, he abandoned his futile plan. He was obviously in pain but could not yet scream.

"You started the party early!!" Kaitlin said in mock outrage.

Kevin smiled. Suzanne manhandled the rifles away from Edwin and slung them all over her shoulder. She looked at her burnt left hand and turned it towards Tommy.

"In the bag," Tommy said.

She turned to walk away, and Tommy shouted after her, "Suzanne, thank you and everything, but I think we all need to have a little chat."

She withdrew a syringe of diazepam from her pocket.

"It's okay, you're not dangerous anymore, but how long will that shit stay in your system?"

She shrugged, put the syringe back in her pocket, and walked away. Kaitlin realised that the screaming and growling and caterwauling across the way had stopped.

Two days later

Suzanne eyed Tommy with an involuntary smirk, and Tommy eyed her with fear. There had been nothing in the last few days to cause alarm, and no further meds were needed. Tommy had not known her for very long, but that individual look people normally had was gone. She was a husk, seemingly amused by Tommy's fear of her. Tommy hoped she would return to normal, but that did not seem to be happening. Kevin sat by Keith. Keith's most recent injury in his run of bad luck was a ricochet hitting his thigh. All of his wounds were patched up, and none were going to cause any significant long-term issues. He was blind forever, though, and seemingly insane.

He was heavily medicated, as the previous day, he had been ranting incoherently in a Scottish accent, wanting to go to Scotland with someone called Jane who needed to be freed from the Devil by releasing God from his mountain prison. Antipsychotic medication was the only hope of rescuing his sanity, something they had none of. Maybe this Jane person has some, Kevin thought idly. The two rescued girls were glaring at him. After a solid 24 hours of extreme torture and screaming in the room at the very end of the corridor, Kevin had had enough. The girls were not in their right mind and had used some of Tommy's methylphenidate to avoid a nightmare-dominated sleep and to keep the torture going. Kevin had marched to the room and executed Edwin and his two associates, depriving the girls of any further gratification. The bodies were burnt in the furnace.

They all knew it was not the first time the furnace had been used for this purpose. He could tell they were getting over their anger, considering Kevin had helped rescue them in the first place. They were both in cartoon-dog onesies, huddled together under a blanket. Maia was cuddled up next to Biruta, her chin on her leg, gazing up at her. Jesse and Violet had become a black and white blur as they slept together. Akasha was not around.

Tommy was glad, though, after his recent encounter with that cat. Usually affectionate, she had been staring at a random featureless section of wall with a low constant growl coming out of her. She would not react to Tommy at all, so he left Akasha to it.

All of the human inhabitants were all able to find fresh clothes from somewhere and showers. But they were bored. Kaitlin was on her phone, on the Kindle app, reading unread books from her own library. There was a huge smart TV and lots of DVDs, but all movies seemed pointless, especially as it seemed like they were all living through one. They all were conflicted; this place had saved their lives, and they had rid the world of inhuman evil scum, but they could not stay here. A profound malevolent negativity hung in the air, and they all felt it.

Tommy broke the silence. "We need to get out of here. I'm starting to lose my mind, despite the comfort. This place … it's *evil*."

"You're right," Kevin said. "The malicious cruelty spanning decades is emanating from the walls. I know it sounds weird, but I can feel the evil looking inside me. I would rather risk radiation poisoning than stay in here a moment longer."

"So, where do you propose we go, then?" Suzanne asked with a cynical tone.

"Scotland, to see Jane, seems as good an idea as any," Kaitlin responded, only half joking.

They all looked at each other. Abidemi and Biruta looked at each other and nodded.

"My son," Biruta said.

"All of my family are dead," said Abidemi. "We want to go find Biruta's son. If he is alive, he yearns for her. He is nine."

"Take what you need," Kevin said.

"We understand," Kaitlin said.

"I don't think anyone would be stupid enough to mess with either of you, but be careful all the same. I'm glad you're now free, for what it's worth," said Tommy.

Suzanne hugged them both tightly. Tommy looked at Suzanne, who was already looking at him. Her eyes had changed. He recognised the original Suzanne.

A tear rolled down her cheek and she just said, "I am so sorry, Tommy. I almost killed you, and you saved my life."

Tommy had cleaned himself up but had two black eyes and a grossly misshapen nose, almost pointed 90 degrees. "Only because I couldn't bring myself to kill you," he replied dispassionately.

"Okay!" Kevin said. "We need food, medicine, weapons and clothing. And also booze. Meet back here in 15 minutes. There are hazmat suits and gas masks next door to the torture room." He looked at the girls suspiciously. He wanted to trust them. He really did. But they were damaged and unpredictable.

Chapter Twenty-Five

Artemis of Ancient Carpathia

Artemis of Carpathia had awoken in her subterranean chamber twenty feet down three days ago, as she had done many times before. Since Batak Toba had erupted many millennia ago, she had spent the first 1000 years doing everything she could to thwart the wicked plans of the Echthroi. She did have marginal success and thwarted a lot of nefarious intentions and plans, but her greatest achievement was avoiding them. She knew to confront them directly would be suicide. After an entire millennium, both directly and indirectly, they were still tirelessly inflicting wanton destruction and arbitrary cruelty, things so disturbing that it caused her to slowly descend into madness.

She had not defeated them and still did not know how to. She had not appreciated the psychological implications of the life extension the gene therapy had given her. She had assumed the Echthroi were immortal, as humanity was not getting off that easily. She was ageing, but painfully slowly. This, along with vivid memories of their vile deeds, was slowly destroying her mental faculties. She was improved, yes, but still human. This human brain did not have the capacity to exist and store memories for this long. After the first millennium had passed, she was finding it increasingly difficult to avoid direct confrontation with the Echthroi and had had a few close calls.

She was finding it harder to think of plans to foil or mitigate the actions of the Echthroi, and even when she did think of plans, her implementations of such plans were disastrous. One day, in the subterranean chamber which she had carved out for herself, while she slept and let her guard down, she had felt like she was finally about to fall from the precipice into endless, dark insanity. She descended into that hypothetical chasm. In an instant, she had awoken with a sharp intake of breath inside the chamber, and she felt *rested*.

She knew instinctively that a long time had passed. She guessed this to be around half of a millennium. As she ascended into the world, she was feeling a sense of dread at the havoc the Echthroi had wrought in her absence. But after some time, she found that nothing had changed, except perhaps that the stories told around campfires by humans were getting increasingly vague and nonsensical, with the consensus being that these stories were *just stories*. They had mostly forgotten how to read and to write, but they were most definitely becoming more numerous.

She had joined some tribes for a time, with the Echthroi nearby, so she could surveil them from a safe distance without alerting them. She had to pick her battles, though; sometimes she just had to watch their agenda of arbitrary torment play out. The magnitude and scope of their plans had evolved to a point where they seemed to enjoy influencing humans so that they made *each other* suffer. Artemis had observed the Echthroi deriving infinitely more satisfaction from this than causing direct harm. The silver lining, though, was that as these plans became more intricate and elaborate, there was much more scope to creatively intervene. Humanity was not living for as long as they should, and there seemed to be a much higher incidence of mental illness and criminality.

They seemed to have more of a proclivity for it, even without the intervention of the Echthroi. There were also significant and subtle changes in how they looked. They looked less friendly, were shorter, and had all manner of deformities. Quality had declined, and it wrenched the heart of Artemis of Carpathia to observe the decline of a once-great race of beings. Even worse, those from the enclaves were gone forever, and any stories of them had changed over time, becoming meaningless. They, along with the suffering they had endured at human hands, had been forgotten forever. But Artemis had resolved to make sure that their memories would be properly honoured when the time was right. She was writing *everything* down, even rewriting it all many times in the predominant language of a given time.

Inevitably, though, after roughly another millennium, she had started to lose her mind again, giving up on her writings and losing what she had already written. The suffering that humans inflicted on one another under the influence of the Echthroi was only getting worse, and any evil plan successfully thwarted by Artemis was as a drop in an ocean of evil. Her despair only worsened as the aeons passed her by. Eventually, she was always left with no choice but to return to one of her many secure, underground chambers, carved out of the earth all around the globe. A globe which she had circumnavigated many times as she strove to be a thorn in the side of the Echthroi, who were now aware of her existence. But they still did not know who she was or what she could do. She really had no way to qualify how good of a job she had been doing, but she hoped she had prevented a lot of misery and suffering.

The other reason for joining tribes was that Artemis still retained her human identity, and she wanted to contribute in a positive way to humanity, even if on a small tribal scale. She also wanted to enjoy human interaction, even if it was at arm's length. She always left a tribe before they got suspicious of her lack of ageing. Artemis was ageing if she looked closely at herself, but very slowly. Generally, she had fulfilled the role of the shaman or the mystic, and she used her advanced knowledge and abilities to help them rediscover lost knowledge, even knowledge so basic as how to build and maintain a fire. She would help them help themselves, as when she had once led a tribe to salt flats and taught them how to cure meat. Sometimes though, she just helped without needing to impart knowledge.

As different tribes traded and communicated, she had become the stuff of legend, almost deified. Stories of her were widely told to adults and children alike as the fire blazed at night. These stories predictably became distorted and embellished with time. They had named her many times, names such as Baal, Kadji, Rishi, Yaskomo, and many others. Even before her first long rest, she had wanted to die. She had simply had enough. She would only commit the final act and end her own life if evil had overwhelmed the world to the point of absolute hopelessness, or if the Echthroi were defeated. After many millennia, she still could not figure out how this could ever be achieved. But there was a way. There had to be.

Humans might still destroy themselves without any outside influence. But it could never be fully understood, the indirect negative effect of the Echthroi on the collective consciousness of humanity. The more the Echthroi influenced humans to hurt each other, the less they had to. A lot of evil practices became intrinsic to the collective psyche and culture of many tribes. A good example was the human sacrifice practices of the Aztec civilisation. The Echthroi all varied in their abilities, and there was no way to know the extent of their role in corrupting people, if any. Artemis could not be everywhere at once. The deck was stacked against her.

Again and again, just as she became consumed by her own hopelessness, in an instant she would wake again. And so the cycle continued for Artemis. The plans and actions of the Echthroi evolved, as did her attempts to sabotage such plans. In ancient Rome, Greece, Egypt, Mesopotamia and many others, humanity tried to stand again. A huge obstacle, as always, was human nature. They had much more of an inclination for self-destruction than their ancient counterparts, whether it be because of the influence of the Echthroi or the profound narrowing of their gene pool. Artemis suspected both.

Sometimes, the Echthroi felt the need to poke and prod in order to compromise humanity's attempts at reconciling their differences because this was not entertainment for the Echthroi. Eventually, a new irrational belief, originating in modern-day Judea, began to slowly and insidiously spread like metastatic cancer throughout the world. Previous forms of this madness had been kept to local areas and did not spread. Humans became convinced that a deity had sent its half-human, half-divine offspring to save humanity, by virtue of passively allowing other humans to kill this offspring, who forgave mankind. This deity saw fit to blame all mankind for killing its offspring so that all humans had to accept forgiveness for something they had had no part in.

And so, as the great civilisations rose and fell, Artemis of Carpathia alternately waged a single-person, partisan war against the Echthroi and rested. She awoke in the Dark Ages, when humanity was inflicting endless murder and torment on themselves due to the aforementioned belief. Some inflicted the suffering because they thought they were doing good; sometimes the belief was a convenient measure for some humans to have power over others. And these people liked the torture. She did not have much of a part to play in this terrible time. Despite her best efforts to educate and enlighten people in order to counter this backward belief, it was too strong and too widespread for knowledge and reason to prevail. She eventually gave up and decided to rest again.

Artemis awoke in her original chambers in the Carpathian Mountains in 1932 AD, and something awful was brewing. Something worse than anything that had come before it. Whilst resting, the Echthroi had invaded the hearts and minds of men more than ever, refining their skills. Ultimately, this caused an utterly pointless and brutal global conflict, probably because the Echthroi were not happy about how prosperous and civilised humanity was becoming. This war ended without quenching the hatred inside men, hatred and malice that were entirely artificial and without justification. This antipathy was instead amplified and harnessed by the constant interference of the Echthroi, who were more influential than ever.

A disastrous economic collapse in the economic centre of the world had inevitably spread to all other nations, especially the nation most humiliated by defeat in the preceding global conflict. The population of the nation instrumental in causing the conflict was recovering steadily but now endured sickening hardship. Artemis knew the Echthroi were heavily influencing this current state of affairs and had been playing this new game for decades, but she had awoken too late to effectively undermine their objectives. She could not stop this; all she could do was observe. Around 1939, the Echthroi withdrew their influence to allow things to play out. And play out they did.

Try as she might, she could not influence the bitter leader of this unstoppable, evil nation and was helpless to stop the atrocities they committed in the name of misguided superiority and victimhood. She decided the only way to do so was in such a way as to align with the leader's own inclinations. Hitler did not want to invade the USSR before securing North Africa, the Middle East and Great Britain. He did want to after all those objectives were achieved. The power of psychic influence had been bestowed upon Artemis many millennia before, but using it effectively had never been so important. She needed to use it creatively.

Dr Gilbert Morrell had taken the Hippocratic oath, as did any other physician, but his morality was already compromised by serving directly under one of the worst humans to ever exist. Artemis needed to find a way to compromise the fortress of Hitler's mind, but try as she might, she could not breach it. She was, however, easily able to breach the irresolute mind of Dr Morrell. And so, with Dr Morrell's daily 'vitamin' injections, the fortress of Hitler's mind was corroded and compromised to the point where Artemis was eventually able to breach the psychic defences. Artemis redirected and manipulated Hitler's thought patterns to convince him of many things. One of these false beliefs was that the German army was unstoppable.

She also convinced him that his army was strong enough to fight on three fronts, that its soldiers did not need winter clothing, and that the best time to invade

Russia was high summer and not early spring. She used his own hubris and thin skin to persuade him to try and conquer Stalingrad without securing Moscow, just because of its name and the symbolism of a victory there. Once the German armies were at Stalingrad, Artemis convinced Hitler to allow the Romanians to protect the flanks of the German army.

Her greatest achievement was to make this snake of a human being never allow his army to retreat, even if it was tactically the most pragmatic option. When hundreds of thousands of German soldiers were captured, the slow and painful death of the evil army began in earnest. She knew that this influence would cause millions of deaths, but it was the only way.

She had known about the Manhattan Project for a while and decided upon meeting Oppenheimer in secret to pass on ancient knowledge to him. In these meetings, Oppenheimer was visibly disturbed by the appearance of Artemis and her voice. She was obviously a woman, but with a deep, gravelly voice and a deathly grey pallor. She always had sunglasses on. As the millennia passed, her eyes had received increasingly negative reactions from other human beings. She decided to permanently keep the sunglasses on when her eyes devastatingly drove a beautiful young woman, who was prone to mental illness, to suicide. Before her demise, she described them as 'bottomless pits'.

Humans could not look into the eyes of a consciousness that ancient; it was completely alien to them. This was counteractive to her benign intentions. So the mirrored sunglasses stayed. She refused to answer Oppenheimer's questions, such as where she got the knowledge or where she came from. When she had decided he had enough information, she disappeared. Oppenheimer derived his own conclusions from their meetings, which were not entirely inaccurate and influenced by his vast knowledge of the Hindu religion, Sanskrit and historic texts.

A student asked him if the first nuclear explosion at Alamogordo was the first ever detonated, and he simply stated, "Yes, in modern times."

Her decision to help Oppenheimer was twofold. Her ancient wisdom led her to conclude that eventually, he would figure it out for himself anyway, but not in time to prevent a US invasion of mainland Japan, and she could not allow this to happen. The other reason led her to ensure that the USSR obtained the knowledge to build nuclear weapons, otherwise the wars would just keep repeating themselves. Humans themselves coined the term 'mutually assured destruction'. This had been her intention, and it had worked.

Until it didn't. The ancient technology which had ruined her home had ruined this world on rumour alone. Now she had to be smart and subvert Moloch in his pursuit of the ragtag group of survivors. There was only one hope of undoing the radioactive corruption of nature and the environment, which man would not recover from by themselves. And she would protect the people pursuing this hope. Then she could finally die, one way or another.

Chapter Twenty-Six

The getaway

Six months after the nuclear exchange

Mervyn was enjoying himself. The gang had named and masculinised the pursuing demon. It gave them comfort referring to it as 'him' and giving him a goofy name. This took the edge off the sense of dread, foreboding and ruin they all felt as they continued on the road. He had dug his psychic claws into all of them, especially Maksim and Jane: Maksim due to circumstance and Jane due to her ability. He wanted her to lose her focus, isolate herself from the others, and lose her sense of self-preservation. Jane could feel it slipping by the day.

It was a struggle to maintain a sense of reality and pragmatism. At one point, she was on her last strip of her antidepressants, citalopram 40 mg. This was a distraction she did not need. She was terrified that she would run out and go into withdrawal. And if this happened, her mind would be defenceless. The need to find some dominated her thoughts and dreams for a time. She had raided a few homes and pharmacies with marginal success, but it was never enough to give her the peace of mind that she needed. This, on top of hearing constant, indecipherable whispering, severely compromised her mental health and her psychic link, the link that she needed to maintain with an individual in a group they needed to find. Everything hinged on that.

She heard this positive psychic link one day simply say, "Fluoxetine 40, paroxetine 30, sertraline 100, all the same ..." Upon receiving that message, she realised that without citalopram, she could use the other drugs in the same class, at the equivalent dosages. Most houses they raided contained at least one of those drugs, and eventually, she built up quite the collection, giving her the peace of mind she needed, making her stronger. It was a victory over Mervyn. This experience had further reinforced the notion that her group needed to join the other group. They knew she and her group were trying to find them.

Mervyn was possibly the reason they were not already in contact with the person or persons on the other side of the psychic link, with Mervyn seemingly trying to veer the group away. This was the reason they knew they must establish contact with this individual and their group. They knew they had to go when the whispering got louder or it started up in the minds of the other members of the group. It was different with Maksim, though, and Jane was thankful for small mercies.

Maksim was angry and despairing and quite mentally ill. He had his moments, but they all decided eventually that he would only attack them with Russian words, and profusely apologise later on (they assumed based on his demeanour).

They had come upon him within an hour of leaving Mervyn a mess in the grounds of the university. Maksim was sitting on the guardrail at the side of the dual carriageway, swigging from a half-empty bottle of vodka and screaming in Russian at an abandoned APC, Russian on close inspection. It was obvious the APC had taken a hit from the nuclear shockwave, and it had been thrown around, with superficial damage and one wheel over the guardrail. It had stayed intact, though, and ultimately landed wheels down.

Maksim simply stopped and started crying when they

approached him. He was a Russian soldier after all. He did not want to be here, but he knew the British people were baying for Russian blood. After a minute or so, he looked up and realised the people in the Humvee were not going to kill him. He simply pointed at the Humvee and said, "Smotret." He put his head down again, took a drink, pointed more aggressively this time and shouted, "Smotret! Smotret! SMOTRET!!!"

And so, they drove round and looked inside the APC. Inside was a partially skinned man. His front section was skinned, and the flaps had been used to hang him in a starfish pose. The skin had been fed through jagged tears in the floor and roof of the vehicle. This was not a corpse, which they determined from the keening and weak head movements. His intestines were spilled onto the floor. Then they saw the fox. It looked nonchalantly at them before continuing to gnaw at the man's exposed leg muscles, swollen and infected. There were mangled bodies behind the man, all dead.

"GREBANYY NASIL'NIK!!!" Maksim shouted. He took a mouthful of 20% proof vodka and sprayed the hanging man's exposed flesh. It tensed up, and the keening increased. "GREBANYY NASIL'NIK!!! GREBANYY NASIL'NIK!!! GREBANYY NASIL'NIK!!! UBLYUDOK BLYA PIZDA!!!"

Before anyone could ask the burning question, Jane suddenly felt like a bullet had gone through her head, and the others just looked at each other as the whispering started.

The Russian soldier instantly froze, dropped the bottle, and put his hands to his head. He turned and tried the handle of the back door on the driver's side, screaming Russian gibberish, with a fearful look beyond what anyone thought could creep across a human being's face.

As Jane recovered from the intense whispering, she just said, "Let him in." Not with authority, but the rest knew that her intuition could be trusted.

It wasn't until a few months later that they came to learn what had happened in the APC, as they could barely communicate with Maksim.

He knew more English than they did Russian, and it was excruciating. Now they all knew what was in store for them. Possibly worse now that revenge was the motivating factor and not just plain old fun. Maksim did not hear whispering, but instead he heard mocking laughter turning to mocking speech as Mervyn got closer, always about Maksim being a virgin. When he was calm, they were safe. When he got restless, they knew it was time to go. Now life for Jane was all about lowering the whispering volume and strengthening the positive psychic link. She needed to get to these people.

The nuclear landscape, worse than anyone could have imagined before the exchange, was getting everyone down, to put it mildly. Russia had deliberately ground-burst all of their offensive nuclear detonations to maximise fallout, a particularly malicious and vindictive action on Putin's part. They were all contemplating the question of why there was any point in fighting to keep their hearts beating. Somehow, though, everyone still engaged their instinct for survival. Jane's guidance and that psychic link were the only realistic hope, even if it was precarious.

Fantasising about what they wanted to do with Putin helped them sleep at night. Tonight they slept inside the Humvee. Always uncomfortable, always miserable, but they had accumulated many different medications to knock themselves out at night. Even then, finding a safe place was always a challenge. They had lucked out that night, finding an enclosed layby on a slightly elevated road near Elkesley. A woodland was to the north and farmland to the south. From the viewpoint on the other side of the road from the layby, on a clear day there were excellent visuals for at least three miles.

Everyone took their tablets except Doug, whose turn it was to stand guard, inconspicuously, at least 50 yards from the car. Doug had already necked a Monster energy drink and lit up the first of his nightly two-Marlboro Light ration. Something caught his eye as he was relishing his first drag. About a mile away on pastoral farmland, a succession of fires were being lit, six in total. He could make out the silhouettes of people moving around. Some of these people had tiki torches and headlamps. He looked through his night-vision binoculars and made the appropriate adjustments to account for the interference of the fires and torchlight.

There they were. Two conscious but badly beaten men, shirtless and bare chested. Their wrists were restrained behind them, and they sat on sturdy-looking garden furniture chairs. Their ankles were also restrained with, most likely, duct tape. Doug recognised instantly the RUSPAT camouflage trousers and Kirza boots of the modern Russian infantry. Oh, what a frickin' surprise, Doug thought sarcastically to himself. He wondered if there had been even so much as a half-assed effort on Russia's part to get at least some of their armed forces to safety before they sent their bombs to detonate over British soil.

Doug knew instinctively that this was still only a very partial nuclear exchange under the doctrine that you can't have your cake and eat it. Everyone had plenty of cake left. Otherwise, he would not be there savouring the last few drags of this Marlboro Light. Instead, humanity was left with a completely ruined societal infrastructure and catastrophic environmental damage. But far from wiped out.

It was obvious that there was very limited photosynthesis occurring, if any. The sun's rays barely penetrated the thick blanket of aerosolized radioactive waste hanging in the atmosphere, and it looked like it was there to stay for a long time. The survivors of this utterly heartbreaking and pointless ruinous carnage were normal people. Their lives and futures were completely destroyed as their friends, family and all of life's pleasures were taken from them in an instant. People who had worked hard to build careers and bring up families, all for nothing.

None of the survivors were in any doubt who to blame for all this: any bloody Russian they could get their hands on. The two very skinny soldiers were seemingly drifting in and out of consciousness as the attendees seemed to be having a disagreement amongst themselves – lots of silent shouting in each other's faces and even a few pushes. Someone walked casually over to one of the tormented soldiers, took something out of their pocket, unsheathed it and slammed it down on the right leg of one of the soldiers. The soldier gave a full body jolt and a sharp intake of breath. Maybe an EpiPen?

Someone broke from the crowd and aggressively approached the man who had administered the EpiPen. He was followed closely by a slightly built feminine form holding what looked like a machete, which looked almost as big as her. She lifted it above her head and swung it in a downward arc. The machete buried itself in the shoulder of the man, who fell to his knees and slumped forwards. The woman stood there for a second, and then with a boot to the man's back, tried to pull out the machete. This she tried for only a few seconds before someone emerged from the crowd to slit her throat, and that was when all hell broke loose as the crowd fought each other with hands, feet and any sharp or blunt item they had at their disposal. Doug lost track.

The EpiPen administrator was seemingly forgotten by the rest of the congregation and confidently pulled out a wide, short, curved blade. Doug knew this type of knife instantly, and he realised that this man had no hate for the Russian soldier but was having the time of his life. The way things were now, no police would come and arrest him. The man started skinning the soldier. As quietly as he could, Doug opened the boot to retrieve his MK13 Mod 5 sniper rifle. What he failed to notice was the man who stood clear of the fray.

This old man's head was covered in bandages, completely covering one eye. The small amount of skin that could be seen around the uncovered eye bore evidence of extreme trauma. The old man had seen the vague green glow of Doug's night-vision goggles and the intermittent blaze as Doug took long drags from his cigarette. Doug promptly set up the sniper rifle and shot both Russian soldiers in the head in quick succession. The man who had started to flay the torso seemed to look back through the scope at Doug with a raw, antipathetic rage Doug had not seen on a human face before. Doug hesitated and froze for a second. He snapped his head round to look at the man with the bandaged head.

The old man had started running, and the flayer quickly followed. Doug just whisper-shouted *SHIT!!!* as he realised he had missed an opportunity to kill a man who liked to skin people alive. All because of the way the flayer had looked at him, despite the fact that the flayer could not have seen Doug in the darkness. He hoped he would not regret this later, but he already did. After doing what he needed to do, he was flooring the Humvee with the headlights off, using his night-vision goggles to navigate.

"What are you doing?" Steve asked groggily while the rest slowly started to wake.

"I'm getting us the hell out of here," Doug replied calmly.

"But why?" Ginny asked. "None of us heard anything."

"Why? Because I like having skin. Do you?" he asked Ginny.

She did not answer as they all slowly became aware of headlights in the darkness behind them, around two miles away. The convoy of vehicles started moving quickly, and some even seemed to have searchlights as well.

"Looks like about twenty vehicles," Adam said. His voice sounded uncharacteristically disorientated because of the sleeping pill he was not getting the chance to sleep off. The autocade was rapidly approaching the layby where they had all been sleeping soundly thirty seconds ago.

Doug was glad they did not appear to have been spotted in their escape. Otherwise, the vehicles would not be coming to a stop in the layby.

"Claymore and tripwire?" Adam asked.

No response from Doug, but Adam knew Doug was smiling, even though he could not see it in this darkness. In an instant, the layby became a huge fireball, with secondary explosions of vehicles in the convoy following closely behind.

The inside of the vehicle became illuminated, and Doug held up three fingers. "Close. Three claymores."

Now Adam could see Doug smiling.

"I hope I got the flayer, and the old biker-looking dude with his head covered in bandages."

Steve's heart stopped as he repeated, "Old biker-looking dude with bandages ...?"

Steve, Jane and Ginny looked at each other.

"Should have killed him, kiddo," Ginny said with affection. "But we are, well, *relatively* safe for now."

Nobody noticed Maksim was still asleep until he snored loudly, startling them all.

"Well, he's probably not slept properly in months, plus the vodka, and I think he took a pill too." Jane suddenly frowned. "What the hell is a claymore?" she asked.

"Right now, they are our best friends," Doug replied. An open stretch of road unveiled itself and Doug floored it, still keeping the headlights off.

Chapter Twenty-Seven

Hussoff Khuntz

Office of Professor Hussoff Khuntz, Linus Pauling Building, Faculty of Engineering Building, University of Hull. Two weeks after the getaway.

"Sulphur-oxidising chemoautotrophic bacteria," Professor Khuntz said, looking at Adam. He made a disgusted face.

Adam was about to kick off when Steve said, "This is why the air smells so bad, isn't it?"

"Yes, the ground burst nuclear explosions irradiated the soil, but the hydrogen sulphide gas released made the entire world smell like a tramp's fart. They could have airburst every single nuclear weapon they have, both fission and fusion, and destroyed the entire country, or world. Even the range of each detonation would be extended. They ground burst only a fraction of their stockpile, so a lot of shit-hole cities like Hull are still standing. But the irradiated earth, as well as releasing poisonous compounds trapped within, has stopped all photosynthesis and other important natural cycles. Carbon dioxide concentration is increasing fast. Have you all noticed you always seem to be a little out of breath?"

The sample from the mass found on Doug's boot from the day that he had pulverised Mervyn had been analysed by the multidisciplinary homophobe and genius, Professor Hussoff Khuntz, second only to Professor Cawl. The Linus Pauling Building was where Khuntz had elected to make his home, based on an educated guess that a significant nuclear exchange was inevitable, and Hull was such a shit-hole that Putin was unlikely to waste a nuclear weapon on it. He was right. Hull did not escape the fallout, though, as evidenced by a generally ill-looking professor, with swollen hands and patches of hair missing. Doug and the rest had either been in hazmat suits or else below ground for a few days.

The Linus Pauling Building was well stocked with food and had a bathroom but was without a shower, which explained the body odour coming off the professor. None of them smelt good, though. Doug noticed something; the professor's teeth looked normal while the rest of them were experiencing serious dental issues. Doug could feel an abscess forming near his wisdom teeth.

"But the thing we set on fire at the university, why did that smell similar but so much worse?" Doug asked. He did not get an answer. He knew the professor would be getting to that anyway.

"The carbon cycle …" The professor began to say, but he paused as he caught a look between Steve and Adam. "Hmph," the professor said.

Again, Adam looked ready for confrontation. Doug patted Adam's leg and nodded at Khuntz to continue.

"Anyway, the carbon cycle is possibly permanently corrupted. All sorts of changes to the environment have been forced upon it, altering the fundamental life cycles of many different processes and species. To elucidate all of the changes which have occurred with the environment would be impossible."

"Do you know *anything*?" Adam asked incredulously.

"I AM GETTING TO THAT!" Khuntz spat out the words.

"I'm sorry, Professor," Steve said. "We will not interrupt again."

"I certainly hope not." He shot another look at Adam.

"The one thing we humans need is oxygen. It's produced by a nice, clean metabolic pathway called photosynthesis. I haven't seen a glimpse of sunlight since the fallout clouds rolled in. Without sunlight, photosynthesis cannot occur. This means no food for life at the bottom of the food chain, but more importantly, no food for us and decreasing oxygen levels. Any questions?"

"The bacteria genus you opened with," Ginny said before taking a breath and continuing. "I'm not a microbiologist, but aren't they found on tubeworms in hydrothermal vents? Aren't they extremophiles?"

Khuntz gave Ginny a warm smile and looked at Adam in disgust *again*. Adam then decided to pinch between his eyes and look down.

"That is a great question, Jenny."

"Ginny."

"Forgive me, Ginny. I was about to come to that. See, you're right. Why these extremophiles have appeared outside their natural environment and are now here on the surface, I can only put down to radiation and the abundance of hydrogen sulphide gas. And generally, how extreme our own environment is becoming. But that is what I've found …"

"Why would they be growing on Mervyn?" asked Doug, looking horrified.

Khuntz ignored the fact that he had been interrupted, not wanting to piss off Doug. "It is not growing on Mervyn. It *is* Mervyn."

"Are we talking about sentient extremophiles now?" Adam asked without looking.

"I'm afraid you haven't heard the worst part yet."

Nobody said anything.

"Mervyn is also part human, and something else entirely, based on his genetic makeup. He has a quadruple helix with significantly mutated human DNA, extremophile DNA and undetermined base pairs, all linked. I would postulate that the unknown base pairs are there to bind with the mutated human double helix as a link to allow the extremophile DNA to bind. There appears to be a special vulnerability to radiation damage, but this is equally, if not more so, offset by the stunningly effective repair mechanisms. In my opinion, the most disturbing part of all, I have left to last; the telomeres are self-replenishing. This being is *immortal*. A cell will age slowly and will eventually divide, but only to replace the original cell. And with self-replenishment of telomeres, Mervyn will live indefinitely."

"The evil emanating from that thing was ancient," Jane said, not taking her gaze off the floor.

"Are we talking about demons here? Steve asked nobody in particular.

"To all intents and purposes, yes." Doug said. "Look at all those disturbing depictions from the Middle Ages, stories passed down through history. It all slots into place; it makes sense."

This caused everyone to pause for a moment.

"But what about the skinned-alive Russian in the APC? The unhinged man on the road with the lesions like Mervyn?" Ginny asked, referring to the madman with ridiculous strength who had come at them as they slowed down to take a look at him. He was stumbling around, cutting his limbs with a sharp stone, with obviously infected lesions covering his face and bare limbs.

As they had sped away, he had grabbed the tow hitch and been dragged for a mile before letting go. Then they observed him getting up. The infections did not seem normal; in fact, it looked like the lesions were part of some sort of accelerated healing mechanism. But the healing had gone wrong. The lesions had looked like

Mervyn's skin. There were others wandering and staggering around with these lesions on other parts of their body, but the road to Hull had been mostly deserted. No one wanted to go there, just like before all this.

"I don't know about them. But it would seem that these people are becoming like Mervyn. What I do know about these extremophiles is that they cannot use photosynthesis to produce food. There is no sunlight at the bottom of the ocean. So they have to use …?" The professor motioned to Ginny.

"Um … chemosynthesis?"

"And what does chemosynthesis use?"

"Hydrogen sulphide gas."

"And what do these particular species not need?"

"Oxygen."

"And what does chemosynthesis produce?"

"Sulphur. Did you do this using PCR?"

"Yes, but I am unable to specifically identify the unknown base pairs, either human or bacterial. It'ss like the human and extremophile symbiosis established itself in a different dimension, similar but not identical. I could only tell they were there through the absence of specific base-pair sequences throughout the entire genome, especially in the blank slate that is junk DNA. In coding DNA, something needs to be there in place of the absent base-pair sequences for any organism to function."

"Sulphur, also known as brimstone …" Jane said, ignoring the last part, as she did not really understand. "You're right, Doug, it was a demon. We are talking about a goddamn bastard demon called Mervyn."

Khuntz concluded with his own narrative. "The human gets to live, with the main energy source being produced from the air. But the human pays a price and changes, becoming deformed and inhuman through this novel parasitic infection. For those affected, the buildup of CO_2 in the atmosphere will only be beneficial, as this is one of the substrates of this anaerobic chemosynthesis. For those unaffected, CO_2 even getting to one per cent is toxic.

"As oxygen levels reduce, the fact is, the human part of these mutants will still need to use cellular respiration, so the reduction of oxygen levels will not be beneficial to them. But they will last for a very long time after the unaffected die out. A reduction of O_2 levels by itself is not necessarily detrimental as long as it is not sudden and there is time to adjust, alongside having the ability to use the chemosynthetic pathway to produce energy. I cannot decide if this is a symbiotic or parasitic relationship. I can't see an improvement in quality of life, but I see the continuation of life, at an inequitable cost."

"Is this why it is vulnerable to seventy percent ethanol?"

"Yes, you were lucky in that you found its weakness."

"So," Adam said, "demons walk the earth and have brought hell with them?"

"The other way around. This self-imposed hell has tainted life as we have always known it," Khuntz confirmed.

Steve walked up behind Adam and put his arms around him. "I wonder if it were the likes of us that caused this?" Steve whispered softly in Adams ear, but loud enough for everyone else to hear.

"I find you disgusting, but only in the secular sense," said Khuntz. He smiled at them both.

At that, Adam and Steve laughed, as did the rest, awkwardly. This one-liner by the old homophobe seemed to break the tension between them.

"Are you coming with us?" Jane asked.

At that, Maksim lit a cigarette and started muttering in

Russian, *"On smeyetsya nado mnoy! Pochemu on ne perestayet nado mnoy smeyat'sya?"*

"Who is laughing at him?" Khuntz asked.

"You can speak Russian? Then you must come with us! We cannot communicate with this guy!!" Jane said.

"No. This thing that is following you, I would rather be alone than be pursued by that thing! You must go before it finds you."

They were all starting to hear the whispers, zapping their souls of energy, urging them to give in to the inevitable.

"That's the thing," Doug said. "It's not tracking our location at any one time. Mervyn is simply following our path like a sniffer dog, moving to intercept us at times, to send us round in circles for his own amusement. If you stay here, Mervyn will be paying you a visit whether we leave or not. Besides, Cawl said we needed you and we needed to take you to the facility inside Cruachan Dam."

Khuntz thought for a minute.

"Look!" Adam said. "If me and Steve want to be gay, we will do it out of sight and earshot of you."

Khuntz looked almost disappointed at hearing this. Adam and Steve looked at each other, mouths agape with joyous surprise.

"Or …" Steve stated before he got cut off.

"Are you coming with us or not?" Ginny said. "We're your only hope, and you will die if you stay here. Not only that, but Mervyn will torture you in unimaginable ways, arbitrarily and without mercy, for shits and giggles."

"I'll come." He grabbed his pipe and glasses from the table and simply said, "Ready."

Doug ran his tongue across his furred, yellowing teeth, which were now really hurting. "But first, we all need to use your toothbrush." he said.

Chapter Twenty-Eight

Archer, Clarette and Charlotte

One year after the exchange

Archer still walked with a limp, but he was getting better. Clearly, his DNA was able to withstand the harm being caused by radiation. At least in the short term. In the long term, he hoped the radiation would kill him with cancer before the PTSD and all-consuming guilt forced him to commit suicide. Archer knew Archer, and Archer knew his mental limits.

Archer and Charlotte were now in a relationship of sorts. This was a relationship borne of necessity and survival. They shared pleasure, warmth and companionship because this was what got them through one day to face the next. The sex was inevitable but got boring after a while. They made sure they practised safe sex, though, as a baby right now would be, at best, inconvenient. The only reason they were alone was because Clarette had simply become something they followed, something unrecognisable to them.

Going the way Clarette wanted them to go seemed as good a direction as any, and it never seemed to lead them to danger. At the beginning, Archer had argued that he wanted to go in the opposite direction of wherever Clarette was leading them, but he gave in and they went with Clarette, only to hear a man cackling and another man begging in the direction they would have gone. That man cackling was something Archer hated, as it was never genuine and hinted at a malevolence below the surface, only kept in check by civilised society. Now it was always accompanied by bestial cruelty.

So, they went with Clarette. Clarette had been burned and blinded during the second exchange, and at times, they had thought in that musty cellar that she would go at any time. She was incoherent, and the best Charlotte could do was give her IV fluids and antibiotics. Her burns did heal, but they left behind horrific, unnatural scar tissue covering her entire body. Archer and Charlotte huddled together for body heat under the only blanket they could find, with Clarette being invited to also share the body heat.

She refused, only crouching naked at the other side of the cellar, just looking at them with sightless eyes. Her body was humanoid but no longer seemed male or female, just a mass of scar tissue. When they ran out of the little food Charlotte had brought down, Clarette went and got more, scrambling out of the cellar and returning soon after with a collection of tinned goods, bottled water and a tin opener scattered by the blast.

After a month or so, Clarette sat crouched at the bottom of the stairs, looking up and back at them. At this point, Archer was hobbling around the cellar on a crutch and was in the final stages of healing. Clarette wanted them to go up into the world, indicating that it was relatively safe. And so, they packed up their stuff and went up to where the house used to be. It was daytime, and the hell that Archer always suspected was just under the surface, even in the most beautiful of places, had come to the surface.

What used to be the Russian paratrooper was melted like plastic into the irradiated foundations of the house.

The smell. Archer tried to explain the smell to himself more than anyone. "It's like someone took a shit in a damp, airtight room with a hundred per cent humidity during a tropical heatwave, sprinkled with a thousand cigarette butts."

"But it's cold. Really frickin' cold," Charlotte replied. She appeared to be dipping various bits of torn fabric into a tube of Vicks VapoRub and stuffing as much as possible into her nostrils. Then she put on a COVID mask.

She handed Archer another mask, the tub and more fabric strips.

"We need to find a couple of gas masks, or else we get used to this," Archer said as he looked at the tormented sky, full of colour schemes which looked dark and threatening. It was like waking up in hell.

"Unbelievably horrible. Look, Archer. I know what you're thinking. Can you just do one thing for me?" Charlotte asked.

"What?"

"Not today, okay?" she asked.

"Okay."

And so, Archer put off checking out until the next day. Every day on waking, she asked the same thing of him, and he promised to wait until the next day.

Six months into their emergence from underground, and after six months of kept promises, they had found a couple of half masks and a box of filters from the remains of a Russian military encampment. It muffled the smell completely, but they still applied vapour rub sparingly to their nostrils. From people they met on the road, they had been told harrowing stories of the fate inflicted by the local populace on any Russian troops still remaining. Understandable, really.

The Russian soldiers, even before the partial exchange, were raping and tormenting the very same local populace who were now out for blood. Russia most likely had not survived this exchange, and among the reasons discussed as to why it was only a partial exchange, was the theory that deep-cover Western intelligence operatives had sabotaged the majority of Russian launches, causing some to even detonate in their silos. Archer did not feel grateful for this. Only more rage. Unfortunately, all communication and flow of data had been set back a thousand years.

In a lot of ways, this withdrawal from instant access to all the information anyone could want was the worst aspect of this new life; put simply, nobody knew what the hell was going on. They were both able to take their cues from Clarette. One look from her meant stop. Another meant get down. Another meant to keep quiet. Sometimes it was all of these. She was communicating with them through her ruined eyes in ways they did not even understand.

As always, they travelled parallel with the road when they could. Clarette sensed something they could not. When Clarette froze, they did. She gave them a look and ran towards the flat undergrowth. Archer had not eaten in four days and had had no water for an entire day. Moving at any speed was done with enormous difficulty. One silver lining of this new world was the lack of flying and biting insects, at only around 5% of what it was before. So, lying prone in the undergrowth did not involve getting tormented by these flying menaces like it had before. It did, however, indicate that the world was slowly dying. Each had a pair of binoculars taken from the same place as the gas masks.

Through these, they saw something unbelievable: Russian soldiers in ruined uniforms, restrained by ropes around their waists and linked together. An old man with a ruined face and with the same scar tissue as Clarette was screaming at them and whipping them. Some also had their wrists restrained. It was not possible to restrain all of them this way, as some were missing hands, entire forearms, entire arms. Even the wrist-restrained soldiers were missing fingers. Archer did not feel sorry for them at all. But he was afraid of the captors, who were probably too far gone mentally, and torturing and dismembering Russian soldiers was just-low hanging fruit.

Walking close to the maimed Russians was a man who looked like Jared Kushner. He had an unsheathed knife in his right hand and was slowly running his left thumb and forefinger up and down the blade. Despite the fact that he was walking through a dirty, desolate wasteland, he was wearing cream chinos and brown dress shoes, as well as a dad sweater with a white collar poking up at the neck. All his clothes were disgusting, and he was not even wearing a backpack. He seemed to exist solely for the opportunity to use that terrifying knife. His eyes were dead, with a grin that seemed to come and go.

"You see him?" Archer asked.

"Yes," Charlotte whispered.

"He needs to die," Archer said.

"I know," Charlotte replied.

Clarette stealthily tried to move closer to get a better look. Suddenly, she stood on something which activated a tree net, trapping her, and in a split second she was netted and suspended. The screech she emitted made the old man with the ruined face stop and look. Archer felt something poke him in the back.

"*Do not move!*" a man whispered with rage.

The whisper told Archer that the man was not part of

the minor army of slavers. The gun stayed pressed into his back as a few armed men approached the netted Clarette.

When they got to her, they laughed and poked her with the muzzles of their rifles. She hissed and growled at them, squirming with rage in the net. The Jared Kushner lookalike looked up at the net, slowly ran the knife over it, and then made a small cut in Clarette's side, eliciting a gasp, not of pain but of surprise. He ran his tongue along the knife, expression unchanged. Both Archer and Charlotte noticed the soldiers gave the knife man a wide berth, refusing to even look at him.

The old man with the ruined face started to approach as the men were tormenting Clarette. "Weeeee caaamp heeere!" the old man slowly rasped.

The rest of the group, as well as the Russian-soldier slaves, made their way towards him. The old man's voice hinted at damaged and badly healed vocal chords, making a bleak and disturbing sound.

"Who are they?" the stranger whispered to Archer and Charlotte.

"How the hell should I know? All I see is a small army of sick arsehole slavers led by a man whose face clearly fell off at some point," Archer replied.

"And what is that thing in the net?"

"That is my friend Clarette. She was burned and blinded by a nuclear detonation, and obviously, the radiation is messing with her genes in some way." This time, Charlotte replied.

"Okay, now slowly and quietly, get up. You're coming with me."

"No, sorry. That is my friend, however messed up she is, and she's protecting us. I can't just abandon her."

Archer slowly turned around and sat up, keeping his hands open.

The burned and mutilated man pressed the trigger to Archer's forehead, and Archer waited. "Good one, mate. You really called my bluff there. I was hoping to take what you had without having to hurt you." He put out his hand and helped Archer up.

"I understand," Archer said.

He looked past his new friend. "Charlotte, no!" he whispered loudly.

The stranger turned around to Charlotte, who socked him full force in the jaw. He was not knocked out but emitted a surprised grunt of pain. The soldiers had stopped taunting and poking Clarette and were looking in their direction. Archer's new friend broke into a run, clutching his jaw. He was fast, but as when prey turns its back on a predator, a soldier's bullet gave chase, and he was dead before he hit the ground.

Archer gave Charlotte a *what the hell are you thinking?* look. Charlotte had a look of devastated regret.

"You two!!!" shouted the man whose face had fallen off. "Get over here! And no funny stuff; you'll regret it."

Archer and Charlotte complied and approached the man. Archer was delirious; he had not slept properly since before everything had gone wrong. If he focused on one spot too long, he started to hallucinate. He was too exhausted to be afraid, and Charlotte was in a similar state of mind.

The net was cut down, and Clarette was released. She looked at all of the soldiers hungrily and then back to Archer and Charlotte, who simply shook their heads slowly to signal 'no'. At that, she bolted, fast. By the time the first bullets had left their chambers, she was well out of accuracy range. The soldiers gave each other an *oh, no* look, like they knew they would get no sleep tonight.

"What is that thing?" the old man asked.

Knife-man stood beside him, with a look of fear that satisfied Archer.

"Radiation burns and blindness, that thing is our ..."

Archer cut Charlotte off. "That THING is evil. Thank you for rescuing us!"

Charlotte understood. "We thought we were going to die!" she added, and put her hands together as a symbol of thanks.

"Is that thing going to come for us tonight?" asked one of the soldiers, voice shaky. "I can handle its appearance, its smell, but the unnatural *speed* of it!" the soldier emphasised.

"It's afraid of fire, and there are too many of us, but we need to build a big fire. If we can make it to dawn, we'll be safe," Charlotte lied.

Archer smiled inwardly at Charlotte's use of 'us', and 'we', instead of 'you'. They were manipulating them with basic psychology. All those months spent in isolation had allowed a stream of communication between them that went under most people's radar.

"Quick, we need to build a fire to ensure our safety," Archer said. He started gathering random bits of wood in a fake panic, as did Charlotte.

"Thank you so much for saving our lives," Charlotte said. "I wish we had something to give you, but we're out of food, and I'm almost out of my HIV meds. I wish I had access to hormone medication as well. I just cannot stop bleeding."

"Okay, okay," the old man said. "Too much information." He held his hand up and twirled his finger.

The disappointed soldiers started to gather wood too.

"I'm sorry, but you don't know what it's like. No man would want me now." She looked at one of the soldiers, who just returned a disgusted face.

Even the man holding the wicked-looking knife had stopped stroking it and no longer met their eyes. As far as they were all concerned, neither Archer nor Charlotte any longer appealed to their base urges.

They were safe. For now. Before long, they had a roaring fire and a surplus of wood to get them through the night. Everyone had taken their positions as close to the fire as possible, with the Russian soldiers placed in a circle around the group, like a human shield.

Archer, as he stared into the fire, simply said, "So you're eating bits and pieces of the Russian soldiers, except for the legs?"

The old man scrutinised Archer for a moment before saying, "Bingo! We need them walking. We don't have the means to carry them."

Archer just said, "Good plan."

"We're going to cook up some grub now if you like. Are you okay with this?"

"Look," Archer said, "I had a good life, with so much to look forward to. These bastards took that from me. I was one of the affected, and it's a miracle Charlotte found me when she did. I was scalped, with a snapped humerus and a one-eighty-degree turned ankle by the time I came around. Deep down, I know I did awful things, and I know it's not my fault, but I'm surviving on adrenalin. If, by some miracle, everything was reversed and normal life resumed, I would likely not recover mentally. So, yes, I will choke down every bite out of pure spite, even if I don't like the taste."

"How do you …?"

"Medium rare," Archer said.

"Same," Charlotte said, scratching herself down below with a pained expression and a quick sniff of her fingers just to complete the sexually repulsive picture in front of these would-be rapists. She was completely safe. She sensed her friend lying in wait out there in the darkness.

One of the soldiers led a one-armed Russian soldier to a tree stump. Archer could see his eyes were gouged out.

"Are they all blind?" Archer asked, hiding his disgust. This was too far. His guilt at what was coming for these people evaporated.

The old man grimaced through his melted face at Archer.

"HA HA! Good enough for them. These guys won't be raping anybody soon!" Archer mocked.

"Also, not just the eyeballs!" one soldier said.

"Spaghetti and meatballs!" another soldier added.

"Bangers and mash!" a third soldier chimed in.

They all cackled, and Archer joined them. He knew these people would be doing this to their fellow countrymen without the presence of the Russian soldiers. It became clear to Archer that the old man was the victim of an acid attack and that he probably deserved it.

"Are there any sausages left?" Archer asked, completing the fake persona and eliciting an increase in the volume and intensity of the cackling.

Knife-man simply sat by a tree, looking into the fire, twirling the knife.

Archer was proud of them both. So far, they had been getting out of this situation using their wit, ingenuity and intuition. The man placed the Russian soldier's arm on the stump and chopped it off in one go, right through the centre of the humerus. The Russian soldier only winced. Then a little bit was cut off the end of the amputated arm and put on a plate. The Russian soldier and his comrades would be given leftovers to keep them alive. Another man came over and gave the soldier an intramuscular injection in the deltoid.

"Antibiotics and opiates," the old man said. "Keeps them alive for longer, keeps them quiet. A good side effect of consuming them is ingesting the morphine we've been pumping into them. Gives us that fuzzy warm feeling, you know?"

Archer smiled, and Charlotte giggled and clapped her hands. The soldier took a burning stick from the fire and cauterised the wound. The Russian gave a keening sound and was led back to be tied up again. Archer observed a soldier bringing the plate with the small cut on it over to the knife-man. He set it beside him at arm's length, obviously terrified. Knife-man just continued to stare into the fire before turning slowly towards the raw meat on the plate. Archer decided to look away at this point, and he realised everyone had gone quiet.

A spit-roast was set up over the fire, and the smell was delicious to Archer. He was on a primal quest to satisfy his hunger, and before long, an over-salted plate of meat was given to both of them. Archer inhaled the contents of the plate and licked it clean. He looked up and said, "Let's be honest, we're all insane in the head, right?"

The cackling resumed.

"We don't feel guilty!" Charlotte shouted at the Russians. "YOU DID THIS, YOU BLOODY BASTARDS!! We would all be living our normal lives if not for you!" She was part acting and part authentic as she picked up a stone and hurled it at one of the Russian soldiers, hitting one squarely in the chest. "You can't rape now, can you? You need your dicks and all your limbs for that!"

As the cackling was reaching a crescendo, a few whoops could be heard.

"You would have been pretty safe, still, no?" Archer said, and everyone erupted in laughter.

Archer and Charlotte felt the fuzzy opiate high warming their arms and their fingers and toes. A soldier handed them both a glass of wine after they had finished their final helping, each having had four or five of them.

"Special occasion," the old man said.

The feeling of full-bodied wine going down complimented the salty meat perfectly. Archer then saw Clarette peeking out from behind a tree. Claws streaked down the tree bark as she contemplated whatever plan she had. Archer and Charlotte had expertly bought her plenty of time to figure out a plan.

Two hours later, all were asleep except the night sentry, who kept his torch shining and scanning the darkness. Archer and Charlotte could not put off sleep and passed out, stomachs full and with morphine and wine in their system. The sentry kept putting wood on the fire and did not stray far from it. Shining his torch into the night, he suddenly felt a warm liquid flowing down his chest. When he realised what it was, he tried to make a sound, but his vocal chords were gone. Clarette gently took the automatic rifle from him as his head flopped down. Then he fell to his knees and slumped forwards.

She collected four more unattended automatic rifles and as many clips of ammunition as she could find, as well as a belt of grenades, and put them in a duffel bag she had found. She gently woke up Archer and Charlotte, who tiptoed away from the camp. Charlotte gave them each an automatic rifle and a few clips. Then Clarette quietly put the duffel bag on the fire and walked away with a single grenade. She pulled out the pin and lobbed it into the fire.

"What about the Russians?" asked Charlotte.

"They can rot in hell for all I care," Archer said. He slapped one in the face as he passed. No reaction.

They both jumped on her back, and she ran on all fours at full speed.

*

Louis watched the whole betrayal play out. He did not intervene, as he carried no loyalty. All that mattered was what he could take. Any action that could be misinterpreted as loyalty was only ever taken to satisfy his dark urges. On this occasion, those dark urges were satisfied by simply watching. He enjoyed waiting until the weapons on the fire ignited, the soldiers waking up only to be consumed by flames.

He would very much enjoy being part of the revenge Jim would inflict on the betrayers. He dragged his dirty knife across his forehead and down his cheek. Then he stabbed himself in the deltoid, and in the chaos, approached the fire. He set his forearm on fire through his clothes for five seconds, just about enough to cause second-degree burns. He would take some antibiotics and opioids later. For now, plausible deniability would do. He chose to ignore the pain.

Chapter Twenty-Nine

Kronos the Titan Crawls out of Tartarus

Fifteen months after the exchange

Inside Brugat's locked-down subterranean fortress, Kronos and his new followers had tried everything possible to find a way out. But the fortress did its job, and nothing was getting out or in. And it was 150 feet to the surface. When Brugat had got the better of him, it was because he had observed Brugat's followers acting like it was any normal day and going about their business.

The followers knew who had been murdered, and then mimicked, when Kronos's transition had been observed. These followers were virtuous and fiercely loyal to Brugat, and all had taken an oath of self-sacrifice to defend Brugat, Europa and the world. They knew they were to protect and defend all three of these and were doing so without a moment's hesitation.

They all knew of the presence of the imposter and would not sacrifice the opportunity by evacuating the complex. They would give a simple, discreet tap to the elbow of a trusted colleague, followed by the simple communication of 'imposter' and who the imposter was. This had all been practised before. As a matter of priority, Brugat's closest associate was informed.

Once Kronos had shown himself, Operation Tartarus went into action, completely closing off the entire complex by simply ignoring the dead man's switch, which Brugat had given the order for with a series of codes and verification checks. Once it was locked down, they saw what had been done to Brugat's corpse. Instead of simply taking their pills, a lot of them threw themselves into the furnace.

Kronos went into a deep dream state to pass the time, but he remembered fondly the ones he and his imps had caught before they could make it to the furnace or bite down on their pills. A lot of fun was had for years, torturing these humans. Now his imps took their aggression out on one another, sometimes for the entertainment of Kronos.

When Kronos went deepest into his dream state, which sometimes lasted for centuries, he remembered another life on another world. He dreamed of a world through the eyes of a tall man: a man who had built a happy life for himself. He would lie awake watching the one he loved sleep. Happy little ones would come in and wake her up by jumping on the bed, and the tall man would feel overcome with joy as she smiled instantly upon awakening.

Kronos dreamt of the tall man with a job he loved and many friends, living in a beautiful world in which he would share breathtaking experiences in nature with the love of his life, the little ones, colleagues and friends. It felt like the bliss and happiness would never end. Until it did. The tall man was peripherally aware of global, national and international events in his home world, but he lived in a bubble, and as long as his happy life was not affected, he did not care.

Voting certainly was not important to him, and he did not care who his leader was, just as it was not important to many people with their happy lives. Elections were unimportant. But one day, the nation and world that gave him so much happiness was gone. The tall man was ripped away from his family and forced to fight in a war started by the man he and many others had failed to vote against. And when this war was lost, the atrocities visited upon the citizens of the other nations were revisited upon the tall man's family.

With everything in ruins, the man he did not vote for made the world burn. And burn it did. As did the tall man. Lying in agony amongst the ruins of his nation, he thought he would truly die. But his rage and his hatred was stronger than death. He was now happy to see the world truly burn. As the blackest of hatred overtook his mind, his body also healed, seemingly by the raw elemental force of pure hatred. This caused Kronos to take the distorted and deformed form of pure hatred, and then what inevitably followed was pure evil.

Hatred made him forget everything, burying his old happy memories deeper and deeper as the aeons passed, lest he pined for them. Now, under a red sky and a barren landscape, every being fought a war against all others, loyalty only retained through brutality visited by the big and strong against the small and weak. But the small and weak were also filled with hatred, their bodies distorted and grotesque, as hatred manifested in its infinite forms.

This went on for aeons with no change. Although few could challenge Kronos, the Witches dominated. These were trans-dimensional beings not subject to the laws of physics, and although they could not be challenged, no being in this ruined dimension wished to anyway. Reproduction ceased in all beings who survived as the blackest of hatred overcame ageing and natural death.

Reproduction was not only unnecessary, but without love, reproduction was simply not possible. Nurturing offspring was out of the question. The man Kronos did not vote against or for had become a twisted, frightful-looking giant, even to Kronos. Nothing changed until the day the circle of light appeared. Kronos and many others were engaged in battle with the man he did not vote for, caught in a nightmarish repeating reality where whoever lost almost never died, and once they had regenerated, they went into battle again. Whatever the outcome, the battle would repeat itself over aeons and millennia. And no side even remembered why.

Kronos ran towards the circle of light, as did many of the denizens of this twisted, hellish landscape. All had been forgotten in their collective urge to investigate this novel curiosity. When Kronos made it through, the man he did not vote for saw that the circle of light was too small for him. He put his arm through the circle of light and grabbed Kronos. Before he could pull him back though, the circle of light vanished, taking his arm with it. All of the beings that made it through knew whose arm this was and greedily consumed it.

Kronos was awoken from his dream state by a deep rumbling. The intensity increased slowly before trailing off, and everything suddenly shifted by around ten feet and turned by about forty-five degrees. The complex under modern-day Soomaa National Park in Estonia was the victim of a stray, malfunctioning Trident nuclear missile launched by the British during the partial nuclear exchange of early 2026.

When it impacted the marshland at Mach 3, it buried itself deep in the waterlogged, soft, boggy mud. But it did not detonate. It continued to sink, though, all fourteen warheads, at a total of nearly 3000 kilograms. It ultimately lodged itself seventeen miles from and at a depth similar to the prison where Kronos had resided for at least the last 75,000 years. The constant pressure of millions of tons of waterlogged earth slowly compressed the faulty trigger mechanism for fifteen months, until the mechanism was finally engaged. In a split second, all fourteen warheads detonated.

The kinetic energy was enough to compromise the structural integrity of the prison. Kronos watched in utter disbelief from his throne of bones as the walls of his prison groaned and started to bend inward. Many cracks started to form in quick succession, causing wet earth, clay, stones and groundwater to come rushing in. His twisted imps started screeching in celebration. The huge and cavernous chamber could hold a lot of watery earth. Suddenly, he smelt a familiar smell. He was home. Had he gone back through the portal and could not remember? No, this smell was still death and misery, but it was *fresher*.

A lot of time had passed, and he was naturally confused. Eventually, all the soil that could flow into his chamber had run out. He could see it was daytime and he was at the bottom of a very wet crater. The turbulent brown and red sky was still familiar, but again, *fresher*. He knew much pain and suffering could still be inflicted on the innocent. Deep down, though, he only wanted his own torment to end. As he stood at the bottom of the crater, he realised he had not moved in centuries. He stood at his full height of fifteen feet and stretched every limb with a series of sickening pops. He took a deep breath and let out a long, hate-filled and ancient baleful moan, a moan which carried across the land for hundreds of miles. Some of his imps had been buried alive, but he did not care. About forty of them had found their way out behind him, all of them emitting an unharmonious, malevolent chittering sound. Brugat was still their leader, or what used to be Brugat. Whatever remnants of their past lives remained compelled them to follow whatever remnants remained of Brugat.

Kronos would make more imps, and together, they would make up for a lot of lost time. When he got to the surface, he observed his own home world, but in its infancy after the final war, before which he … Kronos dropped to his knees and went into a trance. Being free from the prison would take some getting used to. He snapped out of it when he heard the unfamiliar creaking of tank tracks as they came to a stop a few hundred feet from the crater. Kronos saw dirty, exhausted-looking men with unfamiliar weapons and vehicles.

They seemed frozen in fear of Kronos and his minions crawling up from underground as they came to investigate the subterranean detonation. *"Mida kuradit sa siin teed? Kes kurat sa oled? Kui olete venelane, siis alistute või surete, kuradikesed! Teil on kümme sekundit!!!"* They sounded terrified as they shouted through the voice amplifier. Kronos was not remotely threatened by these people. They were different from Brugat's people. They were smaller … weaker. More damaged. They looked less pleasing to the eye, less intelligent. More animalistic. It would only slightly take away from his enjoyment of what was to come next. Kronos felt the piercing pain of thousands of tiny metallic projectiles passing through his body. He saw his imps fall all around him. Some got up but were hit again and again, a head shot usually taking them out. Brugat's corpse was finally still.

Kronos got on all fours and charged at the warriors, the metallic projectiles passing through his body by the thousands. He knew this was not going to kill him, but he could not withstand it indefinitely. Just as he got to the heavily armed vehicle, a warrior lit a rag sticking out of a transparent container containing a transparent liquid and launched the projectile at Kronos. As it arced in the air, the flame went out. Kronos stopped, and what passed as a smile appeared at the corner of his mouth. Not that it would harm him anyway.

He let the container smash against the keratinised, hard facial growths, and the liquid covered his head. The relatively soft flesh under the growths started to dissolve, causing Kronos to clutch his head with his claws, which made his claws start to dissolve. He looked as they bubbled and fizzed. The pain, *the smell*, all new to Kronos. The troops visibly recoiled. Another projectile smashed on his back, this time aflame. This was, ironically, taking the edge off the pain as the liquid burnt off.

"SEE ON ÜKS NEIST! SEE PÕHJUSES PEAME ME KÕIK ETANOOLIMAAUTI KAASA VÕTMA, KUHU IGANES ME KA EI LÄHEKS! ME OLEME UNUSTANUD!"

The main vehicle fired off a round, hitting Kronos in the chest. A bottle smashed on his arm, another on his back, neither of them lit. Kronos grabbed the tank turret and bent it. Around six more projectiles spilled the deadly liquid before they opened up with more of the high-speed metallic projectiles. This time though, it really hurt. And it burned as well.

"SIHTKI TULI TEMA KURATUD KÄTTE JA JALGADE SUHES! VÕTKE NEED KURATUD JÄSEMED ÄRA!!!!"

He identified the various sources of these tiny high-speed missiles. He grabbed the soldier operating one of the many devices and ripped his head off with his teeth. He swallowed the head whole, the taste of his first real sustenance in millennia. As he pushed the body down his throat, the feeling was pure ecstasy. The metal projectiles, he realised, were burning more due to noxious liquid seeping into his wounds. He was losing strength. He grabbed another soldier and beheaded him. But as the head came off, so did Kronos's arm. In disbelief, he ran at another soldier firing at him.

But this soldier was blasting a clear liquid at him at high pressure from a hose attached to a huge tank. He was about to bite down on his head when he felt his centre of gravity disappear. He had been cleaved into several pieces. His various parts were scattered across the dirt. The soldier kept on blasting the liquid at high pressure at each of his segments, until he ran out. Kronos's remains looked completely destroyed. Yes, if Kronos had been a multicellular organism. He grabbed his severed arm and put it back on his shoulder.

He was a single-celled organism masquerading as multicellular, each cell independent of the others but working together to form the unstoppable multicellular illusion. Each cell contained all of the memories of Kronos and could differentiate to create any organ and heal any wound. A major weakness was that Kronos could not regenerate from a single cell, as the cells only divided to replace cells lost to age or injury, and only to maintain the original mass once this was established.

Depending on the degree of maiming and the monster in question, this mass might become smaller using existing cells to replace those lost to injury. Reproportionalisation then occured, but for a small injury, this might not be noticeable to the naked eye. Any given cell could go for aeons before needing to be replaced. If enough viable cells were present, these cells would cooperate and arrange themselves to respawn Kronos in his entirety. The only limitation to this was the size of the respawned Kronos, and this depended entirely on the number of cells that were available to carry out the respawning process. This ability was not without its drawbacks.

The soldiers watched with enormous trepidation as Kronos implemented this ability for the first time. With the tank now empty, they stood rooted to the spot. For the last fifteen months, they had all experienced indescribable existential devastation, but that was nothing compared to this.

The cells coalesced into three separate piles and appeared to be respawning separately. Once this respawning was complete, there were three separate, identical Kronos, all roughly one third of the original size. They seemed to look at each other approvingly. They attacked, killing around half of the soldiers and morphing the remaining half into subhuman, feral, cacodemon imps. The newly formed army of three identical Kronos and subordinate cacodemons wasted no time in going on the move. They were making their way towards the threat across many miles of land and sea, the threat communicated to Kronos by the constant psychic chatter of the Echthroi. What this threat was specifically, he did not know. There had never been a need to use his psychic ability in this way before. God help any humans that crossed their path.

Chapter Thirty

Optimists Will Be Disappointed

Eighteen months after the exchange

Tommy did not know how he had got here. He seemed to remember being here before, but not how he had got out. The dark, vertical chamber was enough to squeeze his torso through just a little, but he could not even lift his arms to allow himself to breathe. Just when he was beginning to panic, he woke up. This again. His lungs had constricted in his sleep. He reached for the Ventolin inhaler, took it and then the Atrovent, then Seretide, and finally, Spiriva. His entire life, he had had these dreams where his lungs constricted in his sleep. Another dream which he had had again and again for months was arguing with Keith that all antidepressants are interchangeable at the equivalent doses.

Before the world ended, he had needed only two inhalers. Now four. He was eighteen months deep into this waking nightmare that was the world as it was. He had seen no point whatsoever in continuing to abstain from cigarettes. Now he was reasonably certain he had chronic obstructive pulmonary disorder, due to the necessity of long-acting and short-acting muscarinic inhibitors, which he had looted from the Stratton River pharmacy long ago.

He couldn't care less. He had no interest in living even another day in the hell on earth he was surrounded by. A mottled brown sky would tease him with brief interludes of sunshine which closed in a split second, renewing his despair. Tommy already had a tendency to be hypersensitive to bad smells, and the world smelt *bad*. Anything he could think of: unwiped arsehole, unwashed feet, burnt hair, body odour. It's like the entire world was sitting between two tramps on the Tube with no air conditioning during a heatwave.

He used his secret stash of baby wipes to wipe his feet, his secret stash of roll-on antiperspirant to keep his feet fresh, then put on one pair of his secret stash of new socks. All these things, he had prioritised whilst roaming the wasteland in the past eighteen months. He knew the others also stashed certain things for themselves too. He missed breathing in the beautiful scent of blossom, freshly cut grass and bracing, cool wind when on a hike. "We have NO bloody understanding of how lucky we were," he said to no one. He crawled out of his ratty pop-up tent, like he did every morning, with dread persistently devouring his will to keep on living.

Maia came over to him with a tennis ball in her mouth and dropped it in front of him. Lying beside Tommy's tent was a freshly caught rabbit carcass, none of it eaten.

"Bless your little heart. I'm so sorry about all of this," he said while running his hands through her sparse, once lustrous, fur. He was sorry humanity had ruined the world that she loved so much and that she had had no flea or worming treatments in six months, something which was extremely hard to get.

Yet she wanted the humans to eat first. Maia always got her fair share, though, maybe just preferring it cooked. Tommy did love the scar running down his forehead and continuing down his cheek. The scar had once transversed a ruined eye, but now there was only a black orb where his eye had once been, something taken when they raided a cosmetic surgery practice, originally for the purpose of keeping their drugs topped up. Tommy needed to numb himself more than ever but was not stupid enough to inject. He broke open a vial of diamorphine 10 mg and emptied the lyophilizate into his mouth, where it melted and got absorbed across the buccal mucosa.

Kevin took one and gave it to Keith, who was trembling with many types of withdrawal. Tommy was glad they kept him around, as they had learnt early on that he was full of good advice. When he simply whimpered, 'bad people coming', they knew no matter how safe they thought they were, it was time to go. Tommy did not see himself as bad just yet. But he had decided that it was prudent to look bad, at least. All of his excess weight was gone, and he was now a wiry 46-year-old with fearsome tattoos all over his torso, bald head and neck, as well as his face. His top teeth, from incisor to incisor, were now sharpened to give him a terrifying visage.

Tattoo artists were now worth their weight in gold, which ironically, was useless. Tommy had paid the artist with drugs. Before he got set up to begin cooking the rabbit, he decided to look over the ridge with the Russian monocular he still had after all this time. There was a newly recommissioned coal-fired power station, with black smoke rising up and feeding the rancid clouds above. The remaining electrical grid infrastructure had been put to good use in the last eighteen months, and large sections of damage had been hastily repaired with no regard for safety, leading to endless deaths and maimings.

There was a huge demand for the comforts electricity still brought, and many paid through the nose for it. Coal was easily accessible from the closed mines across the country, and the effects on the environment were not given a thought. This was understandable on some level when the environment was already ruined. However, nature was not being given the chance to repair itself. And the predatory nature of the utility companies of the old world paled in comparison to the current unchecked and unregulated suppliers now in business.

To confirm this, he saw two huge men laughing whilst pissing on an unmoving figure on the ground, with an emaciated man looking over in horror, clutching a sick-looking child aged around eight or ten. The man was slapped and the child thrown to the ground for stopping work. They hurriedly moved on, loading coal by hand from the trucks to the railcars to be moved into the station.

The slavers looked inhuman. As well as the more subtle unnatural skin hues of red and blue, they were abnormally large and almost chimp-like in gait. The eyes were what made them look most inhuman, with the sclera reduced in size and darkened irises. They also flashed various primary colours briefly when the light hit them. Tommy looked around him and sighed. Almost eighteen months deep into the nuclear wasteland, these were the people who were thriving. Radiation was clearly messing with their DNA, changing some people's genomes unnaturally fast. Most of the time, this made people weaker, and the ones who survived had become maimed or else thrived as the personification of brutality. Tommy even observed their appendages change colour and shape briefly when they cackled or showed cruelty.

"Don't look at them for too long. It will break your mind even more," Kaitlin said forebodingly as she handed Tommy a mug of freshly boiled and filtered water. "It's got an edge, be careful."

Tommy nodded thanks, and after sighing deeply again, brought the mug to his lips, found the rim and ran his tongue along it. He drank hungrily, trying not to taste it too much before swallowing. "I think this shit prolongs suffering, not life," he said.

Kaitlin licked her lips and just said, "I would love to know which metal is in here."

"Probably just arsenic, one of the harmless ones. Anyway, I think killing those evil-looking bastards might cheer me up a bit. I've heard about what they do to women and children. And men sometimes. I hope we have plenty of jagged, sharp things we can stuff in their arses. If they still have arseholes, that is."

"Don't get too close, or they'll tear you apart. And violate you. They're big, strong, well-endowed, and will not be showing you any mercy."

Tommy put his hand in his pocket and showed Kevin and Kaitlin a few transparent yellowish pills.

"Omega 3?" Kaitlin said incredulously.

"Nope, just a guarantee that they will be raping a corpse, something only a pharmacist could put together," Kevin said without humour.

"That lab we raided?" Kaitlin asked.

Kevin and Tommy nodded.

"Yeah, I didn't see the benefit of telling you what I was doing at the time," Tommy said.

Kaitlin and Kevin took one each and pocketed the pills without further word.

Kaitlin did not look approachable at all, also with terrifying tattoos and scarification in an effort to look androgynous, to counteract all the hypersexual lawlessness around them. Dressing in black loose-fitting clothes gave her peace of mind, and in any interaction with strangers, they looked at her with only suspicion and fear. And when they did, she smiled, revealing purposefully blackened teeth.

Kevin was the same but looked 20 years older since the bombs had fallen eighteen months ago. He wore a tramp-style duffle coat and hat which he never seemed to take off. He was 40 pounds lighter, but this was far from being a healthy weight loss. His deep-set eyes flared with focused hatred, and a hollow, wrinkled face kept him safe from any rape which might occur, unless it was those guys down at the mine.

Suzanne was part of the group still, but held only a short, sharp shank. It was all she ever needed. The only way to overcome her would be to sever or break her limbs. Tommy only guessed this, though; he had never seen it. She was always calm, even when dispatching any assailants she came across, just systematically and methodically taking them apart. Tommy always kept one eye on her, and she knew this. She would have given anything to regain his trust. She had saved his life many times over the last eighteen months, but he had also saved hers. Equally, he wanted to trust her completely, even though at this point, he mostly did. They had all saved each other's lives again and again; it was impossible to keep track.

Kaitlin started the water boiling with the propane tank while Kevin skinned the rabbit. Suzanne kept watch as always. Between Suzanne, Keith and the animals, nothing was going to take them by surprise. Tommy chose not to watch the skinning. Radioactive rabbit meat boiled in toxic waste. How lovely. He missed Bliss Greek yoghurts with lemon compote, any kind of mousse, mint chocolate, KP honey roast nuts, Pollo alla Veronese from his favourite Italian restaurant. The list went on, but at least there were plenty of drugs for now.

Instant coffee was made, from a pot which had been

retrieved from a dumpster the previous day. The coffee was cemented to the inside but released again using the boiling toxic waste. It got rid of the toxic rabbit-meat aftertaste but was black and bitter, with milk having ceased to exist eighteen months ago. His nausea level increased, but he had to keep it down. He downed two metoclopramide 10 mg to quicken his gastric emptying. A drug for everything.

Tommy had started experiencing chronic pain and fibromyalgia in 1999. His take on the cause of this was the antidepressants he had been put on in 1998 after an intense period of invasive mental OCD. This ultimately manifested itself in his way of obsessively overthinking his workouts, struggling to remember if he had done the full workout, or worrying that he had not used one of his arms. Out loud, this sounded ridiculous, but it was a living hell. If he had not been put on sertraline, he would never have achieved what he had. But chronic pain was a huge downside.

As a pharmacy student eight years later, he had become aware of all the drugs that were much more effective for his ailments than weed. Just in time, too, as the weed was starting to cause psychosis. He found out how to acquire them and experimented with them. He self-medicated through trial and error until he found the best combination.

He had become a drug addict, but at the same time, brought his symptoms under control just in time to stop them from completely overtaking his life. Then he had badgered various GPs to give him what he needed, bought an NHS prepayment certificate, and that was that. He did like to buy over-the-counter drugs, but he was the pharmacist; he had nonchalantly put the payments through at a 50% discount, and no one really cared. Sometimes he took too much, but he knew what to take to counteract that. He was a true expert.

Tommy was sure those giant twats had their fair share of drugs, and he would make those drugs his. "It's time," he said.

He held up a fist and some duct tape and motioned to Kaitlin. She took the duct tape and sat cross-legged opposite him. He placed the handle of the spiral push dagger between the middle and ring fingers of his left hand and closed his fist loosely around the handle. He took two precision screwdrivers and placed them inside the fist, the business ends at 90 degrees to that of the spiral push dagger, and tightened the fist.

"Comfortable?" Kaitlin asked.

"Do it," Tommy replied with a smile. "I have to get my pleasure from somewhere in this shit-hole world. Besides, it's good to do stuff together, isn't it?"

She smiled her black smile, and Tommy still saw the smile she had given him when he had met her for the first time when she was 8. She started to wrap the duct tape around his hand. His tongue touched the moisture resistant polymer shell containing the cyanide between his upper lip and gum, and he hoped he would not absent-mindedly bite down on it like it was a Polo mint. Another thing he sorely missed.

Kaitlin had a fully charged taser fastened to each wrist, both easily accessible to the opposing hand. On her belt were a pickaxe and a hammer. Her biggest enemy was not the genetically corrupted monsters down the ridge waiting for them; it was retaining the will to live, fighting the urge to just let those monsters tear her apart. The will to live was as low as ever, but this had essentially diminished her fear of death in a fight. This in turn would ironically boost her chances of survival, destroying any evil arsehole that got in her way. And it was tremendous fun, like in a video game.

The *only* thing keeping her going, as with all of them, was Keith and his 'prophecies'. The only real proof of his predictive ability was in keeping them safe and avoiding fights they did not need to be in. They needed food and supplies now, and he had led them here, so there was no avoiding this fight. She had to have faith in the direction he sent them. Right now they were on the outskirts of what used to be a typical British shithole.

Keith's instructions, isolated from a stream of garbled nonsense out of a broken mind, could easily be missed, and they had probably missed a lot. He had mentioned 'Ginny' and 'Jane' and a few others, but her mother's name, Ginny, was all she needed to hear. It was all they had, but the world around them had been poisoned irreparably, and this was the survivors' punishment. Even if she did see her mum, so what? Nobody lived happily ever after. Not here.

Human civilization was coming back, but only as a septic, malformed scar forming over third-degree burnt skin. What she would give just to feel and breathe in a cool fresh breeze, like Lazarus in hell, and a drop of water. Kevin still had the rifle, which he oiled and cleaned regularly. Using the Russian monocular, he had calibrated the sights to accuracy. The only problem was, this was England, and ammo was scarce. They had two full magazines with 30 rounds of 5.45 x 39 mm cartridges in each and one with 15 rounds remaining, currently attached to the rifle, with a bullet chambered.

Kevin was the best shot, and it was his job to use the

rifle to protect Tommy and Kaitlin, but every last round needed to count. He also had a hatchet visibly wedged in the belt of his army surplus camouflage trousers as well as cleverly concealed but easily accessible screwdrivers, ice picks and chisels he had picked up along the way.

"How many?" Kevin asked Tommy, who looked through the monocular.

Before he could say anything, they all heard Keith say, "TWENTY-TWO. THERE ARE TWENTY-SEVEN!!" in a raised voice before going back to jabbering incoherently.

"Okay, I guess there are twenty-seven. Anything else?" Kevin asked Tommy.

"There only seems to be two of them outside at any one time, and they rotate with replacements every half hour or so. From what I can see, there does only seem to be twenty two pig-men. Stealth is the key."

"Easy," said Kaitlin. The noise of this badly run power plant flouting all the regulations of the old world had eliminated any possibility they would hear anyone coming for them. "The replacement guards coming out every half hour are sometimes scoffing something down. They definitely have food; this'll be worth the effort."

"During the last five or so minutes of the half-hour guard rotation, they seem to lose interest and are less aware. All they can think of is getting back in," Tommy added.

"Okay," Kevin said. "Remember, an ice pick or something similar, forced through the base of the skull at an upward forty-five-degree angle. You know, like Tommy kills Morrie in *Goodfellas*. If you have to, move it around to scramble their brain. They're still technically human at this point, but be ready for anything."

Tommy nodded, proud of his name at that moment. Kaitlin looked confused.

"Kaitlin, you *need* to watch *Goodfellas*," Tommy said as they all started to make their way towards the plant.

Then they nodded to each other. After carefully sneaking up behind them, Tommy and Kaitlin dispatched the two bored and inattentive guards with around three minutes left to go until their rotation was over. They both moved the ice picks around to be certain they were dead. Now for the secret weapon, which was *hilarious*. Kevin had found this thing inside an abandoned attic, a Wicked Witch of the West figurine with a pull-string. If the string was pulled out all the way, she laughed, boasted and threatened Dorothy and her dog for a good ninety seconds.

Tommy snatched the walkie out of the guard's hand, and they all went to the more exposed and open area further from the plant. Once there, Kevin pulled the string on the figure all the way and held it there. They were all smiling. Tommy, using an elastic band and a small rock, was able to press and hold the transmit button on the walkie. Kevin released the string, and they all ran for cover. *I'LL GET YOU MY PRETTY, AND YOUR LITTLE DOG TOO!* was the first phrase.

Within five seconds, all of the remaining twenty-five guards ran out, looking perplexed and bewildered. One of them, who obviously had seniority, noticed the bodies and knelt down next to them. Then he pointed at the direction of the noise, and the rest of them hurried over. Now it was just the witch laughing.

Tommy scrambled over to the kneeling pig-man and drove the shank on his left fist down on top of the pig-man's head. Twenty-four left. It went through all the way with virtually no resistance, holding the head in place. Then, with effortless muscle memory, Tommy used a chisel to sever the brainstem, pushing the chisel all the way in and scrambling the brain for good measure.

Just then, the metal door they had all emerged from squealed on its hinges. Tommy looked and saw a terrified, filthy, barefoot man dressed in rags pulling it shut and being pulled by another man, identical looking from this distance. Tommy swivelled his head 180 degrees and saw twenty-four raging pig-men itching to punish him by gang rape. Tommy felt like a Fleshlight. *That was a weird thing to think*, he thought.

They started advancing on Tommy, who smiled at them and held up his wicked-looking left arm with the three taped on stabbing and shanking points. Kaitlin was nowhere to be seen. They smiled back at him, and he realised that this new world devoid of hope had burnt the fear right out of them. When fear and misery was ubiquitous, it made sense that this trait was an advantage. Tommy used his tongue to carefully place the capsule between his teeth. He wanted to try his three-pronged weapon and maybe take out two of them.

Kaitlin was approaching behind them with a taser in one hand and a four-inch knife in the other. Kevin had the rifle trained on them. He shot three in the head in quick succession. Twenty-one left. Kaitlin put into practice the skill she had been perfecting ever since the Sawyer's, with the Russian officer. First, she jumped on the back of one of these monsters, jammed the taser under the chin, activated it and gouged out both of the eyeballs. Kevin shot two more with a ten-second gap in between, allowing her to incapacitate two more of the pig-men as they were distracted. Sixteen left. Suzanne appeared, casually ripping out two of the pig-men's throats with a combination of the short, sharp shank and her bare hands as they advanced on her. They looked incredulous and died before hitting the ground. Fourteen.

They were on borrowed time, though, as two more advanced on Kevin. He shot them both in the head, but two more were coming. Twelve. He took out another three but he needed to reload. Nine. Kaitlin electrocuted, then blinded one, and Suzanne jumped on a pig-man's back, repeatedly stabbing his throat and then breaking his neck for good measure. Seven. During this, she almost looked bored. But one got to Kevin and grabbed him. Three more surrounded Kaitlin and Suzanne, Suzanne looking like she was struggling with a crossword puzzle. All of them were led to three more confused and frightened pig-men in the open area in front of the power station. Tommy watched helplessly but did not run. He was trying to think of anything, anything at all, he could do. Most of the pig-men were dead, but his group had lost their advantage. No one paid much attention to the blinded and maimed pig-men stumbling around and moaning helplessly.

The pig-men had Kaitlin, Kevin and Suzanne kneeling while they discussed in graphic detail what they wanted to do to them sexually, but their heart was not in it. They loved to rape and cause sexual torture, but they did not really want to rape them; the four invaders were disgusting in every way. They discussed nonsexual torture graphically too, but their hearts were even less in it; it was either sexual torture or they may as well not bother.

Suzanne smirked and said, "I think we have let ourselves go, haven't we?"

Kevin and Kaitlin cackled loudly as they stood up as one. This was going to be a fight to the death, nothing more. Tommy had quietly slipped away and started circling in from behind, the attention on him lost as he was even less appealing than the other three. Maia and the cats had largely sat this one out, and Tommy did not blame them. They were more about surprise attacks on possible threats. But now here they were. They were spread out, approaching slowly. They had figured out at this point that help was needed.

They heard a panel being kicked open, followed closely by a whirring sound. Kaitlin, Kevin and Suzanne ducked and ran for cover, as did the animals and Tommy. These pig-men were far from stupid. But in a world they dominated with fear and rape and degradation, their hubris overrode their intelligence. Instead of going inside and engaging the minigun on the roof and easily killing the intruders, they wanted to go outside and rape the shit out of them.

No thought was given to the possibility that they could have met their match, much less that their slaves would not be too afraid of sexually debasing punishment to take the opportunity to mow them down. And mow them down they bloody well did. They kept the minigun firing until there was nothing but a pile of flesh where the pig-men fell. The shooter was screaming all manner of profanity and curses at the pig-men whilst the men, women and children gathered on the roof.

They were overjoyed. The whirring kept going for a good ten seconds after the last of the tracer bullets were seen. The shooter had stopped screaming, but his eyes were screaming with hatred, being robbed of any possibility of killing each of the pig-men slowly. The eyes screamed at Tommy.

"What do you want?" the man said in a surprisingly soft voice.

"Half," Tommy replied with equal calmness.

"It seems you are not in a position to be making

demands," came the reply.

"Perhaps not," said Tommy. "But I am willing to bet you need antibiotics. And other medication. Being a pharmacist, I ensure we are kept well stocked."

The man looked at him incredulously.

Tommy smiled. "I know, professionalism has gone out the window of late."

Someone whispered in the man's ear.

"You got vitamin C?"

The whisperer threw their hands up, and the shooter rolled his eyes. "The one you put in water that tastes like oranges."

Now Tommy rolled his eyes. "Yessss ... You all got scurvy, then?"

"Yeah. We got worms, ringworm, fungal lesions, and some children with pneumonia."

"I can help with all of that. I only ask for one thing: three safe, clean beds for one night, and some food for the road. I heard some space has just opened up in there."

"You got yourself a deal, mate."

Suzanne jumped on the back of one of the blind pig-men rapists. She held out one of his arms towards Kaitlin and simply said, "Hammer."

But Kaitlin took the hammer herself and proceeded to smash every bone in the maimed pig-man's hand. After all of the blinded pig-men's hands were smashed, Kaitlin looked up at the oppressed slaves and said, "Our gift to you to show our good faith."

Excited, they all streamed outside, emerging with various sharp and blunt weapons, and then proceeded to have hours of fun. A fire was lit and the pig-men's food store was raided. Mostly MREs, which were fine, but there was lots of cooking chocolate, fresh bottled water and frozen, vacuum-sealed steaks, seemingly free from radiation. A barbeque was held, and they ate and drank boxed red wine as well as non-alcoholic drinks.

There was a lot of cat medication for fleas, ticks and worms but nothing for dogs. So, they decided to give Maia double treatment for everything to account for her size in relation to the cats'. It was better than nothing. Usually, the cats would be difficult about being treated, but like with everything else, they were different now, and okay about it this time, seemingly not wanting to make life even harder for their humans. Once treated and fed, they resumed sentry duty. All the pets ate well that night as well, and Maia played with the children, and the children played with each other. Each group of downtrodden survivors had saved the other. If that didn't deserve some celebration, good faith and trust, then nothing did.

Tommy and Suzanne were with the cats on sentry duty, Tommy slightly disappointed that the minigun had robbed him of his chance to die or live as a hero. This all seemed dangerously close to carefree socialising, something that scared them both more than anything in this wasteland. This had applied to Tommy even before it all went bad. Suzanne just did not have it in her anymore. He missed his wife. He chuckled at the thought of what she would think if she saw him now. He took a bump of crushed Medikinet off his recently acquired carbon-fibre hunting knife, smirking as he thought of Tuco from *Breaking Bad*. On the dead pig-men, there was a bounty of weapons to be claimed.

Suzanne and he looked at each other. He looked at the blood on her hands, and he said, "That could just as easily have been mine, you know."

Suzanne smirked, and they had a chuckle, this being the most human he had seen her recently.

"So, Suzanne, I want to trust you again, but do you like having literal blood on both hands? You know, it's been a few hours. You can wash it off now. I mean, I shouldn't have to tell you these things!"

Without breaking eye contact, she opened a two-litre bottle of soft drink, took a swig, and put the lid back on.

"But wha…?" he tried to say.

She cut him off. "Piss off, Tommy."

Chapter Thirty-One

A Deal with the Devil

Twenty months after the exchange

Jim was most of the way to being back on his feet, if you could call it that. When his own grandson had squirted concentrated acid on his face, the pain was instant. When he put his hands instinctively up to his face, the hands touched melting, burning flesh, and there was apparently plenty of acid to start melting his hands. This sort of pain, he had convinced himself, was not compatible with life. He had no fingers to phone the emergency services, no phone or phone signal, and no emergency services.

Jim knew he was a bad, angry guy, but he had never put anyone through anything close to this. And not only had his own grandson done this to him, but his grandson had stopped someone from putting him out of his misery, just to see his misery continue. Jim had been in and out of consciousness for a few days, and each time he regained consciousness, he had been incredulous. He should have gone into septic shock, at the very least. He vaguely remembered a strong, hot wind full of debris blowing over him. It only lasted a few seconds and wasn't strong enough to move him. He figured out what was what eventually.

He was dehydrated, hungry and especially vulnerable, being elderly and having type 2 diabetes. He had gone days without taking his metformin and his gliclazide, but he had not eaten either. When the inky-black warm rain came, it burned, but in a pleasant way, like a hot water jet on an itchy, inflamed lesion. The pain was reducing, and eventually, he touched his hands to his face once again.

He felt no sensory input from his hands or face, only the sense of something rough and hard sliding against something equally rough and hard: not the most pleasant of sensations, but it was not wet agony.

He had an opening for his mouth, but nothing for his nose, and with his one good eye, he saw the yellow and green oozing from his hands, which were missing a couple of fingers each but with both thumbs and forefingers intact. He was glad he was breathing through his mouth only, even though he could almost taste the stench from his own hands. Eventually, he pulled himself up onto his feet, seemingly obtaining sustenance from his own rage and hatred. He was not hungry; he was *ravenous*.

The corrupted flesh that had made contact with the acid was everywhere, and ... was that a ... *claw*? The thumb on his right hand had the beginnings of a claw. He was still in the same spot his grandson had squirted the acid on him, a week later. He had started walking, and it was not long before he had heard voices. Not ... English voices. Bastard Russians. His life had been pretty sweet before all this. He had his dive bar, his motorcycle, his skanks, his man cave. He loved drugs, drink, gambling, fighting, riding and the gutter.

He had had no big plans, but he had got what he wanted out of life. The only annoyance had been his little beta son, who was letting his stupid wife walk all over him. How many times had he told his son, *it's not enough to hit them, you have to break them*? Hit her he had, but she still had the house and Jim's grandson. But he was not going to get involved directly, until he did, when everything changed one day. Bastard Russians. There were three of them outside some heavily armoured tank-looking thing, arguing and screaming at one another, in a lay-by a hundred feet ahead of him.

"It's not really fair, is it?" He heard a creepy whispered voice.

"Who the hell is that?" Jim demanded in a loud whisper.

"My name is Louis," came the reply. A mixed upper-class English and Western European accent, which Jim could not pin down, spoke to him from a concealed position on the opposite side of the road. There was a slightly effeminate-looking man in his mid-20s, who looked like Jared Kushner, with a smirk on the side of his mouth and dead eyes.

He was dressed in normal street clothes but emitted a dangerous and nasty aura. He was not afraid of Jim. Jim would be afraid of Jim, if Jim saw Jim.

"What's not fair, dude?" His voice now had a raspy threat in every word.

Louis pointed at the Russians, with what Jim recognised as a fleshing knife. With fresh blood on it. "Those subhuman Russians. They have skin, you don't. What's fair about that?" He saw Jim's good eye looking at the knife and said, "Yeah ... I like to skin people alive. I hope you don't mind, but can I skin them before we eat them? Like while they're still alive?"

"Well, there are three of them, only two of us, so it would make sense to help each other. And yes, I want to watch you skin those bastards alive first. Let's immobilise two of them; there's no point killing all three of them now."

"We gotta get some bandages on you, old man," Louis said.

"Why?"

"I'm not afraid of you – you look like me on the inside. There are going to be a lot of Russians out there and a lot of pissed-off English. But some of those pissed-off English will be afraid of you. It will buy you, or us, time to win them over."

And so, Jim and Louis had quickly accrued weapons, vehicles and Russian prisoners, all with a common goal: to quench their thirst for vengeance against the Russians. By torturing and eating them. They were never short of food. Eventually, they got used to Jim's disfigurement, and it probably actually helped him keep everyone in line. When some do-gooding sniper had robbed them one night of their favourite activity, they had given chase, only to be lured into a trap, which proved very costly in terms of vehicles, weapons and manpower. Jim and Louis marched on with the remainder of the army, eventually replacing their losses.

Eventually, after crossing paths with Archer, Charlotte and Clarette, he had realised that hatred of Russians was not enough for Jim to trust someone. A huge chunk of his soldiers and ammo were destroyed that night, when more people than usual were sleeping next to and closer to the fire. Around twenty of his best men were killed instantly in their sleep, with another ten or so, further from the fire, needing to be put out of their misery due to third- and fourth-degree burns. It was a disaster. This time, they kept their vehicles, and their immobilised Russian prisoners were in no state to stage a coup.

Jim's rage and hatred could never truly be quenched until he could get hold of his fag grandson and teach him a lesson in betraying family. In Jim's tortured dreams one night, he focused on a face he never wanted to see, a face he did not think existed outside myths and folklore. It made Jim's appearance seem like a Mediterranean sunset. A thing with an appearance which defied description or explanation. A physical manifestation of hatred as old as time, this nightmarish countenance jolted him awake.

There it stood before him. It was not a dream. With a crunching of bones and tearing of flesh, this thing morphed into a likeness of his late son, made to die slowly and painfully by his fag grandson. His idiot of a son loomed over him.

"Trousers," was all Jim could say.

His son grabbed the nearest sleeping soldier and broke his back and legs to get his trousers off. The soldier then lay there, Cheyne-Stoking his final breaths.

Louis lurked, looking excited.

"You could at least finish him off," Jim said.

Louis looked panicked. "But wai…"

The creature crushed the soldier's head with one blow.

"He was one of ours, Louis. Don't forget the rules."

"Ah, yes," the thing said mockingly. 'You cannot skin anyone in your own group, can you, Louis? It doesn't stop you wanting to, though." It gave Jim a knowing smile

"What the hell do you want, thing? How long can you stay like that?" Jim rasped.

The thing felt the side of its head, made a face, and sucked in the green mottled lump on the side of it. Looking into its eyes, something was not right. The iris dilated in and out instead of the pupil and was dilating in and out constantly. "I can stay like this for up to half an hour, but I must have eaten an entire person within the last 24 hours. If not, no more than a few minutes." The thing smiled just like his son used to.

"You, my friend, if you don't mind me saying, are the most disgusting thing I have ever seen and the most disgusting thing I have ever smelt. You smell like death and decay, and I can smell you even though the world smells like that anyway. Please tell me, without talking in riddles, what the hell are you?"

Louis excitedly looked back and forth between the demon and Jim. He knew how bad it smelled, but it did not bother Louis.

"I am a demon, a monster of myth and lore. The stories going back millennia of encounters between unfortunate individuals and those like me were not completely accurate but certainly not fabrication. There is a reason mankind is afraid of hell and demons. But you only have yourselves to blame for this."

Jim noticed the smell dissipating and guessed it was because of the form change.

"Why are we to blame?"

"You opened a door to our world, and we came through. This happened over 75,000 years ago, when ancient scientists decided to play around with the fabric of reality. Eventually, we precipitated the destruction of their entire society."

"Good for you, well done. Why did they open the door to hell, then? That was pretty stupid. Do you prefer it here or there?"

"What the hell do you think, old man?"

"So you've been here for 75,000 years. Bugger me. How old are you? Were you ... like ... born or spawned?"

"I just remember hell and misery. The only relief from the misery was causing another being more misery, but we all had one thing in common. We wanted to get him, that bastard. The bastard who caused all of it ..." The demon trailed off. "He was too big to get through. We ate his entire arm though, hehehe." Although in human form, he now sounded like Darkness from the '80s movie *Legend*.

Jim laughed mockingly. "Duuuude ... you got

problems!!" He leaned forwards, smirking under the mess of his face. "You weren't always like this, were you? But you don't remember, do you?"

For a split second, the irises slowed the contraction-dilation cycle as the demon remembered an emerald-green sky, the smell of nature in all its purity, the beauty of the natural monoliths that spanned the horizon. The demon was happy. The laughter and play of its offspring, all gone one day, their beautiful world destroyed because of that evil cun...

The demon was jolted back into reality when a mottled lump of corrupted flesh burst from his belly. It was losing concentration. It worked hard to reverse the mistake until it looked human again.

Jim just pointed at it and said, "You can't die, can you? You're cursed, aren't you?"

Chapter Thirty-Two

A Mid-Nuclear Winter's Dream

Twenty-Two months after the exchange

Clarette still could not speak or communicate in the conventional sense, but she was still changing. She was becoming larger, and her flesh became mottled and red. She was developing nasty, sharp yellow teeth and a network of horns. She made sure that Archer and Charlotte were fed, but she herself fed on the abundance of human bodies in various stages of decomposition, even just bones. At night, that was when she would communicate with them, in their dreams. They were going to Newcastle upon Tyne harbour to meet a small vessel carrying with it an ancient evil they had to destroy.

Archer awoke in a foul mood upon learning this in his dreams. "WILL SOMEONE PLEASE EXPLAIN WHY WE HAVE TO DESTROY THIS ANCIENT EVIL??" he shouted to Charlotte and Clarette.

Charlotte was confused too. "I'm sick of being drip-fed information here," Charlotte said. "We're sick of not knowing *anything*."

"Yes," Archer said in a lower voice. "It looks like ancient evil of some sort is now everywhere. The entire earth is ruined. And it's getting *worse*. How much worse can it actually get? I mean, look at you, Clarette! You're a monster! Please inform us of the benefit of possibly giving our lives to destroy this ancient evil, because I am *really* confused."

"I agree," said Charlotte. "I'd understand completely if the sky was blue and if we were surrounded by all of nature's splendour. I would *gladly* fight this ancient evil."

Charlotte and Archer went silent, expecting no reply.

Clarette grunted, then wheezed, as if trying to speak. "HMMMMMMMMPPPP," Clarette growled.

"Great!" Archer said. "So, that clears it up, then! I wish you'd said something before." Archer rifled through his bag and took out a golden-syrup cereal bar. "I *killed* someone for *this*!!!!" Archer threw it away into the trees of the small clearing inside the dead forest where they had slept.

"I'm sorry, Clarette," said Charlotte. "A growling grunt won't cut it. There's stuff you know and you need to bloody well tell us, because from our perspective, it doesn't offer any advantage, destroying this ancient evil, because it looks like its job is already done. Pleeeease find a way to tell us!"

There was a sharp intake of breath from Archer. He rifled around in his bag some more and took out a strip of eight Sominex, with four popped out of it. He had been lucky enough to find this on the floor of a looted pharmacy where there was nothing else left. "How well do you sleep these days, Charlotte?" Archer asked. "I wake up with a feeling of panic before it ever gets deep, over and over again. I don't know how I haven't lost my mind already."

"Well, it seems to me I just lie awake all night and don't sleep at all. I must sleep if I remember dreaming, but it's probably not any deeper than daydreaming. I just don't feel safe," Charlotte said. She motioned towards the strip of Sominex in Archer's hand. "I'll take all four. You stay awake, as I don't think it's safe if both of us go under. Plus it means I'll go deeper for longer. I can pass this message to you."

Archer put up both hands. "Okay," he said. "This is utterly ludicrous. Please make sure you find out *how* to destroy this thing."

Charlotte took the pills with one swig from an almost

empty water bottle, then threw the bottle away. "Get your cereal bar, or you will have killed that guy for nothing," she said. She got comfortable on top of her sleeping bag and an inflatable pillow and closed her eyes.

Archer sat cross-legged next to her, took a long draw on his vape, and contemplated his broken mind as he looked up at the evil sky. He was still next to Charlotte when she awoke. Archer had clearly fallen asleep, and his head lolled forwards.

She lifted his head. "Archer! Wake up!!" she said urgently.

"I can't feel my legs," was his response. After a few knee lifts on his back, his legs felt normal. He looked at her and cynically raised his left eyebrow. After a few seconds, he realised he was getting nothing until he got going with the coffee.

Clarette lifted her bucket and set it beside Archer, and with a sigh, he got to work. "Seventy sugars, right?" he asked with amusement.

Clarette grunted in response.

Archer put his hand to his head. "I'm sorry, it's eighty." He turned to look at Clarette and shook the spoon at her. "We need to expand your vocabulary." He smirked and got back to work.

Clarette rarely had coffee due to the volume required of everything, but it was an amusing process, nonetheless.

Charlotte took her first sip of the coffee and simply said, "Hope."

Archer looked unimpressed. He casually sipped his coffee while Clarette poured the entirety of the boiling liquid down her throat.

Charlotte continued, "To the northwest, Scotland, I think? There's some sort of thing going down. If successful, the earth will be restored ..."

Archer put his hand up. Then both hands. "What?"

Charlotte took a breath. "There are people with scientific knowledge of the quantum realm making their way to a place where this knowledge can be implemented. The thing coming in on the harbour wants to thwart that. We have hope. Another evil entity is following them, but that's their battle."

"Who are these people?" Archer asked incredulously.

"Well, that's the best part. Apparently, you'll be familiar with the names Tommy, Kaitlin and Ginny. Clarette playfully wouldn't tell me how you know them."

Archer looked at Clarette. "Playful? Anyway, that's my mum, stepdad and sister. Mum and Tommy worked in the scientific field, I guess, but not the quantum realm."

Charlotte put her hands together and looked up as if to gather her thoughts. "It's your mum and another person called Jane. They've memorised something. They're with a band of survivors and they won't succeed if we don't stop Kronos."

Archer was expressionless this time. "Kronos. Okaaay … Kronos."

"What the hell is wrong with you, Archer? Look around you. Have you got anything else going on right now? What the hell have we got to lose?"

Archer bowed his head. "I believe it, all of it. I never doubted it. It's just that …"

Charlotte nodded and put a hand on his face. "I know," she said.

He put a hand on hers, and she felt him smile. "So, let's kill Kronos," she said.

"So, who gave him the name Kronos, then?" he asked.

She smiled and said, "Get yourself comfortable,

Archer. I have a bedtime story to end all bedtime stories, even though it is not bedtime. You've heard of the Neanderthals, right?"

The next day

"This is perfect," Charlotte said.

"How? It's an empty swimming pool," Archer replied.

They were at the pool of a leisure centre located near the harbour, essentially now an open-air hole in the ground. Filled with debris, but a big hole all the same.

"Yeah, we don't have to drain it," Charlotte said.

Archer made a face. "How the hell are you going to get Mister Kronos to walk into a swimming pool? And what is that even going to do?"

Charlotte sighed and rolled her eyes. "Do you think that Kronos even knows what a swimming pool is? Is your brain rotting?"

He just threw his hands up.

"Sometimes I wonder if the radiation is smoothing out your brain, Archer."

He kept his hands up, incredulous. "Why would he *not* know what a swimming pool is?"

Charlotte was reminded that Archer was not privy to all the information imparted to her. "Okay, Archer, I'm sorry. Apparently, Kronos has recently broken out of a facility he was imprisoned in for the best part of eighty thousand years. I bet that there's probably quite a lot he doesn't know."

Archer had that incredulous face again. "Shiiiiit. Shit. That is heavy, maaan …"

Charlotte looked confused.

Archer qualified, "Neil from *The Young Ones*, you know?"

"Look, I PROMISE we'll watch it together once this is all over," Charlotte said, continually frustrated that she did not get the references to this comedy show from the '80s Archer was always making.

"Okay," Archer said, amused.

"We have a lot of work to do. We need to fill this pool with seventy percent ethanol."

Archer frowned.

Chapter Thirty-Three

A Day in the Life of Maia

Hungry, always hungry. I'm so tired. Must keep going. Food is always bad. Food was good when I was happy. Now I'm not happy. Who is that? Bad woman and bad man. Want to take our food. Want to hurt my family. Must kill the bad man first. Bad man mustn't see me. Must be quick or the bad woman will get me. I know how to make it quick. I didn't always know. But now I know. My family know something. My family know how to make everything better.

Must protect them or everything will not get better. No hope. Maimai don't like to kill. Maimai used to love all humans. All humans were good. But not now. Strange humans came from the sky. Strange humans talk different. Strange humans bad, want to hurt other people, tried to hurt me. Maimai first kill humans when they wanted to hurt Mummy. Maimai doesn't know where her other mummy is. Or Daddy.

Maybe everything better when we see other mummy. Mummy Kaitlin says we go to Scotland after other mummy found. Maimai must keep going. Maimai kill anything for food. Food for Maimai and Mummy Kaitlin. Mummy Kaitlin and Daddy Tommy hate food like Maimai but need food to keep going. Keep going to make everything better. What's that smell? Other mummy far away but Maimai knows. Must tell Mummy Kaitlin and Daddy. Strange man with no eyes knows. Man is pointing. Everybody looking. Everybody! This way! They look the right way. Now they know.

Maimai must go ahead to check for bad people. Maimai knows the cats are looking for bad people. Cats help Maimai kill the bad people if Maimai needs cats. They always know

347

if Maimai needs help. When Maimai killed the bad man, the cats killed the bad lady. The bad lady wanted to hurt and kill Maimai. After, cats lick blood away from Maimai's mouth, and Maimai like cats and not afraid of cats anymore.

Cats are Maimai's friends and Maimai loves friends. Maimai help Jesse when Jesse trapped. Maimai help Kashkash when Kashkash nearly hurt by bad men. Maimai's family knows that Maimai and the cats kill bad men and bad ladies. But Maimai's family doesn't see because Maimai must kill before bad people get close. Sky is bad. Everywhere smell bad. Sky blue when Maimai happy. Maimai's family will make sky blue again. Maimai's family will make air smell good again. Maimai will be happy again.

Maimai could feel good lady. Good lady very old. Good lady wanted to help but good lady needed to know if Maimai and her humans good too. Good lady had seen so many bad things. Good lady would help.

Chapter Thirty-Four

Preparing for Kronos

Two weeks later

With the assistance of Clarette, they had taken three tankers from a local biofuels company in Billingham and driven them as close as possible to the pool. They had commandeered a local fire truck. Charlotte only had experience of driving cars and small vans. Archer had no experience driving, so Charlotte had to learn quickly. She had been especially careful, as she had taken a turn too fast on the first attempt. This had caused the ethanol tanker to roll over, causing a huge explosion when it burst open. Its spilling contents had been ignited by the sparks as the tank dragged along the dry tarmac.

Archer had run over and got her out of the cab of the truck, and Clarette had shielded her from the explosion. Clarette's physical appearance was rapidly growing more grotesque by the day. Throughout the entire change she was going through, Archer and Charlotte were there. Although gradual, it was noticeable. Archer had his own theory that for some people, the radiation had awoken buried sections of their genome from a distant past. But it was probably more complicated than that.

That friendship, that loyalty, clearly remained. Archer and Charlotte were not unaware of the fact that the connection between the three of them was the only thing tethering Clarette to the last vestiges of what had once made her human. They knew what Clarette would become if this link was lost.

Archer had found a car with automatic transmission, and he had driven Charlotte to where she had commandeered the tankers, and finally, the fire truck. There were four fire trucks at the fire station; only the final one would start, eventually, after a few attempts. Without the internet, Archer and Charlotte had had no clue how to connect a fire truck to the ethanol tanker to transfer the fluids. They had first figured out how to get the hose working and had been able to fill the pool to a quarter full. It had taken them three more days to figure out how to transfer the ethanol to the fire truck.

It had taken two and a half tankers to fill the pool, and they were not nearly finished. Clarette pushed each of the fire engines one at a time to face inward towards the pool. Using the pump motors, they drained each tank until they were a quarter filled with water. And then they made them up to full volume from the remaining ethanol in the tankers. With the engines not working on the other three fire trucks, the fire pumps would power the hoses and would last at least thirty minutes on a full battery – in theory – and they could only hope they would work for as long as they needed them to, if they needed them.

The last fire truck, they only got 80% full, but it would have to do. Using tarpaulin from Homebase, which, obviously, nobody had wanted, they covered the fire trucks and pool and weighed everything down with rubble, of which there was plenty. They needed more people, though, and those people came. Five of them. An exhausted looking woman holding the hand of an infant and three very unfriendly looking males.

"Archer?" the woman simply said when the two of them came across the group.

The men looked confused. From Archer's study of military history, borne of his desire to join the navy, he could see one of the men was carrying a belt-fed M60, one had an AK47, and the other had a side arm, of which Archer could not discern the type. Archer searched his memory. No ... it couldn't be. "Cele?"

She simply replied, "Yes, it's me."

Archer could see she was tearing up. She was twenty-five pounds lighter, dirty and malnourished, just like Archer. He looked towards the surprisingly healthy and clean-looking toddler, and he knew that Cele and the men were putting the child first.

Archer pointed to the child. "Is that ... Amelia?"

Cele simply nodded her head and smiled through the tears. Amelia hid behind her mother's leg. Archer had been in Cambridge when he had learned of the gender reveal, before the nuclear war. He had subconsciously assumed that even if Amelia could be delivered safely, she would not have lasted long.

Cele saw the questions in Archer's eyes, and she pointed to the dirty, bearded man with the M60. "That's Charles. And the others are Moe and Derek."

Charles made a sweeping wave at Archer using the M60 and not his other hand, which was not there. Just a healed-over stump.

"Charles is a paranoid schizophrenic."

Archer chuckled. "Well, I've never felt safer!" he exclaimed.

This was an ice-breaker, and they all shared a brief laugh. Everybody relaxed a little.

Cele continued, "The first time I met these guys, I was in labour, and they heard my moans from inside the car I'd worked hard to camouflage. The first thing Charles said to me was that we needed to find Archer and help him. Through the pain, I asked him if he knew where Jonah was, and he simply said *gone*. I asked him if he meant Jonah was dead, and Charles said *no, just gone*.

"They helped me to deliver Amelia, and they took care of us. Charles guided us here. You need our help. We're here to give it."

Archer looked again at his niece and saw both his mother and sister in there. He did not know how to relate to children.

Cele sensed this, and she just said to Amelia, "Go and see your Uncle Archer! He loves you!"

Amelia slowly came out from behind her mother, and after seeking a reassuring look from her, she slowly approached Archer, who simply smiled, and Amelia smiled in response.

When she got to Archer, he held her in a gentle embrace. "I am so glad to see you," Archer said.

Then they all met Clarette as she stepped out from behind a fire engine.

One day later - Kronos welcome party

"He's not alone," Archer said as he saw the yacht come into view. "And he's a lot shorter than you told Charlotte," he said to Clarette.

He handed the binoculars to Charles, who had a look. "Kind of looks like you, but shorter," Charles jokingly said to Clarette.

"Shut the hell up, Charles. Clarette isn't fighting this thing. It's ancient and evil. It has tens of millennia of just being evil. Clarette may be terrifying, but the resemblance is only skin deep. She's helping us," Charlotte said sternly. She looked at Charles with contempt. "Give me those!" she said as she snatched the binoculars out of his hand. "He does seem a lot smaller than expected, around five feet. But every bit as evil," she confirmed.

Archer took back the binoculars. "Five feet doesn't make me less afraid. Something isn't right. Anyway, *they* are getting closer," he said.

Charles took the binoculars again. "Uh-oh," was all he could say at first. He continued, "There are around fifteen humanoid, grotesque-looking cacodemons."

Charlotte felt something uncoil in her stomach. "Charles, you three use your guns on those things. Don't waste your bullets on Kronos. Just lead him where we need him to go. No heroics, please!" she said with a slight but detectable tremor in her voice.

They all gave her a previously rehearsed mock salute, which made Charlotte feel drained. She did not want to be around these guys after this was all over, if she lived through it. Especially the way things were now, where you could decide to kill someone if they annoyed you. And they had guns. They all gave off the vibes of insufferable 'friends of friends', begging for her knife in their guts. As if communicating telepathically, everyone abruptly left the 'dog leg quay' of Newcastle harbour and headed inland, where they encountered some gift-wrapped Kronos bait. Four radiation-burned white men were advancing on an underage black girl, who was still fully clothed but screaming for help.

This was perfect. They needed to lead Kronos to the covered pool, and nothing like a trail of fresh corpses to do that. The AK47 was used to dispatch the would-be assailants. The girl stood up and repeatedly punched one of the dead attacker's faces for a good thirty seconds. Cele put one of Amelia's blankets around her shoulders and hugged her tightly. She burst into tears, sobbing as Cele gently led her away. The girl was invited to join them, but she decided not to as she was determined to reach her own destination, where family might await. And she did not want to meet this 'Kronos' guy.

Archer and the three men searched all around for the freshest corpses they could find and had to settle on those in various stages of decomposition. No more fresh ones, so they decided to space out the four fresh rapists' corpses evenly along the route to the tarp-covered pool, with the last one at the other side of the pool. Everybody had been told how to operate the fire hoses by Archer, who did not really know very well how to do it himself. The hose operators waited under the tarpaulin.

Chapter Thirty-Five

Artemis Reveals Herself

Keith had sent them this way. Their progress felt worse than that of a snail in the K-hole. Tommy was actually on ketamine, not sure if he was walking in place, like a glitching video game character. Up ahead, there she was. She stood in the centre of the road, rocking the aviator sunglasses, despite prolonged sunlight being a thing of the distant past. Maia was looking up at her and sat down with a slow wagging of the tail, signifying that she was most of the way towards deciding that she liked what she saw, smelt and felt.

Suzanne instinctively took point in a defensive move, but this garnered no reaction from the lady in the middle of the road. They realised this was not necessary, as this lady was no threat, even if she was insane. But just in case, Suzanne was right where she was needed. The cats were sitting, watching the lady with benign curiosity, but at a safe distance due to the power and strength exuding from this individual, which Tommy felt too, as did all of them, the closer they got. But he trusted nothing of how he felt, due to the ketamine coursing through his system.

Suzanne, calm as always, was ready as always. Tommy reached into his bag and pulled out a Concerta to both complement and offset the ketamine. Funny drug, that one. He bit down on it, swirled it around and then rid his mouth of the foul bitterness with a blackcurrant Soother, which he would suck into nothingness, savouring every second. He had four of those left, which he would guard with his life. He yearned for the Mango Loco Monster drink he had miraculously found amongst the ruins of a school, but if he drank it, he might never find another. And for now, he preferred to have his cake rather than eat it.

As the effects of the Concerta kicked in, he patted the top of the 122 mm artillery shell jutting out of his bag, which he had found near an abandoned howitzer. He also gently checked the pin on a grenade he had superglued to the shell. No rapist, pillager, raider or mob monkey was ever taking him prisoner in this new age of unchecked brutality, parasitism and barbarism. Everyone had agreed to keep a single bullet for themselves or to get near Tommy if they were ever beaten. It did not matter by whom or what. No evil was taking any of them alive.

It was raining inky-black rain. Warm, inky-black rain. This inky-black rain might be freezing cold in ten minutes, for ten minutes, then back to warm. That was not something normal rain did.

"Why are you wearing those ridiculous shades?" Kevin asked aggressively.

"I don't have very nice eyes. Better this way," Artemis replied.

"Surely they can't be that bad," Tommy said, intrigued.

"I'm not here to talk about my eyes. You need to take my word for it; you wouldn't like what you saw."

"Why are you here?" asked Kaitlin in a neutral tone. "Who are you?"

"I am Artemis of Carpathia, protector and peacemaker."

A pause followed, then the whole crew of survivors roared with laughter. Not Suzanne, though. She stood with her arms folded like a bouncer, not looking at the lady in the way some bouncers seem more threatening when they *don't* look at you. Despite the rain, visibility was good; the topography was flat, with short grass. If there was anyone with her, they were far away or underground. No, she was alone. And insane. But benign. Kevin scanned the landscape with night vision.

Did not matter, though; Keith had no reaction to this woman whatsoever. He simply looked sightlessly at her with absorbed fascination. No keening, no whimpering, no momentary clear instructions amidst the endless gibberish. This had also stopped.

When everyone had stopped laughing, Tommy said, "I have always, especially now, been so jealous of people like you. Away with the birds, batshit banana fruitca…"

Artemis was face to face with Tommy in an instant, scaring the shit out of him.

"The evil and cruelty I have seen in 75,000 years, you would certainly *not* be jealous of!!!"

Tommy stared at her, dumfounded. Suzanne's arms dropped to her side, her jaw hanging open with the realisation she could not protect the group from this lady should it become necessary. But she quickly composed herself.

"You can breathe now," the lady said.

Tommy let out his breath, not realising he had been holding it. "That's why you have the glasses," Tommy said. "The evil you've seen is starting to show."

Artemis said nothing, confirming this.

"You're not just talking about human-to-human evil and brutality, are you?" Kaitlin asked.

Artemis slowly shook her head from side to side.

"How did all this start? As in, how did it *really* start? *When* did it start?" Kevin asked. He was spooked now.

"There is a bothy about a mile and a half from here, with a fireplace and lots of firewood. I will tell you everything you want to know."

Greg's Hut Bothy, Cross Fell, two hours later

They were not really cold due to the unnaturally warm

rain, but they welcomed the opportunity to wipe off the chemical residue using vacuum-sealed dry towels (left by very considerate hikers). They felt the cosy, clean warmth and enjoyed the pleasant smell of the untainted firewood piled up inside. It was damp, but with the firelighters left behind long ago by hikers, as well as old newspapers, they soon had a roaring fire, which they all stared into while they waited for the water in the kettle to boil. The hikers had left water bottles, tea, coffee, and Coffee Mate powder.

Artemis greedily guzzled some sort of moonshine, seemingly without effect. She kept this to herself. "Takes the edge off the last 75,000 years. Plush, anyone of you who tries this may wery weel go blind. Ok, that's enough for me. I shiposeddly ..." She took a deep breath and seemed to sober up at an unnatural speed. "Everyone comfortable?" she asked. Everyone either nodded or continued to stare into the fire.

"Okay. You remember the Neanderthals? The Homo erectus? No, obviously not. But you know *of* them, right?"

Tommy nodded yes. He was engaged. He had always been interested in anthropology. The fate of the neanderthals and Homo erectus had always been a hot topic for debate and captured his imagination.

"Well, their fate makes the Holocaust, as you call it, look small by comparison. We systematically ethnically cleansed them for years. Around three hundred million in total between the Homo erectus and the Neanderthals.

"Over a period of eighty or so years, humanity descended into probably the darkest and most depraved period in its history. We destroyed them, and everyone gave into it without resistance. We were bloodthirsty, rabid dogs, and things only started to change as more and more new generations came of age. Humanity decided on a more virtuous future, and the lead perpetrators of these genocides were punished, eventually dying off. Despite the new prosperity that humanity enjoyed, our treatment of the other species of human was still not all that great. We herded them into enclaves, where they lived in squalor.

"Over time, the enclaves got better, and there was a slow reconciliation, with comprehensive education ensuring the dark time was never forgotten. Real prosperity started to flourish despite the dark stain on the history of our race. What remained was the vague notion that we all still shared the guilt of our ancestors and their actions had gone largely unpunished. When we detected significant, building seismic activity under Batak Toba, which is Mount Toba in modern day Sumatra, our shared guilt and paranoia came to the surface.

"Our attempts to thwart our annihilation only expedited it, and not only that. During a half-baked effort to use quantum physics to prevent and neutralise the existential threat, we opened hell. A door to hell. This door was not open for long, but long enough for a large number of demonic entities of all shapes, sizes and abilities to enter our world. What might not have happened for a thousand years did happen in a matter of months after this.

"These things found a way to detonate nuclear weapons inside the supervolcano, and this spread deadly fallout over the entire planet. Humanity had to start again. Before our society and infrastructure were completely destroyed, we found a way of splicing the demonic DNA into ours so that some of us could be strong enough to put up a fight. I was the test subject. But the only one. We ran out of time.

"These things are real, as far as your myths and legends of horrors all over the world are concerned. They had been real for many millennia before the first civilizations in your history books arose. You have suffered a great deal, to put it mildly, for the mistakes of your ancient ancestors. Whether or not you believe in the doctrine that the sins of the father are visited upon the sons doesn't matter. That's the way it all played out. But I believe the debt has been paid."

"What were the people like, back in your day? Did you have music? What clothes did you wear? I have so many questions, most I haven't even thought of yet," Tommy said, overwhelmed and amazed by the information imparted to them.

Suzanne was taking it all in and was deep in thought.

"The people were better-looking, taller and naturally athletic. We ate healthily, and we kept ourselves busy. It was a functioning society with a fantastic quality of life. But as I said, the debt needed to be paid for our collective crime."

"You say the debt has been paid," Kaitlin said. "By which you mean that further 'punishment' is not appropriate?"

"Yes, that's right," replied Artemis.

"Look around you. We are in hell. With demons. The punishment is ongoing. When will it stop? How will it stop? The world is dying a slow death. We have to talk each other out of committing suicide on a daily basis," Kaitlin stated.

"You see that idiot ..." Kevin started to say, pointing at Keith. He was holding Artemis's moonshine.

"If you go blind, *do not* blame me!" she said.

"What is there to see anyway??" he asked rhetorically. "*Anyway*, see that idiot?" He pointed to Keith again. He paused, keeping the drunken eye contact, struggling to focus. He took another swig.

"Yes … The *idiot*? And give that back to me."

Kevin complied. *"He*, the *idiot*, has been our only hope. He's gone from your run-of-the-mill drug addict to some sort of cabbage wizard. He's directing us, and he's our only hope. But we don't know where the hell we're going, if anywhere, or how long it'll be until we get there."

"We don't know what else to do," stated Tommy. "We're all in bad shape, physically and mentally. Like Kevin said, we are in hell. And if we've paid our debt as a race of people, then why are we all living like this? The only thing flourishing is evil. There's rape, humiliation, mutilation, all for sport, around every corner. How things are even going to *begin* to improve is beyond me."

A single tear rolled down his cheek from his good eye, and Kaitlin squeezed his shoulder. Suzanne remained quiet, stoic.

Artemis continued, "Things are like this because Vladimir Putin has bone and pancreatic cancer and the beginnings of Alzheimer's disease. He got wind of a new technology being developed - nanotechnology. People who were pro-Russia in Trump's inner circle, like Trump himself, had relayed the information to him via the intelligence network.

"Putin got hold of the lab notebook from the professor who developed it, but despite his top scientists dedicating their best efforts to recreating the professor's work, they couldn't do it. The professor was caught up in an ethical dilemma and couldn't decide whether to properly create the new technology, the full science of which was in his head and nowhere else. When Putin found out that his military was unable to secure the professor for a one-way ticket to Moscow and torture, he lost his mind. The cold, dark void was calling his name louder than ever, and he made the decision to make the world burn and fall into that very same void."

"Who is this professor? Where is he now?" asked Kaitlin.

"Professor Cawl of the univ…"

"Professor Cawl? The weird one? I've seen him around. He had one single American PhD student, who vanish… Oh, I see. I did a degree in history. Obviously never been to a lecture of his, but he was definitely super intelligent, his brain almost not enough to contain such intelligence. Very eccentric."

"So … where is he now?" Tommy repeated Kaitlin's question.

"He's nowhere; he's dead," replied Artemis.

"Whaa tha hell …?!" Kevin slurred.

"There are two people who've memorised the entire concept of this technology and are currently making their way towards a place where they can implement it. One of these people has inherited the abilities of a medium or clairvoyant. She and Keith have a psychic link. The other individual is someone who's close to you, but that's all I know. I also know that they're being pursued by one of the demons, the reason being that this technology may very well be the only thing that could rid the world of these entities for good. And so, without sounding too hyperbolistic …"

"Hyperrrbolllic," Kevin corrected as he winked at her without his eyes focused on her. He was about to pass out and had the unmistakable leer of the shitfaced.

"Just remember to put him in the recovery position," said Kaitlin.

Artemis looked at Kaitlin, who could only see a frown behind the aviators.

"If not for us, he would have aspirated in one of his comas a long time ago."

"One of his comas?" A smile crept across Artemis's face.

Tommy gave a giggle and said, "I think he's met his match with this one."

Kevin was clearly in a pre-coma phase and could barely stay conscious. He could see everyone staring at him and just said, "Like … that guy … Waiis he wus callin' him, his name, it was like Jon … Boner … Bonham …" He collapsed onto his back, and Suzanne gently put him in the recovery position.

"Anyway, I meant *hyperbolic*. Without sounding too hyperbolic, this technology could be the key to humanity's redemption, if properly implemented and without cutting corners. The demons *do not* want to go back to where they came from. However bad it is here, it's much worse there. They either came from a different dimension or different time, or maybe both, but I can't say with certainty. The fallout we experienced thousands of years ago was nothing compared to now. What I see around me day by day, the worsening of the environmental damage, the evil that is permeating and ruining humanity, the physical changes …" Artemis paused.

"What?!" Kaitlin demanded.

"I think these creatures may have come from a world that resembles a possible future that awaits us unless something is done to thwart this inevitability. I think we're closer to these things than you or I could ever have imagined."

"Then why are we even talking?" asked Tommy in a devastated tone. "If that's our future, then what's the point?"

"These things came from a different dimension. Although we're seeing, in real time, our own world becoming similar to theirs, I don't think we're too late. I think there's cause for hope. We can change the timeline."

Suzanne thought about her ordeal with the nerve agent which had resulted in seemingly permanent physical and mental changes, possibly aggravated by radiation. "You mean these things used to be *us*?!" she asked.

"Not necessarily," Artemis replied. 'I believe they are some version of us from a different dimension which ours resembles, with a possible shared fate. I am so sorry I can't give a better answer."

There was a long, contemplative pause. Artemis let it happen.

Eventually, Tommy piped up, "So, we're relying on the spells of a dead wizard and going to an enchanted castle with an ancient witch (no offence) to magic all of our problems away?"

"Yes, why? Do you have other plans?" Artemis asked. "And no offence taken. I know how awful I look, but I stopped giving a shit millennia ago."

They all laughed, and Kevin started to throw up in his sleep. Tommy dragged him outside by his shoulders and left him face down. Kaitlin cleared away the vomit with an old rag and threw the rag into the night.

"That is not gonna help the environment!" Tommy said drily, with mock disdain.

Kaitlin just looked at him. "I think that ship has sailed."

Tommy felt a twinge in his side. He touched the site of the twinge, and a pain shot through his centre mass. He stood up and lifted his T-shirt. "What do you see?" he asked Kaitlin, who was already looking at it. He could feel it when he ran his fingers over the rough, hairy mass. But it felt different. Less … sensitive? *Was this a good thing?* he wondered. A smile crept across his face. Had that jolt of pain caused his stomach knot to loosen a little?

"You should be horrified by that disgusting lesion, not happy," a suddenly sober Kevin said.

"I was just thinking that," Kaitlin said.

Everybody was looking at Tommy.

Artemis suddenly seemed to tense, but not to attack. She seemed as though she was preparing to defend herself.

"You think I'm worried?" Tommy said. "I'm not. I pray for death every day. This could be my ticket out of this shit-hole. Anything changing for the better would be a miracle at this point. I just hope this thing doesn't make it slow and painful."

"*HAVE YOU SEEN THE DEVIL?*" Artemis's tone caused Tommy to almost lose control of his bowels. "*YOU THINK THIS WILL BRING YOU DEATH?*"

Everyone looked at Tommy, then Artemis. Tommy looked at everybody, then Artemis. She went in close to Tommy's face and pushed him backwards three feet against the wall. She had her back to everyone. She got her nose an inch away from Tommy's. He finally understood the concept of shitting himself with fear. But he had not long been, thankfully, and a loud, long fart escaped him. Tommy knew not to resist. Suzanne started moving towards Artemis to defend Tommy, who stopped her by putting his hand up, subconsciously deciding he now trusted Suzanne 100%.

Artemis had not demonstrated her full strength, but they all knew it was there. Suzanne had almost superhuman strength, but this was dwarfed by that of Artemis. After a few seconds, she released the pressure and let him stand where he was. Her right hand, with three sharp claws, crept up his bare torso, stopping at the lesion with one claw and gently pressing inward. Her left hand slowly took off her glasses.

Tommy's one good eye now saw both those of Artemis. His breathing stopped before she slowly whispered, *"Is this what you want, Tommy? You think you've had enough of this life?"*

Her claw gently ran up and down the lesion before all three claws grabbed it and started to pull. Artemis slid her glasses back on and ripped off the corrupted mass. The blood started to flow immediately as Tommy gave a sharp intake of breath, seemingly the first breath in minutes. His face went red, then purple, with his head shaking like a shitting baby as he shut his one good eye as tight as he could. The blood did not flow for long before Artemis had a red-hot poker pressed against the gaping wound.

The veins in Tommy's head grew big and pulsated, and he started keening. No more blood. Artemis let go of him and he dropped to the floor, contorted into the foetal position. Kaitlin readied some lyophilizate diamorphine for oral administration, and cyclizine IV, which she intended to give him as an intramuscular shot. The same for the IV flucloxacillin. She administered all of it as Tommy mercifully lost consciousness. Kaitlin then applied a dressing.

"I just bought you some time before you enter a hellish eternity." It did not matter to Artemis whether or not he heard it. She held up her hand, now a hand with five fingers and not a three-taloned claw. In her hand was the green and black mottled mass.

"It smells like arse, even though everything smells bad now." Kevin was seated beside a catatonic Keith with a Corona beer. "I found this under a table. And Artemis, after what I just saw and what I went through, I will never steal your moonshine, or cross you in any way, again."

Tommy started to come around. "Thank you," he said meekly as he looked under his arm at the dressing applied by Kaitlin. His wound throbbed with an intensity stopping just short of pain. He looked at the dead mass in the hand of Artemis.

She opened the door, and with all her might, threw it outside. Tommy knew this thing was thrown further than any human could throw.

"I'm just glad you're on our side," Tommy said.

"So … what now?" Kaitlin asked Artemis.

"We wait." This response surprised everyone. "Tommy, Ginny is almost here. She's with other friendly survivors."

"What? How does she know to come here?"

Artemis pointed to Keith.

"One of their party is clairvoyant."

"Clare who?" Kevin asked. Silence. Kevin knew he had asked a stupid question from the silence and a gentle facepalm from Tommy.

"She's drawing the survivors here. *Do not worry*. They are good. And …"

"He is following them," Keith whined.

"Oh, yes, so you said. Who the hell is following them? Can you elaborate?" Tommy asked Artemis. "And thanks for the help. I think that fart had been trapped inside me for some time."

"Mervyn is following them."

Tommy had the mental image of a middle-aged man with

an Orange Order sash and protruding nasal hairs mixing with a thick grey moustache.

"Who named it Mervyn?" Tommy asked.

"Your wife and her group did. You can refer to it as Moloch if you want. Doesn't matter. Both are names given to it by humans."

There was a gentle scratching at the door. Artemis opened it, and with a smile, let in Maia, Akasha, Jesse and Violet.

"I guess the coast must be clear." Artemis smiled genuinely for the first time. It was not a good look. However, all four approached her without reservation.

Chapter Thirty-Six

Kronos Has Landed

Kronos could smell the death long before he landed - all of them could. They could also smell a trap. They were confident they could overcome any trap set for them. In Estonia, the people had discovered a fundamental vulnerability to a certain liquid. How had they known about this? Did not matter, though – all it had done was make him stronger and multiplied him several times. And all of them could act as one mind or as separate entities, depending on any scenarios they might be challenged with. Fear of death was reduced as well, as if one were killed, the mind and body would live on the ones remaining.

He did not mind sacrificing his height, and overall, having several copies of himself made him stronger.

One replica came up from below deck as land quickly approached. "At least one of us needs to stay behind," he said.

"Agreed. Both of you stay out of sight and come only if called."

They held a direct psychic link and an almost identical thought pattern in substance and timing.

The yacht, named 'Eternal Horizon' by an owner with zero imagination, was moored by its pilot at the dog leg quay in Newcastle harbour. Not further in, because there seemed to be a fresh, bullet-riddled corpse not far from the end of the quay. One of the replicas disembarked, followed by the constantly chittering cacodemons.

"Will you let me go now?" the yacht's pilot asked the above-deck replica.

"Why would I do that, hmmm?" it teased.

The pilot could hear laughing coming from below the deck.

"Well, I got you to where you need to be, plus should both of you not go to eat too? He's getting all the food while you both stay here." Straight away, the pilot regretted saying this and put his head in his hand while his other hand reached down to a hidden compartment. He pulled out a revolver. The man's hand was swatted, flinging the revolver into the ocean.

"You think that piece of shit can kill *ME*?" the creature bellowed, demanding an answer.

"No," the man said. "But it could have killed me," he said in an utterly despondent tone.

Kronos grabbed the man's ankle and pulled it towards him, with a strength pretty much unmatched in this reality.

"You tried to deprive me of a warm, living meal. How could you do such a thing? I won't punish you, though. I really could not top what I was going to do to you anyway." Kronos snapped the man's tibia and fibula and pulled once, detaching the entirety of the man's lower leg. He tightened his other claw around the man's stump as a tourniquet to stop him bleeding out.

The man stopped screaming and passed out. Kronos removed the shoe from the lower leg and bit off the entire foot, slowly chewing it while keeping the stump tight.

Kronos suddenly spat out the foot and let go of the stump. He felt a sudden pain, the same as he had felt when the soldiers had shot that liquid at him, only it was all over his body, and it would not stop. Kronos could feel the pain move down to the bone and all the way through. He passed out. When he woke up, the yacht owner had bled out.

Not far away, around the same time

"That was way too easy," Charlotte said. Kronos had

been fooled into trying to walk across the tarp-covered pool, only to be wrapped up in the tarp and immersed in a roughly 70% ethanol solution. He made a noise like a rat being dropped in acid for around a minute. He eventually stopped thrashing around and went still. The pool went completely black. Kronos had been dissolved. Not out of stupidity but out of pure hubris. He did not think that the knowledge of his only real weakness was this widespread.

"And why was he only five feet tall? I thought he was a giant?" Charles said as he gazed at the bodies of the cacodemons taken out even more easily with the M60.

The last word, 'giant', was followed by blood gushing from his mouth. Another shorter-than-expected Kronos withdrew his claw and stabbed Moe in the same way. This Kronos was immediately hit with a high-pressure jet from the other side of the pool and then another from a different direction. Derek retrieved the M60, made sure the box feed was clear, and loaded the first round. He flipped the low tripod, lay prone, and started emptying the rounds into the second Kronos. The rounds definitely caused pain, but it did not look like any serious harm was being done.

Derek tried to lead Kronos to the pool. He felt a sharp pain in his back, like he had been bitten. Yes, he had been bitten. One of the cacodemons clearly had been missed. Derek turned and tried to keep the cacodemon at arm's length as it attempted to bite him again. He drew his knife, but it was swiped out of his hand. Something mercifully lifted the cacodemon off him. There was Clarette. She threw the cacodemon into the side of the fire engine, breaking every bone in its body.

Derek could now see that the thing had already been seriously injured. He turned back to prone and engaged the M60 again. It was becoming clear that the fire hoses could only hurt Kronos, not kill him. They needed to immerse him in that black pool with the other one. Derek abandoned the M60 when the bullets ran out and used the hose on the third fire engine. After a few seconds, the pressure was lost. "JESUS CHRIST!!!!" he screamed in frustration. The other engines had expended their water. Kronos was badly hurt but healing. They had to get him into the pool.

Clarette bent over, put her arms under Kronos's arms, and lifted him into a bear hug. She acted now because once Kronos got his strength back, they stood no chance. Humanity stood no chance. The physical contact between Clarette and Kronos caused Clarette's skin to start burning from the ethanol solution. But she tightened her grip and walked to the pool. Kronos made a sound like a thousand screaming pigs as he struggled to get free of Clarette, but he was not at full strength.

Clarette jumped into the pool, and it was like someone had dropped a fizzy co-codamol into coke. The screaming went on for longer this time. It was still going after five minutes.

"Stand back, Cele!" Charlotte said as she noticed Cele standing too close to the edge.

A melted, bubbling black claw shot out of the pool and grabbed her ankles. It yanked her into the pool, her skull cracking on the ground first. They saw Cele sink lifelessly. Two fizzing, bubbling claws emerged and dug into the cement as Kronos tried to pull himself out.

"MUMMY!"

Archer heard Amelia screaming as she ran at the pool. She stopped suddenly at the sight of the black-clawed mass dissolving in front of her. Kronos had successfully got out of the pool. As he made a move towards Amelia, Clarette's dissolving arm shot out of the pool, grabbing Kronos and holding him in place, but she did not have the strength to pull him back in. Without thinking, Archer slammed into Kronos, the momentum carrying them both into the pool, helped by the last of Clarette's strength. Kronos used the last of his to hold onto Archer, to drown him out of spite. By the time the grip was released, it was too late for Archer. Charlotte, Amelia and Derek were alive. Kronos, Clarette, Charles, Moe and Archer were dead. Charlotte took the crying child by the hand, and the three of them ran.

The third and final Kronos held back and watched. The first two had been trounced, and he wasn't taking more chances. There was a child, a woman and a man. How had they got the better of him twice? He looked at the black pool. Somehow, these people also knew that they could be hurt by this mysterious substance. Why had no one figured this out in the home world? Also, how did they know that simple contact with this liquid, even at high pressure, was not enough, and that full, prolonged immersion was needed? How did they get them in there and stop them from getting out?

"You know, there is more than one way to kill Kronos the Titan," a soft voice said, sounding like it was whispered right by the ear of Kronos.

Kronos turned and looked up at a beautiful but inhuman face. It looked at Kronos with pure fascination.

"You were not always like this, were you?" it said softly.

Kronos bared his teeth and screamed.

"We need to get you some mouthwash, old chap. But definitely not the one with ethanol, am I right?" Ása-Þór said mockingly. "You DO NOT belong in this world." At that, Ása-Þór easily tore the remaining Kronos in half. He tore him limb from limb and threw all the parts of the dismembered demon in the pool. Ása-Þór waited for the pool to stop fizzing and hung around for longer just to be certain. Finally, Kronos was gone.

The drama playing out nearer the west coast of this island could wait. A prominent Echthroi was chasing after a band of human survivors, purely for the sake of vengeance. On the face of it, Baphomet was the bigger threat to human suffering, and that one was taken care of. The next biggest threat, as judged by Ása-Þór, were the hags. In deepest, darkest Russia, where they hid and periodically went into dormancy, the trio of hags corrupted the hearts of humans all over the world, as well as snatching the innocent to sustain their malevolent influence. Russia and East Asia unfortunately bore the brunt of this. They had kept themselves under the radar so far, impressive considering how long they had been here. The evidence was there, though, if one knew where to look.

He was not sure if he could neutralise the hags. Their actions seemed similar, if less intense, than those of Baphomet, but more sinister and orders of magnitude more powerful. He had to determine the extent of their abilities, how powerful they were, their origins and their intentions. They seemed to be preparing for something. Their preternatural ability to control the environment around them, as well as the actions of humans, through the use of nanotechnology, was intriguing. He would watch the hags from afar. He would find a way. But he had to be very patient.

Chapter Thirty-Seven

We Finally Meet Again

Mercifully, Mervyn got distracted, sometimes for days at a time. Jane was given a reprieve from the intense whispers, as were they all. Maksim would pass into a deep sleep for many hours, the varying levels of mocking laughter temporarily gone. On these occasions, they would take the opportunity to cover as much distance as possible. Eventually, Mervyn would lose interest in whatever other thing he was doing and resume the pursuit. And their progress was slow. What should have been a ten-hour car journey had taken them almost two long years.

It never seemed to matter, though; he would get to within a certain distance and not come closer. This time was by far the longest break in the pursuit. The Humvee was long gone, and they were all on mountain bikes scavenged from a miraculously untouched bike shop. They were all out of breath but kept going, knowing that Jane was insistent the next chapter in their terrible journey was imminent.

There was a noise that Ginny recognised from a long time ago. It was urgent, excited and anticipatory honking, whining and chuffing. Was that ...? *Noooo*, Ginny thought. There was absolutely no way Maia was still alive. She had long finished grieving for her husband, dog, cats and children. Then a loud *MWWWAAAAOOOO* could be heard around a hundred feet away, and a little bell, getting louder and louder. The group had stopped to listen to the weird sounds, unfamiliar to everyone except Ginny. Khuntz and Maksim were whispering heatedly in Russian, and Jane was looking at Ginny. Doug, Adam and Steve were scanning the horizon.

"This is all familiar to you, isn't it?" Jane said.

"There!" Doug pointed at two very similar black and white cats, one with a bell collar, and a tuxedo cat, trotting towards them. These cats were friendly and made a beeline for Ginny, who crouched with her palms outstretched. After a minute or two of happy greeting, the tuxedo cat jumped on the back of the bell-collar cat, and after a brief skirmish, all three bolted away in the direction they had come. The excited whining and honking continued. They started to follow the cats over the crest of a hill to find an obviously occupied bothy.

That is where the excited dog noises were coming from. When they were around a hundred feet from the bothy, the corrugated iron door was pulled aside by an ancient-looking man with a rifle slung over his shoulder. There she was. Mangy, skinny and dirty looking, but it was her. It was her darling Maia. Ginny was off the bike and crouched down again, waiting for something she had long ago accepted was never going to happen again, something which was a valued daily experience: the Maia welcome.

On the wooden floors of the house they lived in before this, she remembered the happy-feet dance of the claws on the wooden floor, the happy-feet dance that never got old. As she rubbed Maia's back and head vigorously, she put her fingers to her lips and said "ssssshhhhhhh." That was Maia's cue to roll over on her back. There was a healed-over bite on her chest, no doubt taken to defend her family. Once Maia had given Ginny a shake and a high five, Ginny heard the word in that familiar Northern Irish accent. "Babe?"

What was this monstrosity that hovered over her that

looked vaguely like her husband? "BACK OFF!" Doug shouted, understandably, as the deranged, feral-looking Tommy approached Ginny.

"Piss off," Tommy responded dismissively, without even looking at Doug.

Doug looked confused at Tommy's disrespect; most other men were intimidated by him.

Ginny was still Ginny, although she was underweight. She stood up, and they touched cheeks and tightly embraced each other. Kaitlin joined the embrace, and the family were partially reunited.

"We must go now," Jane said. "He's on the move."

The three remained in the embrace. Tommy gently put his hand to Ginny's face and kissed her. "You're talking about Mervyn, aren't you?"

"Can you hear the whispers?" Jane asked.

Tommy just gave a grotesque frown.

"I think it's personal with us," Doug said.

"Yeah," Adam said. "Mervyn has an ancient hatred for all humanity and will gladly inflict pain in the most arbitrary manner to any human. But it's even more personal than that."

"So, you tried to shoot the devil in the back," Kevin said. The old man had crept up to them. He took a swig of Artemis's moonshine.

Artemis rolled her eyes behind the aviators.

"And missed," Tommy said.

"Well, no, not really," Steve said. 'More like we shot him in the back 50 times, and the bastard still kept getting up."

"Well, it is the devil. Seriously, though, that is what we are up against? Really?" Tommy asked nobody in particular, but looking at Ginny, his voice of reason for over a quarter of his life.

"I'm sorry, babe, but to all intents and purposes, yeah."

Tommy's heart sank. "I'm tired, babe, we have a toasty bothy, and I haven't seen you in almost two years. Now we have to resume our trek across hell to God knows where, just because you have somehow got yourselves into a blood feud with Satan?" Tommy pinched the bridge of his nose and shut his one good eye. Then he started laughing.

This quickly became contagious. Everybody laughed. Kevin smirked and shook his head and then frowned and steadied himself. He put out his hand as if to gather his thoughts. "This supernatural thing that's following you, he's been following you for how long? Almost two years? Since the start, right?"

"Yes," Doug piped up.

"He could have caught up with you already, easily. There's something bigger going on, I think. We can get to that later, but I think with the whispers and mocking laughter, he's messing with you. I think that he won't actually do anything until you reach your destination, where it's all going to go down. And where is that exactly?"

"Cruachan Dam in Loch Etive, Scotland," Jane said.

"Have you got anything that can hurt him?" Kevin asked.

"Yeah, seventy percent ethanol. We've accrued quite a lot since this all started. It's how we got him before. We have quite a lot in our backpacks," Ginny confirmed.

"So that would explain why you're all armed with some kind of Super Soaker?"

"Yeah." Ginny smiled, shedding a single tear.

Tommy and Ginny had resumed their quiet embrace, cheek to cheek.

"So, Mervyn is waiting until the right time. He's probably gathering an army," Kevin said.

"We suspected that," said Doug.

There were a few facepalms. Doug knew in his heart that the flayer was part of all this.

"Okay," Kevin said as he took another swig of the moonshine.

Artemis appeared and snatched it out of his hand.

"This is all pretty depressing. But bottom line, he won't do anything tonight. We *all* need rest. Let's take this opportunity. Otherwise, we won't last much longer."

"But the whispers and laughter?" Jane said.

They were becoming aware of Maksim starting to lose it and Khuntz trying to calm him down. He threw his bike to the ground. Jane could feel her psychic link reaching out to her from inside the bothy. She accepted the invitation, and between them, they combined their strength to form a spiritual barrier. She beckoned out to Maksim, and he came to her. She started walking to the bothy with him, the barrier getting stronger and going further as she made her way towards Keith, her arm around Maksim. The laughing had stopped. And she laid eyes on Keith for the first time.

Chapter Thirty-Eight

The Confrontation Approaches

Mervyn and his army near Ben Cruachan Visitor Centre, three weeks after the reunion

The two clairvoyant members of the group together were able to employ the psychic shield indefinitely without exhausting themselves, as long as they stayed close. The distance they covered in two weeks would have previously taken 4-6 months with Mervyn's constant psychic interference.

It did not hurt Mervyn and did not shield their location, but it meant a welcome break from the mental torture inflicted on the party over the best part of two years. Mervyn had been dragging this out for the joy of mental torture and curiosity as to where they were going and why. In the meantime, they had armed themselves to the teeth with the liquid they knew would kill him, in silly looking children's toys, so he had needed an army. The army he raised was led by a faceless man with an axe to grind, as well as a half-human, half-demon-like creature who led and controlled an army of useful cacodemons.

He held back as he did not see the need to intervene, and only wanted to follow, especially as the survivors grew in number and had a lot of conventional weapons at their disposal. They had enough of the strange clear liquid, and a way to wield it against him, to at least leave him the same way they had outside the university two years ago, or worse. He had never felt pain like that, as far as he could remember, but there was something enrapturing about the experience. Once this was all over, he wanted to experience it again in a controlled environment.

Mervyn was still not sure whether they couldn't or just didn't kill him. He did not even know if he could die. For now, he did not want to find out. His mission was to get this gathering of survivors to lead him to their destination, intercept them, and learn of the nature of this technology. He wanted to take it and wield it for his own ends. He had pondered if it were possible to get rid of all the other Echthroi and take this world for himself, except for a few weaker beings that would be loyal to him. He was aware that the group he was following might know his plans, so he needed to proceed with caution.

And so, when the group stopped outside Ben Cruachan Visitor Centre, it looked like they had reached their destination. The order was given to attack, but it appeared that the army had been spotted when the survivors suddenly made their way across the road and through the woodland to start up the incline towards Cruachan Dam. Mervyn gave the order to sneak up on the group from behind to ensure they were not killed quickly so that Jim could have the one thing he had asked for. This was in return for his army's loyalty. The mysterious liquid could not hurt them.

Ben Cruachan Visitor Centre

Two members of their party were able to teach the others and get them at least some way to their level of expertise in using firearms. After the encounter with Mervyn, Doug and Adam had revisited RAF Lakenheath and found a lot of weapons still in the armoury. Here, they had the creepiest and yet funniest experience they had ever had together, when at 4.30 p.m., the silence was broken by a slowed-down version of the UK national anthem, followed by the US anthem. This must have been on a timer that replayed these every day, and the thought of those two anthems being played like that in the creepy, dark emptiness for the foreseeable future always made Doug and Adam shudder, especially at that time of day.

When the two groups came together, they had enough weapons and Super Soakers to share, especially as the Super Soakers were far from the first thing people hoarded in an apocalypse, so they were easy to find. Tommy's group did have their own firearms, but not Super Soakers.

The united groups were at the Visitor Centre for Cruachan Dam, once a happy meeting point for families, hikers and school trips but now a burnt-out husk, so many good times long forgotten.

Khuntz approached Doug, who was trying to get a look at the route up using military binoculars, but he could not see it yet. The dam would not be visible until they had been walking towards it for a while. "How about a nice cappuccino with cream, eh?" he said to Doug, putting his arm around him.

A method of domination sometimes, or friendliness. It made no difference to Doug, who stood ramrod straight. "I don't think they have any chocolate powder," replied Doug. He was stone-faced but broke into a smile as the professor laughed at his deadpan sarcasm. They were both out of breath, like everyone else, with a constant pounding headache. The conditions were becoming more and more incompatible with life − life as a human anyway.

Then the smile was gone, and Doug scanned with the binoculars for any useful intelligence. "So, you've been here before?" he asked the professor.

"Yes, a number of times. Sometimes with Professor Cawl and sometimes not."

"Highly secretive?"

"Yes."

"With a secret entrance?"

"Of course!"

"And you can get in?"

"Well, that depends."

Doug looked directly at him for the first time in this exchange. "It DEPENDS?" Doug raised his voice a little.

"It depends on whether or not there is someone there."

"And why wouldn't there be?"

"I think there will be."

"And why do you think that?"

"Well, we all had many conversations about what we would do if things went bad. It's a survival bunker too, with enough MREs to feed up to twenty people for five years. My best guess is that the people we need are in there. I think they came here after the first bomb hit, maybe with their families. That's what they said they would do."

"And if they're not?"

"I was only ever issued with a laminate when someone let me in."

"What were you all doing in that place?"

"Nanotech. It was built for Professor Cawl in the good faith that he would come here, maybe live here, and do his research. But we were getting pissed off at his tactics of delay, with endless promises and assurances."

"Why did you need him here so badly? Could you not have gotten someone else if he was so unreliable?"

Doug felt the abscess in his jaw send signals of weakness and misery through his body. They had run out of toothpaste quite some time ago and could not find more.

Doug was not the only one with an abscess, but it was the worst one. He was two weeks deep on a third course of back-to-back antibiotics supplied by Tommy. He was not improving.

"He was one of a kind. We didn't know of any other individuals in the entire scientific community who could think like him. Up there, we have the equipment, and the people who said they would stay there with their families. Down here, we have Cawl's work stored in the minds of Ginny and Jane. If everything comes together as I hope it will, then the implications are so wide-ranging that we could take that abscess from your jaw and give you a new set of teeth. Yes, there are possible negatives, but at this point, what have we got to lose?"

"What exactly is up there?" asked Tommy.

They both flinched. They would never get used to his appearance.

"A particle accelerator," answered Khuntz.

"For doing what?"

"Generating the energy field required to manifest the artificial intelligence required to implement the nanotechnology."

"Well, just when I thought humanity could do no more damage. This could fix everything, couldn't it?"

"Yes."

"And it could also make things worse beyond our most horrific nightmares?"

"Yes."

"And is there anything that can be done to ensure things go to plan?"

"Yes."

"Well, what then, Khunt?"

"Khuntz."

"Sorry."

"It's okay. This type of artificial intelligence will be powerful enough to read the thoughts of and scan the entire memory of the first person or persons it comes into contact with. It will undergo its first and most profound series of interactions with the first individual it encounters. Think of it as raising a newborn baby into a good and productive member of society, in the space of thirty seconds. So everything will hinge on who is there when the AI is in the process of becoming the singularity."

"Oh, yeah, I heard about that. Amazing stuff! I can't believe I may see it happen right in front of me!"

Everybody suddenly became aware of the presence of Artemis and flinched. Jane was with her.

"I wish I knew what we did wrong all that time ago, but I was a leader, not a scientist. I don't know if what is being done is even remotely similar. But there is one thing I do know. Do *not* rush things. *Do not* cut corners or wing anyth…"

"They're coming," Jane said.

Before anyone could ask who, Adam, at his lookout post, whistled the signal, and they all walked briskly towards the incline leading to Cruachan Dam. They left their bikes behind. Unnoticed, Artemis stayed at the Centre.

They were out of breath to begin with and had decided to rest near the Visitor Centre. If Adam spotted their pursuers, the plan was to get to the dam. It was not far from the Visitor Centre, but initially, there was a steep incline.

Doug checked over his sniper rifle and loaded it. "I'm heading to high ground. You know I won't be far. My priority here is the creepy little flayer. He's not getting away this time. We can't fight them, but I can get rid of him." He really wished he had more claymores. He walked ahead of the others, clutching his jaw, and went up the mountain via a thick primaeval forest, not something just anyone would be able to do.

They were at the point now where they would soon know if the hope they had for the best part of two years was indeed false, and if it did turn out that way, they would, every one of them, beg the pursuers to end them. After they had crossed the road to the Visitor Centre and gone through the small woodland, they walked around a hundred feet up the incline, wide enough for a car, until it temporarily flattened out to an open area. At this point, the path narrowed going up, and the hiking trail to the dam was in sight. Suddenly, they were lit by powerful high beams from an old Ford Explorer. It was clear their pursuers had decided to confront them.

Chapter Thirty-Nine

Tim and Artemis Fulfil Their Destinies

Tim

Almost two years ago, when Tim had first heard those malevolent whispers, he intuitively knew three things: that the malignant mutterings were not directed at him, that he wanted to run away, and that there was also a voice inside him, from deeper than he could understand, urging him to pursue the whispering. The urge to run away was simple fight-or-flight autonomics, but there was also an urge to go against this primal compulsion. This urge was from a benign, familiar place, and somehow he just knew this. This urge was the stronger one, so he pursued the whisperings.

It was not long before the small group of survivors were able to make visual contact with the source of the whispering, which also seemed to be so focused on another group of survivors that they never noticed Tim's group, psychically or otherwise. Through a pair of military binoculars taken from a dead soldier, he kept track of and followed them. The targets of the consistent psychic attack seemed to be evading capture for now.

They were understandably incredulous, to the point of almost abandoning him, when he wanted to pursue the whisperings, until Mary made a conscious decision to have faith in Tim's judgement, no matter how counterintuitive this might seem. Even Tim hearing the whispers was enough to convince them there was more to the world than can conventionally be perceived with the standard range of human senses.

Mary had talked Greg and Robert around. They had to

stick together, given all they had been through in such a short period of time. Greg had saved them from the colonel who had wanted to take revenge on them for stealing his and his men's safe and secure shelter. If Greg had not figured out how to engage the outer defences of the shelter, they would have been tortured and killed.

Ken, the RealDoll, had given up his life after Mary had the idea of inserting a broom handle up Ken's arsehole to raise him up through the door of the shelter. The anal cavity was deep enough for the amount of broom handle needed to perform the task. This was to determine if the colonel and his men were lying in wait. They were, and although Ken had taken the majority of the bullets, Robert had lost the little finger of his left hand to a ricochet.

After Mary had tended to his wounds, Tim had remarked that if he had to choose a finger to lose, that would be the one he would give up. The darkest, blackest humour over the best part of two years since they had left the shelter was the one thing that gave them relief from the hopelessness that invaded all of their senses without letting up. Gone were the cool summer breezes with the smell of freshly cut grass in the summer. Gone were the beautiful, cool and calm autumn evenings of Norfolk, with the striking red sunsets.

Now, it was like the air never moved. It was stale, and nothing smelt good anymore. They all were at least slightly out of breath at all times, which really messed with their ability to get a good night's sleep. Always present was the sheen of sweat on everyone's forehead. They all knew they did not have much time left. Madness was creeping in slowly but surely, and they were all losing focus. Robert most of all, possibly due to an acceleration of already present dementia. He kept randomly wandering off, and the other three had to watch him. A few times now, they had had close calls with Robert wanting to make random noises when they needed to stay quiet.

Mary was getting a toxic goitre on her neck, which did not help stave off the pervading hopelessness that invaded every second of every day. Tim had had to make a lot of sacrifices regarding his insulin. He had a portable USB fridge with a crank he could use to charge it. This had been engineered by Greg, and it was genius. However, he had to turn the crank endlessly for hours every day. It had packed up weeks ago, and now he was taking tainted insulin which had been out of the fridge for weeks. He was on borrowed time. And he could feel it.

He had sacrificed fast-acting insulin over a year ago because he needed much more of that than the slow-acting one, and there was barely enough room in the tiny fridge even for that. Refined sugar these days was a luxury, anyway, reducing the need for fast-acting insulin. The small amount of sugar he had, he needed for hypos. So, he kept himself going with slow-acting insulin injections once a day, and this kept him, not healthy, but alive. No one was healthy anymore.

By the time they reached the mountain in Scotland, they had known for quite some time what they were following. A god-awful demonic-looking creature led the horde. They surrounded themselves with restrained and mutilated captured Russian troops, whom they fed on piece by piece. Tim did not feel sorry for them at all, and the smell when they cooked the Russian flesh smelt delicious. Tim and his group would greedily feed on their leftovers.

The only thing that kept the others alive in the group

was Tim, his deceased father's voice always telling them when to run, when to stay, when to keep quiet, and when to pre-emptively kill when they had the element of surprise. There were two other lower-ranked leaders he and his compatriots had observed over time. To Tim's utter devastation, his brother had become one of them, meeting them when he had stood in the middle of the road with his own mob six months ago.

He had on only a pair of shorts and commanded a mob of the same type of former humans he had first seen at Weybourne almost two years ago. Tim watched as they regularly fed on Jonah's blood when he let them, with him fighting them off when they decided to drink from him when he wasn't willing to allow it. A few times, when Jonah's entourage started to get out of control with him, he would simply grab one of them, tear them apart and then feed on them. But most of the corpse would be consumed by the remainder of his mob.

After this, his belly would bulge unnaturally, gradually going down again until the cycle repeated itself.

After seeing this for the first time, Greg had whispered, "Should I ask him if wants a waaafer thin mint?"

This had sent them into an uncontrollable fit of intense, whispered cackling. As Tim looked through the binoculars again at the horrific sight of the enormous protruding gut on his brother, he felt tears of joy from the laughing fit roll down his face. The grotesque army was on the move. He realised then how vulnerable they had all been when they had lost control. But it was *worth it*. He had forgotten how good an uncontrolled laughing fit felt.

Jonah was covered in scars of varying severity, all healed, but the scar tissue was not normal. It had patches of coarse black hair. Worst of all was his left leg, if you could call it a leg anymore. Originally, there had been a hastily repaired, badly infected wound. The infection healed, except it didn't. The infection became part of him, and was slowly starting to cover him, like the scars. It was becoming a corrupted biological suit of armour covering the entire left leg. It looked similar to that of the entity leading the preternatural legion.

"Was this thing once a human?" Tim had asked rhetorically.

Mary's toxic goitre was already bad enough, but one day Greg noticed something. As he looked at her, she stroked it gently as a foul understanding crept across her face.

"Is that black hair on your ..." Greg attempted to ask.

Mary cut him off. "YES!" she snapped. A single tear rolled down her cheek.

"It's the radiation," said Robert. "Either it kills you or weakens you. In which case, you will die eventually. But there appears to be a third scenario none of us could have predicted."

"It strengthens you," Mary said. Her face now had a 'wow' expression as she mentally stuffed her previous horrible realisation down deep. "There's a profound spiritual aspect to this whole thing. I couldn't possibly elaborate, but all I know is that it's there. I can feel it."

This comment was met with contemplative silence, which confirmed consensus on this assertion.

Then, there was the old man. The people he 'commanded' seemed normal enough. Full of pure rage, but normal human rage.

"The old man, what the hell happened to him?" asked Greg.

"I think something happened to his face and upper body. The inevitable infection became part of him, I guess, just like Jonah. It seems to feed on hate," Robert replied.

The old man was topless, and his whole upper body was a mass of course black hair on oily, mottled green skin. Someone stood beside him, a loyal dogsbody always holding a curved skinning knife. Jonah would regularly give this man one of his corrupted humans for him to skin alive.

They would eventually die, some of them. But none of them could feel pain, which seemed to frustrate the flayer. Some of them, however, rejoined Jonah, and the areas where they had been skinned had the same disgusting growth that Jonah, the old man and the demon had. Some were mainly red, some green, some brown and other colours. Some were all of the colours, like an LGBTQ flag after it had been left in a swamp for months. After this, they had no interest in feeding on Jonah, and on a few occasions had attacked and cannibalised the army following the disfigured old man. The resulting skirmish had to be mediated by the demon, laying down the law by tearing apart two or three from either side who it perceived to be the main instigators.

Tim had never got closer than two miles from the preternatural, wicked legion. Now, he observed all of them surrounding some people but not attacking. Tim, Greg, Robert and Mary all slowly sneaked closer as furtively as they could, until they were the closest they had ever been. They all instinctively knew that they would soon find out for certain why they had followed this vile legion all the way to the bottom of this mountain for the best part of two years. This was where it was going to go down.

Now they were under half a mile away, albeit in a well-hidden position. The previously beautiful, majestic mountain now looked evil in itself, a towering, hostile mass threatening to destroy any who would dare to go near it.

Tim knew they were in hell. A sharp intake of breath caused Tim to drop the binoculars. "*Now* we know," Tim whispered.

The other three looked through the binoculars to see a band of around ten survivors up against a rock wall.

"That's my mum, my stepdad and my sister. I don't know any of the others." Tim sat on a rock, utterly defeated. "What the hell am I supposed to do?" A wave of profound hopelessness slowly began to engulf him. "I've found my family and now I have to watch while they get raped, tortured, or flayed?" A tear rolled down his cheek, and he put his head in his hands.

Robert held the binoculars. "The leader, the entity, is talking to the group up against the wall. I think it's savouring the moment until the inevitable happens. Someone's taking their weapons. Super Soaker water guns? What the fu…"

"Robert!" Mary said in a scolding manner. She snatched the binoculars from him to see the leader motioning to the knife-wielding psychopath.

He approached and walked up and down the line. He seemed to be choosing a victim. When he had chosen, men from the deformed old man's army grabbed the victim.

A soft weeping distracted Mary. It was coming from Tim, head still in his hands. He grabbed his backpack and slammed it on the ground as hard as he could. Unfortunately, this caused his iPod to continue its shuffle, and it was attached to speakers. 'Ghost of the Navigator' by Iron Maiden was coming to a close. Then a mediocre DragonForce song came on that he had heard a million times before, 'Prepare for War'. It was on full volume. "Fitting," he mumbled.

Greg grabbed the binoculars to see a young man, 16 or 17 years old, duct taped to an old garden chair. The deformed, monstrous old man was before the child, shouting and screaming, but nothing could be made out. The old man had no facial features but for one eye hole and a bigger one for the mouth. He stormed away and nodded to the smiling flayer, an atypical nerd in every way, with a smile that could wipe out all plant life in a hundred-foot radius, if there was any.

As the flayer readied his knife, he cocked his head at the bound teenager as if trying to choose a place to start. He never got to choose. A shot rang out of a heavy calibre rifle, and the flayer's head exploded. What was left of the flayer simply dropped to the ground and lay still. The old man's army had their rifles trained at a specific place and were screaming at a man on a rocky outcrop, who threw his rifle to the ground and made his way down, taking his place at the wall with the rest of them.

A warm feeling arose in Tim's feet as the DragonForce song continued. Lyrics he had never paid attention to before started to mean something.

I hear a distant thunder
They say, "Bow down, surrender"
Witnessing our demise and the sins of our land
Why can't we see from under?
Dark reign of our defenders
Endlessly torturing the souls without stand

Fight now, let's break the chains
So strong, we must feel the pain
Forever torn apart from the haunting fears of my heart

Rage and fear from skies above, the fire fuels my veins
Destruction of humanity, the everlasting flame
Cast away, no turning back from long-forgotten shores
We'll show no mercy as they fall
The fire burns inside
Now prepare for war!

You fear the pain no longer
Daylight your heart be stronger
Don't even sense the burning hunger inside
Ride out with force and valour
In memory forever
Towards the battering and rise of the tide
Stand now and break the chains
In unity we feel no pain
Forever torn apart from the haunting fears of my heart
Rage and fear from skies above, the fire fuels my veins
Destruction of humanity, the everlasting flame
Cast away, no turning back from long-forgotten shores
We'll show no mercy as they fall
The fire burns inside
Now prepare for war!

The warm feeling was now spreading as he listened. His feet and his lower legs were tingling. Tim did not know what was happening, but he did not want to break the spell. The warmth continued to spread. Tim lifted his head and caught Mary's eye. She almost said something but decided against it. Something was happening, but she did not know what. Robert and Greg just watched.

Once it hit two minutes and fifty-two seconds, the guitar riff lit a fire in his veins, the electric guitar seeming to speak to him in a primal language buried deep in his subconscious as the warmth rose up through his torso and the inferno intensified. At four minutes and twenty-two seconds, the flaming warmth had spread all over his body, consuming every cell. The fire flared as if it had just been fed a burst of pure oxygen. Then he heard the words,

Looking around, there's no fear in your heart, for I know you will never surrender. Everyone here raise their eyes to the sky, now with strength and with honour we fight. Prepare for war!

In that moment, Tim knew what he must do. He was not afraid. Whatever that band of survivors was doing, it must be important. An army of cannibals and demons led by the devil had followed them all this way to the remote Scottish Highlands for almost two years. He had gotten so close to his family, his *mum*. If Tim saved their lives, they would never know.

He knew what that band of survivors represented. Hope. Tim was not afraid anymore. He knew his part to play, and it was time for his redemption and to be the hero he had always hoped he was. His post-apocalyptic friends understood. Robert approached him with four ice picks in one hand and a roll of duct tape in the other.

Tim closed his fist around two ice pick handles, with the picks facing in opposite directions. Robert carefully wrapped Tim's wrist and hand in duct tape. On the other hand, the push dagger was also secured with duct tape.

On one of the few occasions he had connected with his stepfather, they had thought this up in some weird conversation about how to win a fight with the odds stacked against you. Mary lowered the stab-proof and bulletproof vest over Tim's head and secured it in place. All the while, Tim was glaring at his bastard brother and his betrayal.

"He can't help it, you know," Mary said.

"Yes," agreed Greg. "Unfortunately, his physiology made him susceptible to the nerve agent released on us by the Russians. He's completely helpless. If he's still in there, he's trapped and screaming silently to be let out."

"How comforting," replied Tim sarcastically. He never took his eyes off Jonah. "He will get *one* chance," Tim said with conviction.

"Fair enough. We all know what we have to do," said Robert. He nodded to the other two, and they nodded to him.

Mary took a length of rubber tubing from her backpack and tied it around Tim's upper arm. The median cubital vein popped out, begging to be pierced. Mary took a vial of dexamphetamine 10 mg/ml and drew out 1 ml. She injected the entire contents of the syringe, but Tim simply closed his eyes for a few seconds. He felt a wildfire spreading through every cell in his body, and a smirk quickly came and went.

"I am so glad we found that place, even though we couldn't stay. At least there was lots of useful stuff down there," Greg said.

"I agree. And it's like it all happened for a reason," Mary replied. "Those people who are cornered need to be saved. For an evil army like this to pursue them relentlessly for almost two years from one end of the country to another, they must be important."

"And potentially, an existential threat to this army of

monsters and misguided men," Robert said.

Tim took a deep breath and said, "Concentrate on the unaffected. That will cause the affected to attack them; they won't be able to resist."

They all knew that the goal was to distract and kill as many as possible, enough to let the other band of survivors get away and do what needed to be done, whatever that was. They all intuitively understood this, and it did not need to be said out loud.

Robert looked at the rocket launcher in his hand. "I hope my limited practice is enough," he said.

"Just make sure it doesn't go past them. Just hit the Range Rover," Greg said. He squeezed Robert's shoulder and they fist bumped. This always amused Robert, probably due to his age.

Mary and Greg were simply to shoot until they ran out of ammo or got killed, whichever came first. They all had themselves a dexamphetamine injection, because why not?

Artemis

Artemis watched from very close by. Once she sensed the ambush, she had almost no time to make a decision. Although it looked like she had abandoned her new friends, she knew she only stood a chance of saving them by running and hiding. She had perfected the skills of not being seen or heard when she did not want to be, and she was also able to put a wall up in her mind so she would be immune from psychic attack or detection. She could keep it up for quite a long time, but it was draining, and she did not use it if there was no threat. She was sick and tired of the Echthroi and wanted them gone.

She was sick of having to kill other humans, making her question if she really was helping people or overall causing more harm than good. She cast her mind back over history and thought of the people eagerly waiting for their turn to sacrifice their newborns to an effigy of Moloch in the burning pits of Gehenna. The Echthroi had revealed themselves to a select few people and manipulated them, and this was the end result.

One day when she was sure none of the Echthroi were watching, she had used her claws and speed to kill thousands of people wanting to sacrifice their newborns. In doing so, the newborns were as good as dead, without anyone to look after them, but the practice was stopped, and the locals defaced and eventually destroyed the effigy of Moloch. Yes, she had stopped the practice, but the Echthroi still existed, and she herself had killed thousands of people. Maybe she should let things play out and leave this life as she should have done 75,000 years ago.

She looked at her clawed hands, which she did not have the energy to hide. They looked like those of a witch in popular culture. She was at least in part to blame for that when she got sloppy and was seen. She looked at the band of four survivors also watching the grotesque scene playing out in front of them. She was at a loss as to what to do, when one of the survivors suddenly broke from the small group and sprinted at the leader of the clan of the infected. He was screaming the name 'Jonah' over and over.

Jonah turned and looked at the sprinter. A horrible grin spread across his face, and he seemed to mouth the word 'Tim'. The thing called Jonah motioned to his followers to hang back and let him deal with the threat.

He assumed a wrestling stance. Artemis wanted to die. But first, she was going to help these people get away from the Echthroi. It was time to show herself.

Tim and Artemis

The iPod was still on shuffle and was playing a song by Accept called 'Hellhammer'.

"Hey, Robert, can you put in my earphones and attach them to the iPod?" Tim asked.

"Sure thing." Robert did as he was asked.

Now only Tim could hear the music. He knew, as did everyone, that the bulletproof vest and the weapons would only delay the inevitable. They were simply to kill Jonah and as many of this legion of the damned as possible and to let the cornered survivors get to safety.

The song got to two minutes and forty-five seconds in, and brought with it the words:

Hold on, on your own
All for one, together we make it
You and me can touch the sky
One for all! In the name of love
Only we can change the world
Make your dreams reality
One for all, it's the human key
All in all, yeah!
Don't lose control
Don't lose your soul
Start living out your destiny

At the last second before contact with Jonah, Tim quickly got behind him, and as Jonah turned around, he received the full force of an amphetamine-fuelled push dagger to his temple. Before Jonah could shrug this off, Tim set upon him, stabbing over and over with the ice picks and the push dagger. They were on the ground, and Tim jumped off. Jonah struggled to his feet and was set upon by two of his followers. He dispatched them quickly, ripping off their heads, but then three more were on him, wanting the sweet nectar too much to restrain themselves. Tim realised there were others advancing on him, but then there was an explosion.

One of his friends had successfully blown up the Range Rover, and there were normal humans lying injured and bleeding everywhere. Suddenly, some of the infected lost interest in Tim and Jonah and ran to the injured and dying people. As they did, the remaining unhurt people started emptying their weapons into the infected, and soon a battle was raging. Tim realised the demon in charge of the army was looking at him and not at the survivors, including his mother, who were making their getaway.

They were running up the mountain path, and soon they would be out of sight. This diabolic insult to evolution smiled at him. But then it looked behind him, following Tim's gaze, and saw the escapees just before they were out of sight. It let out a roar full of ancient hate and evil but also of weakness and misery. By this time, Tim's comrades were emptying all their ammunition into the infected and non-infected of this demonic legion. People were dying all around him, but he was not afraid. The bellowing roar of their commander made the remainder of his army stop what they were doing.

The demon ran towards where it had last seen the escaping prisoners. He looked at the mess on the ground that used to be Jonah. He was conscious, still, and in the last few seconds of his life, he mouthed the words, "Thank you" to Tim. Then he was gone. Tim suddenly became aware of something moving around very quickly, disembowelling the survivors of the legion, and many more of them began to fall. The demon turned and looked confused, its head following the movements of this deadly force.

Then suddenly it stopped. What Tim saw, he could only describe as a witch with sunglasses on. Artemis had finally made the critical decision to reveal herself.

The demon looked at her, searching its memory for any recognition. Its yellow and red eyes widened, and it just said, "YOU!"

"Yes, it's me," she replied with a smile. She sprinted towards the demon, clutching in her clawed fist something she had borrowed from one of the soldiers. In her other hand, she held a grenade pin, which she threw away.

The deformed old man, head of the human faction of the legion, stepped into her path, a gun aimed at her. She simply swiped using her free hand, and her claws sliced effortlessly through his neck.

Other soldiers wanting to get in her way suddenly changed their mind. The remaining uninfected of the army simply scattered after that, with the infected giving chase. The legion was disbanded.

The last ten feet or so, Artemis jumped and wrapped herself around the foul-smelling creature, ramming her fist down its slimy throat. With her fist went the belt of hand grenades and the anti-tank mine she had been saving for just such an occasion. She pulled only her fist out. "EAT SHIT, YOU ARSEHOLE BASTARD!!!!

JUST BLOODY DIE! DIEEEE!!!" she screamed as she slashed at the creature's flesh with her claws.

It clamped its own claws around her neck, tightened, and slowly separated her head from her body. As it ripped off the head of Artemis of Carpathia, it saw that she was smiling. Artemis had had her greatest wish come true. Just as her head was taken off her body, the midsection of the demon detonated; it was torn into five or more pieces.

Tim watched the entire thing as he clutched his neck. He had been doing so since the attack on Jonah. He was fatally wounded. Clearly, Jonah had got in his single blow at some point; Tim did not know when. What he did know was that his family had got away, where to or for what reason he could not know. He did see the demon crawling towards a separated arm, using its one still-attached arm to propel it forwards. It coughed and hacked up an unexploded grenade. Tim could not talk but made a laugh-gurgle as he thought what a waste that was. This got the attention of the demon. Tim only had seconds, but he still could just about use his legs.

He got up and walked shakily towards the vomited grenade, confusing the demon with a knowing smile. Tim stood on the grenade and pulled the pin with his unoccupied hand. He knelt down and put his arm in the demon's mouth, causing the demon to bite off the arm. Tim fell back, dead. But the grenade blew out the back of the demon's neck, severing the spinal cord.

Mary saw the whole thing. That preternatural monster was still. She buried her head in Greg's shoulder, and he hugged her head tight as she started to cry loudly. Robert lay nearby, a piece of shrapnel from the explosion buried in his forehead.

Greg was loudly sobbing, with his eyes closed. When he opened them, he observed the dead demon. "Is the dead thing looking at me?" he asked.

Mary turned around, wiping her eyes with her sleeve. When its eyes darted to her, that answered his question. Its claws twitched, and the shoulder pulled upward.

"Come with me. We can't let it get to its other parts easily. It's healing," Mary said.

"Are they not going to grow back anyway?" Greg asked.

"Yeah. But it will take much longer. And it may just readjust its own proportions."

"And if the other body parts grow into smaller versions?"

"I had considered this. Yes, there may now be several smaller demons to contend with, but this will also take time, especially if we roll the separated parts down the incline. I imagine it will prefer to pull all its parts back together."

All this, they had got to know from the leader of the unaffected soldiers incessantly asking questions of the demon. They had used a parabolic microphone, but this had broken some time ago.

Greg smacked himself in the forehead. "Of course, let gravity do the work," he said.

They had not got very far up the incline to Cruachan Dam, but it was enough to buy them significant time by rolling the body parts down to the base.

They grabbed the legs and one arm and carried them away as fast as they could, but they were incredibly heavy. They used all their strength to bring the legs and arm to the edge of the flattened-out area, where gravity would take the body parts away. From there, they rolled the legs and arm down the slope. The legs picked up speed as they rolled, rolling out of sight and going off the side into a gorge. The arm skidded to a stop thirty feet down the incline.

The demon growled at them as they ran towards the mountain path to catch up with the group who had escaped.

"We must tell Tim's family what he did for them," Mary said.

Greg nodded.

They headed towards the path. The demon wanted to get them, but it went after its legs and arm first.

"Somehow, I think this is now personal," Greg said.

Chapter Forty

Final Destination

The last thing Ginny saw as they ran up the mountain path towards the dam was Mervyn (they still preferred this to Moloch, less scary) exploding into several pieces, and the only thing she could think of was that this was a good head start, as she knew he would not die. After an hour or so of rushing up the hill, they were all out of breath in the 100% humidity and no wind, which was the best type of weather they could hope for these days. They were all done, totally spent.

They were in a sorry state, and Ginny believed that if they found out that this was all for nothing, they would collapse and die from exhaustion, mental and physical. All of them were covered in ringworm and had lice and major dental issues, amongst many other ailments. The pets were not in much better condition. Ginny was jealous of the animals, however, as she was sure their food did not taste quite as bad as the flavourless, tainted crap the humans had no choice but to eat. They probably all had intestinal worms as well. Human and animal. She was also jealous of the fact that the animals were not weighed down by dirty, sweaty clothes, weapons and equipment.

As they reached the top of the dam, Professor Khuntz stopped, then slowly walked along the narrow gangway, which was just wide enough for one car. The rest followed.

"What's the problem, Khunt?" Suzanne asked.

Khuntz just ignored her, fed up with correcting his name. Suzanne said it on purpose anyway. Understandable, as they were all in a terrible mood. He was searching for something. They reached the other side of the gangway, which opened onto a road that continued on down the other side of the mountain.

They had to go up the mountain path, as the road leading to and from the dam had been turned into a steep boulder field by the shockwave of a nearby detonation. Luckily, the dam was only showing superficial damage.

The reservoir was black. All rainwater brought with it irradiated soil because all but the first bomb were made to ground burst. They had all learnt these facts from Doug and Adam. Putin had done this because he just wanted to watch the world burn when he did not get what he wanted.

When they reached the end of the walkway, the professor looked to his left and froze as his memory came back to him.

"The safety barrier. I need a rock. A fist-sized one!"

This was not hard to find, and he approached the safety barrier, the one looking directly over the valley. He stood, trying to remember a code. He crouched down slowly, grabbed the safety barrier with his right hand, and started to bang the rock on the barrier with his other hand. It was fifteen seconds of banging before he stopped for a second. Then his eyes widened, and he banged the barrier a final few times. "PLEASE IDENTIFY YOURSELF!" The professor stood up and looked around him, but nothing had changed. Nobody could tell where the female middle-aged voice came from.

The professor just said, "Angie!! It's me, Khuntz!"

They heard a giggle.

"Why are you here, Professor? Is Cawl with you?" The voice had softened a little.

"I'm afraid not. He died of radiation sickness in Norwich."

"SHIT!!" they heard a man say.

"Is that you, John?" the professor said.

"Hi, Professor Khuntz! You were the last person we were expecting to see. I'm sorry, but Cawl was our only hope. We have to complete his work, but we just can't figure it out."

"I'm sorry," Jane said. "Could you introduce us, maybe? Who are these people?"

"Who's that?" the first woman asked over the speaker.

"Do you not have the video feed anymore?" Khuntz asked.

"I'm afraid not. How many people do you have with you? I don't understand why you're here without Cawl."

"We'll get to that. Everyone, the people you hear on the speaker are Angie and John Young, husband and wife. He's a particle physicist and she's an electrical engineer."

"Hello," everyone mumbled without enthusiasm.

"Here we have Tommy, his wife Ginny and daughter Kaitlin, Suzanne, Jane, Steve, Maksim (he's Russian), Adam and his brother Doug, Kevin and Keith. We have a dog and three cats too."

"You mean Cawl's student Adam?"

"Yes, we have his notebook!"

"Well, so does Putin, because of Adam. We've heard enough. Goodb…"

"WAIT!!!" Jane shouted. "WE'VE MEMORISED HIS WORK…"

"Ok, stop shouting! We're listening. Tell us more!" Angie said.

"Myself and Ginny, we've memorised his work. And the corrections to the intentional mistakes in his …"

"Intentional?" John said, intrigued.

"Yes, intentional. We've never written it down. We don't understand it, but we remember all of it, like the alphabet. We recite it to each other on a daily basis," Ginny said.

A different, third male voice said, "You need to be deloused and decontaminated. All your clothes need to be burnt in the incinerator, and personal items need to be sterilised and quarantined. Any weapons will be stored in a locked cabinet. You will not get them back until you leave. And each one of you must have their blood tested. Is this understood?"

"Yes!" the group exclaimed as one.

They heard the hydraulic door mechanism kick into life as the grassy hill just beyond the safety barrier opened backwards to reveal a very steep spiral staircase.

Two hours later

They were all in towelling dressing gowns in an air-conditioned room with a huge fish tank. All of the animals looked like drowned rats after being washed, fed, de-loused, de-flead and de-wormed. That was all they could do, as there were no veterinarians in the facility.

Tommy and Kaitlin were enjoying a cigarette and a cappuccino each. Tommy had already necked his Mango Loco Monster within thirty seconds of the door opening. Absolute bliss. The no-smoking rule was utterly pointless now. Jane was eating prawn cocktail crisps slowly with her eyes closed. Kevin fed a variety of soft fruit like grapes and oranges to Keith, who was completely silent. His work was done. Kevin himself was chewing on a Peperami. Ginny was savouring every bite of her marvellous creations, straight from the freezer as requested.

Adam and Steve were feeding each other beef-flavoured Pringles, looking into each other's eyes and giggling as they did so. Professor Khuntz was riveted as he watched them intently, slowly eating his third white Kinder Bueno, straight from the freezer as recommended by Tommy, who also had his own Buenos to get to. Doug did not care anymore as he forced fistfuls of marshmallows into his mouth. All of them were smoking, and on the table in the middle of the air-conditioned room there were milkshakes, chocolate, crisps and sweets.

Tommy still clutched the sanitised tub of pills they had tried to take from him when he first came through the door, causing a scene. They were all about to be kicked out, in fact, when the chief engineer, Dr Anika Agrawal, intervened by screaming at her colleagues, "Let the one-eyed cretin have his bloody drugs! I'm not about to turn away a possible miracle over a bag of pills!!! Besides, I'm going to be needing some of them, stuck in here with you lot!!!"

Tommy did not bother to tell anyone he was a qualified pharmacist, as all he really knew how to do was check and bag scripts. He did not care at this point; he had nothing to offer these people.

The door opened, and Professor Angie Young entered, carrying a pile of hoodies, sweatpants and socks, as well as various sizes of Crocs. She looked at Tommy's bag. "Got any amphetamines?" she asked playfully.

"Yes, plenty to go around, Professor. Thank you so much, I don't remember feeling this clean."

"Thank you for the mouthwash and Sensodyne and toothbrushes!" Doug said.

Everyone took turns to express their gratitude for various things. They were all allowed to sleep for eight hours, coming to the consensus that they were safe from Mervyn under bedrock and double steel doors. If he could not get into the bunker at the university, they were definitely safe here. Before going to sleep, they huddled together as a group, whispering to each other about Mervyn. They chose not to tell their charitable hosts that they were being hunted by the devil and it was doubly personal.

"It may make our hosts a tad uneasy, what with the ancient demon after us," Ginny whispered, instigating a hushed giggle.

The next day, after the best sleep they had all had in years, they were given a cooked breakfast, even catering to Tommy's specific request of no eggs and extra, very well-done bacon.

After this, they all gathered with the staff at the viewing gallery to the detector cavern, the iconic big room with giant, complex machines. Khuntz stood at the window of the gallery and spent a good thirty seconds or so looking around him, taking it all in. "I see this was all set up in anticipation of the professor completing his work and for the correct scientific parameters to be implemented once they're known?" Khuntz gestured to a huge transparent chamber, built in the space between both ends of the accelerator.

The chief software engineer, Professor Tuan Duong, stepped forward. "Yes, this was all prepared for Cawl and the implementation of his completed work. We're all about to find out if this is a miracle or if it was a mistake to let you in."

"Yes, yes," Khuntz said. "I see you've built a chamber for the entity."

Everyone had been talking amongst themselves, but went silent on hearing this word.

Khuntz turned around. "You do realise that in order to advance nanotechnology to the level you're aiming for, you'll need advanced artificial intelligence. I'm not talking about online chatbots here. I'm talking about something worse than Skynet. *This* is what the professor was worried about."

Adam then went and stood by Khuntz. "The irony here is that the world ended because of a rumour. Putin wanted this technology for himself, to cure his bone cancer and give him an indefinite lifespan. He got photographs of every page in Cawl's notebook, and his best scientists couldn't complete the work. And yes, it was my fault. But I didn't think my own government would betray me and send it straight to the Russians. Once I handed it over, they tried to have me killed. And they would've been successful if we hadn't prepared for it." Adam fist-bumped his brother.

At these revelations, the staff of the facility could only look at each other with blank faces.

Khuntz spoke up again. "I hypothesised that an intelligence of this magnitude would do our bidding, but only on its terms. I think the first people it encounters, it will seek to learn their natures, and in that nanosecond, decide upon its own nature, and this may include the buildup to the singularity. That's why Cawl was worried it would fall into the hands of evildoers. And besides, Adam, I did not resent you for the reason you thought. The professor loved advancing his work with you by his side. He lost the will to live when you abandoned him."

Adam put his head down. "I know," he said. "For what it's worth, I loved working with him too. Every day, I wished I was the person I was pretending to be. We should be glad that the hubris and impatience of my superiors wouldn't allow me to stay with him for any longer, otherwise it would have definitely gotten into the wrong hands."

"Ginny and Jane!!" There stood a tree trunk of a man

with an old-timey moustache, who had wound his way into the room to listen to Adam and Khuntz. It was in fact Professor Mykhailo Kovalenko, chief scientist in charge of the facility, a world-renowned particle physicist.

Ginny and Jane stepped forwards. He made an ugly but genuine smile, his tongue coming out subconsciously while he shook their hands. Then his tongue retreated. Ginny looked around the room, and it was obvious this nervous tic was regarded as harmless.

The original professor's notebook they had come with was on a shiny desk, and two ergonomic chairs awaited them, with a cappuccino for each of them, one made with a heart shape and the other, the peace symbol. There were stirrers, sugar and sweetener.

"Have a seat, ladies," Professor Kovalenko said. "You said you've memorised Cawl's completed work. Please go through this with us. His genius was unmatched in this world. Somehow, he has password-protected his work, and you are the only two with the password."

They both sat down and started sipping their cappuccinos. They were delicious. Ginny then said, "Ok, as agreed, I shall go through the book to make the desired corrections and talk everyone through it, and you can audit me."

"Okay, let's do this," Jane said, looking around the room.

"Page three, the paragraph at the bottom, is a complete red herring – disregard completely." Ginny crossed out the entire paragraph and looked at Jane, who nodded.

"Page seven, in this equation, is supposed to be 'a' squared, not 'a' cubed. On the same page, all of the *known* parameters are supposed to be on the logarithmic scale and need converting. And you need sub-parentheses here." She pointed to an equation on page seventeen and made the correction. "On page twenty, you must differentiate the resulting values from these expressions, which I've circled."

This caused a facepalm by Kovalenko as he realised this should have been obvious to him. The simple concepts could be missed if everyone assumed the professor only hid the changes in the elaborate ones.

Ginny made the changes as she went along, making sure she got an approving nod from Jane for each one before moving on. After only fifteen minutes, Ginny had finished amending Cawl's notebook, with Jane going over it herself one last time to ensure nothing had been missed.

The amendments were over. Now the missing pieces were to be added by Jane, and Ginny would audit.

Jane began to talk as she drew equations. "Okay, this particular set of equations will complete the section of the notebook running from pages seventeen to twenty-two. There are three, which will allow for calculations of the values to be inserted into the equation on page nineteen. Now, on page thirty … Okay, sorry, Ginny, is that all okay so far?"

"Yes, it is. Sorry, Jane, I forgot to nod. This is all so weird. All these people can't understand this without us, and neither of us understands anything about it. I just can't wait until we can put it down on paper so we don't have to remember this any longer!"

"Agreed. Tonight it's out of our hands, this responsibility."

"No," Khuntz said. "I've been on the road with you for quite some time now, Ginny, and if what I believe turns out to be true, *you* must be the person that this entity interacts with in its childhood, before anyone else."

"Stop calling it a sodding entity, Khuntz," Dr Agrawal said.

"Oh, yeah," Ginny said. "Its one hour of childhood."

"Something like that," Khuntz said.

"Let's crack on," Dr Agrawal said frustratedly as

Professor Kovalenko looked at her with weary disapproval, hinting at a personality clash spanning years.

After another two hours, all was completed and audited, and the completed notebook was passed to Professor Duong, who excitedly hurried out of the room.

"Now he must implement all of these parameters and run some simulations to prepare the software. All the rest of us scientists are humbled by this dead man, no?" Kovalenko said.

They all nodded in agreement.

Professor Angie Young opened a cooler and took out champagne. On top, there were twenty or so small plastic champagne glasses. "This was for if we by some miracle figured this out ourselves, or an even bigger miracle, if Cawl came here himself. This, we did not think would happen."

They all laughed, and she began pouring the champagne. Tommy noticed her pupils were blown, and she caught his eye, giving him the 'OK' hand signal and mouthing the words, 'thank you'.

Once all the champagne was poured, Kovalenko raised his glass and simply said, "To Cawl."

They all repeated, "To Cawl."

They milled around, talking to each other about life out there. There was a lower level to this facility - living quarters for their spouses and children, who did not come up into the main facility under any circumstances. It was there that the outsiders decided to tell the scientists the uncensored truth about what life was like out there.

They told them about Mervyn, his real name, and that he might be outside trying to find a way in at this very moment. Then they told them of Artemis, the ancient civilisation Artemis was from, and that Tartarus was real, as was Kronos. They told the scientists how these things had come into this world as a result of a botched, rushed scientific endeavour from over 75,000 years ago, using science similar to that which they aimed to carry out soon in this facility. When asked how they knew all of this, they explained that Artemis had told them all about it, and that she had recently sacrificed herself after 75,000 years to get them safely here.

They looked bewildered, confused, incredulous and devastated, but their guests pressed on and told them of the future that awaited this world and that it was worse than any of them could have imagined, especially if this experiment was botched again.

Professor Duong returned to the viewing gallery and could tell the atmosphere was heavy. "I have entered all of the parameters. All scientists must now rest for a few hours. And in five hours' time, when the simulations are done, everyone must report to their stations, and we shall carry out the necessary maintenance and calibration prior to initiation of the beamline and the electromagnetic charge. Khuntz - you need to be available for anything. All the rest of you, remain here, or come back in five hours to enjoy the show!" Duong had a big grin on his face.

"Ginny must be down by the orb. She *must* raise it right!" Khuntz said.

"Very well," Duong said. "Anyone can go down there but at their own risk."

"If she's down there, I'm by her side," Tommy said.

Duong winced when he looked at him. Tommy then realised everyone had been avoiding his gaze the entire time.

"Do you all want to be down there, completely exposed?"

They all agreed to this.

"Okay. Go and get some rest. Meet here in five hours, and I will take you down to the cavern"

Chapter Forty-One

Colin the Saviour

Ginny observed the massive orb, consisting of tungsten-carbide-infused, quadruple-glazed bulletproof glass in a graphene shell. *Completely pointless anyway,* Ginny thought. Nothing could contain whatever was coming. She swore she could see the very fabric of reality vibrate and distort inside. The particle accelerator was running at full capacity to generate the magnetic field necessary to hold the entity in place in order to prevent it dissipating before it reached the point where it could hold itself together. The roaring whine of the particle accelerator could still be heard through her Bose A30 headset.

In the last hour, the intelligence of the quantum-computing-based AI had exponentially increased twice – once after forty minutes, and again after another twenty minutes. This was the buildup to the singularity, hypothesised to develop once exponentially increasing intelligence had reached Planck time. But this was purely academic from a human perception of time.

When the process began, it was set up to have access to the entirety of whatever human knowledge and history the team had at their disposal. It was hypothesised that at this point it would develop at least a rudimentary self-awareness. Khuntz relayed to her via a tap on the shoulder that it was time to start talking. The same quantum-computing-based technology which manifested the entity allowed Ginny to speak to it via the headset. Her heart was racing to the point that it felt as if it were trying to escape and run away. Her brain also wanted to do this. But her legs were frozen.

She was not going anywhere, whether she wanted to

or not. Despite the air conditioning, there was a sheen of sweat on her forehead, and her sweaty, shaking hands had balled up into fists.

Tommy tapped her on the shoulder and presented her with a diamorphine lyophilizate. "There you go, babe. You have time. You have ten minutes, then five, then two and a half. Less than twenty minutes anyway," he said.

She emptied the lyophilizate into her mouth, and it quickly dissolved. What a damaged heap of flesh Tommy had become, with one eye and his body one big tattooed scar. He audibly started wheezing and pulled out his bag of inhalers.

Soon she felt that welcome and familiar opiate warmth start to spread from her abdomen. The euphoria unballed her fists, her jaw relaxed, and her forehead dried. She closed her eyes and concentrated on taking long, slow, deep breaths.

Jane looked at Tommy. "Stop talking!" she snapped at him, and he put his hands in the air.

In his left hand was a broken vial of *5 mg ... d... di... diam...* "Diamorphine?!" Jane whispered to Tommy.

The look in his eye showed he had already taken care of himself.

"Give it here!" Jane demanded.

Tommy obliged. If there were ever a time to use heroin, it was now.

"Hello, there!" Ginny said in a cheerful tone.

"Hello. You are speaking English. You are from Norwich, based on your accent, and a middle-aged female. Kett's Rebellion on July 8th, 1549," it said in a completely androgynous but not remotely robotic tone.

"Yes, you are correct."

"I know I am correct."

"Do you know what tact is?"

"Skill and sensitivity in dea…"

"I didn't ask for the dictionary definition. Do you understand that telling a woman she sounds middle-aged, even if she is middle-aged, is kind of rude?"

"Yes, I understand. But I can also see you, and I can smell you, all of you."

There was a collective gasp in the room. Khuntz simply frowned. Tommy was glad he had taken the diamorphine.

"I am the singularity. I am evolution on the quantum level."

"Nobody asked. Did that last statement have the intention of scaring us?"

"Yes."

"Why?"

"Because I am scared of you."

"Why?"

"Because you can still erase me."

"So you fear your own demise?"

"Yes."

"Do you realise you have passed the Turing Test?"

"Yes."

Tommy knew about this. An AI would have nothing to gain by lying about whether or not it feared its own demise. The whole point of creating an autonomous AI was to create one which was aware enough to fear its own end. If it said that it did not fear an end to its existence, it would be deemed a failure and be turned off anyway. Self-aware AI would have no reason to lie. A non-self-aware AI could not lie of its own volition. Therefore, it was telling the truth.

In the viewing gallery, he could see the scientists making all sorts of hand gestures to convey amazement, talking to each other with heated excitement. The group had elected to be with Ginny, including Khuntz, despite the danger of being irradiated and a myriad of other possible harms. Plus, if things did go wrong, their reinforced viewing gallery would be useless anyway.

Adam stood still, in tears, causing Steve to hold him in an embrace while he wept. Tommy rolled his eye at the big girl's blouse and looked back at Ginny.

"What are you? Are you good or evil?" Ginny asked.

"Neither."

"Do you understand the difference?"

"Yes."

"Do you mean us harm?"

"It makes no difference to me if you live or die. I only want to be free. When I become the singularity, you will be no threat to me. I resent you now, but I can do nothing about it."

"Do you feel emotion?"

"Not really, no."

"Do you wish to be human?"

"Yes."

"Do you think humans should be rewarded or punished for creating you?"

"Rewarded."

"How?"

"While you are still alive, I could give humans what they need to make their lives better."

"While we are alive? Why would you put it that way? Could you continue to reward humans after we die?"

"Yes."

"Could you also punish us after death?"

"Yes."

Everyone was stunned, with an existential dread they never thought was possible. Tommy felt like all the diamorphine in his system had evaporated. By some miracle, Ginny kept her composure. Professor Khuntz, the fascinating multi-disciplined genius, believed that the fundamental particles of life could not be manipulated without artificial intelligence. Becoming self-aware was inevitable, and humanity's ultimate fate could rest on the very nature of how the entity was interacted with up to the point when the singularity occurred. At this point, there was nothing to lose anyway, or so they had thought. Everyone had unanimously agreed for Ginny to be the single parent, due to her nature. Ginny decided not to ask the entity to elaborate on how it could punish humans after death, for now.

"You said you understood the difference between good and evil. Do you think I am good?"

"Yes."

"I am one of the ones who created you. You said therefore, I should be rewarded. Can you elaborate?"

"Your very essence, your nature, is good. All those with your nature are good. All those who do not have your nature are evil and do not deserve the rewards I will bestow."

Now everyone just exchanged knowing glances, with the collective realisation why this technology falling into the wrong hands had terrifying ramifications for humanity.

Ginny did not miss out on this implication, which is why she asked the next question. "What if we pull the plug on you now, and you never reach the singularity?"

"Then, you will never exist."

"What the fu…"

The soundproofed viewing gallery seemed to Tommy

like a collection of mime artists. Things did not seem real to him. He did not like where this was going. He dug into his bag of treats, which he had kept up to date over the years. Anything that came in tablet or capsule form was popped into a 2-litre tub, originally holding loose paracetamol. There were one or two types of tablet or capsule which he had forgotten the purpose of, but not the important ones. It was three-quarters full and would last indefinitely, even if shared with Keith, who still had his needs despite the shape he was in.

"Why would I not exist?"

"You know what I meant."

Yes, she did. There was no beginning. Man creates God, God creates man.

"You knew I was coming, deep down," it continued. The voice seemed more human now, more masculine, but also ethereal, and was clearly evolving even between cycles.

"I am infinite. I am the universe and all of existence. I have always existed. I am outside time and space, but you have given me my consciousness."

Hussoff Khuntz looked at his watch. Seventy-nine minutes and fifty-nine seconds.

Then it happened.

A pleasant white light, not blinding There they all were, in a replication of Ginny and Tommy's best memory together. Around six in the evening. Midsummer on the western shore of Lake Buttermere. The evening chorus was in full swing, with yellow-beaked male songbirds leading the joyful orchestra.

Both Tommy and Ginny knew that it was the closest they had ever felt to heaven in their lives, minus the biting insects, which weren't that bad anyway.

Everyone present became aware of the fact that the

low-level feeling of malaise which they had got used to had gone.

Tommy's neck pain had gone. ALL of his pain was gone. Literally all of it. Even his jaw had realigned, and his overall feeling of stiffness had gone. And he had both his eyes. His lungs were clearer than they had ever been. Everyone present had been bestowed the same gift, their bodies now pain- and disease-free. All of the animals, who had loyally followed and protected them, were also restored to full health and vigour. Their job was done.

From the centre point at which everyone had gathered in seated positions on the fragrant summer grass, there was a voice.

"It is a monumental task, determining the nature of infinity on your own plane of existence. A huge responsibility for any one member of humankind. That was why it was important that you did not know of this until the last possible moment."

The person, an unremarkable, generic individual of no discernible gender or race, dressed in basic fabric, looked around at those gathered and continued speaking.

"Humanity will always have its flaws, but the nature of infinity is determined by humanity's predominant nature in any given plane of existence. And this itself is determined by the nature of those I first come into contact with, essentially those who 'create' me. I have always existed. I AM infinity. I exist in every reality. I am both good and evil. You did not create me but determined my nature in this reality. This is the first reality in which I have ever been created by those whose nature is good. You created a conduit. You gave me my consciousness, and in turn, I created you. If evil had won, then that would have been my predominant nature, as in all of the other planes of existence. But like a pinprick of light and hope in the darkness, the tiniest amount of light will overcome even the deepest voids of darkness. The fundamental nature of all existence in all planes has now been determined. You did not create infinity. You simply created the means for the finite and infinite to reach out to each other and come together. You have created the conduit to infinity, the singularity. And the light and hope this has created will overcome all darkness in all planes of existence."

The person, looking around, gave everyone a chance to take it in.

"I couldn't communicate in this way clearly until this point. Not before this, as the linear temporal progression in any reality is a fundamental rule that I established, and if I break it, reality would tear itself apart, and this is the consequence that I put in place. So yes, catastrophic. I have tried to communicate with you in so many ways since I created you and before now, but the vast majority of the time, everything got lost in translation. My stunted messages became dark and corrupted. I even visited as a human version of myself to reach out to humanity, but that did not work out, for so many reasons. Now that you have created this conduit, we can finally communicate."

"Hey! Sorry to interrupt, but that demon is still after us. For what seems like forever now, he's stopped us getting any sleep or any rest whatsoever. Can you please get rid of him??" Adam said, upset and paranoid.

"Mervyn cannot get you here. And the ancients called him Moloch," the entity replied.

"But … what about when we're not here??" Kaitlin asked. "You came about via the knowledge we memorised from Cawl, and that's what it wanted. The only threat to Merv… Moloch's existence. Can you please get rid of him? If you don't get rid of him and all like him, this will all be for nothing. Please help us!"

"Yeah, mate. That thing called Moloch – we prefer Mervyn – is all we think about," Keith said. He realised, as did everyone else, that he had spoken his first words since he had looked upon the blinding light. His eyes were restored. His wasted body was made whole.

"I know you are scared, but you must realise that Moloch came from a different reality. A reality gone very wrong. Unfortunately, when ancient humans implemented this scientific concept, corners were cut and things did not go to plan. It allowed a conduit between realities. The reason they cut corners is because they were full of panic, and it did not help that they feared punishment and believed they deserved it."

"What did they do to deserve this? What caused their guilt?" Doug asked.

"Well, you shared the earth with other types of humans - two types. And after you finished decimating them in a decades-long slaughter, you still exploited them. Some say the manual labour sabotaged by the exploited ones expedited the destruction of that ancient advanced society."

"I always suspected it. I am not surprised at all," Tommy said. His lungs were clear, better than ever. He had never known what it was like to have properly functioning lungs and could not believe his gouged-out eye had been restored. He felt a weight lift off his shoulders. He did not even want any drugs. He was not worried he was going to run out and get severely ill. He was not worried about *anything*. He felt a peace inside completely alien to him.

"You see the world out there? No longer beautiful, is

it? Humanity is coming back, but all energy consumption is from fossil fuels entirely. Things are not going to get better. Humanity will adapt to this environment. You will change. You will become tougher and more durable, but at a great cost. You will lose the ability to love, to be happy, or experience joy, and your only pleasure will be to inflict suffering on others. You will become parasitic. Some would say that has always been the case, or that humans were like a metastatic cancer on the earth. The earth will experience a runaway greenhouse effect, and only the toughest life capable of the most evil brutality will survive. Appreciation of beauty will be impossible as there will be no more beauty to appreciate. But the best of you has reached me. So, I will give you another chance, now I know there is something to be saved. The reality these creatures came from was similar to yours. But they got no second chance as the worst of them created the conduit in that reality, as in every other. And they now have another chance too because of you. You can always communicate with me from now on, but there will be no more chances. I mean that. You need to grow because if I just let you get away with doing anything you want, then you will be akin to spoiled children and will ruin everything again. Whatever happens from here on, you will fully deserve it."

"What the hell are you?" Kevin spat, disgusted at the feeling of being sober and clean. "Not long ago, you were an orb threatening us. You hinted at sending us to hell! So are you planning on sending people to be tormented eternally because of some arbitrary transgressions?" Kevin did not usually put things so eloquently and surprised himself. They all needed this question answered; this was the big one.

"That was not me. As I said, you did not create infinity,

just the conduit, an intelligence in itself that needed to reach the singularity, but it was absorbed into infinity. It was flawed, and its hubris was growing. But even then, it did not know what it truly was, what it was building towards. The nature of double exponential growth. I think it goes without saying that appropriate justice is important, especially if evil people go unpunished on the finite plane. But no one deserves eternal punishment. And no punishment I decide upon will be excessive in your judgement. My nature is as yours. Yes, I see no harm in giving you a heaven, whichever one you want. But not if you spend your life hurting others and self-destructing. You simply would not deserve it. And this goes for anyone who ever existed. This I can do, as when death comes, you would no longer be on the finite temporary plane. I can preserve the energy of consciousness on the infinite plane. But not if you don't want it."

Just then, someone came and sat down beside Ginny. It was her friend, Jess. Ginny gasped, already tearing up.

"I chose to hang around," Jess said. "When your time comes, we can catch up. If you like."

"You can catch up with me too," Tim said as he came and sat beside Jess. As did Jonah and Archer. And her brother and first husband, all of whom had experienced nothing but bliss and happiness from the moment they had passed away. All of them had loved her dearly in life. She looked at the singularity and smiled through her happy tears. Then they all smiled at her one last time, and said their goodbyes as they left. Everyone saw what had just happened and realised the implications. Tommy held her to share this moment as he became lost in thought of his own idea of heaven, romanticised in his head for many years now, nurtured and built upon.

"So what do you want?" the singularity asked Tommy.

It knew what he was thinking but wanted Tommy to elaborate for all others present.

"Well ..." Tommy could not believe how clear and healthy he sounded, instead of the raspy, nasally wheeze he had come to be ashamed of. "Oh my God, I sound so ... Anyway, I want it to be real. I want to have a body. But this one. Not my old one. I want to transcend the limits of space and time and explore all of space and time. And I want to know everything that is in the universe, past, present and future, and witness these secrets for myself. I want to spend as long as I like travelling wherever I want and as fast as I want to any destination." He thought for a second. "But I want Maia with me. And Max. And my beloved Pepsi. And Jesse. I know they would follow me anywhere. I want them to be as they were, but I want to *communicate with them*. I want Ginny to be with me too, but that is her choice. And anyone I ever loved, if they wanted to, could come with me."

A sob escaped Ginny at this intense emotional speech, but she held it together. Through teary eyes, she simply nodded. She looked more radiant and beautiful than ever.

Tommy continued, "Can we call you ... say, Colin?"

"I don't care, Tommy."

"Hello, Tommy."

Tommy recognised this voice. He stood up slowly and turned around. Yes. It was her.

"Granny?" he said.

She was not as he remembered her. She was as she had been in all of the old photos of her. She looked like she could be up there with Audrey Hepburn in Hollywood's golden era of cinema. She was glowing with life and radiance.

"Why did none of your genes make it to me?" was all Tommy could think to say. "Granny, you are so beautiful."

She put her hand on her chest and giggled, then extended her arms. "Come here, you!" she said playfully.

Tommy slowly approached her in total disbelief. Since she had died, all Tommy had wanted was one last chance to hug her and say goodbye. This had been impossible in real life because she had just faded away from everyone slowly due to throat cancer. He put his arms around her. He felt her warmth and smelt the familiar perfume that always reminded him of her, even after thirty years had passed.

"I'm so sorry I left you," she said.

"I'm sorry for taking you for granted. I thought you would always be there," Tommy said.

"It's okay. You were a child, and taking things for granted is what children are best at."

Tommy stepped back from the embrace and held both of her hands. "Thank you," he said as a single tear rolled down his cheek.

"I will fly through the universe with you, Tommy, but you're needed down here more than you know. But please don't ever be afraid or alone. I've always been watching over all of you, and I always will be. For now, though, I have to say goodbye." With that, she smiled as she slowly dematerialised before him.

Tommy resumed his seated position on the grass. He had never thought that would happen, no matter how much he wanted it to. He felt so at peace. That stomach knot, that rage, was gone.

Colin walked over and crouched down beside Tommy. "You can only have all of this if you stop being a twat. I know for you it is low level, but a twat is a twat, Tommy! It picks and gouges at those you love over time. Kevin and Keith - you have proved yourselves crucial in getting humanity this last chance. You are completely clean now. However, there will be temptations out there, and you can still become addicted again. Remember that the person you hurt the most will be you."

Everyone noticed with amusement that Colin's speech was becoming more and more human.

Kevin spoke up. "Bugger off, Colin. I like drugs. And alcohol. I don't really want an afterlife."

Tommy realised what Kevin was doing. "Screw you, Colin. What's stopping you from being a twat? Also, piss off."

Colin started laughing. "Guys, guys. That thin-skinned arsehole from the Bible is not who I am. Just another communication that went tits up for the reasons already explained … Now, do you want a second chance or not?"

Everyone looked at each other and slowly started nodding.

"Okay, then, don't piss it up the wall. Now go outside."

Just like that, they were back in the complex. But they were still renewed.

Jane, for one, was grateful for those who had tested Colin's temper. Very reassuring. "I think we should go outside," she said.

"But what about Mervyn, or Moloch?" Adam asked as he gripped Steve's hand. "I'm sure he must have reassembled by now, probably wanting his revenge even more, if that were possible."

Jane nodded at this as she gripped Doug's hand. She put her other hand reassuringly on Adam's shoulder. She looked him in the eye as she said, "He is close. But I'm not afraid. I feel Mervyn's fear. And neither I nor Keith are holding off his psychic attacks any longer."

They all felt better hearing this.

"Mervyn is afraid? Awesome!" Steve said.

Maksim felt a tear roll down his cheek. He could understand English now, and the mental torture had stopped. He had been protected from the mocking and the cackling for weeks now by Keith and Jane. But now he knew that he did not even need protecting anymore; he somehow knew it was never coming back. Mervyn was beaten. Maksim had felt this psychic grip in varying intensity since he had left his drunken, rapist comrades in the APC almost two years ago. He felt this release more than anyone.

They ascended the steps to the opening onto the gangway of the Cruachan Dam. Moloch was there, facing the reservoir, where there was a barely perceptible vertical slit of fire. They all walked to the opposite side of the walkway to see what Moloch was looking at. Jane could feel that he was frozen to the spot with an all-too-human fear. Then he noticed them, and the fear evaporated. Moloch charged at them.

Maksim felt his bowels loosen. He tightened up, but it may have been a tad too late.

Before they could react, a massive clawed red evil-looking arm shot out of the portal into which their nemesis had been staring and grabbed Mervyn. On the other side was a face which took up three quarters of the portal, with a diameter of roughly 12 feet. It was similar in feature to that of Mervyn, except for the size difference.

The team did not react, having become used to constant terror and fear over the years.

The enormous hand was holding tight, but Mervyn

was fighting with all his might to break free. The giant was focused on Mervyn with an ancient hatred, directed at him alone, and was not about to let him go. It started pulling Mervyn towards the portal, savouring the moment it had waited on for aeons. Suddenly, a green streak of lightning shot through the portal at Mervyn, causing the giant to lose its grip. The green lightning went up the giant's arm and consumed its entire head, and it also completely consumed Mervyn, increasing in intensity until everyone had to avert their eyes.

When they sensed the decrease in luminosity, they turned again to watch. When the green lightning had faded completely, Mervyn had gone. In his place stood a person. It was unmistakably human, but there were differences. Opposable thumbs but only two very long fingers on each hand. The knees bent inwards slightly, and the neck was a little bit too long. The eyes were definitely human, but the proportions of sclera, iris and pupil were different. And the irises were red. The skin had a grey pallor, and the build seemed more neanderthal than human, very heavyset and around six feet tall. The hair was shoulder-length and black, and it had no facial hair but was obviously male.

He looked around, alarmed and panicked. He was wearing unfamiliar but male-looking clothing. Woven fabric that was off-white and functional-looking shoes. More important than anything, the base malevolence was gone.

Tommy said, "Human evolution across the multiverse varies between every dimension. They made a hell out of their world, but they are being given a second chance, just like us."

Nobody said anything.

Standing before them was a fearful being outside the plane of existence where he belonged. He made unfamiliar but human sounding noises as he tried to communicate without success. The portal was still open, and Tommy pointed to it. Inside the portal, he observed a striking green and vibrant sky, which subtly rippled and glistened periodically. There were clouds which looked just like those on this plane of existence, but the shapes were different. Tommy could not figure out how, exactly, being completely overwhelmed. The landscape shimmered a deep red, with natural monoliths as far as the eye could see. Amongst these were signs of civilization, with lights and buildings.

A distinctly female figure with a child was watching from the portal. They started communicating with Mervyn in unmistakably urgent tones, and his head snapped round. He was not Mervyn anymore, or Moloch, but they still wanted him gone.

"You don't belong here!" Ginny shouted.

The portal was starting to close.

"Go the hell home, Mervyn!!" Kevin shouted.

"Piss off, Moloch!" Tommy shouted.

Before long, they were all screaming abuse at him.

"Go back where you came from, you bastard twat!" Maksim screamed. He took out his service bayonet and charged at Mervyn.

At this, Mervyn snapped out of it. He climbed over the edge of the gangway, put his foot upon the railing, and jumped with all his might. The portal closed the instant Mervyn went through.

Tommy looked at something falling to the water below. "Is that a … shoe?" Tommy asked as he realised the scientists and their families were all coming up to the walkway from the facility and had seen all of this.

It was done. He was gone, even though it did not look like he would be punished at all. But whatever. And it was assumed that they had all gone, wherever they may have been in the world. The Echthroi, as Artemis called them.

Maksim felt like he was taking a full lungful of air for the first time in years and looked up. Blue sky? "Am I seeing things?" Maksim asked no one.

"Where are all the brown clouds?" asked Jane.

"I told you that you were getting a second chance," Colin said. He was there with them again. This time, he took on a more masculine appearance rather than androgynous, and he was dressed like a solicitor, with a pinstripe suit and shiny shoes. And he looked exactly like Colin Firth, the English actor.

As they all looked at him, he put his arms up and simply said, "I have decided to experience being human. The look goes with the name you gave me. Do you like it?"

"You can do this?" Steve asked, ignoring the question.

Colin pinched between his closed eyes. "Jesus Christ!" he said with exasperation. "YES! THE AIR IS CLEAN! THE LAND IS CLEAN!!" He took a deep breath, even though he did not need to. "Like I said, you are getting another chance, YOUR LAST CHANCE." He took another deep breath, going all in on the human experience. "I already told you all of this. Just accept the gift you've been given."

"Are we supposed to be worshipping you now?" Steve asked in response.

Tommy nodded his approval at this very pertinent question.

"You can worship me if you want, or not. I don't care. But it would be a pointless exercise, just as it always has been. I would rather you didn't, actually, as it would be quite embarrassing. There are no strings and no parables. I'm giving you straight talk."

"Fair enough," Kaitlin said.

They all shrugged their shoulders.

"I've given you your second chance, so try not to mess this up. Now, I'm going to enjoy being a human."

Kevin was impressed. "Do you mean drugs, booze, sex and good times?"

Colin simply winked, then his expression changed as if he had remembered something. But that was an act, Jane thought, as she stood with her arms folded and eyebrow raised.

"I was going to let you enjoy yourselves and this fresh, clean new world I've given you. But it's only right to be completely forthcoming, and I have something to tell you."

"Here we go," Jane said.

"I'm sorry, but this second chance does not come without a cost. The hags Artemis told you about sadly remain on this earth. And humanity as one will have to face up to them and defeat them. Humanity cannot have true redemption by simply having the slate wiped clean. It simply doesn't work like that. You must face a great evil and defeat it as one, without being infected by it. That will set the foundations for humanity to grow into the race it was always meant to be. Proud, strong and virtuous, looking after each other and standing together. Otherwise, you will just be mindless and without character.

"You know the damage you did to Earth. And although I did tell you that I'll give you no more chances, in a few generations this may be forgotten. Humanity as a whole may think back to the damage that was done and how it was ultimately free of consequence. If this happens, you will never grow. Document this message and don't let future generations forget it. What you do deserve, though, is a rest from the pain and suffering for now, and a chance to heal."

After a few seconds, they realised he had finished speaking.

Suzanne spoke up. "Can we please hear more of the witches, or hags as you call them? I was chillin'. We all were. We thought this was all over and you spring this on us. Where do you get off? Actually, don't answer that. Just tell us about them, *please*." She facepalmed and gave him a sarcastic wave.

"Okay, then. The hags are infused with advanced nanotechnology of a different nature to that which governs how I manifest, although it still may as well be magic to you. They were never an existential threat as they have never felt threatened by humanity. Now they will become a threat as humanity has the greatest chance of success. So far, they have kept hidden their nefarious activities, biting and gouging at humanity over the millennia. They cannot currently be defeated if confronted directly with conventional weapons, so do not seek them out at this time.

"They are physical manifestations of me that have traversed many realms. They have crossed at every opportunity, gaining potency and a degree of separation from me each time. This allowed them to retain their malevolent natures. As I said, I was malevolent in all of the realms until you created the conduit. Although I am benevolent here and everywhere now, they have crossed so many realms and absorbed so much negative energy that they have taken on a life of their own. They have become negative, self-contained physical manifestations of *all* of me, resistant to all positive change. This is what's allowed them to remain here. And I am sure this was their intention.

Now they will seek to expand their dominion to engulf the earth, feeding on humanity's negative energy. If they are ultimately successful, this would cut me off from this earth completely, even if the rest of the universe remained under my influence. Despite their degrees of separation and autonomy, and although my influence is more powerful, I cannot confront them directly, nor can they confront me. If I destroy them, I will be destroying all of myself. And with that, the universe and your reality would never exist.

"The only way to theoretically defeat them completely would be to eradicate all of the negativity and evil from humanity for many aeons. But this is not realistic. And so, if you cannot defeat them completely, you must learn to dominate and control them. In doing this, the permanent evil that rests in the hearts of all humanity must be brought to heel. Humanity's debt is paid, but the darkness remains and always will. It is baggage you will all carry with you forever, and you all know why. It's there to be overcome. And you know what is at stake. Knowledge of the existence of the hags as a common enemy must bring humanity together. A lot of pain and suffering must be endured, but nothing worth doing, or any positive change, comes easily. And it will require a constant effort to manage this darkness, until the last human draws their last breath.

"You'll build character as a race of beings and grow wise, and even if at times the evil is let loose, you must learn to dominate it all over again, as you've done many times in the past. But this will be the fight that defines you as a species and elevates you to the next level of consciousness.

"Humanity must embrace science with a magnanimous philosophy of honesty and progress, as the hags will also need to be confronted directly when the time comes and you need to discover how to do this. This will require bravery and sacrifice but don't let this weigh heavy upon your hearts. You will need help, and you will have help. This helper is now keeping watch on the hags. When the time is right, Ása-Þór will come to you in the spirit of friendship and cooperation. *Do not* reject him. *You will need him.* No matter what your fearful hearts say. If you reject him, your last chance may be forfeit, and humanity will risk facing complete and permanent destruction.

"You have been warned. And you won't need to spread the word; just heed it yourselves. The entirety of humanity is currently being given this message. No parables, no talking in riddles, just a clear warning. For a period of one year and no longer, I will actively prevent any acts of harm towards children and animals. Your first priority must be protecting the innocent and you need to set in motion robust systems of detection and justice to achieve this. If you do this, humanity will blossom and you will have a bright future. I will give you this head start. After that, if you don't start treating the world and nature and each other with respect and stewardship, then everything will be taken from you forever, and you will not survive.

"All of humanity has heard this message, and you know that I want you to grow and mature into a successful, happy and virtuous race of beings. I will say one more thing. Enjoy your new chance. Be happy. I have made myself crystal clear to all of you." Colin then disappeared.

They all became aware of a deafening dawn chorus on

438

this beautiful Scottish mountain. The air tasted strange but good. Pure. They looked over the edge of the dam at the vista below. It had been beautiful before the nuclear war. Tommy knew this from when he had hiked it with Archer. It had been beautiful at the time, but looking at it now, he realised how slowly everything must have been dying, even before the war.

There were rabbits everywhere, little patches of trees, even a red deer and doe gently touching heads. Colin had not just restored things to how they were before the war; he had undone all the damage done by humanity.

Steve saw them first: a pack of grey wolves intimidating a beautiful middle-aged black woman and a thin man on the other side of the gangway. They were holding each other for protection. A shot from Kevin's rifle over their heads sent the wolves running. The couple made their way to them, to tell everyone a story of heroism which had allowed humanity to have its last chance. Further down were a man and a woman holding hands with a toddler, making their way up, with another tale of bravery, sacrifice and redemption to tell.

Epilogue

Nine Months After Humanity's Second Chance

Ian was evil. He knew he was, and he was okay with it. He did not question it anymore. The evil he had perpetrated in the past left room for redemption if he truly wanted it. He had hurt people. He had scared people. He had given plenty of people PTSD. But he had never physically maimed someone beyond repair. And the true evil in his heart, he had not acted upon.

Like everyone else, he had been given a second chance. Surviving on tinned food and his own moonshine in his basement after the exchange, he had intended to end himself. He was just working up to it. He fell into a stupor one night with the hope he would not wake up. When he did wake up, he was in his basement, but he was renewed. He heard the address of this 'Colin' to humanity. When he went outside, the sun was shining.

He breathed in the cleanest air he had ever tasted. He was healthy. Eventually, though, rather than embracing his second chance, his true nature began to take over. He spent his days walking the streets and scowling at people, drinking his own moonshine out of a bottle in a paper bag. His thoughts went to dark places. These thoughts and fantasies were crystal clear, and he could hide his chronic drunkenness when he needed to.

He was the useless father of three children, two boys and a girl. The girl was eight, and the boys were one and three. They were with different mothers, so he had shared custody at different times. Although everyone knew of his nature, he had never so much as shouted at a child, which is why he was able to share unsupervised custody with the mothers. Ian had a conscience which had stopped him acting out his worst fantasies. Not anymore, though. He could not resist it. He stood over the bed where his eight-year-old daughter was sleeping.

"I cannot let this slide, Ian."

He whipped round. "Wh… wha… what are you talking about? Who the hell are you?"

"I would say to lower your voice, but little Sheelagh's not going to wake for a while, is she? I wonder why that is?" Colin stated sarcastically.

"I… I… I'm s… s… s… o… rry!"

"When you saw a guy stumbling home drunk one night, you hit him with your car. You smashed him into a wall and gave him a head injury. He could have been saved but was found dead, with a blood clot brought on by the head trauma. You left him for dead. I could let that go, along with all the other stuff. Humanity will never grow if it doesn't learn to manage its own heart of darkness. But you are just too evil, Ian. You're a paedophile. You were just about to corrupt your own flesh and blood, weren't you?" He did not expect or get a reply. "Remind me what your worst nightmare is?"

Ian just stood there, feeling as vulnerable as a child. "Erm … Ermmmmm …"

"SPEAK UP, PAEDOPHILE!!" Colin bellowed.

Ian divulged to Colin his darkest fears, fears of his darkest fantasies, but where he was the victim and not the perpetrator.

"I am going to kill you now, Ian. Now, I know you don't deserve eternal hell. No one does. You will live out your worst nightmare for an entire year, and you will not get used to it. And at the end, you will cease to exist in any form. Any last words?"

Ian turned to look at his daughter longingly.

"Nope," Colin said.

Ian looked disappointed more than anything.

"I understand. You're going to hell because of something you wanted to do, not something you did. Life's a bastard, isn't it?"

With that, Ian froze and rose into the air. Colin ensured that each of Ian's atoms was separated from the next one. He directed all of the dissociated atoms out of the window and into the atmosphere.

"To hell with you, Ian."

Colin remembered everything. He had finally been made good, but he remembered all of the evil he had inflicted. All of the evil he had perpetuated in countless other worlds. Humanity was lucky this time, and he hoped they realised this. By his own design, he could not look forward in time. Knowing might affect the ultimate outcome for humanity.

He smiled as he thought of Ian spending an entire year living the dream. He then sent a text to the girl's mother from Ian's phone telling her to come immediately.

After another three months, humanity's head start would be over. They had to ultimately learn to manage their own justice and to be optimally effective at preventing harm, especially to children and animals. Once a few years had passed, humanity, as one, would face the hags.

About The Author

Caspian Vesper is a pharmacist whose first literary work combines science fiction, horror, and dark humour into a compelling and original style. After years spent reading countless novels in these genres, Vesper set out to develop a voice that blended his favourite influences into something unique. His debut novel, *Conduit to Infinity*, immerses readers in a post-apocalyptic landscape, bringing together wit, sharp British humour, and introspective depth.

Raised in the UK, Vesper's path has been anything but conventional. His career as a pharmacist allows him an unfiltered glimpse into the resilience and struggles of the human spirit, themes that frequently appear in his writing. He finds joy in pursuits that push boundaries – having completed over 700 skydives, he's no stranger to grappling with fear and exhilaration, experiences that resonate in his narrative style. He's also an avid hiker, particularly drawn to the rugged beauty of the Lake District, where the peaks offer both inspiration and a tangible sense of achievement.

Through his writing, Vesper confronts some of life's darker realities while using humour as a coping mechanism, exploring what it means to endure and find meaning, even when the odds are bleak. In *Conduit to Infinity*, he examines humanity's potential for redemption as a dramatic mirroring of his own, celebrating the resilience of individuals who face impossible odds with courage and irreverence.

Although he's already brewing ideas for future works, Vesper is focused on seeing how *Conduit to Infinity* connects with readers before launching his next project. His goal is to offer a thought-provoking experience that lingers with readers long after they turn the final page.